Praise for GREGOR

Also by Gregory Benford

EATER
COSM
THE STARS IN SHROUD
JUPITER PROJECT
IF THE STARS ARE GODS *(with Gordon Elklund)*
FIND THE CHANGELING *(with Gordon Elklund)*
SHIVA DESCENDING *(with William Rostler)*
TIMESCAPE
AGAINST INFINITY
ARTIFACT
HEART OF THE COMET *(with David Brin)*
A DARKER GEOMETRY *(with Mark O. Martin)*
IN ALIEN FLESH
MATTER'S END
FOUNDATION'S FEAR

The Galactic Center Series
IN THE OCEAN OF NIGHT
ACROSS THE SEA OF SUNS
GREAT SKY RIVER
TIDES OF LIGHT
FURIOUS GULF
SAILING BRIGHT ETERNITY

Worlds Vast and Various

STORIES

GREGORY BENFORD

An Imprint of HarperCollinsPublishers

Individual story copyrights can be found on pages 311–312, which serve as an extension of this copyright page.

EOS
An Imprint of HarperCollins*Publishers*
10 East 53rd Street
New York, New York 10022-5299

Copyright © 2000 by Abbenford Associates
Cover art by Rick Sternbach
ISBN: 0-380-79054-8
www.eosbooks.com

Library of Congress Cataloging in Publication Data:
Benford, Gregory, 1941–
    Worlds vast and various : stories / Gregory Benford.
        p. cm.
    Contents: A calculus of desperation—Doing alien—In the dark backward—The voice—Kollapse—As big as the Ritz—The scarred man—World vast, world various—Zoomers—High abyss—A worm in the well—A dance to strange musics—Afterthoughts.
    ISBN 0-380-79054-8
    1. Science fiction, American. I. Title.
PS3552.E542 W6 2000
    813'.54—dc21   00-031789

First Eos trade paperback printing: October 2000

Eos Trademark Reg. U.S. Pat. Off. and in Other Countries, Marca Registrada, Hecho en U.S.A.
HarperCollins® is a trademark of HarperCollins Publishers Inc.

Printed in the U.S.A.

RRD   10   9   8   7   6   5   4   3   2   1

To the editors who helped shape these stories:

Greg Bear
Gordon Van Gelder
Scott Edelman
Elizabeth Mitchell
Ed Ferman
Robert Silverberg
David Hartwell
Stanley Schmidt
Jennifer Brehl

Contents

A Calculus of Desperation

Amy inched shut the frail wooden door of her hotel room and switched on the light. Cockroaches—or at least she *hoped* they were mere cockroaches—scuttled for dark corners. They were so big she could hear them bumping into the tin plating along one wall.

She shucked off her dusty field jacket, threw it at the lone pine chair, and sprawled on the bed. Under the dangling, naked lightbulb she slit open her husband's letter eagerly, using a dirty fingernail. Frying fat flavors seeped through the planking but she forgot the smells and noises of the African village. Her eyes raced along the lurching penmanship.

> *God, I do really need you. What's more, I know it's my "juice" speaking—only been two weeks, but just at what point do I have to be reasonable? Hey, two scientists who work next to disasterville can afford a little loopy irrationality, right? Thinking about your alabaster breasts a lot. Our eagerly awaited rendezvous will be deep in the sultry jungle, in my tent. I recall your beautiful eyes that evening at Boccifani's and am counting the days . . .*
>
> *This "superflu" thing is knocking our crew people down pretty fierce now. With our schedule already*

packed solid, now comes two-week Earth Summit V in São Paulo. Speeches, press, more talk, more dumb delay. Hoist a few with buddies, sure, but pointless, I think. Maybe I can scare up some more funding. Takes plenty juice!—just to keep this operation going! Wish me luck and I'll not even glance at the Latin beauties, promise. Really.

She rolled over onto her side to ease the ache in her back, keeping the letter in the yellow glow that seemed to be dimming. The crackly pages were wrinkled as if they had gotten wet in transit.

A distant generator coughed, stuttered, stopped. The light went out. She lay in the sultry dark, thinking about him and decoding all that the letter said and implied. In the distance a dog yapped, and she smelled the sour lick of charcoal on the air. It did not cover the vile sickly sweet odor of bodies left out in the street. Already they were swelling. Autumn was fairly warm in this brush-country slice of Tanzania, and the village lay quiet with the still of the fallen. In a few minutes the generator huffed sluggishly back into its coughing rhythm and the bulb glowed. Watery light seeped into the room. Cockroaches scuttled again.

She finished the letter, which went on in rather impressively salacious detail about portions of her anatomy and did the job she knew Todd had intended. If any Tanzanian snoops got into her mail, they probably would not have the courage to admit it. And it did make her moist, yes.

The day's heavy heat now ebbed. A whispering breeze dispersed the wet, infesting warmth.

Todd got the new site coordinates from their uplink, through their microwave dish. He squatted beside the compact, black matte-finish module and its metallic ear, cupped to hear a satellite far out in chilly vacuum. That such a remote, desiccated, and silvery craft in the empty sky could be locked in electromagnetic embrace with this place of leafy heaviness, transfixed by sweet rot and the stink of distant fires, was to Todd a mute miracle.

Manuel yelled at him in Spanish from below. "Miz Cabrina says to come! Right away!"

"I'm nearly through."

"Right away! She says it is the cops!"

The kid had seen too much American TV. *Cop* spun like a bright coin in the syrup of thickly accented Spanish. Cops. Authorities. The weight of what he had to do. A fretwork of irksome memories. He stared off into infinity, missing Amy.

He was high up on the slope of thick forest. Toward him flew a rainbird. It came in languid slow motion, flapping in the mild breeze off the far Atlantic, a murmuring wind that lifted the warm weight from the stinging day. The bird's translucent shape flickered against big-bellied clouds, and Todd thought of the bird as a gliding bag of genes, biological memories ancient and wrinkled and yet still coming forth. Distant time, floating toward him now across the layered air.

He waved to Manuel. "Tell her to stall them."

He finished getting the data and messages, letting the cool and precise part of him do the job. Every time some rural bigshot showed up, his stomach lurched and he forced down jumpy confusions. He struggled to insulate the calm, unsettled center of himself so that he could work. He had thought this whole thing would get easier, but it never did.

The solar panels atop their van caught more power if he parked it in the day's full glare, but then he couldn't get into it without letting the interior cool off. He had driven up here to get a clear view of the rest of the team. He left the van and headed toward where the salvaging team was working.

Coming back down through kilometers of jungle took him through terrain that reflected his inner turmoil. Rotting logs shone with a vile, vivid emerald. Swirls of iridescent lichen engulfed thick-barked trees. He left the cross-country van on the clay road and continued, boots sinking into the thick mat.

Nothing held sway here for long. Hand-sized spiders scuttled

like black motes across the intricate green radiance. Exotic vi-
tality, myriad threats. A conservation biologist, he had learned
to spot the jungle's traps and viper seductions. He sidestepped
a blood vine's barbs, wisely gave a column of lime ants their
way. Rustlings escorted him through dappled shadows which
held a million minute violences. Carrion moths fluttered by on
charcoal wings in search of the fallen. Tall grass blades cut the
shifting sunlight. Birds cooed and warbled and stabbed insects
from the air. Casually brutal beauty.

He vectored in on the salvaging site. As he worked downslope the insecticidal fog bombs popped off in the high canopy.
Species pattered down through the branches, thumped on logs,
a dying rain. The gray haze descended, touched the jungle
floor, settled into nooks. Then a vagrant breeze blew it away.
His team moved across the hundred-meter perimeter, sweeping uphill.

Smash and grab, Todd thought, watching the workers in
floppy jeans and blue work shirts get down on hands and knees.
They inched forward, digging out soil samples, picking up
fallen insects, fronds, stems, small mammals. Everything, anything. Some snipped samples from the larger plants. Others
shinnied up the slick-barked trees and rummaged for the resi-
dent ants and spiders and myriad creatures who had not fallen
out when the fog hit them. A special team took leaves and
branches—too much trouble to haul away whole trees. And
even if they'd wanted to, the politicos would scream; timbering
rights here had already been auctioned off.

Todd angled along behind the sweeping line of workers, all
from Argentina. He caught a few grubs and leaves that had
escaped and dropped them into a woman's bag. She smiled
and nodded respectfully. Most of them were embarrassingly
thankful to have a job. The key idea in the BioSalvage Program
was to use local labor. That created a native constituency wher-
ever they went. It also kept costs manageable. The urban North
was funding this last ditch effort. Only the depressed wages of
the rural South made it affordable.

And here came the freezers. A thinner line of men carrying Styrofoam dry ice boxes, like heavy-duty picnic coolers. Into these went each filled sack. Stapled to the neck of each bag was a yellow bar-code strip giving location, date, terrain description. He had run them off in the van this morning. Three more batches were waiting in his pack for the day's work further up the valley.

His pack straps cut into his roll of shoulder muscle, reminding him of how much more remained to do. To save. He could see in the valley below the press of population on the lush land. A crude work camp sprawled like a tan fungus. Among the jungle's riot of emerald invention a dirt road wound like a dirty snake.

He left the team and headed toward the trouble, angling by faded stucco buildings. Puddles from a rain shower mirrored an iron cross over the entrance gate of a Catholic mission. The Pope's presence. Be fruitful, ye innocent, and multiply. Spread like locusts across God's green works.

Ramshackle sheds lay toward the work camp, soiling the air with greasy wood smoke. In the jungle beyond, chain saws snarled in their labors. Beside the clay ruts of the road lay crushed aluminum beer cans and a lurid tabloid about movie stars.

He reached the knot of men as Cabrina started shouting.

"Yes we do! Signed by your own lieutenant governor *especial!*"

She waved papers at three uniformed types, who wore swarthy scowls and revolvers in hip holsters.

"No, no." An officer jerked a finger at the crowd. "These, they say it interferes with their toil."

Here at the edge of the work camp they had already attracted at least fifty. Worn men slouched against a stained yellow wall, scrawny and rawboned and faces slack with fatigue. They were sour twists of men, *maraneros* from the jungle, a machete their single tool, their worn skins sporting once-jaunty tattoos of wide-winged eagles and rampant bulls and grinning skulls.

"The hell it does." Cabrina crossed her arms over her red jumper and her lips whitened.

"The chemicals, they make coughing and—"

"We went through all that with the foreman. And I have documents—"

"These say nothing about—"

Todd tuned out the details and watched lines deepen in the officer's face. Trouble coming, and fast. He was supposed to let Cabrina, as a native, run the interference. Trouble was, these were macho backcountry types. He nodded respectfully to the head officer and said, "Our schedule bothering them?"

The officer looked relieved to deal with a man. "They do not like the fumes or having to stay away from the area."

"Let's see if we can do something about that. Suppose they work upwind?"

So then it got into a back-and-forth negotiation. He hated cutting in on Cabrina but the officer had been near the breaking point. Todd gradually eased Cabrina back in and the officer saw how things were going to go. He accepted that with some face-saving talk and pretty soon it was settled.

Todd walked Cabrina a bit back toward the jungle. "Don't let them rile you. Just stick to the documents."

"But they are so stupid!" Flashing anger, a wrenched mouth.

"Tell me something new."

Their ice van growled into view. It already had the sample sacks from the fogging above. Time to move a kilometer on and repeat the process. All so they could get into this valley and take their samples before these butchers with their bovine complacency could chop it down for cropland or grazing or just to make charcoal. But Todd did not let any of this into his face. Instead he told Cabrina to show the van where to go. Then he went over and spoke to several of the men in his halting Spanish. Smoothing the way. He made sure to stand close to them and speak in the private and respectful way that worked around here.

*   *   *

Amy followed the rest of her team into the ward. It was the same as yesterday and the day before. All beds filled, patients on the floors, haggard faces, nurses looking as bad as the patients. The infection rate here was at least eighty percent of the population. These were just the cases which had made it to the hospital and then had the clout to get in.

Freddie went through the list prepared by the hospital director. They were there to survey and take blood samples but the director seemed to think his visitors bore some cure. Or at least advice.

"Fever, frequent coughing, swellings in the groin," Freddie read, his long black hair getting in the way. He was French and found everything about this place a source of irritation. Amy did not blame him but it was not smart to show it. "Seven percent of cases display septic shock, indicating that the bloodstream is directly infected."

"I hope these results will be of help to your researches," the director said. He was a short man with a look that alternated between pleading and outright panic. Amy did her best to not look at him. His eyes were always asking, asking.

Freddie waved his clipboard. "All is consistent with spread directly among humans by inhalation of infected respiratory droplets?"

The director nodded rapidly. "But we cannot isolate the chain. It seems—"

"Yes, yes, it is so everywhere. The incubation period of the infection is at least two weeks, though it can be up to a month. By that time the original source is impossible to stipulate." Freddie rattled this off because he had said the same thing a dozen times already in Tanzania.

Amy said mildly, "I note that you have not attempted to isolate the septic cases."

The director jerked as if reprimanded and went into an explanation, which did not matter to anyone but would make him feel better, she was sure. She asked for and received limbic fluids, mucus, and blood samples from the deceased patients.

The director wanted to talk to someone of higher authority, and their international team filled that need. Not that it did any good. They had no vaccine, no real advice except to keep the patients cool and not to use sedation which would suppress their lung function. They told him this and then told his staff and then told him again because he just kept looking at them with those eyes. Then they went away.

In the next town Amy got to a telephone and could hook up her modem. She got an uplink with only a half hour wait. They drove back into the capital city over dusty roads while she read the printouts.

Summary View.
    This present plague is certainly a derived form of influenza. It is well known that the "flu" virus undergoes "antigenic" drifts—point mutations in the virus's outer protein coat which can enhance the ability of the virus to attack the human immune system. New pandemic viruses emerge at unpredictable intervals on the order of decades, though the rate of shifts may be increasing. The present pathogenic outbreak, with its unusual two- to three-week incubation period, allows rapid spreading before populations can begin to take precautions—isolation, face masks, etc. Fatality rate is 3% in cases which do not recover within five days. Origin: The apparent derivation of this plague from southern Asia has been obscured by its rapid transmission to both Africa and South America. However, this Asian origin, recently unmasked by detailed hospital studies and demographics, verifies the suspicions of the United Nations Emergency Committee. Asia is the primary source of "flu" outbreaks because of the high incidence there of "integrated farming," which mingles fowl, pigs, and fish close together. In Southeast Asia this has been an economic blessing, but a reverse-spin disaster for the North. Viruses from different species mix, recombining and undergoing gene reassortment at a rapid rate. Humans need time to synthesize specific antibodies as a defense. Genetic

aspects: Preliminary results suggest that this is a recombinant virus. Influenza has seven segments of RNA, and several seem to have been modified. Some correlations suggest close connection to the swine flu derived from pigs. This is a shift, not a simple drift. Some recombination has occurred from another reservoir population—but which? Apparently, some rural environment in southern China.

She looked up as they jounced past scrubby farmland. No natural forest or grassland remained; humans had turned all arable land to crops. Insatiable appetite, eating nature itself.

Nobody visible. The superflu knocked everybody flat for at least three days, marvelously infective, and few felt like getting back to the fields right away. That would take another slice out of the food supply here. Behind the tide of illness would come some malnutrition. The U.N. would have to be ready for that, too.

Not my job, though, she thought, and mused longingly of Todd.

São Paulo. Earth Summit V, returning to South America for the first time since Summit I in the good old days of 1992. He was to give a talk about the program and then, by God, he'd be long gone.

On the drive in he had seen kindergarten-age children dig through cow dung, looking for corn kernels the cows hadn't digested. The usual colorful chaos laced with gray despair. Gangs of urchin thieves who didn't know their own last names. Gutters as sewers. Families living in cardboard boxes. Babies found discarded in trash heaps.

He had imagined that his grubby jeans and T-shirt made him look unremarkable, but desperation hones perceptions. The beggars were on him every chance. By now he had learned the trick which fended off the swarms of little urchins wanting Chiclets, the shadowy men with suitcases of silver jewelry, the women at traffic lights hawking bunches of roses. Natives didn't get their windshields washed unless they wanted it, nor did they say "No" a hundred times to accomplish the result. They just held up one finger and waggled it sideways, slowly. The pests magically dispersed. He had no idea what it meant, but it was so easy even a gringo could do it.

His "interest zone" at Earth Summit V was in a hodgepodge of sweltering tents erected in an outdoor park. The grass had been beaten into gray, flat blades. Already there was a dispute between the North delegates, who wanted a uniform pledge of seventy-five percent reduction in use of pesticides. Activists from the poor South worried about hunger more than purity, so the proposal died. This didn't stop anyone from dutifully signing the Earth Pledge which covered one whole wall in thick gray cardboard. After all, it wasn't legally binding.

Todd talked with a lot of the usual Northern crowd from the Nature Conservancy and World Wildlife Fund, who were major sponsors of BioSalvage. They were twittering about a Southern demand that everybody sign a "recognition of the historical, biological, and cultural debt" the North owed the South. They roped him into it, because the background argument (in Spanish, so of course most of the condescending Northerners couldn't read it) named BioSalvage as "arrogantly entering our countries and pushing fashionable environmentalism over the needs of the people."

Todd heard this in a soft drink bar, swatting away flies. Before he could respond, a spindly man in a sack shirt elbowed his way into the Northern group. "I know who you are, Mr. Russell. We do not let your 'debt swap' thievery go by."

BioSalvage had some funding from agreements which traded money owed to foreign banks for salvaging rights and local labor. He smiled at the stranger. "All negotiated, friend."

"The debt was contracted illegally!" The man slapped the yellow plastic table, spilling Coke.

"By your governments."

"By the criminals!—who then stole great sums."

Todd spread his hands, still smiling though it was getting harder. "Hey, I'm no banker."

"You are part of a plot to keep us down," the man shot back.

"By saving some species?"

"You are killing them!"

"Yeah, maybe a few days before your countrymen get around to it."

Two other men and a woman joined the irate man. Todd was with several Northerners and a woman from Costa Rica who worked for the Environmental Defense Fund. He tried to keep his tone civil and easy but people started breaking in and pretty soon the Southerners were into Harangue Mode and it went to hell. The Northerners rolled their eyes and the Southerners accused them in quick, staccato jabs of being arrogant, impatient, irritated when somebody couldn't speak English, ready to walk out at the first sign of a long speech when there was so much to say after all.

Todd eased away from the table. The Northerners used words like "proactive" and "empowerment" and kept saying that before they were willing to discuss giving more grants they wanted accountability. They worried about corruption and got thin-lipped when told that they should give without being oppressors of the spirit by trying to manage the money. *"Imperialista!"* a Brazilian woman hissed, and Todd left.

He took a long walk down littered streets rank with garbage. Megacities. Humanity growing by a hundred million fresh souls per year, with disease and disorder in ample attendance. Twenty-nine megacities now with more than ten million population. Twenty-five in the "developing" world—only nobody was developing any more. Tokyo topped the list, as always, at thirty-six million. São Paulo was coming up fast on the outside with thirty-four million. Lagos, Nigeria, which nobody ever thought about, festered with seventeen million despite the multitudes lost to AIDS.

He kicked a can and shrugged off beggars. A man with sores drooling down his face approached but Todd did not dare give him a bill. Uncomfortably he wagged his finger. Indifference was far safer.

Megacities spawned the return of microbes that had toppled empires down through history. Cholera, the old foe. New antibiotic-resistant strains. Cysticercosis, a tapeworm that invades the brain, caught from eating vegetables grown in the city's effluent. Half the world's urban population had at least one skin rash per year.

And big cities demand standardized, easily transported foods. Farmers respond with monocrops, which are more vulnerable to pests and disease and drought. Cities preyed on the cropland and forests which sustain them. Plywood apartment walls in Nagasaki chewed up Borneo's woodlands.

When he reached his hotel room—bare concrete, tin sink in the room, john down the hall—he found a light blinking on the satellite comm. He located the São Paulo nexus and got a fastprint letter on his private number. It was from Amy and he read it eagerly, the gray walls around him forgotten.

> *I'm pretty sure friend Freddie is now catching holy hell for not being on top of this superflu faster. There's a pattern, he says. Check out the media feeding frenzy, if you have the time. Use my access codes onto SciNet, too. I'm more worried about Zambia, our next destination. Taking no recognition of U.N. warnings, both sides violating the ceasefire. We'll have armed escorts. Not much use against a virus! All our programs are going slowly, with locals dropping like flies.*

The sweetness of her seemed to swarm up into his nostrils then, blotting out the disinfectant smell from the cracked linoleum. He could see her electric black hair tumbling like rolling smoke about her shoulders, spilling onto her full breasts in yellow candlelight. After a tough day he would lift her onto him, setting her astride his muscular arch. The hair wreathed them both, making a humid space that was theirs only, musk-rich and silent. She could bounce and stroke and coax from him the tensions of time, and later they would have dark rum laced with lemon. Her eyes could widen with comic rapt amazement, go slit-thin with anger, become suddenly womanly as they reflected the serenity of the languid candle flame.

Remember to dodge the electronic media bloodhounds. Sniffers and lickers, I call 'em. Freddie handles them for us, but I'm paranoid—seeing insults spelled out in my alphabet soup. Remember that I love you. Remember to see Kuipers if you get sick! See you in two weeks—so very long!

Todd's gray computer screen held a WorldNet news item, letters shimmering. His program had fished it out of the torrent of news, and it confirmed the worst of his fears. He used her code-keys to gain entry and global search/scan found all the hot buzz:

SUPERFLU EPIDEMIC WIDENS.
SECRETARY-GENERAL CALLS FOR AIR TRAVEL BAN.
DISEASE CONTROL CENTER TRACING VECTOR CARRIERS.

(AP) A world-sweeping contagion has now leaped from Asia to Africa and on to South America. Simultaneous outbreaks in Cairo, Johannesburg, Mexico City and Buenos Aires confirmed fears that the infection is spreading most rapidly through air travelers. Whole cities have been struck silent and prostrated as a majority of inhabitants succumb within a few days.

Secretary-General Imukurumba called for a total ban on international passenger air travel until the virus is better understood. Airlines have logged a sharp rise in ticket sales in affected regions, apparently from those fleeing.

The Centers for Disease Control is reportedly attempting to correlate outbreaks with specific travelers, in an effort to pinpoint the source. Officials declined to confirm this extraordinary move, however.

He suspected that somebody at the CDC was behind this leak, but it might mean something more. More ominously, what point was there in tracing individuals? CDC was moving fast. This thing was a wildfire. And Amy was right in the middle of it.

He sat a long time at a fly-specked Formica table, staring at the remains of his lunch, a chipped blue plate holding rice and beans and a gnawed crescent of green tortilla. Todd felt the old swirl of emotions, unleashed as though they had lain in waiting all this time. Incoherent, disconnected images propelled him down musty corridors of self. Words formed on his lips but evaporated before spoken.

She hated autopsies. Freddie had told her to check this one, and the smell was enough to make her pass out. Slow fans churned at one end of the tiny morgue. Only the examining table was well lit. Its gutters ran with viscous, reeking fluids.

The slim black woman on the table was expertly "unzipped"—carved down from neck to pelvis, organs neatly extracted and lying across her chest and legs. Glistening tubes and lumpy vitals, so clean and smooth they seemed to be manufactured.

"A most interesting characteristic of these cases," the coroner went on in a serene voice that floated in the chilly room. He picked up an elongated gray sac. "The fallopians. Swollen, discolored. The ova sac is distended, you will be seeing here. And red."

Amy said, "Her records show very high temperatures. Could this be—"

"Being the cause of death, this temperature, yes. The contagion invaded the lower abdomen, however, causing further discomfort."

"So this is another variation on the, uh, superflu?"

"I think yes." The coroner elegantly opened the abdomen further and showed off kidneys and liver. "Here too, some swelling. But not as bad as in the reproductive organs."

Amy wanted desperately to get out of this place. Its cloying smells layered the air. Two local doctors stood beside her, watching her face more than the body. They were well-dressed men in their fifties and obviously had never seen a woman in a position of significance in their profession. She asked, "What percentage of your terminal cases display this?"

"About three-quarters," the coroner said.

"In men and women alike?" Amy asked.

"Yes, though for the women these effects are more prominent."

"Well, thank you for your help." She nodded to them and left. The two doctors followed her. When she reached the street her driver was standing beside the car with two soldiers. Three more soldiers got out of a big jeep and one of the doctors said, "You are please to come."

There wasn't much to do about it. Nobody was interested in listening to her assertion that she was protected by the Zambia-U.N. terms. They escorted her to a low, squat building on the outskirts of town. As they marched her inside she remarked that the place looked like a bunker. The officer with her replied mildly that it was.

General Movotubo wore crisp fatigues and introduced himself formally. He invited her to sit in a well-decorated office without windows. Coffee? Good. Biscuit? Very good. "And so you will be telling now what? That this disease is the product of my enemies."

"I am here as a United Nations—"

"Yes, yes, but the truth, it must come out. The Landuokoma, they have brought this disease here, is this not so?"

"We don't know how it got here." She tried to understand the expressions which flitted across the heavyset man's face, which was shiny with nervous sweat.

"Then you cannot say that the Landuokoma did not bring it, this is right?"

Amy stood up. General Movotubo was shorter than her and she recognized now his expression: a look of caged fear. "Listen, staying holed up in here isn't going to protect you against superflu. Not if your personnel go in and out, anyway."

"Then I will go to the countryside! The people will understand. They will see that the Landuokoma caused me to do so."

She started for the door. "Believe me, neither I nor the U.N. cares what you say to your newspapers. Just let me go."

There was a crowd outside the bunker. They did not retreat when she emerged and she had to push and shove her way to her car. The driver sat inside, petrified. But nobody tried to stop them. The faces beyond the window glass were filled with stark dread, not anger.

She linked onto WorldNet back at the hotel. The serene liquid crystal screen blotted out the awareness of the bleak streets beyond the grand marble columns of the foyer.

PULLDOWN SIDEBAR: News Analysis
MIXED REACTION TO PLAGUE OUTBREAK

Environmental Hard Liners Say "Inevitable" (AP) . . . "What I'm saying," Earth First! spokesman Josh Leonard said, "is that we're wasting our resources trying to hold back the tide. It's pointless. Here in the North we have great medical expertise. Plenty of research has gone into fathoming the human immune system, to fixing our cardiovascular plumbing, and the like. But to expend it trying to fix every disease that pops up in the South is anti-Darwinian, and futile. Nature corrects its own mistakes." . . . Many in the industrialized North privately admit to being increasingly appalled with the South's runaway numbers. Their views are extreme. They point to how Megacities sprawl, teeming with seedy, impoverished masses. Torrents of illegal immigration pour over borders. Responding to deprivation, Southern politico/religious movements froth and foment, few of them appetizing as seen from a Northern distance. "The more the North thinks of humanity as a malignancy," said psychophilosopher Norman Wills, "the more we will unconsciously long for disasters."

Amy was not really surprised. The Nets seethed with similar talk. Todd had been predicting this for years. That made her think of him, and she shut down her laptop.

He stopped at the BioSalvage Southern Repository to pick up the next set of instructions, maps, political spin. It was a huge complex—big, gray, concrete bunker-style for the actual freezing compartments, tin sheds for the sample processing. All the buzz and clatter of the rest of Caracas faded as he walked down alleys between the Repository buildings. Ranks of big liquid nitrogen dewars. Piping, automatic labeling machines, harried workers chattering in highly accented Spanish he could barely make out.

In the foyer a whole wall was devoted to the history of it. At the top was the abstract of Scott's first paper, proposing what he called the Library of Life. The Northern Repository was in fact called that, but here they were more stiff and official.

A broad program of freezing species in threatened ecospheres could preserve biodiversity for eventual use by future generations. Sampling without studying can lower costs dramatically. Local labor can do most of the gathering. Plausible costs of collecting and cryogenically suspending the tropical rain forest species, at a sampling fraction of 10-6, are about two billion dollars for a full century. Much more information than species DNA will be saved, allowing future biotechnology to derive high information content and perhaps even resurrect then-extinct species. A parallel program of limited *in situ* preservation is essential to allow later expression of frozen genomes in members of the same genus. This broad proposal should be debated throughout the entire scientific community.

Todd had to wait for his appointment. He fidgeted in the foyer. A woman coming out of the executive area wobbled a bit, then collapsed, her clipboard clattering on marble. Nobody went to help. The secretaries and guards drew back, turned, were gone. Todd helped the woman struggle into a chair. She was already running a fever and could hardly speak. He knew there wasn't anything to do beyond getting her a glass of water. When he came back with one, a medical team was there. They simply loaded her onto a stretcher and took her out to an unmarked van. Probably they were just going to take her home. The hospitals were already jammed, he had heard.

He took his mind off matters by reading the rest of the Honor Wall, as it was labeled. Papers advocating the BioSalvage idea. A Nobel for Scott. Begrudging support from most conservation biologists.

Our situation resembles a browser in the ancient library at Alexandria, who suddenly notes that the trove he had begun inspecting has caught fire. Already a wing has burned, and the mobs outside seem certain to block any firefighting crews. What to do? There is no time to patrol the aisles, discerningly plucking forth a treatise of Aristotle, or deciding whether to leave behind Alexander the Great's laundry list. Instead, a better strategy is to run through the remaining library, tossing texts into a basket at random, sampling each section to give broad coverage. Perhaps it would be wise to take smaller texts, in order to carry more, and then flee into an unknown future.

"Dr. Russell? I am Leon Segueno."

The man in a severe black suit was not his usual monitor. "Where's Confuelos?"

"Ill, I believe. I'll give you the latest instructions."

Back into the executive area, another new wrinkle. Segueno went through the fresh maps with dispatch. Map coordinates, rendezvous points with the choppers, local authorities who would need soothing. A fresh package of local currency to grease palms, where necessary. Standard stuff.

"I take it you will be monitoring all three of your groups continuously?"

An odd question. Segueno didn't seem familiar with procedures. Probably a political hack.

"I get around as much as I can. Working the back roads, it isn't easy."

"You get to many towns."

"Gotta buy a few beers for the local brass hats."

"Have you difficulty with the superflu?"

"Some of the crew dropped out. We hired more."

"And you?"

"I keep away from anybody who's sniffling or coughing."

"But some say it is spread by ordinary breath."

He frowned. "Hadn't heard that."

"A United Nations team reported so."

"Might explain how it spreads so fast."

"*Sí, sí.* Your wife, I gather she is working for the U.N.?"

"On this same problem, right. I hadn't heard that angle, though."

"You must be very proud of her."

"Uh, yes." Where was this going?

"To be separated, it is not good. Will you see her soon?"

No reason to hide anything, even from an officious bureaucrat. "This week. She's joining me in the field."

Segueno chuckled. "Not the kind of reunion I would have picked. Well, good luck to you."

He tried to read the man's expression and got nothing but a polished blandness behind the eyes. Maybe the guy was angling for some kind of payoff? Nothing would surprise him anymore, even in the Repository.

He stopped off in the main bay. High sheet-metal ceiling, gantries, steel ramps. Stacks of blue plastic coolers, filled with the labeled sacks that teams like his own sent in. Sorting lines prepared them further. Each cooler was logged and integrated into a geographical inventory, so that future researchers could study correlations with other regions. Then the coolers went into big aluminum canisters. The gantries lowered these into permanent place. Tubes hooked up, monitors added, and then the liquid nitrogen pumped in with a hiss. A filmy fog, and another slice of vanishing life was on its way to the next age.

Todd wondered just when biology would advance to the point where these samples could be unfolded, their genes read. And then? Nobody could dictate to the future. They might resurrect extinct species, make leopards again pace the jungle paths. Or maybe they would revive beetles—God must have loved them, He made so many kinds, as Haldane himself had remarked. Maybe there was something wonderful in those shiny carapaces, and the future would need it.

Todd shrugged. It was reassuring to come here and feel a part of it all.

Going out through the foyer, he stopped and read the rest of the gilt lettering on polished black marble.

We must be prudent. Leading figures in biodiversity argue that a large scale species dieback seems inevitable, leading to a blighted world which will eventually learn the price of such folly. The political impact of such a disaster will be immense. Politics comes and goes, but extinction is forever. We may be judged harshly by our grandchildren, our era labeled the Great Dying or the Age of Appetite. A future generation could well reach out for means to recover their lost biological heritage. If scientific progress has followed the paths many envision today, they will have the means to perform seeming miracles. They will have developed ethical and social mechanisms we cannot guess, but we can prepare now the broad outlines of a recovery strategy, simply by banking biological information. These are the crucial years for us to act, as the Library of Life burns furiously around us, throughout the world.

He left. When he got into his rental Ford in the parking lot, he saw Segueno looking down at him through a high window.

*   *   *

He had not expected to get a telephone call. On a one-day stop in Goias, Brazil to pick up more coolers and a fresh crew, there was little time to hang around the hotel. But somehow she traced him and got through on the sole telephone in the manager's office. He recognized Amy's voice immediately despite the bad connection.

"Todd? I was worried."

"Nothing's gone wrong with your plans, has it?"

"No, no, I'll be there in two days. But I just heard from Freddie that a lot of people who were delegates at the Earth Summit have come down with superflu. Are you all right?"

"Sure, fine. How's it there?"

"I've got a million tales to tell. The civil war's still going on and we're pulling out. I wrote you a letter, I'll send it satellite squirt to your modem address."

"Great. God, I've missed you."

Her warm chuckle came through the purr of static. "I'll expect you to prove it."

"I'll be all set up in a fresh camp, just out from Maraba. A driver will pick you up."

"Terrif. Isn't it terrible, about the Earth Summit?"

"Nobody's immune."

"I guess not. We're seeing ninety percent affliction in some villages here."

"What about this ban on passenger travel? Will that—"

"It isn't sticking. Anyway, we have U.N. passes. Don't worry, lover, I'll get there if I have to walk."

He got her letter over modem within a few minutes.

We're pinning down the epidemiology. Higher fevers in women, but about 97% recover. Freddie's getting the lab results from the samples we sent in. He's convinced there'll be a vaccine, pronto.

But it's hard to concentrate, babe. This place is getting worse by the hour. We got a briefing on safety in Zambia, all very official, but most of the useful stuff we picked up from drivers, cops, locals on street corners. You have to watch details, like your license plates. I got some neutral plates from some distant country. People sell them in garages. Don't dare use the old dodge of putting a PRESS label on your car. Journalists draw fire here, and a TV label is worse. Locals see TV as more powerful than the lowly word-artists of newspapers. TV's the big propaganda club and everybody's got some reason to be mad at it.

We got a four-wheel job that'll go off-road. Had to be careful not to get one that looked like a military jeep. They draw fire. We settled on a white Bighorn, figuring that snipers might think we were U.N. peacekeeping forces. On the other hand, there's undoubtedly some faction that hates the U.N., too. Plenty of people here blame us—Westerners—for the superflu. We get hostile stares, a few thrown rocks. Freddie took a tomato in the chest today. Rotten, of course. Otherwise, somebody'd have eaten it.

We go out in convoys, seeking superflu vectors. Single cars are lots more vulnerable. And if we break down, like yesterday, you've got help.

I picked up some tips in case we come under fire. (Now don't be a nervous husband! You know I like fieldwork . . .) Bad idea to ride in the back seat of a two-door—hard to get out fast. Sit in the front seat and keep the door slightly open so you can dive out. Windows open, too, so you can hear what's coming down.

Even in town we're careful with the lights. Minimal flashlight use. Shrouds over camera lights as much as you can. A camera crew interviewing us from CNN draped dark cloth over their heads so nobody could see the dim blue glow of the viewfinder leaking from around their eyes.

Not what you wanted your wife to be doing, right? But it's exciting! Sorry if this is unfeminine. You'll soon have a chance to check out whether all this macho stuff has changed my, uh, talents. Just a week! I'll try to be all frilly-frilly. Lover, store up that juice of yours.

He stared at the glimmering phosphors of his laptop. Superflu at the Earth Summit. Vaccine upcoming. Vectors colliding, and always outside the teeming city with its hoarse voices, squalling babies, and swelling mothers, the rot of mad growth. Could a species which produced so many mouths be anything more than a blight? Their endless masses cast doubt upon the importance of any individual, diminished the mind's inner sense.

He read the letter again as if he were underwater, bubbles springing from his lips and floating up into a filmy world he hoped someday to see. He and Amy struggled, knee-deep in the mud of lunatic mobs. How long, before they were dragged down? But at least for a few moments longer they had the shadowy recesses of each other.

He waited impatiently for her beside his tent. He had come back early from the crew sites and a visit to the local brass hats. It had gone pretty well but he could not repress his desire for her, his impatience. He calmed himself by sitting in his canvas-backed chair, boots propped up on a stump left by the land clearing. He had some background files from Amy and he idly paged through them on his laptop. A review paper in *Nature* tried to put the superflu in historical perspective.

There were in fact three bubonic plagues, each so named because the disease began with buboes—swollen lymph glands in the groin, armpit, neck. Its pneumonic form spread quickly, on breaths swarming with microorganisms, every cough throwing microorganisms to the wind. A bacterial disease, the bacillus *Pasteurella pestis,* was carried by fleas on *Rattus rattus.*

In assessing the potentials of Superflu, consider the first bubonic pandemic. Termed the Plague of Justinian (540–590), who was the Caesar of the era, it began the decline of the Roman Empire, strengthened Christianity with its claims of an afterlife, and discredited Roman medicine, whose nostrums proved useless—thus strangling a baby science. By the second day of an ever-rising fever, the victims saw phantoms which called, beckoning toward the grave. The plague ended only when it killed so many, up to half the population of some cities, that it ran out of carriers. It killed a hundred million, a third of the region's population, and four times the Black Death toll of 1346–1361.

Our Superflu closely resembles the Spanish Influenza, which actually originated in Kansas. It was history's worst outbreak, as rated by deaths per day—thirty million in a single fall season of 1918. The virus mutated quickly. Accidental Russian lab release of a frozen sample in 1977 caused a minor outbreak . . .

He lay on his cot, waiting for the sound of his jeep, bearing Amy. Through the heavy air came the oddly weak slap of a distant shot. Then three more, quick.

He stumbled outside the tent. Bird rustlings, something scampering in the bush. He was pretty sure the shots had come from up the hill, where the dirt road meandered down. It was impossible to see anything in the twilight trees.

He had envisioned this many times before but that did not help with the biting visceral alarm, the blur of wild thoughts. He thought he had no illusions about what might happen. He walked quickly inside and slapped his laptop shut. Two moths battered at the lone lantern in his tent, throwing a shrapnel of shadows on the walls, magnified anxiety.

Automatically he picked up the microdisks which carried his decoding routines and vital records. He kept none of it on hard disk so he did not need to erase the laptop. His backpack always carried a day's food and water, and he swung it onto his back as he left the tent and trotted into the jungle.

Evening falls heavily beneath the canopy. He went through a mat of vines, slapping aside the stinging flies which rose angrily.

Boots thumping behind him? No, up on the dirt road. A man's shout.

He bent over and worked his way down a steep slope. He wished he had remembered to bring his helmet. He crouched further to keep below the ferns but some caught him in the face. In the fading shafts of green radiance he went quietly, stooped forward. Cathedral pillars of old trees were furred with orange moss. The day's heat still thickened the air. He figured that if she got away from them she would go downhill. From the road that led quickly into a narrowing canyon. He angled to the left and ran along an open patch of rock and into the lip of the canyon about halfway down. Impossible to see anything in there but green masses.

There was enough light for them to search for her. She would keep moving and hope they didn't track her by the sound. Noise travels uphill better in a canyon. He plunged into lacerating fronds and worked his way toward where he knew a stream trickled down.

Somebody maybe twenty meters ahead and downslope. Todd angled up to get a look. His breath caught when he saw her, just a glimpse of her hair in a fading gleam of dusk. Branches snapped under his boots as he went after her. She heard, as he had hoped, and slipped behind a tree. He whispered, "Amy! Todd!" and there she was suddenly, gripping her pop-out pistol.

"Oh God!" she said, and kissed him suddenly.

"Are you hurt?" he whispered.

"No." Her eyes ricocheted around the masses of green upslope from them. "I shot the driver of my jeep. In the shoulder, to make him stop. I had to, that Segueno—"

"Him. I wondered what the hell he was— Wait, what'd you shoot at after that?"

"The jeep behind us."

"They stopped?"

"Just around the curve, but they were running toward me."

"Where was Segueno?"

"In my jeep."

"He didn't shoot at you?"

"No, I don't think—"

"He probably didn't want to."

"Who is he? He said he was with World Emergency Services—"

"He's probably got a dozen IDs. Come on."

They forked off from the stream. It was clearer there and the obvious way to go so he figured to stay away from it and move laterally away from the camp. The best they could do would be to reach the highway about five kilometers away and hitch a ride before anybody covered that or stopped traffic. She had no more idea than he did how many people they had, but the follow-up jeep implied they could get more pretty quickly. It probably had good comm gear in it. In the dark they would take several hours to reach the highway. Plenty of time to cover the escapes but they had to try it.

The thin light was almost gone now. Amy was gasping—probably from the shock more than anything else, he thought. She did look as though she had not been sleeping well. The leaden night was coming on fast when they stopped.

"What does he—"

She fished a crumpled page from her pocket. "I grabbed it to get his attention while I got this pistol out." She laughed suddenly, coughed. "He looked scared. I was really proud of myself. I didn't think I could ever use that little thing, but when—"

Todd nodded, looking at the fax of his letter, words underlined:

God, I do really need you. What's more, I know it's my "juice" speaking—only been two weeks, but just at what point do I have to be reasonable? Hey, two scientists who work next to disasterville can afford a little loopy irrationality, right? Thinking about your alabaster breasts a lot. Our eagerly awaited rendezvous will be deep in the sultry jungle, in my tent. I recall your beautiful eyes that evening at Boccifani's and am counting the days . . .

"He thought he was being real smooth." She laughed again, higher this time. Brittle. "Maybe he thought I'd break down or something if he just showed me he was on to us." Todd saw that she was excited still, but that would fade fast.

"How many men you think he could get right away?"

She frowned. "I don't know. Who is he, why—"

He knew that she would start to worry soon and it would be better to have her thinking about something else. "He's probably some U.N. security or something, sniffed us out. He may not know much."

"Special Operations, he told me." She was sobering, eyes bleak.

"He said he was BioSalvage when I saw him in Caracas."

"He's been after us for over a week, then."

He gritted his teeth, eyeing the inky jungle. Twilight bird calls came down from the canopy, soft and questioning. Nothing more. Where were they? "I guess we were too obvious."

"Rearranging Fibonacci into Boccifani? I thought it was pretty clever."

He had felt that way, too, Todd realized ruefully. A simple code: give an anagram of a mathematical series—Fibonacci's was easy to remember in the field, each new term just the sum of the two preceding integers—and then arranging the real message in those words of the letter. A real code-breaker probably thought of schemes like that automatically. Served him right for being an arrogant smart-ass. He said, "I tried to make the messages pretty vague."

Her smile was thin, tired. "I'll say. 'God, I do need more juice at next rendezvous.' I had to scramble to be sure virus-3 was waiting at the Earth Summit."

"Sorry. I thought the short incubation strain might be more useful there."

She had stopped panting and now slid her arms around him. "I got that. 'This "superflu" thing knocking people with two-week delay. Juice!' I used that prime sequence—you got my letters?"

"Sure." That wasn't important now. Her heart was tripping, high and rapid against his chest.

"I . . . had some virus-4 with me."

"And now they have it. No matter."

Hesitantly she said, "We've . . . gotten farther than we thought we would, right?"

"It's a done deal. They can't stop it now."

"We're through, then?" Eyes large.

"They haven't got us yet."

"Do you suppose they know about the others?"

"I hadn't thought of that." They probably tracked the contagion, correlated with travelers, popped up a list of suspects. He and several others had legitimate missions, traveled widely, and could receive frozen samples of the virus without arousing suspicion. Amy was a good nexus for messages, coded and tucked into her reports. All pretty simple, once somebody guessed that to spread varieties of the virus so fast demanded a systematic, international team. "They've probably got Esther and Clyde, then."

"Damn!" She hugged him fiercely.

Last glimmers of day gave a diffuse glow among the damp tangle of vines and fronds. A rustling alerted him. He caught a quick flitting shadow in time to turn.

A large man carrying a stubby rifle rushed at him. He pushed Amy away and the man came on, bringing the rifle down like a club. Todd ducked and drove a fist into the man's neck. They collided. Momentum slammed him into thick ferns. Rolling, elbows jabbing.

Together they slammed into a tree. Todd yanked on the man's hair, got a grip. He smacked the head against a prow of limestone that jutted up from the leafy forest floor. The man groaned and went limp.

Todd got up and looked for Amy, and someone knocked him over from behind. The wind went out of him, and when he rolled over, there were two men, one holding Amy. The other was Mr. Segueno.

"It is pointless to continue," Segueno called.

"I thought some locals were raiding us." Might as well give it one more try.

No smile. "Of course you did."

The man Todd had knocked out was going to stay that way, apparently. Segueno and the other carried automatic pistols, both pointed politely at his feet. "What the hell is—"

"I assume you are not armed?"

"Look, Segueno—"

They took his pack and found the .38 buried beneath the packaged meals. Amy looked dazed, eyes large. They led them back along the slope. It was hard work and they were drenched in sweat when they reached his tent. There were half a dozen men wearing the subdued tan U.N. uniforms. One brought in a chair for Segueno.

Todd sat in his canvas chair and Amy on the bunk. She stretched out and stared numbly at the moths that still flailed against the unattainable lamp.

"What's this crap?" Todd asked, but he could not get any force into his voice. He wanted to make this easy on Amy. That was all he cared about now.

Segueno unfolded a tattered letter. "She did not destroy this—a mistake."

His letter to Amy. "It's personal. You have no right—"

"You are far beyond issues of rights, as I think you know."

"It was Freddie, wasn't it?" Amy said suddenly, voice sharp. "He was too friendly."

In the fluttering yellow light Segueno's smile gleamed. "I would never have caught such an adroit ruse. The name of a restaurant, a mathematical series. But then, I am not a codebreaker. And your second paragraph begins the sequence again—very economical."

Todd said nothing. One guard—he already thought of the uniformed types that way—blocked the tent exit, impassive, holding his 9mm automatic at the ready. Over the men outside talking tensely he heard soft bird calls. He had always liked the birds best of all things in the jungle. Tonight their songs were long and plaintive.

Segueno next produced copies of Amy's letters. "I must say we have not unpuzzled these. She is not using the same series."

Amy stared at the moths now.

"So much about cars, movement—perhaps she was communicating plans? But her use of 'juice' again suggests that she is bringing you some." Segueno pursed his lips, plainly enjoying this.

"You've stooped to intercepting private messages on satellite phone?"

"We have sweeping authority."

"And who's this 'we' anyway?"

"United Nations Special Operations. We picked up the trail of your group a month ago, as the superflu began to spread. Now, what is this 'juice'?"

Todd shook his head silently, trying to hear the birds high in the dark canopy. Segueno slapped him expertly. Todd took it and didn't even look up.

"I am an epidemiologist," Segueno said smoothly. "Or rather, I was. And you are an asymptomatic carrier."

"Come on! How come my crew doesn't get it?" Might as well make him work for everything. Give Amy time to absorb the shock. She was still lying loosely, watching the moths seethe at the lamp.

"Sometimes they do. But you do not directly work with the local laborers, except by choice. Merely breathing in the vapor you emit can infect. And I suspect your immediate associates are inoculated—as, obviously, are you."

Todd hoped that Cabrina had gotten away. He wished he had worked out some alarm signal with her. He was an amateur at this.

"I want the whole story," Segueno said.

"I won't tell you the molecular description, if that's what you mean," Amy said flatly.

Segueno chuckled. "The University of California's Center for

Molecular Genetics cracked that problem a week ago. That was when we knew someone had designed this plague."

Todd and Amy glanced at each other. Segueno smiled with relish. "You must have inoculated yourselves and all the rest in your conspiracy. Yet with some molecular twist, for you are all asymptomatic carriers."

"True." Amy's eyes were wary. "And I breathed in your face on my way in here."

Segueno laughed sourly. "I was inoculated three days ago. We already have a vaccine. Did you seriously think the best minds in medicine would take long to uncover this madness, and cure it?"

Todd said calmly, "Surprised it took this long."

"We have also tracked your contagion, spotted the carriers. You left a characteristic pattern. Quite intelligent, using those who had a legitimate mission and traveled widely. I gather you personally infected hundreds at Earth Summit V, Dr. Russell."

Todd shrugged. "I get around."

"To kill your colleagues."

"Call it a calculus of desperation," Todd said sharply. "Scientists are very mobile people. They spread a virus real well."

"A calculus? How can you be so—" Segueno caught himself, then went on, voice trembling slightly. "As an epidemiologist, I find puzzling two aspects. These strains very in infectivity. Still, all seem like poor viral design, if one wants to plan a pandemic. First, they kill only a few percent of the cases. Even those are mostly the elderly, from the fever." He frowned scornfully. "Poor workmanship."

"Yeah, I guess we're just too dumb," Todd said.

"You and your gang—we estimate you number some hundred or more, correct?—are crazy, not stupid. So why, then, the concentration of the disorders in the abdominal organs? Influenza is most effective in the lungs."

Amy said crisply, "The virus had proteins which function as an ion channel. We modified those with amantadine to block the transport of fusion glycoproteins to the cell surface—but only in the lungs." She sounded as though she were reciting from something she had long ago planned to say. It was as stilted as the opening remarks in a seminar. "The modification enhances its effect in another specific site."

Segueno nodded. "We know the site—quite easy to trace, really. Abdominal."

"Game's over," Todd said soberly. The CDC must know by now. He felt a weight lifted from him. Their job was done. No need to conceal anything.

"This 'juice,' it is the virus, yes?"

Amy hesitated. Her skin was stretched over her high cheekbones and glassy beneath the yellow light. Todd went over and sat beside her on the cot and patted her hand reassuringly. "Nothing he can do anyway, hon."

Amy nodded cautiously. "Yes, the virus—but a different strain."

Todd said wryly, "To put a li'l spin on the game."

Segueno's face pinched. "You swine."

"Feel like slapping me again?" Todd sat with coiled energy. He wished Segueno would come at him. He was pumped up from the fight earlier. His blood was singing the age-old adrenaline song. The guard was too far away. He watched Todd carefully.

Segueno visibly got control of himself. "Worse than that, I would like. But I am a man with principles."

"So am I."

"You? You are a pair of murderers."

Amy said stiffly, "We are soldiers."

"You are no troops. You are—crazed."

Her face hardened with the courage he so loved in her—the dedication they shared, that defined them. She said as if by rote, "We're fighting for something and we'll pay the price, too."

Segueno eyed Amy with distaste. "What I cannot quite fathom is why you bothered. The virus runs up temperature, but it does not damage the cubical cells or other constituents."

"The ovarian follicles," Amy said. "The virus stimulates production of luteinizing hormone."

Segueno frowned. "But that lasts only a few days."

"That's all it takes. That triggers interaction with the follicle-stimulating hormone." Amy spoke evenly, as though she had prepared herself for this moment, down through the years of work.

"So you force an ovarian follicle to rupture. Quite ordinary. That merely hastens the menstrual cycle."

"Not an ovarian follicle. All of them."

"All . . . ?" His brow wrinkled, puzzled—and then shock froze his face. "You trigger all the follicles? So that all the woman's eggs are released at once?"

Amy nodded. "Your people must know that by now, too."

Segueno nodded automatically, whispering, "I received a bulletin on the way here. Something about an unusual property . . ."

His voice trickled away. The moths threw frantic shadows over tight faces that gleamed with sweat.

"Then . . . they will recover. But be infertile."

Todd breathed out, tensions he did not know that he carried now released. "There. It's done."

"So you did not intend to kill many."

Amy said with cool deliberation, "That is an unavoidable side effect. The fever kills weak people, mostly elderly. We couldn't find any way to edit it out."

"My God . . . There will be no children."

Todd shook his head. "About fifteen percent of the time it doesn't work through all the ovarian follicles. The next generation will drop in population almost an order of magnitude."

Segueno's mouth compressed, lips white. "You are the greatest criminals of all time."

"Probably," Todd said. He felt suddenly tired now that the job was done. And he didn't much care what anybody thought.

"You will be executed."

"Probably," Amy said.

"How . . . how could you . . . ?"

"Our love got us through it," Todd said fiercely. "We could not have children ourselves—a tilted uterus. We simply extended the method."

Amy said in her flat, abstract tone, "We tried attaching an acrosome to sperm, but males can always make new ones. Females are the key. They've got a few hundred ova. Get those, you've solved the problem. Saved the world."

"To rescue the environment." Todd knew he had to say this right. "To stop the madness of more and more people."

Segueno looked at them with revulsion. "You know we will stop it. Distribute the vaccine."

Amy smiled, a slow sliding of lips beneath flinty eyes. "Sure. And you're wondering why we're so calm."

"That is obvious. You are insane. From the highest cultures, the most advanced—such savagery."

"Where else? We respect the environment. We don't breed like animals."

"You, you are . . ." Again Segueno's voice trickled away.

Todd saw the narrowed eyes, the straining jaw muscles, the sheen of sweat in this tight-lipped U.N. bureaucrat, and wondered just how a man of such limited horizons could think his disapproval would matter to them. To people who had decided to give themselves to save the world. What a tiny, ordinary mind.

Amy hugged her husband. "At least now we'll be together."

Segueno said bitterly, "We shall try you under local statutes. Make an example. And the rest of your gang, too—we shall track them all down."

The two on the cot sat undisturbed, hugging each other tightly. Todd kissed Amy. They had lived through these moments in imagination many times.

Loudly Segueno said, "You shall live just long enough to see the vaccine stop your plan."

Amy kissed Todd, long and lingering, and then looked up. "Oh, really? And you believe the North will pay for it? When they can just drag their feet, and let it spread unchecked in the tropics?"

Todd smiled grimly. "After they've inoculated themselves, they'll be putting their energy into a 'womb race'—finding fertile women, a 'national natural resource.' Far too busy. And the superflu will do its job."

Segueno's face congested, reddened. Todd watched shock and fear and then rage flit across the man's face. The logic, the inevitable cool logic of it, had finally hit him.

Somehow this last twist had snagged somewhere in Segueno, pushed him over the line. Todd saw something compressed and dark in the face, too late. *My mouth,* he thought. *I've killed us both.*

Segueno snatched the pistol from the guard, and Todd saw that they would not get to witness the last, pleasant irony, the dance of nations, acted out after all.

It was the last thing he thought, and yet it was only a mild regret.

Doing Alien

I remember how Mitchell was putting the moves on some major league pussy when the news about the aliens came in.

That Mitchell, he stopped in mid-line and cocked his big square head and said kind of whispery, "Double dog damn." Then he went back to the little redhead he had settled onto the stool next to his, way down at the end of the mahogany bar at Nan's.

But I could tell he was distracted. He's the kind of fella always drawn to a touch of weirdness. At Mardi Gras he just loved the confusion, not being able to tell guys from gals, or who was what, the whole thing. Weirdness.

He left with the redhead before ten, which was pretty quick even for Mitchell. When he's headed for the sheets there isn't much can get in Mitchell's way. But he kept glancing over at the Alphas on the TV. Going out, he gave me the old salute and big smile, but I could tell he was thinking off somewhere, not keeping his mind and his hands on the redhead. Which wasn't like him.

Mitchell's been my buddy since the earth's crust cooled off. I can read him pretty well. We graduated high school about the time the dinosaurs started up,

and went into farm equipment sales together when there were
still a few nickels to make in that game. I've seen Mitchell
bare-ass in the woods howling around a campfire, watched him
pulling in six-foot tuna off the back of McKenzie's old boat,
laughed when he was drunk up to his eyeballs with a big brassy
broad on each arm and a shitass happy grin. For sure I know
him better than any of his goddamn two ex-wives or his three
kids. None of them'd recognize him on the street, pretty near.

So when the Alphas showed up right here in Fairhope I
could tell right away that Mitchell took it funny. These Alphas
come in slick as you please, special escort in limos and all.
They go down to the wharf and look at the big new Civic
Center and all, but nobody has a dime's worth of idea what
they're here for.

Neither does the escort. Two suits on every Alpha, dark
glasses and shoulder-slung pistols and earplug radios and the
like. You could see it plain, the way their tight mouths
twitched. They dunno from sour owl shit what to expect next.

For sure nobody thought they'd go into Nan's. Just clank on
in, look around, babble that babble to each other, plunk down
on those chrome stools.

Then they order up. Mitchell and me, we was at the other
end of the bar. The Alphas, they are ordering up and putting
them down pretty quick. Nobody knows their chemistry but
they must like something in gimlets and fireballs and twofers,
cause they sure squirt them in quick.

Pretty soon there's a crowd around them. The suits stand
stiff as boards, but the locals ooze around them, curious. The
Alphas don't pay any attention. Maybe they're used to it or
maybe they don't even know people are there unless they need
something. Way they act, you could believe that.

But Mitchell, he keeps eyeing them. Tries to talk to them.
They don't pay him no never mind. Buys one a drink, even,
but the Alpha won't touch it.

I could see it got to him. Not the first day maybe or the
second. By the third, though, he was acting funny. Studying

them. The Alphas would show up at Nan's, suck in plenty of the sauce, then blow out of town in those limos.

News people around, crowds waiting to see them, the whole goddamn shooting match. Made Fairhope hell to get around in.

I was gone three days to Birmingham on a commission job with International Harvester, so I didn't see what started him on it. I come into town all busted out from chasing tail in Birmingham and first thing you know, phone rings and Mitchell wants help.

"I'm in that beat-up shack back of Leroy's TV," he said.

"That place's no bigger'n a coffin and smells worse."

"They spruced it up since Briggs run that poker game in here."

"So who you pokin' there now?"

"Fred, your dick fell off your IQ would be zero."

"That happen, what'd I need to think for?"

"Get your dumb ass over here."

So I did. Walk in on Mitchell in a chair, this brunette working on him. First I figured she was from over Bessie's, giving him a manicure with her kit all spread out. Turns out she's a makeup gal from clear over to New Orleans. Works Mardi Gras and like that.

Only she's not making Mitchell up to be a devil or in blackface or anything. This is serious. She's painting shellack all over him. He's already got a crust on him like dried mud in a hog wallow, only it's orange.

"Christ on a crutch," is all I can say.

"Mix me a bourbon and branch." Mitchell's voice came out muffled by all these pink pancake-size wattles on his throat, like some kind of rooster.

So I do. Only he doesn't like it, so he gets up and makes his own. "Got to add a twist sometimes," he says.

Mitchell was always picky about drinks. He used to make coffee for the boys, morning after a big carouse, and it had to be Colombian and ground just so and done up in this tricky filter rig he made himself out of tin sheeting.

That's how he was with this makeup girl, too. She layered on ridges of swarthy gum all down his arms, then shaped it with little whittling tools. She was sweating in that firebox shack. Mitchell was too, under all the makeup.

I'm wondering what the hell, and Mitchell says, "Go take a squint, see if they're in Nan's yet."

So I'm catching on. Mitchell's always had something working on the side, see, but he takes his time about letting on. Kind of subtle, too. When Mr. Tang moved into Fairhope with his factory, Mitchell was real respectful and polite and called him Poon for a year before that Tang caught on.

As I go out the shack and down the alley I see why he used that place. I angle across Simpson's parking lot and down by those big air conditioners and pop out on Ivy right next to Nan's. That way, none of the suits can see you coming. Slip in the side door and sure as God's got a beard, there's three Alphas. Got a crowd around them but the room is dead quiet. People just looking and wondering and the aliens drinking.

I'd heard that plenty of fast-lane operators were trying to get information out of Alphas, seeing as they got all this technology. We didn't even see them coming, that's how good their stuff is.

First thing anybody knew, they were bellying up to Venus, this other planet out there. Covered in clouds, it was. Then the Alphas start to work on her. First thing you know, you can see those volcanoes and valleys.

Anybody who can clear up muggy air like that inside a week, you got to pay attention. Turned out that was just cleaning off the workbench. Next they spun a kind of magnetic rod, rammed it in at the pole, clean down into the core of the whole damn planet. Easy as sticking an ice pick through an apple. Only the ice pick was hollow and they sucked the liquid metal out of there. Up the rod like it was a straw, and out into space. To make those metal city kind of things, huge and all.

That's when people started getting really afraid. And some others got really interested. The way they figured, any little scrappy thing you got from an Alpha might just be a billion-buck trick.

That's the scoop I heard on CNN coming down from Birmingham, anyway. Now here was the whole circus in Fairhope, big as life and twice as ugly. Snoops with those directional microphones. Cameras in the backs of vans, shooting out through dark windows. Guys in three-piece suits kind of casual slouched against the bar and trying to get an Alpha to notice them.

So back I go. Mitchell is getting some inflated bags stuck on him by the makeup girl. Bags all over his back and chest and neck even. He's all the Alpha colors now, from Georgia clay red here to sky blue there.

"Three of 'em sucking it up in there," I said.

"Holy shit, let's go," Mitchell croaks back at me. The girl had fitted him out with this voice-box thing, made him sound like a frog at the bottom of a rain barrel.

The girl pats him all over with that fine, rusty dust the Alphas are always shedding. She straightens the pouches so you can hardly see that his arms are too short for an Alpha.

"Let's make tracks," Mitchell says, and proceeds to do just that. Alpha tracks, fat and seven-toed.

We go across the parking lot, so the escorts can't see. In a minute we're in Nan's. The other Alphas don't take any notice of Mitchell but all the people do. They move out of the way fast and we parade in, me a little behind so it'll seem like I was just a tourist. Mitchell's got the Alpha shuffle down just right, to my eye.

Bold as brass, he sits down. The suits look at each other, dunno what to do. But they buy it, that Mitchell's one of them.

The Alphas still don't notice him. Bartender asks and Mitchell orders, making a kind of slithery noise.

He slurps down two drinks before anything happens. An Alpha makes a gesture with that nose thing of theirs and Mitchell does, too. Then there's some more gesturing and they talk like wet things moving inside a bag.

I sit and listen but I can't make sense out of any of it. Mitchell seems to know what he's doing. He keeps it up for maybe five more minutes. I can see it's wearing on him. He gives me the signal.

I clear some space for him so he can get back up—that crap he was wearing weighs real considerable. He gets up smooth and shuffles some and then we're out the door. Free and clean. We got back to the shack before we let go with the whooping and hollering.

We pull it off four more times in the next three weeks. Each time the Alphas take more notice of Mitchell. Hard to know what they think of him. The girl comes over from New Orleans and does him up, getting better each time. I keep an ear open for word on the street and it's all good.

Or seems so to me, anyway. Everybody thinks Mitchell's the real thing. 'Course that's people talking, not Alphas. After the fourth time I couldn't hold back anymore. "You got some money angle on this, right?"

"Money?"

"What I want to know is, how you going to get anything out of them?"

"I'm not in for money."

"You figure maybe you can get one of those little tool kits they carry? They don't look hooked on real firm or anything."

Mitchell grinned. "Wouldn't try that, I was you. Fella in Cincinnati went to lift one, came up an arm short."

"Then what the hell you in for?"

Mitchell gave me this funny look. " 'Cause it's *them.*"

I blinked. "So goddamn what?"

"You don't get it, Fred. Thing about aliens is, they're alien." In his eyes there's this look. Like he was seeing something different, something important, something way bigger than Fairhope.

I couldn't make any more sense out of what he said after that. That's when I realized. Mitchell just wanted to be close to them, was all.

That pretty well took the wind out of my sails. I'd figured
Mitchell was on to something for sure. I went with him one
more time, that's all. And a few days later I heard that the
same Alpha was coming back to Nan's every day, just sitting
and waiting for more Alphas to come in, and hanging out with
them when they did.

It went that way for a while and I was feeling pretty sour
about it. I went on a carouse with the Perlotti brothers and
had me a pretty fair time. Next morning I was lying in bed
with a head that barely fit in the room and in walks Mitchell.
"Heard you maybe needed some revivin' from last night."

He was grinning and I was glad to see him even if he did
waste a slab of my time. We'd do little things like that for each
other sometimes, bring a fella a drink or a hundred dollar bill
when he was down and could sure use it. So I crawled up out
of bed and pulled on some jeans and went into the kitchen.

Mitchell was filling a pot and popping open one of his Colombian coffee packs. I got some cups and we watched the
water boil without saying anything. That's when it happened.

Mitchell was fooling with the coffee and I was still pretty
bleary-eyed, so I'm not sure just exactly what I saw. Mitchell
was stirring the coffee and he turned to me. "Ummm. Smell
those enzymes."

He said it perfectly natural and I wouldn't have taken much
notice of the funny word. I looked it up later at the library and
it's a chemical term, I forget what it means. Mitchell would
never have said something like that. And I wouldn't have given
it any mind, except that just then his arm stuck a little farther
out of the denim work shirt he had on. He has big arms and
thick wrists. As the shirt slid up I saw the skin and curly hair
and then something else.

At first I thought it was leather. Then it seemed like cloth,
real old fabric, wrinkled and coarse. Mitchell turned further
and looked at me and that's when I heard the sound of him
moving. It was like dry leaves rustling. Old and blowing in a
wind. In the next second I caught a whiff of it and the worst

smell I ever knew came swarming up into my head and I finally really saw what the thing next to me was.

I don't want to describe that. It sent me banging back against the plywood wall of the kitchen and then out the door. The smell stayed with me somehow even in the open. I was off into the pines way back of my place before I knew it.

I had the shakes for hours. Made myself circle around for three miles. Got to my sister's place. Didn't tell her anything about it but I think she might of guessed. I was pale and woozy.

I got my truck and went off to Pensacola for a week. There was maybe some work there but it didn't pan out and I hadn't gone for that anyway.

I didn't go back into my place for another week. And I was real careful when I did.

It was all picked up, neat as you please. Not a sign. Mitchell was a fine man but he would never have done that.

I stood in the kitchen and tried to work out what had happened, how it had been. Couldn't. There was that one second when I saw straight into whatever was there and being Mitchell, and that was all.

He had tried to blend in with them. And I'd helped him. So in some way maybe this was the reverse. Or a payback, kind of. Or maybe a signal or something. No way to tell.

Only, you know what I think? I figure there isn't any Mitchell anymore. There's something else.

Now, could be there's still some Mitchell in there, only he can't get out. Or maybe that thing's Alpha for sure. I guess it could be something in between. Only thing I know is, it isn't anything I ever want to know.

Maybe it's something I can't know. Thing about aliens is, they're alien.

They say that one Alpha still hangs out at Nan's. I haven't been to check. I don't even walk down that part of town anymore.

In the Dark Backward

The fearful wrenching snap, a sickening swerve—and she was there.

Vitrovna found herself in a dense copse of trees, branches swishing overhead in a fitful breeze. Shottery Wood, she hoped. But was the time and place truly right? She had to get her bearings.

Not easy, in the wake of the Transition. She was still groggy from stretched moments in the slim, cushioned cylinder. All that aching time her stomach had knotted and roiled, fearing that intercession awaited the Transition's end. A squad of grim Corpsmen, an injunction. A bleak prospect of standing at the docket for meddling in the sanctified past, a capital crime.

But when the wringing pop echoed away, there was no one awaiting to erase her from time's troubled web. Only this scented night, musky with leaves and a wind promising fair.

She worked her way through prickly bushes and boggy glades, using her small flashlight as little as she could. No need to draw attention—and a white beam cutting the darkness of an April night in 1616 would surely cause alarm.

She stumbled into a rough country lane wide enough to see the sky. A sliver of bleached moon, familiar starsprinklings—and there, Polaris. Knowing north, she reckoned from her topo map which way the southward-jutting wedge of Stratford might be. This lane led obliquely that way, so she took it, wind whipping her locks in encouragement.

Much still lay to be learned, she could be far off in space and time, but so far the portents were good. If the combined ferretings and guesses of generations of scholars proved true, this was the last night the aging playwright would be afoot. A cusp moment in a waning life.

Up ahead, hollow calls. A thin blade of yellow as a door opened. A looming shamble-shadow of a drunken man, weaving his ragged course away from the inky bulk of an inn. Might this be the one she sought? Not the man, no, for they were fairly sure that graying Will had spent the night's meaty hours with several friends.

But the inn might be the place where he had drunk his last. The vicar of Stratford's Holy Trinity Church, John Ward, had written years after this night that the bard had "been on an outing" with two lesser literary lights. There were probably only a few inns in so small a town, and this might be the nearest to Shakespeare's home.

Should. Might. Probably. Thin netting indeed, to snare hard facts.

She left the lane and worked through brush that caught at her cloak of simple country burlap. A crude weave covering a cotton dress, nothing lacy to call attention, yet presentably ladylike—she hoped. Considering the sexual fascinations of the ancients, she might easily be mistaken for a common harlot, or a village slut about for a bit of fun.

Any contact with others here would endanger her, to say nothing of definitely breaking the Codes. Of course, she was already flagrantly violating the precepts regulating time travel, but years of preparation had hardened her to that flat fact, insulated her from any lingering moral confusions.

She slipped among trees, trying to get a glimpse through the tiny windows of the inn. Her heart thudded, breath coming quick. The swarming smells of this place! In her antiseptic life, a third-rank Literary Historian in the University Corps, she had never before felt herself so immersed in history, in the thick air of a world innocent of steel and ceramic, of concrete and stale air.

She fished her senso-binoculars from her concealed pack and studied the windows. It was difficult to make out much through the small, warped panes and heavy leading, behind which men lifted tankards and flapped their mouths, illuminated by dim, uncertain candles. A fat man waved his arms, slopping drink. *Robustious rothers in rural rivo rhapsodic. Swill thou then among them, scrike thine ale's laughter.* Not Will's words, but some contemporary. Marlowe? Whoever, they certainly applied here. A ragged patch of song swept by on the stirring wind, carried from an opening door.

Someone coming out. She turned up the amps on the binoculars and saw three men, each catching the swath of lantern light as they helped each other down stubby stairs to the footpath.

Three! One large, balding, a big chest starting to slide into an equatorial belly. Yet still powerful, commanding, perhaps the manner of a successful playwright. Ben Jonson?

The second younger, short, in wide-brimmed hat—a Warwickshire style of the time, she recalled. It gave him a rakish cast, befitting a poet. Michael Drayton?

And coming last, tripping on the stair and grasping at his friends for purchase, a mid-sized man in worn cloak and close-fitting cap. *Life brief and naught done,* she remembered, a line attributed—perhaps—to this wavering apparition. But not so, not so.

The shadowy figure murmured something and Vitrovna cursed herself for her slowness. She telescoped out the directional microphone above the double barrels of the binoculars. It clicked, popped, and she heard—

"I was then bare a man, nay, a boy still," the big man said. "Big in what fills, sure speak." The wide-hatted man smirked.

"Swelled in blood-fed lustihead, Ben's bigger than stallions, or so rumor slings it," the cloaked figure rapped back, voice starting gravelly and then swinging tenor-high at the sentence's end.

The tall man chuckled with meaty relish. "What fills the rod's same as fills the pen, as you'd know better."

So this was the man who within a few years would say that his companion, the half-seen figure standing just outside the blade of light cast by the inner inn, was "Not of an age, but for all time." Ben Jonson, in breeches, a tuft of white shirt sticking from an unbuttoned fly. A boisterous night for all.

"Aye, even for the miowing of kitticat poetry on spunk-stained parchment, truest?" the cloaked man said, words quick but tone wan and fading.

"Better than a mewling or a yawper," the short man said. All three moved a bit unsteadily round a hitching post and across the yard. Jonson muttered, laughed. She caught the earthy reek of ale. The man who must be Drayton—though he looked little like the one engraving of his profile she had seen—snickered liquidly, and the breeze snatched away a quick comment from the man who—she was sure now—must be Shakespeare. She amped up the infrared and pressed a small button at the bridge of the binoculars. A buzz told her digital image recording was on, all three face-forward in the shimmering silver moonlight, a fine shot. Only then did she realize that they were walking straight at her.

Could they make her out, here in a thicket? Her throat tightened and she missed their next words, though the recorder at her hip would suck it all in. They advanced, staring straight into her eyes—across the short and weedy lawn, right up to the very bushes that hid her. Shakespeare grunted, coughed, and fished at his drawers. To her relief, they all three produced themselves, sighed with pleasure, and spewed rank piss into the bushes.

"The one joy untaxed by King or wife," Jonson meditated.

The others nodded, each man embedded in his own moment of release, each tilting his head back to gaze at the sharp stars.

Then they were done, tucked back in. They turned and walked off to Vitrovna's left, onto the lane.

She followed as silently as she could, keeping to the woods. Thorns snagged her cloak and soon they had walked out of earshot of even her directional microphone. She was losing invaluable data!

She stumbled onto the path, ran to catch up, and then followed, aided by shadows. To walk and keep the acoustics trained on the three weaving figures was all she could manage, especially in the awkward, raw-leather shoes she had to wear. She remembered being shocked that this age did not even know to make shoes differently curved for left and right feet, and felt the effect of so simple a difference within half a kilometer. A blister irked her left heel before she saw a glow ahead. She had given up trying to follow their darting talk. Most was ordinary byplay laced with coarse humor, scarcely memorable, but scholars could determine that later.

They stopped outside a rambling house with a three-windowed front from which spilled warm lantern light. As the night deepened a touch of winter returned. An ice-tinged wind whipped in a swaying oak and whistled at the house's steep-gabled peak. Vitrovna drew as near as she dared, behind a churning elm.

"Country matters need yawing mouths," Shakespeare said, evidently referring to earlier talk.

"Would that I knew keenly what they learn from scrape and toil," Drayton said, voice lurching as the wind tried to rip it away from her pickups.

"A Johannes Factotum of your skinny skin?" Shakespeare said, sniffing.

Vitrovna translated to herself, *A Jack-Do-All of the senses?*—though the whole conversation would have to be endlessly filtered and atomized by computer intelligences before she could say anything definitive. If she got away with this, that is.

"Upstart crow, cockatrice!" Jonson exclaimed, clapping Shakespeare on the shoulder. All three laughed warmly.

A whinny sped upon the breeze. From around the house a boy led two horses. "Cloddy chariot awaits," Drayton said blearily.

Shakespeare gestured toward his own front door, which at that moment creaked open, sending fresh light into the hummocky yard where they stood. "Would you not—"

"My arse needs an hour of saddle, or sure will be hard-sore on the ride to London tomorrow," Jonson said.

Drayton nodded. "I go belike, to see to writ's business."

"My best bed be yours, if—"

"No, no, friend." Jonson swung up onto a roan horse with surprising agility for one so large. "You look chilled. Get inside to your good wife."

Ben waved good night, calling to the woman who had appeared in the doorway. She was broad and sturdy, graying beneath a frilly white cap, and stood with arms crossed, her stance full of judgment. "Farewell, Anne!"

Good-byes sounding through the frosty air, the two men clopped away. Vitrovna watched Shakespeare wave to them, cloak billowing, then turn to his wife. This was the Anne Hathaway whom his will left with his "second-best" bed, who had saddled him with children since his marriage at eighteen— and who may have forced him into the more profitable enterprise of playwriting to keep their household in something resembling the style of a country gentleman. Vitrovna got Anne's image as she croaked irritably at Shakespeare to come inside.

Vitrovna prayed that she would get the fragment of time she needed. Just a moment, to make a fleeting, last contact—

He hesitated. Then he waved his wife away and walked toward the woods. She barked something at him and slammed the door.

Vitrovna slipped from behind the elm and followed him. He coughed, stopped, and began to pee again into a bush.

An ailment? To have to go again so soon? Stratford's vicar had written that on this night Will "drank too hard," took ill, and died of a fever. This evidence suggested, though, that he knew something was awry when he wrote his will in March, a few weeks before this evening. Or maybe he had felt an ominous pressure from his approaching fifty-second birthday, two days away—when the fever would claim him.

All this flitted through her mind as she approached the wavering figure in the wood-smoke-flavored, whipping wind. He tucked himself back in, turned—and saw her.

Here the danger made her heart pound. If she did something to tweak the timeline a bit too much—

"Ah! Pardons, madam—the ale within would without."

"Sir, I've come to tell you of greatness exceeding anything you can dream." She had rehearsed this, striving for an accent that would not put him off, but now that she had heard his twangy Elizabethan lilt, she knew that was hopeless. She plowed ahead. "I wanted you to know that your name will be sung down the ages as the greatest of writers."

Will's tired, grizzled face wrinkled. "Who might you be?"

—and the solidity of the past struck her true, his breath sour with pickled herrings and Rhenish wine. The reeking intensity of the man nearly staggered her. Her isolated, word-clogged life had not prepared her for this vigorous, full-bodied age. She gulped and forced out her set speech.

"You may feel neglected now, but centuries hence you'll be read and performed endlessly—"

"*What* are you?" He scowled.

"I am from the future. I've come backward in time to tell you, so that such a wonderful man need not, well, need not think he was just a minor poet. Your plays, they're the thing. They—"

"You copy my lines? 'The play's the thing.' Think you that japing pranks—"

"No, no! I truly am from the future, many centuries away."

"And spring upon me in drafty night? I—"

Desperately she brought up her flashlight. "Look." It clicked on, a cutting blue-white beam that made the ground and leaves leap from inky presences into hard realities. "See? This is a kind of light you don't have. I can show you—"

He leaped back, eyes white, mouth sagging. "Uh!"

"Don't be afraid. I wondered if you could tell me something about the dark lady in your sonnets, just a moment's—"

"Magic!"

"No, really, it's just a different kind of lantern. And your plays, did you have any help writing them?"

He recovered, mouth curving shrewdly. "You be scholar or rumormonger?"

"Neither, sir."

His face hardened as he raised his palm to shield his eyes from the brilliance. "Think me gut-gullible?"

"You deserve to know that we in the future will appreciate you, love you, revere you. It's only justice that you know your works will live forever, be honored—"

"Promising me life forever, then? That's your cheese?"

"No, you don't—"

"This future you claim—know you something of my self, then? My appointed final hour?" His eyes were angry slits, his mouth a flat, bloodless line.

Was he so quick to guess the truth? That she had come at the one possible moment to speak to him, when his work or friends would not be perturbed? "I've come because, yes, this is my only chance to speak with you. There's nothing I can do about that, but I thought—"

"You tempt me with wisps, foul visions."

Did he suspect that once he walked into that house, lay upon his second-best bed, he would never arise again? With leaden certainty she saw him begin to gather this, his mouth working, chin bobbing uncertainly.

"Sir, no, please, I'm just here to, to—"

"Flat-voiced demon, leave me!"

"No, I—"

He reached into his loose-fitting shirt and drew out a small iron cross. Holding it up, he said, "Blest be he who spares my stones, curst be he who moves my bones!"

The lines chiseled above his grave. So he had them in mind already, called them up like an incantation. "I'm sorry, I didn't mean—"

"Go! Christ immaculate, drive such phantoms from me! Give me a sword of spirit, Lord!"

Vitrovna backed away. "I, I—"

—and then she was running, panicked and mortified, into the woods. In her ears rang a fragment from *The Tempest*,

What seest thou else
In the dark backward and abysm of time?

In the shimmering cylinder she panted with anxiety and mortification, her skin a sheen of cold sweat. She had failed terribly, despite decades of research. All her trial runs with ordinary folk of these times who were about to meet their end, carried out in similar circumstances—those had gone well. The subjects had welcomed her. Death was natural and common here, an easeful event. They had accepted her salute with stoic calm, a quality she had come to envy in these dim eras. Certainly they had not turned their angers on her.

But she had faltered before Shakespeare. He had been larger than life, awesome.

Her recordings were valuable, yes, but she might never be able to release them for scholarly purposes now. She had wrenched the past terribly, exciting the poor man just before death's black hand claimed him. She could never forget the look of wild surmise and gathering panic that worked across that wise face. And now—

She had stolen into the University Corps Facility, slipped into the machine with the aid of friends, all in the service of true, deep history. But if she had changed the past enough to send a ripple of causation forward, into her own era, then the Corps would find her, exact the penalty.

No time to think of that. She felt the sickening wrench, a shudder, and then she thumped down into a stony field.

Still night air, a sky of cutting stars. A liquid murmuring led her to the bank of the Big Wood River and she worked her way along it, looking for the house lights. This route she knew well, had paced it off in her own era. She could tell from the set of the stars that she had time, no need to rush this.

Minutes here took literally no time at all in the stilled future world where machines as large as the cities of this age worked to suspend her here. The essence of stealing time from the Corps was that you took infinitesimal time-wedges of that future world, undetectable, elusive—if she was lucky. The Corps would find her uses self-indulgent, sentimental, arrogant. To meddle so could snuff out their future, or merely Vitrovna herself—and all so a few writers could know for a passing moment of their eventual high destiny? Absurd, of course.

July's dawn heat made her shed her cloak and she paused to get her breath. The river wrinkled and pulsed and swelled smooth against the resistance of a big log, and she looked down through it to an unreadable depth. Trout hung in the glassy fast water like ornaments, holding into the current. Deeper still a fog of sand ran above the gravel, stirred by currents around the pale round rocks.

The brimming majesty of this silent moment caught at her heart. Such simple beauty had no protection here, needed none.

After a long moment she made herself go on and found the house as faint streamers traced the dawn. Blocky, gray poured concrete, hunkered down like a bunker. A curious, closed place for a man who had yearned to be of the land and sky. In 1926 he had said, "The real reason for not committing suicide is because you always know how swell life gets again after the hell is over." Yet in this spare, beautiful place of rushing water and jutting stone he would finally yield to the abyss that had tempted him all his wracked life.

She worked her way up the stony slope, her Elizabethan shoes making the climb hard. As she reached the small outer

door into the basement, she fished forth the flex-key. Its yellow
metal shaped itself to whatever opening the lock needed, and
in a moment she was inside the storage room, beside the heavy
mahogany rack. She had not seen such things except for photographs. Elegant machines of blue sheen and polished, pointful
shapes. Death solidified and lustrous. They enchanted her as
she waited.

A rustling upstairs. Steps going into the kitchen, where she
knew he would pick up the keys on the ledge above the sink.
He came down the stairs, haggard in the slack pajamas and
robe, the handsome face from photographs now lined and
worn, wreathed by a white beard and tangled hair. He padded
toward the rack, eyes distant, and then stopped, blinking, as
he saw her.

"What the hell?" A rough voice, but recognizable.

"Mr. Hemingway, I ask only a moment of your time, here
at the end. I—"

"You're from the IRS aren't you? Snooping into my—"

Alarm spiked in her throat. "No sir, I am from the future.
I've come backward in time to tell you, so that so wonderful
a man need not—"

"FBI?" The jowly face clouded, eyes narrow and bright. "I
know you've been following me, bribing my friends."

The drinking, hypertension, hepatitis, and creeping manic depression had driven him further even than her research suggested.

She spread her hands. "No, no. You deserve to know that
we in the future will appreciate you, love you, revere you. It's
only justice that you know your works will live forever, be
honored—"

"You're a goddamn federal agent and a liar on top of that."
His yellowed teeth set at an angry angle. "Get out!"

"Remember when you said that you wanted to get into the
ring with Mr. Tolstoy? Well, you have, you did. You're in his
class. Centuries from now—"

A cornered look came into the jumping eyes. "Sure, I've got six books I declare to win with. I stand on that."

"You have! I come from—"

"You a critic? Got no use for sneaky bastards come right into your house, beady-eyed nobodies, ask you how you write like it was how you shit—"

He leaned abruptly against the pinewood wall and she caught a sour scent of defeat from him. Color drained from his wracked face and his head wobbled. "Future, huh?" He nodded as if somehow accepting this. "God, I don't know . . ."

She stepped back, fear tight in her throat. Earlier in this year he had written, *A long life deprives a man of his optimism. Better to die in all the happy period of unillusioned youth, to go out in a blaze of light, than to have your body worn out and old and illusions shattered.* She saw it now in the loose cant of mouth and jaw, the flickering anxiety and hollow dread. The power of it was unbearable.

"I . . . I wanted you to know that those novels, the short stories, they will—"

The sagging head stopped swaying. It jerked up. "Which have you read?"

"All of them. I'm a literary historian."

"Damn, I'm just read by history professors?" Disdain soured the words.

There were no such professions in her time, just the departments of the Corps, but she could not make this ravaged man understand that. "No, your dramas are enjoyed by millions, by billions—"

"Dramas?" He lurched against the wall. "I wrote no dramas."

How to tell him that the media of her time were not the simple staged amusements of this era? That they were experienced directly through the nervous system, sensory banquets of immense emotional power, lived events that diminished the linear medium of words alone to a curious relic?

"You mean those bum movies made from the novels? Tracy in *The Old Man?*"

"No, I mean—we have different ways of reading the same work, that is all. But for so long I've felt the despair of artists who did not know how much they would mean, poor Shakespeare going to his grave never suspecting—"

"So you know what I'm down here for?" A canny glint in the eyes.

"Yes, of course, that's why I came."

He pulled himself erect with visible effort. "If you're not just another shit artist come here to get a rise out of me—"

"I'm not, I'm a scholar who feels so much for you lonely Primitivists who—"

"That's what you call us? Real writers? *Primitives?*" Jutting jaw. "I'm going to kick your goddamn ass out of here!"

His sudden clotted rage drove her back like a blow. "I meant—"

"Go!" He shoved her. "Hell will freeze over before I'll give in to a lard-ass—"

She bolted away, out the basement door, into the spreading dawn glow. Down the rocky slope, panic gurgling acid in her mouth. She knew that years before this, when asked his opinion of death, he had answered, "Just another whore." Yet there was something new and alive in his face just now, fresh fuel from his sudden, hugely powerful anger, some sea change that sent into her mind a wrenching possibility.

She looked back at the house. He was standing there thin and erect, shaking a knotted fist down at her. She reached the dawn-etched river and punched the summons into her controls and then came the wringing snap and she was in the cylinder again.

Vitrovna let a ragged sigh escape into the cool, calming air. This one was as unsettling as the last. The old man had seemed animated as she left, focused outside himself by her visit. He had kept her off balance the entire time.

Now she saw her error. The earlier tests with ordinary people, whose deaths did not matter in the flow of history, had misled her. In person Shakespeare and Hemingway loomed immensely larger than anyone she had ever known. Compared with the wan, reasonable people of her time, they were bristly giants. Their reactions could not be predicted and they unsettled even her, a historian who thought she knew what to expect.

Vitrovna leaned back, shaken and exhausted. She had programmed a long rest after this engagement, time to get her thoughts in order before the next. That one, the great poet Diana Azar, lay as far ahead in centuries as the gap between the last two, yet her simple dress should still pass there and—

A slim man materialized at the snub end of the cylinder. He wore a curious blue envelope which revealed only head and hands, his skin a smooth green.

"Ah," he said in a heavily accented tenor, "I have intersected you in time."

She gasped. "You—how? To catch me while transporting—"

"In your age, impossible, of course." He arched his oyster-colored forehead, which had no eyebrows. "But when you are in Transition we of your far future may snag you."

She had thought for decades about what she would do if caught, and now said cannily, "You follow the Code standards for self-incrimination?"

She blinked with shock when he laughed. "Code? Ancient history—though it's all the same here, of course. I am not one of your Corps police."

"Then you're not going to prosecute—"

"That was an illusion of your time, Vitrovna. You don't mind me using your first name? In our era, we have only one name, though many prefer none."

"But how can you . . ."

He languidly folded his arms, which articulated as if his elbows were double-jointed. "I must first say that generations far beyond yours are eternally grateful to you for opening this possibility and giving us these historical records." He gestured at her senso-binoculars.

"Records? They survived? I mean, I do make it back to my—"

"Not precisely. But the detailed space-time calculations necessary to explain, these you would not understand. You braved the Codes and the Corps quite foolishly, as you have just discovered—but that is of no import to us."

She felt a rush of hope, her lips opening in expectation. "Then you've come to rescue me from them?"

He frowned, a gesture which included his ears. "No, no. You feared the Corps' authority, but that was mere human power. They vaguely understood the laws of acausality, quite rightly feared them, and so instituted their Code. But they were like children playing with shells at the shore, never glimpsing the beasts which swam in the deeps beyond."

Her seat jolted and she felt queasy. He nodded, as if expecting this, and touched his left wrist, which was transparent.

"The Code was a crude rule of thumb, but your violations of it transgressed far beyond mere human edicts. How arrogant, your age! To think that your laws could rule a continuum. Space-time itself has a flex and force. Your talk with Hemingway—quite valuable historically, by the way, considering that he was not going to ever release his memoir, *A Moveable Feast,* when he went down into that basement. But even more important was what he wrote next."

"Next? But he—"

"Quite. Even so, rather less spectacular than your 'apparition' before Shakespeare. As his shaky hand testified, you cause him to gather his notes and scraps of plays. They kept quite well in even a tin box, wedged in with the corpse. A bounty for the critics, though it upset many cherished theories."

"But he still died of pneumonia?"

"You do not have miraculous healing powers. You simply scared him into leaving something more of a record."

"Still, with so much attention paid to the few records we do have, or *did* have, I—"

"Quite." A judicious nod. "I'm afraid that despite our vastly deeper understanding of these matters, there is nothing we can do about that. Causality will have its way."

The cylinder lurched. A raw bass note. "Then how—"

"Not much time left, I'm afraid. Sorry." He leaned forward eagerly. "But I did want to visit you, to thank you for, well, liberating this method of probing the past, at great personal sacrifice. You deserve to know that our epoch will revere you."

He spoke rapidly, admiration beaming in his odd face, the words piling up in an awful leaden weight that sent bile-dark fear rushing hotly through her, a massive premonition.

"So Vitrovna, I saw the possibility, of making this intersection. It's only right that you know just how famous you will be—"

The sensation of stepping off a step into a dark, unending fall.

Her speech. He was giving her own speech, and for the same reason.

The Voice

"I don't believe it," Qent said sternly.

Klair tugged him down the musty old corridor. "Come on, turn off your Voice. Mine is—I showed you."

"Stuff on walls, whoever heard of—"

"There's another one further along."

Down the narrow, dimly lit hallway they went, to a recessed portion of the permwall. "See—another sign."

"This? Some old mark. What's a 'sign' anyway?"

"This one says"— she shaped the letters to herself carefully—"PASSAGE DENIED."

Qent thumbed on his Voice impatiently. He blinked. "That's . . . what the Voice says."

"See?"

"You've been here before and the Voice told you."

"I let you pick the corridor, remember? A fair trial."

"You cheated."

"No! I can read it." Read. The very sound of the word made her pulse thump.

Qent paused a second and she knew he was consulting the Voice again. "And 'read' means to untangle things, I see. This 'sign' tells you PASSAGE DE-NIED? How?"

"See those?—they're letters. I know each one—there

are twenty-six, it takes a lot of work—and together they shape words."

"Nonsense," Qent said primly. "Your mouth shapes words."

"I have another way. My way."

He shook his head and she had to take him on to another sign and repeat the performance. He grimaced when the Voice told him that, indeed, the markings meant ALDENTEN SECTOR. "A trick. Your Voice is on. You just rigged your touchpad—"

"Here, take my insert!" She thrust it into his hand and made him walk to the next emblem. "MANUFAC DIST, that way."

"I know an arrow when I see it," he said sarcastically. "But the rest of it—what's DIST mean?"

She had hoped he wouldn't ask that. "Maybe it means a place."

"Like a neighborhood?"

"Could be—in fact, yes, 'district.' If there wasn't room to write it all out, they'd shorten a word."

"And who were 'they'? Some magicians?"

"The ancients, I guess."

He was working his way around to being convinced, she could see. "They left wall marks? What for, when the Voice—"

"Maybe they came before the Voice."

"But what possible use—"

"I learned all this from those old papers I uncovered in the Historical Section. They were called 'Bills of Lading' but there were enough words—"

"How do you know you can 'read' something? I mean, without checking with the Voice?"

"I know. The letters group together, you see—MANUFAC is just 'man' and this upturned letter is the sound 'you,' and—"

"You're going too fast." He grimaced, obviously not liking this at all. He was a biology specialist and tolerated her interest in antiquity, but finally he said, "Okay, show me again. Not that I really believe this, but . . ."

*   *   *

They spent the next few days in the oldest precinct of the Historical Sector, searching out corridors that the Imperium had not gotten around to Voicing. Klair read him signs and he started picking up the method. Progress was slow; reading was hard. Letters, words, then working up to grasping how sentences and then paragraphs had their logic and rhythms, their clues about how to extract meaning.

Still, it wasn't as though he were some Deedee, after all. After a while she recalled from her Educational Specialty training that Deedees were actually officially called the Developmentally Delayed. So if someone had once taken just the first letters of both words, that was how they had gotten their name.

Everything went well between them and they got to like having their Voices off while they strolled through the antiquated hallways, making sense of the signs.

The Voice was always available if they needed it. Link-chips embedded near both ears could pick up the pervasive waves of CompCentral. They only had basic link, no frills but constant access. Like everybody, they had used the Voice more as time went on; it was so easy.

But reading gave them a touch of the past and some silence. It was a relief, really.

They had kept their Voices nearly always on. It was easy to get used to the Voice's silky advertisements that floated just within hearing. You could pay the subscriber service for the Voice and have no ads, but none of their friends did: it was far too expensive. And anyway, the ads told you a lot about people. There was a really interesting one for sperm and egg donors to the gay/les bank, a Meritocracy program to help preserve the Gay Gene. It had zoomer sonics and life histories and everything. You could amp it and hear a whole half-hour show if you wanted. For free, too. But most weren't anywhere near that good, so they were glad to be rid of them.

Reading, though, grew on them. There were advantages to reading old signs that the Voice didn't bother to translate. They showed off to a few friends but nobody believed they could really read the curious markings. It had to be some trick, for sure. Klair and Qent just smiled knowingly and dropped the subject.

Not that it was all good. At an old intersection Qent honored the GO signal by reading it, rather than listening to his Voice. The signal was off synch and he nearly got flattened by a roller car.

They debated whether to tell anyone in authority. After all, maybe nobody knew this.

"Ummm, no," Qent said. "Look at it this way—carrion eaters rule the world, in their way. Because nobody cares. Nobody wants what they like."

"So we'd be fools to make other people like reading?"

"Demand rises, supplies fall. Suppose everybody wanted those old books you found?"

She had to admit it was a sobering possibility. The carrion-eater analogy came out of his biology training, and he couldn't resist adding, "It's a smart strategy. When times are tough on everybody, the buzzards just get more to eat."

The thought was so disgusting she decided to forget about the whole question.

They came to like strolling the byways of the Megapolis, ferreting out the antiquated secrets of the signs. Lovers often find their own rituals, and this was a particularly delectable one.

Outside one vaultway there were clearly marked instructions on how to spin a dial and get in. They had to work on it for quite a while but finally they made it work. The door swung open on primitive hinges and they walked into a musty set of rooms. Exploring them proved boring; just stacks of locked compartments, all without signs. Until a guard came in with a drawn zapper.

"How'd you kids get in here?"

"It was open, sir," Qent said. He had always been quick, and Klair supposed his answer was technically correct. She had opened the door.

"How the hell—? Well, get out. Out!"

He was confused and worried and hardly gave them more than a brief search. Qent asked to see the zapper, imitating a dumbo kid, and the guard brushed them off, still puzzled.

Until the vault she had not realized that her hard-won trick was anything more than a delicious secret. Klair was a scholarly type and enjoyed her hours of scanning over the decaying sheets she found in the Historical Sector's archives.

The fat ones she learned were called "books" and there was even an entry in the Compendium about them. The Voice recited the entry to her in its soft tones, the ones she had chosen for her daily work. She used a more ornate voice for social matters and a crisp, precise one for directions. In normal life that was all anyone needed, a set of pleasing Voice agents.

There was hardly any delay when she requested the book entry, and the Voice told a marvelous tale. There were many kinds of books, including one called "novel." This meant new, the Voice said. But the one novel Klair found in the dank, dark Antiquities Vault was obviously old, not new at all. Such confusions were inevitable in research, she realized.

Books were known also as buchs in some ancient sources, it said, in the confusing era when there were competing Voices. Not really even Voices, either, but whole different speech-methods, before Standard was discovered.

All that happened in the Narrow Age, as antiquarians termed it. A time of constrained modes, hopelessly linear and slow. People then were divided by their access to information. Thank goodness such divisive forces were now banished.

They now lived in the Emergent Age, of course. The Voice had emerged from the evolution of old style Intelligent Agents, on computers. Those would perform fetch-'em tasks. Gradually, people let their Agents do more and more. Agent merging led to more creativity, coming from the overlap of many voices, many threads in a society where all was open and clear to all, available through the Voice.

"What sop!" Qent said to this, and she sort of agreed. The Narrow Age sounded fascinating, with its books and reading. The tingling thrill of being able to hold a year's worth of Voice talk in your hand, opening it to anywhere you chose, picking out lore at will—it captivated her.

Of course, she knew the Voice was superior. Instantly it could skip to any subject or even word you liked in any record. It would explain in private, sounding just like an enormously smart person speaking to you alone, in your head. Everybody had one and could access it with an internal signal.

She looked up the Voice itself in one of the old books. The words were hard to follow and she began to wish for some way to find out what they meant. Sounding them out was hard because, even when she knew the word, the mapping from letters to sounds followed irregular rules. "What's the point of that?" Qent asked often, but he kept at it with her.

The books said that the Voice had started as an aid to people called "illiterates"—and Klair was startled to find, consulting the Voice, that everybody was one. Except her and Qent, now.

Once, lots and lots of people could read. But as the Voice got easier to use, a certain cachet attached to using only the Voice. Independence from linear "print-slavery" became fashionable, then universal. After all, the Voice could pipe the data you needed on fast-flow, a kind of compressed speech that was as fast (or in fact, by that time, faster) as people could read.

Most people got their information by eye, anyway. In a restaurant, they ordered chicken by touching the drumstick icon, or fish by the fish-stick icon. And of course most of their time they spent at entertainments, which had to be visual, tactile, smell-rich—sports, 3Ds, sensos, a-morphs, realos.

She found it quite delicious to have an obscure, secret talent that none of her friends even guessed. She was going to have a party and show them all, but then she saw the big letters in the Boulevard of Aspiration, and things got complicated.

*   *   *

Qent said, "I make it to be—

SAVVY THIS? MEAT 13:20 @ Y."

Skeptically he eyed the poorly printed letters written in livid red on a blue wall.

"Somebody did that by hand," Klair marveled.

"Writing by yourself? How?"

"I hadn't thought anybody could. I mean, machines make letters, don't they?"

"You're the one who read all those historical books. Printing machines gave way to Voice machines, you said."

Klair traced a hand over the misshapen letters. "It's like making a drawing, only you try to imitate a machine, see? Think of letters as little art objects."

"This isn't an art exhibit."

"No, it's a message. But maybe I can . . ."

By luck she had in her side-sack her latest cherished discovery, a fat book called "Dictionary." It had many more words in it than the Voice, approximating and vernacular. Big words that nobody used anymore, hadn't used for so long even the Voice didn't know them. It even told her that "@" meant "at," but not why.

"Here." She pointed forcefully at the tiny little entry. "Meat is the flesh of an animal."

"Animals do that. I heard that people used to."

"Primitivo!" she said scornfully.

"It may mean that in there, but it *sounds* like 'meet.' "

"Somebody made an error? Confusing the sound with another word?"

"Somebody wants people who can read the sign to meet them."

"Other readers."

"Where?" He frowned.

"It says 'Y.' That's not a word."

"Maybe it's an abbreviation, like that MANUFAC DIST?"

"No, too short."

He snapped his fingers. "Remember where the Avenue of Aspiration branches? You can look down on it from the balcony of the Renew building. From above, it looks like that letter."

"Let's be there, then."

They showed up, but nobody else did. Instead, at the Y another crude hand-lettered sign said

MEAT CORRIDOR 63,
13:30 TOMORROW, BLOCK 129

They went home and turned off their Voices and talked. Most couples silenced the Voice only during sex. This was merely polite, even though of course no other person could be sure it was off nowadays, what with the new neuroactivated models.

They went home and sped-read some ancient texts. There was a thick book titled *The Lust of the Mahicans* that Qent had seen on senso. She read it—her speed was a lot higher than his—but it wasn't anything like the senso he had seen. There was no sex in it at all. Just stares of infinite longing and heavy breathing and pounding pulses and stuff like that. Still, she found it oddly stirring. Reading was funny that way.

They could not get their minds off the sign. Qent was out of sorts, irked that others had mastered their discovery. He groused about it vaguely and found excuses to change the subject.

Klair didn't see it possessively. After all, the higher moral good was to share. Reading was wickedly single-ist. Was that why she liked it so much? A reader was isolated, listening to a voice no one else could take part in. That led to differences and divisions, friction and clashes.

Still, the rapture of reading—of listening to silent sounds

from ages past—was too, well, perhaps the right word was titillating.

She was excited by the prospect of other readers. Inevitably, they went to the site.

The man who slouched beside a rampway was not impressive. Medium height, his crimson codpiece was three years out of date. His hair was stringy and festooned with comically tattered microbirds. He said nothing, simply handed them a sheet. Miserably printed sentences covered both sides. The first paragraph was enough for Klair:

THE SECRET ASSEMBLY OF READERS MUST UNITE! WE HAVE A TALENT THE MASSES CANNOT UNDERSTAND. THEY WILL FEAR US IF THEY KNOW. A BROTHERHOOD AND SISTERHOOD OF READERS IS THE ONLY SOLUTION TO OUR ISOLATION. ARISE!

"What cliché sop!" She thrust the sheet back at him.

"True, though."

Qent said sharply, "Just tell us what you—"

"You never know when the Voice is on," the man said mysteriously.

Klair said, "And your printing is awful."

"Better than yours," he said shrewdly.

"That's not the point," Qent said. "We demand to know—"

"Come on. And shut up, huh?"

They were in a wildness preserve before the man spoke. "I'm Marq. No Voice pickups here, at least according to the flow charts."

"You're an engineer?" Klair asked, admiring the oaks.

"I'm a philosopher. I make my money engineering."

"How long have you been reading?"

"Years. Started with some old manuals I found. Figured it out from scratch."

"So did we." Qent said. "It's hard, not being able to ask for help from the Voice."

Marq nodded. "I did. Dumb, huh?"

"What happened?"

"Some Spectors came by. Just casual talk, y'know, but I knew what they were after."

"Evidence?" she asked uneasily.

"When I asked the Voice there was a pause, just a little one. A priority shift, I know how to spot them. So I broke off and took the books I had to a hiding place. When I got back there were the Spectors, cool as you like, just kind of looking around my room."

"You didn't tell them . . . ?" she asked.

"You got to give them something. I had a copy of this thing about books that I couldn't understand, *Centigrade 233.* Kept it buried under a pseud-bush bed. They were getting funny on me so I took it out and gave it to them."

She blinked, startled. "What did they do? Arrest you?"

Marq gave her a crooked grin. "Reading's not illegal, y'know. Just anti, that's all. So they let me off with six weeks of grouping."

"Wow, do I hate those," Qent said.

Marq shrugged. "I did the time. They poked at me and I had to pretend to see the light and all. They kept the book."

"You're brave," Klair said.

"Just stupid. I should never have asked the Voice."

Qent said earnestly, "You'd think the Voice would encourage us to learn. I mean, it'd be useful in emergencies. Say the Voice goes down, we could read the info we'd need."

Marq nodded. "I figure the Voice reads. It just doesn't want competition."

She said, "The Voice is a machine."

"So?" Marq shrugged again. "Who knows how smart it is?"

"It's a service," Qent said. "That's all."

"Notice how it won't store what we say?" Marq smiled shrewdly.

Qent nodded. "It says it's trying to improve our memories."

"Reading was invented to replace memory," Klair said. "I read it in a history book."

"So it must be true?" Marq shrugged derisively, a gesture that was beginning to irk Klair a lot.

She hated politics and this was starting to sound like that. "How many books have you got?"

"Lots. I found a tunnel into a vault. I can go there anytime."

Qent and Klair gasped at his audacity as he described how for years he had burrowed into sealed-off chambers, many rich in decaying documents and bound volumes. He spoke of exotica they had never seen, tomes which were nothing but names in the Dictionary: Encyclopedias, Thesauruses, Atlases, Almanacs. He had read whole volumes of the fabled Britannica!

Would he trade? Lend? "Of course," Marq said warmly.

Their friendship began that way, a bit edgy and cautious at the margins, but dominated by the skill and secret lore they shared. Three years of clandestine reading followed before Marq disappeared.

He wasn't at any of their usual meeting places. After all this time, they still did not know where he lived, or where his hoard of books might be. Marq was secretive. They searched the sprawling corridors of the complexes, but were afraid to ask the Voice for any info on him.

The Majority Games were on then, so the streets were more crowded than usual. Most people were out all the time, excited and eager and happy to be in the great mobs that thronged the squares. The Games took up everybody's time—except, of course, the three hours of work everyone had to put in, no exceptions, every laborday. Klair and Qent broke up to cover more ground and spent a full week on the search. Many times Klair blamed herself for not pressing Marq about where he lived, but the man was obsessively secretive. "Suppose they grab you, make you tell about me?" he had always countered.

Now she wondered what the Spectors would do if they uncovered a lode of books like Marq's. Send him to Advanced Treatment? Or was there something even worse?

She came home after a day of dogged searching and Qent

was not there. He did not appear that evening. When she awoke the next morning she burst into tears. He was gone that day and the one after.

On her way back from work, a routine counseling job, she resolved to go to the Spector. She halfheartedly watched the crowds, hoping to see Marq or Qent, and that was how she noticed that three men and a woman were moving parallel to her as she crossed the Plaza of Promise. They were all looking some other way but they formed four points of the compass around her with practiced precision.

She walked faster and they did too. They looked stern and remorseless and she could not lose them in the warrens of streets and corridors near the two-room apartment she shared with Qent. They had waited five years to get one with a tiny balcony. Even then it was just two levels up from the muddy floor of the air shaft. But if you hooked your head over to the side you could see some sky that way.

Klair kept moving in an aimless pattern and they followed. Of course she did not want to go to the apartment, where she would be trapped. But she was tired and she could not think of anything else to do.

They knocked a few minutes after she collapsed on the bed. She had hoped they might hold off for a while. She was resigned. When she spun the door open the person she least expected to see was Marq.

"You won't believe what's going on," he said, brushing past her.

"What? Where have you—"

"The Meritocrats want us."

"For what?"

"Reading!"

"But the Voice—"

"Keeps people out of touch and happy. Great idea—but it turns out you can't run everything with just the Voice." He blinked, the merest hesitation. "Somebody's got to be able to access info at a higher level. That was our gut feeling, remember—that reading was different."

"Well, yes, but the Spectors—"

"They keep people damped down, is all." A slight pause. "Anybody who's got the savvy to see the signs, the grit to learn to piece together words on their own, to process it all—those are the people the Merits want. Us!"

Klair blinked. This was too much to encompass. "But why did they take you away, and Qent—"

"Had to be sure." He gave his old familiar shrug. "Wanted to test our skills, make sure we weren't just posing. People might catch on, only pretend to read, y'know?"

"I . . . see." There was something about Marq that wasn't right. He had never had these pauses before . . . because he wasn't listening to the Voice then?

She backed away from him. "That's marvelous news. When will Qent be back?"

"Oh, soon, soon." He advanced and she backed out onto the balcony.

"So what job will you do? I mean, with reading in it?"

They were outside. She backed into the railing. The usual distant clatter and chat of the air shaft gave her a momentary sense of security. Nothing could happen here, could it?

"Oh, plenty. Looking up old stuff, comparing, y'know." He waved his hands vaguely.

It wasn't much of a drop from here. Over the railing, legs set right . . .

"It's good work, really."

Could she could get away if she jumped? Marq wasn't the athletic type and she knew that if she landed right on the mud below she wouldn't twist an ankle or anything. She had on sensible shoes. She could elude him. If she landed right.

She gave him a quick, searching look. Had he come here alone? No, probably there were Spectors outside her door, just waiting for him to talk her into surrendering. Stall for time, yes.

"How bad is it?"

He grinned. "You won't mind. They just access that part of your mind for three hours a day. Then they install a shutdown on that cerebral sector."

"Shutdown? I—"

"So you don't need to read anymore. Just during work, is all. You get all you need that way. Then you're free!"

She thought it through. Jump, get away. Couldn't use the Voice for help because they could undoubtedly track her if she had her receiver on. Could she get by just reading the old signs?

Suppose she could. Then what? Find some friends she could trust. Stay underground? How? Living off what?

"It's much better. Qent will be back soon and—"

"Hold it. Don't move."

She looked down the air shaft. Was the jump worth it?

You spool out of the illusion and *snap*—back into the tight cocoon. The automatic sensory leads retract, giving your skin momentary pinprick goodbye kisses. Once more you feel the cool clasping surfaces of the cocoon. Now you turn and ask, "Hey, where's the rest?"

Myrph shrugs her shoulders, still busy undoing her leads. "That's all there was, I told you."

"Maybe it's just damaged?"

"No, that's the end of the cube. There must be another cube to finish the story, but this was the only one I found back in that closet."

"But how does it end? What's she do?" You lean toward her, hoping maybe she's just teasing.

"I dunno. What would you do? Jump?"

You blink, not ready for the question. "Uh, this reading thing. What is it, really?"

Myrph frowns. "It felt like a kind of your own silent voice inside your head."

"Is it real? I mean, does reading exist?"

"Never heard of it."

"So this isn't an historical at all, right? It's a fantasy."

"Must be. I've never seen those things on walls."

"Signs, she called them." You think back. "They would have worn away a long time ago, anyway."

"I guess. Felt kinda strange, didn't it, being able to find out things without the Voice?"

You bite your lip, thinking. Already the illusion of being that woman is slipping away, hard to fix in memory. She did have a kind of power all on her own with that reading thing. You liked that. "I wonder what she did?"

"Hey, it's just a story."

"What would you do?"

"I don't have to decide. It's just a story."

"But why tell it, then?"

Myrph says irritably, "It's just an old illusion, missing a cube."

"Maybe there was only one."

"Look, I want illusions to take me away, not stress me out."

You remember the power of it. "Can I have it, then?"

"The cube? Sure."

Myrph tosses it over. It is curiously heavy, translucent and chipped with rounded corners. You cup it in your hand and like the weight of it.

That is how it starts. You know already that you will go and look for the signs in the corridors and that for good or ill something new has come into your world and will now never leave it.

Kollapse

When the Kollapse came, Wirehead jumped to his feet, knocking over his stand of compact disks with a clatter. He picked up his Kollapse Kit 2.4, his own design, and slung it over his back. It weighed over twenty kilos— nobody on the Net used old-fashioned English units— and he waddled as he started directly for the front door of his family home.

In the street people were looking around in wonder, trying to figure out what to do. They murmured to each other, mere gossip and speculation, no real data.

He avoided their questions. If they had not prepared for this day, if they did not have the database to fathom how the threads of complexity in modern society could warp and buckle under the sheer stress of the modernity of it all, that was their problem. He had said this many times on polisci.talk.com, one of the Net bulletin boards devoted to earnest and insightful discussions of just such possibilities—no, certainties, Wirehead reminded himself—as the Collapse. Or the Kollapse, as some of the more hip and aware guys on the Net called it.

He went back inside and took the extra set of keys to the family car from the secret place he had hidden them, right beside the car itself in the garage. He hit the button for the automatic garage door opener and nothing happened. So the electrical grid had gone out already. Very well; that just verified one of his predictions in "Overture to the Krunch," a piece he had written for Apocalypse.on-line.net over two years ago. It had even been excerpted on *HotWired,* the online magazine.

He pulled the release cord on the door opener and grunted as he heaved upward on the door handle. It slid up with a metallic clatter that sounded to Wirehead like the death rattle of civilization itself. He could hear his parents calling his name in the house but he ignored them because of course they had no application now to the problems of this wholly new and transformed world.

Wirehead got into his father's car and backed out into the street. There was a change in the tenor of the background noises. People were shouting angrily, others were simply alarmed, their cozy routines disturbed, the infinite buffet of services at an end. Pathetic voices, unable to deal with even so predictable a phenomenon as a power failure. Nineteenth century tech, yet most people did not understand even the rudiments of it.

He drove toward the east, which he had decided in his careful plans of several years before afforded the best escape route. In his rearview mirror—more exactly, in his father's, since Wirehead spent all his money on computer gear and Net online costs and had nothing left for lesser hardware like cars—he saw his parents come out of the house and begin to run after him. They were both nearly fifty and therefore hopelessly mired in the thought patterns of the dead past. He stepped on the gas. The full-throated growl of the engine, another piece of antiquated tech but still useful, filled him with purpose. Soon his parents dwindled away in the rearview mirror even though they had begun running with surprising speed. His father lasted longer, though of course that came from the pointless sports his father had wasted time on instead of sharpening his computer skills. That was the old way, and the Kollapse would sweep aside men like his father. His mother was just a woman. Neither would fit the world that was being born today.

As he left town he saw a lot of other people doing the same. How had his Tactic #1, "Escape from the disintegrating infrastructure," leaked out to the rabble? Probably some hacker breaking into his super-secret personal computer files. He mentally tipped his hat—though of course no one he knew wore a hat, and those with caps wore them backwards—to the info-thief who had gotten past his digital snares and protocols.

But then he realized that no one could have gotten to his files because they were all on floppy disks, tucked right into his Kollapse Kit 2.4. No one could access them through the Net. That meant that these people around him had devised the same tactic. A scowl crossed Wirehead's face, but he then reasoned that these mundanes would soon thin out. They were probably driving to take shelter with their relatives or some other antique notion. Time would prove their folly.

He had barely reached a wooded area before the car coughed and glided to a stop. A simple inspection of the car's old fashioned dashboard showed an analog needle which registered gasoline reserve. It read zero. His father's fault, of course, another example among many of lack of foresight, by a generation now completely out of date.

He got out of the car. There were no gas stations nearby. He hefted the Kit pack and set out. When he did pass near a gas station, there were a lot of people there. He stood at a distance and watched them bicker with the owner over paying for gasoline, and when a fight broke out he wisely turned away into the woods. Incredible, arguing over the exchange of useful fluids for useless, symbolic paper. He had no money to buy anything, because in the new order about to descend upon the world in the wake of the Kollapse, all value would be digitized.

The masters of that new millennium would be those who had the Net skills to manage the innovative regime.

Shouts. He studied the gas station through binoculars. A man was waving a gun.

How pointless. Power would not come from old methods. That man was mired in the past.

He struck out with the sure, steady gait of one who has the future in his pocket and knows it.

Soon dark came. He had always thought of the Kollapse coming with the morning, representing as it did a new day in human consciousness, so the fall of dusk was a little unsettling. Already the woods had petered out and he was heading into grasslands. Best to get as far as possible. He had a flashlight with him, a real gem, only thirty grams and surprisingly powerful. In the excitement he had forgotten to take it out of the Kollapse Kit 2.4, and when he did now it gave no light because, of course, it was solar powered.

For weeks he had been meaning to recharge the batteries. Well, he couldn't do everything. He put it away and forged on. Bushes brushed him in the gathering gloom and then he sprawled headlong into a ditch. He lay there calculating his best move. He was not injured but after a while he decided that perhaps he should stop anyway.

He lay there in the night and watched a satellite skim across the horizon. To be so visible it had to be in low orbit, probably specially launched for surveillance.

He fell asleep shivering. Kollapse Kit 2.4 had no room for bulky things like blankets, which could be acquired later anyway in exchange for far more valuable data. The thin silvered sheets he had instead helped some, but weren't really comforting.

At dawn he surveyed the terrain ahead. Rugged, just the thing to stop the mindless hordes from following him. He climbed a hill and looked back. Through his pocket binoculars he watched a distant highway, packed to a standstill with traffic, a perfect metaphor.

Time for breakfast. He got out his laptop and set it on its black plastic mat. All the gear in the Kit was black, the only hip color. A black cord led to a solar array.

He powered up and felt the gigabytes surge beneath his fingertips. He accessed his hard disk library and found EDIBLE PLANTS OF NORTH AMERICA. A quick word search found his area, and on the screen popped up three-color displays of leaves, berries, and roots. In a few seconds he held color hardcopy from his printer, a marvel of compactness. He spent the half hour allotted in his schedule searching for these as he hiked along, but the hardcopy colors did not match very well with those in nature. It occurred to Wirehead that maybe he should have done some field research about this. Still, that would have taken valuable time, too, he reasoned. He could not risk eating anything potentially poisonous so he slogged on.

The few scattered houses he avoided. They had no satellite dishes in view and so were probably not tied into the Net and would be left behind in the New Info Order. Reorganizing the world would be by definition a global problem. How could this point have eluded them?

At lunchtime, without any foraged berries or leaves, he kept his strength up with the one can of warm Jolt cola he had brought. This did not quiet his rumbling stomach so he used his remaining water reserve to dissolve some bouillon cubes. These were beef bouillon and quite salty. When he had planned his Kollapse Kit 2.4 the bouillon was to accompany the chopped berries and roots around a crackling fire. Drinking salty cold water in scrub desert, though, just made him thirsty.

By this time he had gotten a sunburn even though he was wearing a cap. He wore the cap backwards of course, so that he did not look like a dork. It had a team emblem above the bill, but he never wasted his time watching such stuff and did not know what team the emblem represented, or even what sport. The sunburn itched a lot. He spent all his time indoors, on the Net, or else in the virtual reality setup he had built himself, complete with data gloves and spex. He thought about the cool recesses of cyberspace while his tongue rasped on his lips like a file on rock.

He reached Focus Point 3.5 in early afternoon. It was a cave in a folded sandstone ridge. He had picked it himself from a detailed topographical survey, available on ftp@geosurv.gov. The survey had not shown that below the cave was a steep drop—the resolution was only five meters—into thick brambles. Wirehead discovered this while inching along the ridgeline. He had chosen to approach Focus Point 3.5 from above so that he could see and assess whoever had already reached it. Planning was paying off. Peering over the edge, he slipped and tumbled down—by the cave, then over the drop.

Getting out of the brambles and putting bandages on several parts of himself took longer than he had allowed in his plans. It was already late afternoon when he flopped at the entrance of the dusky cave. He lay there panting and noticed that his shoes had worn down considerably, even though they were made of the latest high-impact plastics.

No time to search for firewood. He was tired anyway. He lay there and thought about ice cream until he heard footsteps.

It was HeavyLink, marching along under an antique Desert Storm field helmet. Wirehead recognized HeavyLink and the helmet from the picture posted on the Kollapse bulletin board. He had never met HeavyLink before, of course, because there was no need to travel in real space when your mind was free in cyberspace.

"Hi," he said.

"Uh, hi." HeavyLink was shorter than Wirehead had expected, somehow, with a big belly.

"Glad ta meecha, Heavy." Wirehead shook hands. HeavyLink's grip was soft.

"We're in the big-time, Wired."

Wirehead's real name was Arnold, like Schwarzenegger, but on the Net he was Wirehead@user.web.com. and preferred to stay that way even face-to-face.

"Dig, that's your own Kit, right?" Heavy always used retro 60s slang.

"Kollapse Kit 2.4, my own design."

"Mine is, too." Heavy grunted as he let his Kit pack thump to the floor of the cave. "Apocalypse Angel '96."

To Wirehead it looked like an ordinary wilderness backpack with APOCA ANGEL stenciled across the back in flaming red.

One of the sore spots on the Kollapse bulletin board was that some people just wouldn't agree on a standard terminology for Kits. Some used the clear, orderly number system, just like for software, while others like HeavyLink slapped on the year when they'd conceived the plan of their Kits.

Covering his annoyance, Wirehead started breaking out some of his gear. It was all custom, hardwired for the Kollapse, high bandwidth. "I figure it was the currency tumble," Wirehead said.

"Huh?" HeavyLink was unpacking, too. "Howzzat?"

"International trading broke down, 'cause somebody finally hacked the Treasury Exchange."

"Total B.S."

Wirehead bit his inner lip but kept calm. HeavyLink was a neo-Netter compared with Wirehead, and you had to tolerate some crap from them sometimes. "Most probable cause of all, Syntho said."

"No way." Syntho was a GEnie megahacker who had broadcast on all the boards an elaborate scheme for breaking into the Exchange. "That was just PR he put out."

"He said he was spreading it so that the proper authorities could prevent any really bad guys from spiking in," Wirehead said.

HeavyLink made an imitation fart sound, pretty authentic. "That was pure cover. He just wanted credit for the idea, is all."

"Okay then, so what *did* cause the Kollapse?"

"Obvious. Somebody hacked the *credit* info, all the bank records, the works."

Wirehead frowned. "I heard of that somewhere."

"Sure, in *How to Surf the Coming Catastrophe.*"

"I've got that on floppy."

"So do I."

"Maybe I'll read it right now."

HeavyLink kept unpacking his gear. "Who's got the time?"

"You mean you didn't read it either?"

HeavyLink shrugged. "Slid my eyes over the abstract in the Squeezed Books CD listing."

"I've got that, too." Wirehead didn't like being down on data, but at least he had it in the two dozen CDs he carried, right next to the built-in CD reader on his laptop, cozy as anything.

A big black slab like a huge single wing came shooting over the horizon. To Wirehead it looked a lot like the paper airplanes he had sailed in grade school. "Stealth bomber!" he cried in surprise, his war gaming years coming back in a rush.

The shock wave knocked both of them over. The dark wedge fled over the horizon, leaving a thin white trail that quickly evaporated.

"War!" HeavyLink shouted. "Not some systems hacking—war."

"I would have heard about it on the Net. I was online when the Kollapse started and—"

"It's plain as DOS, man." HeavyLink slapped the last of his setup together. "I'll get online and *show* you."

Wirehead was not going to be outdone in the field quite so easily. He had his laptop out and popped the short cable to a disk like an upside-down Frisbee. Its rim flared out rather than turning in, but guys in the biz called them thrower disks anyway, because pointed at the sky they could throw messages clear around the Earth. The disk had an aluminum base with holes punched in the struts to reduce weight. Top of the line.

He powered up. The whine of the hard drive was a comforting song, in the strife of the moment. Up came his operating system. Effortlessly he punched in single-key commands that brought on whole slabs of software, customized for just this moment. "Way past wicked fast, man," HeavyLink whispered with approval, and then bent to his own setup.

Wirehead loved the warm, blissful rivulets that trickled up his spine, pure cyberpleasure, as his laptop ran five different search programs on true, thirty-two bit, interthreaded preemptive multitasking. Micro macho to the max! Rapt, he watched the entire computing power of western civ, circa 1972, labor in his lap. The flat panel adjusted the slanting sunset glare with no problem, sharp and true, full color, high res.

His dish worked the exact microwave frequency of the geo-synchronous satellite, with high signal-to-noise ratio. He got through the usual blocks and soon was acing the protocols in highly select channels: NorAmComm, WorldNet, ZyncOn. His search pattern covered the whole range.

Only, nothing was coming in. "Blank, nada, zero," he muttered as he slapped three of the search patterns onto the Windows display at once. Not a burble of traffic.

"No pace in the pixels," he muttered, feeling uneasy. He let the patterns run background and resorted to the highest level he had, a program he had gotten on the sly from a pirate bulletin board operation.

Nothing. Here he had the computing power that could have run the whole Apollo moon landing, dedicated to making Donald Duck, in a spitting rage, pop up in icon to tell him there was nothing, nothing at all, frying on any search.

"It's . . . it's all *gone*," he muttered.

HeavyLink looked over his own laptop screen. "I can't believe it."

"The whole Net. Down." Wirehead caressed his keyboard, filling the soft green background with yellow type. Meaningless, but reassuring.

"You don't suppose . . . ?"

"That the Net itself . . . kollapsed?"

"Naw. Can't be."

"Maybe it was the I Squared Conspiracy."

HeavyLink frowned. "What's that?"

"Iran-Iraq. I read about it on the Armageddon Age bullboard."

"Huh. Ask me, it was the Japanese."

"Or else an eco-kollapse."

"Or OPEC making a power grab again."

"Or Earth First! monkeywrenching."

"But . . ." HeavyLink's eyes were plaintive. "How'll we ever *know?*"

"Let me think about that a moment." Wirehead always said that to gain time.

HeavyLink tapped away at his laptop—a standard item, off the shelf. His setup was a kludge, Wirehead looked away in quiet disdain. HeavyLink lacked some bandwidth, for sure. After a while HeavyLink's fingers stilled. Silence fell in the gathering cold of early evening. A dry wind blew through the cave mouth, moaning softly. Wirehead had waited for this dramatic moment, when all hope was lost in his online buddy. He began to speak.

"Do you know what most people are, Heavy?"

"Uh, mundanes?"

This was the usual online term for outsiders, but Wirehead waved away the word. "Amoebas is a better term."

"Huh?"

"All an amoeba knows of its watery world is what it physically bumps into. It has no buffers. If it meets a poison, it learns of it just as it dies. People—*ordinary* people—are like that."

"And us . . . ?"

HeavyLink was not slow, just younger on the Net. Wirehead smiled enigmatically. "Evolution gave more complex organisms better buffers. In animals, vision and scent. In ordinary people, ideas. To us, the *Net*."

"Oh, I see. But look, with the Net down—"

"That is temporary. I am talking about the far horizon of this Kollapse, HeavyLink. I am looking beyond the moment."

"Yeah, but—"

"Shall I tell you what I see?"

HeavyLink blinked and nodded. Wirehead had found that people on the Net reacted well to visionary talk. That was in text format, of course. He was thrilled to find that the same rhetoric worked in person. Maybe dealing with people in the flesh was not as hard as he had thought. He would have to rethink that, sometime, maybe examine the disaster of his high school years.

"I see the obsolete, falling by the wayside in this Kollapse. I see even the young, their thin cries echoing, calling for help. For a savior, a true leader, someone to point the way. For vision, for inspiration, for data, for a plan."

"And that's . . ."

"*Us*. We are the future."

"Not without the Net we aren't."

"But the Net is merely down for a moment. HeavyLink, we've planned for this for years. When Chaos stalks the streets and valleys of the world, only the Net can bring Order. And we, as Net veterans, will be the only leaders who can show the way."

"We all thought the Net would make it through."

"It will. And we will rule, those who know how to use it. *Think*, man! There won't be newspapers, TV will be babbling sensationalism, the politicians won't know zip! Only *we'll* be able to cope."

"I don't think so." HeavyLink had finished packing up. He stood.

"What you think now doesn't matter." Wirehead kept his voice calm, reasonable. "We'll get things sorted out, and soon enough—"

"You've got to live that long first," HeavyLink said.

He took from his Kit pack a pistol. "Smith & Wesson," he said fondly. "Top grade. Chromed, too."

Wirehead blinked, shocked. "What? Physical violence? That's hopelessly twencen!"

"That's what we're still in, y'know—the twencen. Now if you'll just hand over your food . . ."

"All I've got is a few packages of, well, candy bars."

"Let's have 'em, then." HeavyLink crooked a finger.

"But you can't *mean* this. We're buddies, in the Net together."

HeavyLink said softly, almost gently, "It ever occur to you that you never even seen me before today?"

Wirehead opened his mouth but he could think of nothing to say. HeavyLink stuffed the candy bars into his pack, grunted as he slung it over his shoulder, and started off into the wilderness.

"Stop! You and I, together we can inherit the whole world!"

HeavyLink looked back and grinned. "You can have my half."

Wirehead shouted his worst curse at the dwindling figure. "You're—you're a *flamer!*"

They found Wirehead a week later.

The National Guard patrol had already gotten tired of dealing with the Net users who had, in a curious imitation of lemming behavior, taken the rumor runaway on the Net as the signal for the demise of all order. The Net Krash had driven hordes of users onto the highways and into the confused countryside. The troops referred to them as "wireweenies" and were tired and resigned when they came upon the body.

Wirehead had died of thirst, apparently, lips and tongue leathery and purple. His arms were wrapped around his laptop and satellite dish, as if to draw energy from them.

As Big as the Ritz

It is youth's felicity as well as its insufficiency that it can never live in the present, but must always be measuring up the day against its own radiantly imagined future—flowers and gold, girls and stars, they are only prefigurations and prophecies of that incomparable, unattainable young dream.
            —F. Scott Fitzgerald
               "The Diamond as Big as the Ritz," 1922

Kings and fools
Make their own rules.
            —Joan Abbe

1

A lingering respect for the niceties of an Earthside education was the bane of the asteroid communities. Yearly it drained them of their brightest young men and women.

Thus the parents of Clayton Donner persistently pressured him to attend Harvard or Cambridge or Tokyo General, picking these names from a list as unfathomable as a menu in Swahili. Each locale was pictured in verdant 3D as a cultured pinnacle, a doorway to a different life.

The asteroids had been colonized by those who respected no conventional wisdoms but instead made their own. Those ancestors, now in their vacuum-dried graves, would have wrinkled their noses at the odor of flatlander-envy that pervaded the discussions of Clayton's destiny. The boy was quick, studious, clever. He would have made a fine metal-ceramics man, biointegrater, or snythominer. Instead, his parents relentlessly pressured him into an Earthside education extracted from books rather than from the gray tumbling worlds.

After his first year flatside, Clayton was a convert to their cause. For a young man a career is a distant, fuzzy goal. Earth was concrete and *fun.* Gaudy. Effervescent. Deliciously lurid. A banquet, topped off by the chemical consolations of civilization. He visited what was left of Africa, sampled the original abode where men had evolved, and came away with both a skin rash and a faint incredulity that anything worthwhile could have started there.

The east coast of the Americas was rather better, though clearly past its great days. The focus of Earthside economic life had shifted to the pan-Pacific nations over a century before. The snug, smug eastern streets were steeped in murky history and claustrophobic assumptions. Clayton stayed in the Ritz-Carlton Hotel in Boston, spending a week's worth of his father's profits in two days. The building was well-preserved, eccentric by modern standards, and impressed him deeply with its timeless gilded swank. He tasted the now-rare lobster and savored the heady fragrances of orderly decline. A woman he met in the bar seemed to find his asteroid origins fascinating, exotic, and within a few hours she was in his bed. It was a perfect setting to lose his virginity. He was only mildly disturbed when, the next morning, she firmly showed him the Greater Boston price sheet and luxury tax scale. He irritably paid up, resolving that the experience would not blemish his memory of the Ritz and its majesty.

He had ended up at UCLA, his ability and personality profile matched with the school's needs and strengths by an elaborate

trait-sifting program; the education of the young was too important to be left to their vagrant tastes.

Like virtually everyone's, his life appeared dull from the outside, or at best made of elements from a soap opera, while
from inside it had all the sweep and grandeur of *War and Peace*.
Clayton went through the usual undergraduate crises. He
learned to conceal his naive assumptions and be shocked at
nothing. Fashion allowed one to be occasionally stunned, but
only within severe limits. Dismay, however, was his for the
asking; it implied a certain haughty despair. He tried the various exploits—sexual, social, hallucinogenic—appropriate to his
age. Struggling, he invested ideas from survey courses, earnest
late-night bull sessions, op-ed pages, and other fast-thought
franchises. He imagined that he was crossing new frontiers,
when in fact he was only crossing into Iowa; billions had been
there before. He did not suspect that a decade later he would
find these pulse-quickening reaches not a little boring.

In his second year he met Sylvia. She was different from the
other students—intent, dedicated, severe. Her devotion to the
cause of selfless politics was already well-known at UCLA. He
was mildly attracted to her, despite her habit of wearing loose-
fitting, dowdy attire in dull browns and grays.

She was known as Sylvia Hammersmith at UCLA, but that
meant little—at that time students often adopted the names of
famous people as a gesture. As the young grew more and more
alike, devices to distinguish themselves became ever more enticing. Sylvia's taking the name of an explorer, fatally crushed on
Venus the year before, seemed only a mild affectation.

When he discovered her true last name, however, his interest
deepened. Compared to any savvy Earthy, Clayton was still
downright naive. Still, he sized up Sylvia quickly and judged
his best approach. She wore a perpetual frown, assaying even
casual remarks for their moral gold, so—intuiting rapidly—he
decided not to mention his major subject of study, Comparative
Astrophysics. Instead, he talked endlessly of his minor area,
Analytic Economic Morality.

He was, without thinking about it very much, solidly for Earthside's social shibboleths of the era—strict equality of pay for all, abolishment of all inherited wealth right down to items of clothing and furniture, and numerous measures to alleviate any trace of economic envy. The university incorporated these ideas as best it could, but found difficulty staffing the scientific fields, since technical talent could easily find work elsewhere. Support for progressive ideas centered, naturally enough, among the professoriat devoted to such subjects as Greek pottery and interpersonal dynamics.

These notions met with Sylvia's approval, and she opened up a bit. He learned of her laughing, pouting mouth, her glinting sea-blue eyes, her natural and unstudied grace. Quickly he became entranced. He was a man of the world now; certain mature delights should naturally come his way.

All the same, he was amazed when she invited him to spend December at her father's. Though this might be customary if she lived on Earth, or even in one of the crystalline orbital cities, she casually revealed that she was Sylvia Townsworth Rollan. Her father was founder of the most bizarre enterprise in the solar system: Brotherworld. It orbited at a steep tilt to the ecliptic, about two astronomical units away from the sun. Getting there would have taken expensive weeks by conventional transport.

Until this moment his interest in Sylvia had largely centered upon the pure, pointed lust of a young man. Mores of other eras had swung back to a constraining reticence in matters sexual. Clayton was well-socialized, and believed various unsupported assertions that had the effect of delaying marriage, postponing children, and generally defusing the explosive power of adolescent sexuality. Sublimation is a subtle game, one the twenty-second century played well. His warmly remembered night in the Ritz now seemed to be a gauzy treat, unreal, like cotton candy at a circus.

Ambition he had a-plenty. After Sylvia's invitation, he went immediately to his Major Tutor and asked advice. The gray-haired woman listened attentively, then said flatly that he must go, of course. There was no question. It could make his career.

Clayton was slightly shocked to find his own secret thoughts so freely voiced. He observed a quickening in the Major Tutor's manner, a fine-drawn anticipation of possible benefits to herself. Clayton remarked that he was reluctant to mix his regard for Sylvia and his other interests, especially since she had such, well, fixed views.

The Major Tutor pursed her lips, tapping a stylishly yellow fingernail on her amber desktop. She began a set-piece mini-lecture on devotion to the profession, on taking every opportunity in a field where such things came seldom these days, on understanding that in such circumstances he could allow no niceties.

Clayton had heard it all before but believed it anyway. He could see the elements of personal advancement in this, but something deeper drove him and the Major Tutor as well: curiosity. Among those souls of true scientists, this was the ultimate addiction that could not be deflected. Both of them wanted to *know*. If minor deception was the price, so be it.

The Major Tutor observed that he would, of course, need special equipment. She could arrange that. But even more important was care, a sense of timing, even downright guile. Clayton understood.

His Major Tutor gave him confidential summaries of Brotherland's construction, or rather, what little was known about it. The utopian colony, established on Brotherworld, was the great enigma of the day. What's more, Dr. Rollan had been acquiring advanced technology of an unsettling kind: plasma containment vessels, superstrong magnets, high-quality ceramics and alloys. Could he be building something even stranger than Brotherworld?

These questions the Major Tutor implied with raised eyebrows, and gave him an inventory of recent purchases by the colony. Clayton tucked it away for study at the site.

The task was not without risk. Clayton was an adventurous

type, though, determined to get his kicks in life, even if some of
them were in the face. He left his Major Tutor firmly resolved.

He accepted Sylvia's invitation, and changed his major subject to Undeclared, in case she should be of suspicious mind.
Indeed, some of his friends did mention to him, as he was
packing, that Sylvia had casually inquired into Clayton's do-
ings. They took it as a sign of female caution; courtship was a
rite given much thought in this era, and the preliminaries were
often the most rewarding aspect. They slapped him on the back,
made nudge-nudge wink-wink jokes, and gave unsolicited and
rather explicit advice.

Clayton took the precaution of leaving behind any reading
cylinder that could give away his interests. Instead, he took
microtexts on social responsibility, even one that denounced
the anarchist-cum-free capitalist asteroid communities from
which he came. He halfway agreed with the book, anyway.
The 'roid clans were rude, unsubtle, even loutish, compared
with the fine manners and delicate social distinctions com-
monly found in California. The books had a point.

2

They took a standard commercial fusion liner from Earth to
Ceres, the conjunction being good. It made the trip under boost
at full grav and arrived in five days. There they changed to a
slingship. Its electromagnetic accelerating rings squashed them
at three gravs for aching tendon-stretching moments, then
abruptly set them free on a long arc across the solar system,
out to the motes of asteroids. The ship moved like a darting
wisp among the stately slow sway of worlds.

Their target was a lonely, rolling hunk of iron called Hellbent. The other people on the slingship were rough, silent types,
ill-kempt and grimy, with little hope of ever getting far enough
ahead to afford a true, full-water bath, or food not force-grown,
or clothes of something finer than the fibrous weaves they wore.

All Hellbent men and women sucked a lean milk from bare, spongy rock. Economics had decreed Hellbent's smelted products valuable for one booming generation, and had then snatched away its blessings, leaving only a shadowy clan that had too much invested to leave the place. The large docking cylinders and electromagnetic accelerators were leftovers of the glory days, patched up now as the buttress of the economy. Clayton and Sylvia found the maze of sheet-metal corridors forbidding and chilly. The sheen of bare phosphors made them squint.

As they waited near the air lock for her father's shuttle, Sylvia asked, "Did you see that skinny man on the slingship?"

"Uh, yes."

"He was an astrophysicist, I'm sure of it."

"Why?"

"The way he looked at us. He knows who I am."

"Maybe he just thought you were good-looking."

She shrugged this off, impervious to compliments. "*And* his fingernails were clean."

Clayton hid a grin. "A sure sign."

He sighed, and felt an itchy sensation as he breathed in. Hellbent was so poor they ran their public rooms at zero humidity. In their hour-long wait the system could extract a gram or two of vapor from their breath and sweat, an involuntary tax of fluids.

His home was never *this* badly off. Clayton felt a twinge of guilt at thinking of his parents, laboring in the chilly grit of a rockworld not greatly different from this. He should visit them, but the cost was prohibitive. Sylvia had paid all the expenses this trip; he could never have afforded it. One of Clayton's classmates had even suggested that as long as he was out this far, he might as well nip over and look in at home, too—all this said with an oblivious groundhog smile, never thinking that Clayton's parents were on the other side of the solar system from here. To Earthsiders, like New Yorkers of the centuries before, everything beyond their neighborhood was a single, amorphous Elsewhere.

The shuttle arrived with a clanging thump. When the thrumming pumps had stilled, the two of them floated into the bare, gloomy loading bay. A silvery body nestled there, sleek and chromed. From its nose a powerful beam of ruddy light turned and regarded them like a malignant eye out of the coagulated night. As they glided forward, Clayton saw it was a shapely fusion flitter, gleaming with polish. The slim craft was studded with portals that winked and sparkled as he passed, looking exactly like enormous green and yellow jewels. Its nose was subtly asymmetric, and spindly guidance rods studded its sides, deftly functional. It was a work of art.

Two men, dressed in Spartan simplicity, stood inside the welcoming ramp. Clayton saw instantly that they were Brothers, the famous product of Dr. Leon Rollan's cloning experiment. And indeed, he could not tell one Brother from the other.

"Welcome to the Gates of Paradise," one said, giving Clayton a warm handshake.

"I'm, uh, pleased to enter," Clayton replied.

The Brothers greeted Sylvia even more warmly, as was fitting. Clayton glanced back and saw a small clutch of Hellbent's miners, muttering to each other and staring with frank, wide-eyed awe at the magnificence of the shuttle. The well-lit interior had upholstery of woven silk and linen. Here and there were plump pillows of subtly stated opulence. The bulkheads were a deep ebony, adorned with crescents of glittering rubylike stones and iridescent splashes of some blue-white jewels. It all represented the firmament itself, artfully arranged to lead the eye from one glowing high point to another.

"Incredible!" Clayton cried out.

"Oh, this is the old one," Sylvia said.

"There are others?" Clayton could not take his eyes off the rich fabrics.

"Oh yes." Something flickered in her eyes, and he guessed that she saw a sudden contradiction springing up. She believed in selfless politics, yet had grown up among wealth such as this. Perhaps she was a classic TwenCen liberal, able to hold such a contradiction in a mind that chose to see only what it desired.

"So much . . ." he hinted delicately.

"We have to keep up appearances, or my father's economic position in the macroeconomic community will suffer."

"Oh, yes, quite reasonable. People do pass judgment, don't they?" It felt lame, somehow, but her sunny smile banished his frown.

An alabaster dome topped the passenger lounge, a miniature copy of the famous mosque in Cairo he had seen the year before—except even more glorious here, in a sun-defying white.

"Of course." Sylvia gestured lazily at the Hellbent miners, who now crowded around the foot of the ramp. "It's for them, really. They like to see how well a truly different system works."

Soon they were boosting at a steady 1.5 gravs, the ship humming with solid assurance through slick blackness. Clayton could tell immediately from several constellations, and the orange disk of Jupiter aft, that they were arcing above the ecliptic. Hellbent was merely the nearest 'roid to Dr. Rollan's famous experiment. Hellbent chanced at this moment to be close to the point where Brotherland intersected the ecliptic plane every eighteen months in its oblique path. Lonely miners perceived Brotherworld as a glittering, sparkling speck high up in the darkness, orbiting serenely above the affairs of ordinary men.

Clayton saw it within a few hours. The Brothers kept to their business, scarcely sparing more than a few phrases after their warm greeting. They spoke to each other in a strange argot, which Clayton could not penetrate, so he turned to staring dreamily out the faceted portals. These were unusual in design, not giving a clear vision at all, but rather a series of refracted images, as though peering through a jewel. Certainly the sculpt-engineer had gone to a great deal of trouble to create the effect.

The multiple perspectives complemented the design of the walls, but Clayton found it hard on the eyes.

Through this layered set of images Clayton first saw the glowing eye of the Vortex. It was burnt-gold near the center, brimming with crisp light. Around it was a halo of red, and then an encircling, smolderingly blue haze. He strained to see the very center and was rewarded with a tiny, virulent twinkling. At first he could not be sure it was not an optical trick of the odd portal. The dot flickered like a will-o'-the-wisp in a distant, churning fog. Clayton felt his breath quicken, a tingle of excitement. The dab of light hardened. He was sure now. The dazzling white speck was the roiling glow emitted by matter as it cried out in its incandescent agony, flaring brightly for one long groaning instant before it plunged forever down the yawning Schwarzschild throat of a black hole.

3

A massive star at the endpoint of burning has a central temperature of ten billion degrees and is nearly a billion times more dense than iron. Unable to burn any longer, its core collapses, the nuclei there break apart, and implosion begins. There is a "bounce" and the implosion turns into the classic supernova explosion. Matter initially near the stellar core rapidly expands and cools. Often the core left behind forms a neutron star or a black hole. These bizarre end products of stellar death throes were the principal focus of much of TwenCen astronomy.

—VALERIE THOMPSON, 2078
Supernova Debris (2nd edition)

The glory of Dr. Rollan's artful empire unfolded in concentric rings: the Vortex. Its fuzzy, glowering blue rim was a disk of dust that slowly spiraled inward, toward its death. As dust swarmed ever nearer the hole, friction among the particles heated them. Stirred by magnetic fields to a turbulent frenzy, they radiated. Farthest out, a blue oxygen line dominated the emission, giving this rim the color of a week-old bruise. Farther in, the faster-circling gas sputtered with an angry red. Radiation stole angular momentum from the dust. This minutely affected the orbiting particles, lowering them slowly inward.

Clayton quickly calculated in his head. It would take years for a dollop of dust to bleed inward, into the next band, a brimming mustard circle. Then the compressed dust flowed into the sunlike, white-hot hub where a fraction of its rest mass energy was released, fully thirty percent. There lived the black hole, the dynamo that made this work.

"You can't see the hole," Sylvia said helpfully. "It's only a speck, anyway, no bigger than your fingernail."

"Uh, amazing." He must not appear to know very much.

"See the collectors?"

A wide array of photon collectors orbited above and below the luminous disk. Sylvia said, "They provide the energy we sell to the interplanet runs."

Clayton watched the filmy sheets turn in their own elliptical orbits, feasting on the light that burst from the rim of the black hole. They were hundreds of kilometers away, but the scene was lit with dazzling intensity. The collectors beamed microwaves across the solar system, he knew, providing in-flight power to ships. That cut transport costs enormously. Rollan had been the first to provide the service.

"I don't follow the details, but it *is* lovely, isn't it?" Sylvia said with little-girl wonder.

Clayton agreed, but yawned and languidly said, "Uh-huh." He shouldn't seem too interested, and would make some sketches as soon as he was alone.

He allowed himself one more moment of rapt appreciation. The Vortex glowed with the mere waste energy of vast forces at work. The disks turned, huge economic flywheels steadily rendering ordinary asteroid debris into limitless wealth.

"There's home!" Sylvia cried.

Until now the banks of dust above and below them had hidden the jewel of the system.

Farther out, beyond the blue band, all was a mottled darkness, blotting out the stars behind. Farther still, the infalling dust thinned. Beyond this shroud, Clayton could see the true marvel, the Hoop.

It was a thin glowing strip, as ripely blue-green as Earth on a summer's day. The inner rim of the Hoop was lit by the glow of the Vortex, its light funneled out and focused on the Hoop by the scalloped plates of the dust. This conserved most of the radiance and delivered it to the Hoop, bringing warm temperatures to its delicately contrived biosphere.

Clayton knew from sketchy information available through the UCLA library that a monolayer shield floated on top of the Hoop's atmosphere. He could see the sheen of Vortex-light scattered by that thin air-trapping film, high above a cotton-ball cluster of cirrus. Below, basking in radiance, were shimmering lakes and softly undulating hills. At the "equator," the inward curve of the Hoop, a long lake stretched, dividing the span.

Sylvia said excitedly, "Have you ever seen anything so beautiful?"

"Never," he said with complete conviction.

"The forests, the green hills . . ." Sylvia peered dreamily at the swelling Hoop. "Our Eden . . ."

Clayton realized she meant the "natural" beauty of the Hoop; he had thought she meant the marvelous engineering that made the thin slice of biosphere possible. He suppressed a disbelieving smile.

They slid outward toward the Hoop. He guessed the entire Hoop was a few kilometers thick, and they were only perhaps twenty kilometers from the black hole itself. Yet the tiny sucking mote provided brimming light for an entire ecology.

The hills swept by, revolving cool and serene, as he watched. The Hoop circled the Vortex every seven minutes, a giant bicycle tire without spokes. But perspectives were awry here. The irreality of a glowering, gnawing mass-eater so near to placid forests was too jarring. He shook his head, dazed.

A faint pattering came through the alabaster dome of the improbable ship.

"Ah!" one of the Brothers said. He hastily dipped the nose down toward the Hoop.

"What was that?" Clayton said, alarmed. Any accident so near the virulent maw—

"A small error," Sylvia said calmly. "We probably hit a cloud of dust that strayed from its course, is all." She smiled with the confidence of a person for whom the technical problems were always someone else's. Clayton had noted that she was becoming more easygoing, less severe, as they voyaged out from Earth's bright confusions.

Once told, he understood. The infalling dust was supposed to be channeled down in a parabola, flowing above and below the Hoop by a wide, safe margin. Some errant matter had brushed them.

They descended rapidly. As they dropped toward the slowly gyrating Hoop, the Brother pilots warbled to each other in their strange, insular tongue. The ship looped outward and passed over the nightlike outer side of the Hoop, where ice rimmed the terminator. The Hoop eclipsed the Vortex and darkness descended. Beneath the sole luminescence of the distant speck of the Sun the ice was blue.

"My father says this is where the past ends," Sylvia said, her face pensive and distant.

He reminded himself that to her this spectacular vista was as homey as a backyard. yet he could see that homesickness welling up in the expectant pout of her mouth. Her high cheekbones gave her a severe, imperial look; the mouth belied that now. She was a woman of profoundly felt currents, emotions that at UCLA had found expression in ideas. Now her depths emerged. Her contradictions only made her more alluringly mysterious to him.

"And this"—Clayton had not yet digested the spectacle of the Vortex—"is the future?"

"Why, of course." To her the intricate waltz of light and

matter, wheeling here in infinite black, was the family farm, a fact of nature.

He had thought of her as a kinswoman of sorts, reared in a place more like his 'roid origins than the comfortable plush of Earth. But this place, despite his preparation, was bizarre to him. He began to understand how different she was, and felt the tug of a sublime strangeness. He remembered his Major Tutor's calculating eyes and a confusion of motives swirled in him for a moment. Only the grandeur of the spectacle outside made him put all thoughts aside.

They came over the rim of the Hoop, clouds allowing brief glimpses through to the verdant fields. From the Vortex a wedge of light poured outward, trapped between the blankets of infalling matter. The twin sheets of dust resembled plates that necked in to intersect at the hot central spark. As they converged the plates glowed, giving the bands of blue and yellow and brilliant white that he had seen earlier.

They arced around the face of the Hoop, toward the permanent high noon of the equator. The monolayer sheen was turquoise here, with distorted cumulus clouds wedged against its restraining boundary by the rising heat from below.

There—a lessening. The entrance hole, a swiftly forming leak in the system that allowed ships in and out. It would be open for mere moments.

They turned and glided through it, thrusters focused down now. Here the jockeying was difficult. The ship went through the hole, through thick cloud layers, and emerged suddenly above a careening landscape. The Brothers worked furiously now, vectoring sidewise and up, and now down and aft, as they matched velocities and accelerations in an intricate gavotte, descending toward their landing field.

The ship, so graceful in vacuum, now seemed to have the aerodynamic properties of a brick. Clayton shrank into his couch, dizzy.

What would seem a simple problem in vector mechanics back at UCLA became a sickening whirl. He felt the eternal power of matter over abstractions. This was nothing like piloting among serenely orbiting asteroids.

Thumps, rattles, a hollow *whoosh*. Landfall.

The side of the ship furled up. Clayton followed Sylvia down the ramp into the lush valley. A golden haze hung idly over the vast sweep of lawns, azure lakes, and artfully arranged forests. Above, the Hoop curved away in both directions, arching up into a blue fog. In the middle distance groves of oak studded the tawny hills, reminding him of California. Farther away, rough masses of pine swathed the rumpled land in a grip of dark blue-green.

"It's . . . lovely," he said.

Three deer emerged from a grove of elms nearby, never giving them a glance, and meandered into a wooded gully. A falcon wobbled on changing air currents high overhead, then began a descending gyre. Above all this hung the incessant Technicolor blaze of the Vortex.

"Hail!" came a voice nearby.

Clayton turned to see a ruddy-faced man who seemed about sixty walking stiffly toward them. The famous Dr. Ludwig Rollan showed his years, yet his eyes vibrated with resolve beneath the golden glow of the haze.

The next moments' customary greetings went by Clayton without leaving any lasting impression, for he was fascinated by Rollan's presence. It is common to be so overwhelmed by the celebrity of the great that at first the actual person seems unreal, too compact and mortal to have been the source of such renown. Clayton had never met anyone of remotely the stature or mystery of this tanned, fuzzy-bearded man who shook his hand slowly, blue eyes self-assured and calm and questioning. He could think of absolutely nothing worth saying. His mind hung in a vacuum, spinning fruitlessly as Sylvia hugged and kissed her father and peppered the grizzled, indulgent man with questions. They exchanged affectionate jokes.

Then Dr. Rollan said, as if prompting Clayton, "I gather you are a young man deeply committed to our ideas here."

"Sure am," Clayton said, without specifying which ideas he meant. This place was certainly ripe enough with demonstrated ideas, with practical applications of huge forces.

"Fine!" Dr. Rollan slapped Clayton on the back with gusto. "Out here we used to get lots of the other kind, you know, good Clayton."

Clayton nodded, supposing that Rollan meant the grimy, no-nonsense inhabitants of the asteroids, perhaps begging for handouts. They were interrupted by Rollan's dog, a mongrel who seemed to become immediately fond of Clayton's leg. On Earth dogs were rare, other than as a delicacy, and Clayton did not know how to respond. The dog was ardenting embracing his knee. Rollan was distracted, pointing out the sights, so Clayton gave the dog a quick, experimental kick. It backed away.

Dr. Rollan took them to a handsome dinner in a vast, green stone country house, termed the Hostel. "Just something the Brothers made up as a greeting," he said, ushering them into a vast communal dining hall. "Do you know what this is?" he asked Clayton.

"Well, uh, a cafeteria," Clayton said uncertainly.

"No!" Dr. Rollan cried good-naturedly. "It is our equivalent of church."

They stood watching the throng for a moment, and soon Clayton saw what he meant. The Brothers dined with a ritual seriousness, passing food and observing social graces with a deadpan earnestness. Evidently the sharing of food was a crucial observance to them.

Clayton found it unnerving—a huge long room filled with Brothers and Sisters who looked exactly like each other. Dr. Rollan had cloned them all from the cells of a great genius of the last century, a social philosopher who had updated Marx and mix-mastered in a blend of Oriental religion, self-help, and moral philosophy. The high steepled wall above bore the statement.

A WEED IS MERELY A PLANT SOMEONE DOESN'T LIKE

Clayton frowned, trying to figure out the implications. Rollan's dog reappeared, this time eyeing Clayton's leg avidly but keeping a respectful distance. He glowered; it cowered. Fascism evidently worked with dogs, Clayton deduced.

"The Brothers and Sisters, they're really all alike?" he asked, to be saying something.

"Exactly," Dr. Rollan said.

"Nothing's *perfectly* copied every time," Clayton said.

Dr. Rollan answered crisply, "Circus knife-throwers know it is possible to be perfect, and one had better be in *anything* truly earnest."

"Yes, sir?" a Brother answered at the doctor's elbow.

"Oh, I didn't mean you, Ernest. Meet Clayton."

Ernest was a burly version of the others, obviously the product of an extensive exercise program. He wore his shirt open to the navel, where a mat of brown hair exuded a husky scent. Clear blue eyes regarded Clayton closely. There were three women behind him blank-faced, obviously waiting until his attention returned to them.

"Glad to shake the hand of anybody can give the Miss a good time," Ernest said, pinching Clayton's hand in a vise-like handshake.

"The . . . the Miss?"

"Miss Sylvia," Ernest explained. "She's the untouchable around here."

"Ernest means I don't take part in their sexual calisthenics," Sylvia explained lightly.

"Not genetically allowed, you see, good Clayton," the doctor said. "Would pollute the strain."

"Ah." Clayton liked something in Ernest's direct, gruff manner and was pleased when they sat at a table together. They all called Dr. Rollan the Handyman, as though he were some mere technical assistant. Clayton thought this odd, and even stranger that Dr. Rollan beamed at the nickname. There were greetings all around, but then the Brothers and Sisters fell into

rapt conversation with each other, leaving the three genetically
different people to themselves.

Food arrived, succulent and steaming. All vegetarian, of course.
It was passed on plates of a hard, black, heavy substance which
Clayton guessed must be a product of the Vortex itself, matter
transmuted by the intense heat of the inner accretion disk.

Ernest quickly downed several glasses of sweet wine, smacking his lips and pronouncing in detail its qualities. "Try more,
good Clayton," Ernest said, slopping some on the table as he
refilled Clayton's glass.

"Uh, thanks." He wished everyone wouldn't use the "good"
preface, though he noted others routinely using it. It reminded
him of old ideas about conditional training. Ernest began telling
stories about the farming and labor of the Hoop, dominating the
table talk for a while. They were seldom quick and light, and
each had a point delivered with the leaden quality of pig irony.

Clayton got on well enough with Dr. Rollan, discussing his
parents' asteroid community and the ever-changing economics
of the Belt. The doctor had once been a rockhound himself and
still remembered much of what a catch-as-catch-can existence it
was. At first the venerable man merely nodded and grunted
assent, but as Clayton described his father's company and their
hardships, Rollan began to break in with stories of his own,
snippets of information, good-old-days counterexamples.
Slowly, listening respectfully, Clayton knitted together a picture
of the man, filling in the space that had remained obscure in
the biographies he'd read.

4

Rollan had found the Vortex entirely by accident.

He was born Norman Vladimir Rollan, son of good New
Socialist parents in Middle Europe. At that time the planners
were attempting to arrest the long economic slide of his native
land, and so sent teams into the newly opened asteroids. Their

National Mission was to return raw materials for smelting in high orbit.

Rollan was fully committed to the ideals of his government, and volunteered for prospecting duty. This was a chancy affair, involving long low-energy orbits between likely asteroids. Exploratory robots, however intelligent, had failed; they had no intuitive feel for the crannies that concealed lucrative metal deposits.

The North Americans had gotten to the obvious candidate 'roids long before, so the European prospectors were forced to explore lesser targets—those with odd spectra, or hard-to-reach orbits out of the ecliptic plane.

Rollan was not a lucky prospector. He turned up countless examples of the most common 'roid—a spongy assemblage of boring elements, with no seams of rare metals. He failed to find even one carbon-rich rock, which would at least have paid his expenses.

He was on his final run, having boosted up to three km/sec at an angle of thirty-seven degrees out of the ecliptic plane, fatalistically pursuing a lumbering mountain of unpromising rock. He never reached it. Fifteen hours after his pulsed launch in a cramped, one-man slingship, Rollan registered a flash of X rays that looked like the preliminary burst from a solar flare. Normally the warning system would give him an hour to find a 'roid and hide behind it, out of the sleet of protons spewing from the sun.

But when Rollan swiveled his 'scope around to confirm, the sun was an ordinary disk. Turning, he found that the radiation came from a spot high above the ecliptic. Unless he had ventured off on this oblique orbit, he would not have been within range to pick it up.

He tracked the spiky, slow-simmering X rays for hours. They came from a pinprick of UV emission that was swooping down toward the asteroid belt.

Rollan expended his remaining reserve fuel and met the firefly dab of yellow. As he approached he expected it to swell into a 'roid profile. Instead, he nearly collided with it, believing it must be still a long distance away. Only his acceleration meters warned him, seconds before it was too late, of a sudden steepening of the local gravitational potential.

It was a black hole, the first ever found in the solar system— still grinding up and devouring the small rock it had intersected, yielding the burst of X rays.

Rollan was a competent astrophysicist and he knew a fortune when he saw one. Observation of distant quasars had shown that their dazzling energies came from matter processed by vast black holes at a galactic center. Matter cast into a disk around a black hole could yield an entire menu of radiation, exotic materials, and useful high-energy particles.

He also knew the hole was dangerous. His Earthside training had included elementary magnetic fusion methods; this qualified him to fly a solo slingship craft and make his own repairs. That came in handy.

He fashioned a magnetic trap for the hole, keeping a respectful distance. The hole, despite containing the mass of a medium-sized asteroid, was only a millionth of a centimeter wide. Rollan's magnetic bottle could be strong but crude.

Slowly, gingerly, he towed it back to a grubby 'roid station, where he kept silent about the contents.

Only when he reached the tinny magnificence of Ceres Station did he begin to use the hole, injecting ordinary dust and extracting energy by driving magnetohydrodynamic generators. Electrical power was still at a premium, and he—or rather, his National Mission—prospered.

The hole was kept a secret, but even its profitability did not stave off the effects of a general economic recession. Rollan's National Mission folded up. Most of his countrymen went home, but Rollan managed to keep the hole—he had never revealed, even to his superiors, what fed the generators.

These hard times were the crucible that hardened and shaped Rollan. The decline of the New Socialist nations—democratic or totalitarian, first world or tropical, strict or reformist—led him to believe that only a wholly fresh kind of society could bring about the aims of the old utopian thinkers. With the hole, he began a series of brilliant economic coups, manufacturing exotic materials and plasmas for anyone who could pay. He brought his own asteroid and moved it to a concealing orbit at a steep tilt to the ecliptic. This isolated him from the Belt society, allowing time to refine ore as he refined his own ideas.

He hired trusted assistants, all ideologically pure. He went on frequent, high-boost journeys to Earth, carrying his wares, and returned with huge credit balances payable in the banks of the Belt. He was an early investor in the self-replicating robot companies, buying over a third of them in the first decade of the industry.

Then came the long plateau of his life. He traveled little and worked ever harder. Inevitably, news of the hole escaped. Eager, ferret-eyed scientists came to inspect. The nations of Earth attempted to confiscate it. The Belt laid claim to "mineral rights." The systemwide economic community demanded that it be classified as a natural resource, the "proper heritage of all mankind."

In a sense, it was. Astronomers had long believed that the solar system began with a nearby supernova explosion. It had occurred in a star of about ten times our sun's mass, blowing outward a huge expanding shell of debris. A sector of this outrushing, highly radioactive junk collided with a neighboring dust cloud, compressing it.

Once begun, gravitational contraction proceeds apace. Within a thousand years the jolt applied by the supernova made the dust cloud shrink into a sputtering, newborn star, with an attendant disk that would eventually form planets.

All this could be deduced from the unusual concentrations of rare elements in present-day meteorites. The radioactive elements of the original supernova had long since decayed into daughter and granddaughter elements, a telltale signature of a violent birth for the solar system.

What had *not* been anticipated, though, was the fate of the original supernova remnant. A black hole formed, from matter crushed inward while most of the dying star rushed outward. The hole was of relatively unimportant mass, scarcely more than a mountain's. It was swept along in the chaos and currents of the explosion, and eventually formed part of the collapsing cloud that made the solar system. It apparently reached the imploding dust cloud late in the formation, and took up an orbit not fully aligned with the ecliptic. This gave astronomers a fix on the original rotation axis of the supernova star, and helped formulate detailed numerical studies of the titanic event that had given birth, eventually, to all humanity.

Rollan didn't give a damn. He regarded astrophysics as a mildly interesting but fundamentally useless activity, unless it could be used to extract further wealth from the hole. After giving the scientists minimal time to study the hole—now surrounded by a complex system of infalling asteroid dust, transmutation cylinders and furiously working robots—he closed the entire community to outside visitors.

Earth had long maneuvered to gain control of the hole. Rollan favored neither Earth nor the asteroids, on grounds that it was silly to select one bull over another on the basis of the beauty of its horns, when what mattered was that you lived in a china shop.

He maneuvered the 'roid Belt interests into successfully countering Earth. In return they asked for preference in patents derived from the hole. Rollan freely gave that, demonstrating again his balancing act between the two economic giants. However, patent rights were all he would grant. All else was cloaked in isolation.

Scientists came to inspect and were turned away. Observations from afar were neatly blocked by the huge clouds of asteroid matter that Rollan sent orbiting in toward the hole, masking whatever enormous engineering feats were going on. Specialists hired for the tasks were sworn to secrecy. Their memories were wiped clean when they left Rollan's employ.

As the years stretched on, no scientists ever managed to wangle an invitation to see Rollan. He evaded government surveys of his holdings, keeping all but a few workers at a great remove from the actual hole site. Rumors circulated that his self-replicating machines were roving the high-azimuth orbits above and below the belt, searching for raw materials not claimed, or even other black holes.

The happy years of progress and expansion were punctuated by Rollan's marriage to a woman of the Lunar Nirvana Colony. The Nirvanites' short-lived experiments in "human-animal genetically altered communality" had led to public outrage. There were some interesting, unanticipated side effects, however. The breakup of Luna Nirvana greatly enhanced the market in collies and cougars who could take care of the children and run the house, too. It created a whole new industry in big game hunting, promising more nearly even odds.

But the experience left Rollan's wife a shattered vessel, a docile receptacle for his idealistic impulses. Sylvia was their only child. Inspired by his vision, Rollan thereafter devoted himself to the cloning program necessary for the new society he envisioned.

5

Generally ignored in twentieth century astrophysics was a hard problem—what happens to the bulk of the mass ejected from a supernova? Does it all turn to mere drifting interstellar dust, as many supposed?

The explosion occurs in the "carbon flash," when the carbon nuclei begin to collide and fuse. The energy released by carbon-burning heats the core without letting it expand, vastly increasing pressure. This means carbon-level nuclei can remain bonded into a solid form even as they are ejected in the explosion.

—Supernova Debris

Morning. As Clayton awoke he saw drowsily that multicolored streamers of light lanced across his room, rippling the far wall with elegant traceries of shifting blues, greens, and oranges. This resonated with his Technicolor headache, a memento of the sweet wine from the night before. He groped from the bed.

Through curiously thick windows he saw the great planes of the accretion disk, a broad stripe that ran straight across the sky. A pale eggshell-blue stretched away into oblivion, merging with the fuzzy vision of the Hoop itself, arcing up and away. The spectacle turned dry equations into exotic flourishes of almost kinesthetic delight. He longed to see better, to be able to pick out the robot shepherds who tended the accretion disk. They would be mere dots against this magnificence, lost in the glare, but they could tell him much from their location and movements. His heart pounded.

He tapped the window. It gave back a solid *thunk*. He felt its slick surface, marveling at the density and thickness of the glass. Each pane was faceted at its edges, refracting splashes of light. Even for a man of Rollan's expansive style, it seemed an incredible indulgence.

"Good morning, sir," a voice said behind him.

He turned. It was Ernest, the man from dinner yesterday.

"Are you ready for your bath, sir?" Ernest asked, holding out a towel.

"Well, sure." He hadn't expected such service. And Ernest's respectful "sir" he liked better than "good Clayton." Ernest was so devoted to Sylvia that Clayton automatically took him for a rival. It was reassuring that the man apparently knew his place.

Clayton began to shed his pajamas, but Ernest knelt before him and undid the buttons, saying, "Allow me." As the man slid the pajama bottoms off, he observed Clayton's state of tumescence (caused by the vision of the accretion disk, plus a full bladder) and offered to provide any sexual service required.

"Uh, well, no, ah—no, not my kind of thing," Clayton gasped.

"You're sure?"

"No!"

"Perhaps one of the Sisters, then? I can summon Pauline or Hadley quickly, they are nearby."

"No, no, nothing thanks."

Ernest nodded gravely and then smiled. "Anything you want, that's what you'll get. Our ideal is selfless service here, sir."

"So I see," Clayton muttered.

"Hot rosewater and vanilla soap?"

"What?"

"Followed by a plasma ionizer rinse," Ernest suggested. "Stimulates the body, while quieting the mind." He nodded significantly at the still-horizontal member.

"Yes," agreed Clayton, smiling inanely, "as you please."

The bath was reached by a slick slide down from his room. The swift journey surprised him, even with Ernest's warning. He plunged into a communal bath, an opulent bowl that was unpopulated save for himself.

Ernest stood at the edge and asked solicitously, "Music, 3D?"

He selected a melody that featured flutes, their notes dripping like a waterfall. Through the translucent walls he saw a moving shadow and abruptly realized that he was surrounded by an immense aquarium. Huge fish, clearly the offshoots of the old Lunar Nirvan experiments, swam in amber light, gliding without curiosity up to the walls and peering at him. They mouthed something but he could not make it out. A poem, perhaps. The fish had been good at that, were frequently published. He wondered what they ate.

He had only a few minutes before breakfast to draw sketches of the Vortex and Hoop, from memory. At the ample meal they were surrounded by the hubbub of the communal dining room. Brothers and Sisters everywhere brought forth and devoured huge glittering plates of eggs, toast, cereal, ham. Following Uniformism beliefs, the ham was a vegetarian substitute, but Dr. Rollan assured them that it tasted remarkably like true pig flesh. Systematically they ate and left. Clayton could not keep track of the streams of bodies or follow their odd accents.

"They all seem to be about, uh . . ." Clayton began.

"Twenty-five, on the nose," Dr. Rollan said. "They all came out of the cooker at exactly sixteen when I started the experiment, nine years ago."

"They're all sort of older brothers and sisters to me," Sylvia said. Clayton noticed she had forsaken her constant Earthside garb of severe pants and blue cotton work shirt. Now she wore a little white gown that came to just below her knees. He liked especially the wreath of marigolds clasped with slender blue slices of stone in her hair.

"All the same genotype," Clayton said. "And you hold the patent?"

"I have published the specs," Dr. Rollan said. "Anyone can clone more Brothers and Sisters if he or she likes."

"They *are* handsome," Clayton said politely. Actually, he was already tiring of them.

"A simple formula, really," Dr. Rollan said. "I hired the best DNA artists to make me a chain with no inherited diseases, yes. That much is commonplace. But fashioning the right personality mix and making it breed true in the conception tubes—that was no trifling matter."

"I see," Clayton said. "To get the right sort of worker for—"

"No, no!" Dr. Rollan was agitated. He stopped slicing the blue-brown fake ham and frowned furiously. "The exact personality type does not matter. I know my ideas are not widely known in the reactionary citadels of Earth—and of course they are roundly despised among the 'roid rabble—but you must have gotten some misinformation somewhere."

"I just—"

"The point is that those societies contain a contra*dic*tion, a dialectical one, if you will. Earth, with its billions of citizens, preaches the virtue of tolerance, of passivity, of conformity. But who does it reward? The heads that poke up above the crowd! It is impossible to free them of their adulation of the special unless it becomes impossible to *be* special!"

"That's a scientific fact," Sylvia put in. "Father gave Brotherland its own dialect, too—it's the easiest way to program their worldview."

"Ah."

"You are training to be a social scientist, Mr. Donner," Dr. Rollan went on, cutting his cube of ham precisely into smaller brown cubes, all alike. "You must realize the central problem! One cannot carry out reproducible experiments on human societies. They are not a controlled environment."

"Well, yes."

"So I constructed this world, to prove that Uniformism will work. Here we can illustrate the central tenets of progressive thinking, begin the true evolution of Post-Socialist man."

"Through controlled experiments."

"Yes. We will demonstrate that Uniformism produces more material goods, higher pleasures, healthier bodies."

"And you'll drive the 'roids into a depression, by outcompeting them."

Dr. Rollan chuckled. "It is *they* who preach the virtue of their vaunted free markets."

"But my father's operation—"

Dr. Rollan smiled shrewdly, his eyes rolling upward in amusement. "Free markets . . . can be costly."

When he returned to his room, Clayton quickly finished unpacking. He assembled the telescope that he had dismantled and hidden among his belongings. It was stubby and could not give fine resolution, but it did not need to. Its heart was a spectrum analyzer that attached like a lamprey to the base.

Clayton pointed the telescope at the huge strip of light that hung like a ribbon wrapping the sky. He would have liked to do this outdoors, but there he would have been quickly spotted.

He sighted the telescope through the thick windows and thumbed the instrument into action.

Rollan's ingenious design of the inflowing matter made astrophysical observation of the black hole impossible from a great distance. The infalling matter masked the hole except for the thin wedge in the equatorial plane—which was blocked by the Hoop itself.

Clayton focused the telescope on each of the Technicolored bands of the accretion disk in turn. The spectrum analyzer recorded emission lines, buzzing and humming to itself. There was a wealth of information here, and Clayton began to perspire slightly, his heart thumping. He punched in commands for a finer scan and then heard the door behind him opening.

"Clayton!"

He jumped. It was Sylvia.

"I, uh, I'm—"

"You *must* come to see the harvesting. The entire quadrant is there!"

He stood speechless for a moment before realizing that Sylvia could not see the telescope behind him. "Well, sure, just give me a minute, huh?"

"Just one!" she cried happily, and left.

He quickly stripped the telescope into its components and hid them.

As a Festival of Commonality, it left Clayton feeling curiously left out. The Brothers and Sisters harvested their wheat, all right, using lightweight machinery and considerable skill. But they chattered together in the indistinguishable patois that was beginning to irritate Clayton.

They all referred to Clayton as "sir" on the few occasions when they addressed him. Clayton felt rather swell about this until Sylvia mentioned that to be exalted above the commonality was in fact a denigration, so "sir" was a term of polite contempt. Ernest had used it, he recalled, in very nearly every sentence since this morning. Had the man become surly over his romance with Sylvia? Or from Clayton's rejection of his advances? Clayton studied Ernest's brooding face, but could read nothing. Though Ernest looked like all the other Brothers, a certain musky confidence hung about the man, though unescorted by very much apparent cleverness. He decided the man was either very deep or very shallow, and as with many people, it was difficult to tell which.

Dr. Rollan tried to labor with them, sweating profusely, stripped to the waist. The man was old, of course, even neglecting the times he had spent in the cold-sleep vaults while his self-reproducing machines had built the Hoop. He so earnestly wanted to be included among the Brothers and Sisters that he ran the risk of overtiring himself. Indeed, he quickly became ashen-faced and had to sit down. Clayton had to admire the chaste and consistent selflessness in the man.

"See how . . . well they . . . work together," Dr. Rollan observed while he shakily took a drink at the water trough.

Clayton agreed. He and Sylvia watched from the side of the fields, since he, as an outsider, was not allowed to take any part in the joy of production. Sylvia was in rapture. She confided to Clayton that she loved everything in nature, except perhaps anchovies.

Dr. Rollan said meditatively, gesturing at the laboring lines, "They are the future, young man. Superior to the mess humanity has made of itself."

Like most idealists, Dr. Rollan loved mankind in principle and disliked it in very nearly every particular. "Do you plan to spread the Brotherhood and Sisterhood?" Clayton asked mildly.

"Where?" Dr. Rollan seemed genuinely puzzled.

"Perhaps to those new worlds discovered around Tau Ceti?"

"Good lord," the old man said crankily, "I wouldn't *run away* from the problems of the human race. We have to face them here."

Clayton nodded, but frowned.

*   *   *

That night Clayton could not sleep. The vegetarian diet had proved an ineffective cushion for the weight of wine that had landed on it. Still, he was too cautious to go wandering about on his own. Best not to arouse suspicions.

He sat up reading, and quickly grew tired of reviewing the old text, *Supernova Debris*. It was the last major work on the subject. Dr. Rollan had denied scientists access to the black hole and to Brotherland, so astrophysics had gained little from his discovery. *Supernova Debris* contained many speculations that could not be verified.

He put it aside and turned to an old text on social theory, tracking down details of the half-remembered Model of Utopias, a classic treatise created by the nearly unreadable but famous social theorist and nudist, Darko Drovneb. Brotherland seemed to have all the characteristics. The textbook discussion rang uncannily true.

The Brothers and Sisters made a point of communal values, keeping their culture pure and without diversity. Rollan's program of genetic uniformity helped that, and also aimed at the second Drovneb characteristic: no change with time. Experiments required unchanging conditions, after all. Even more important, change implied that something had been wrong before.

Drovneb's third signature—a nostalgic and technophobic atmosphere—fit, too. The Hoop was a giant farm, recalling Earth of centuries ago. And the Brothers and Sisters knew little or nothing of machines beyond their farming equipment. Robots and Dr. Rollan made the Hoop work, with nearly everything technical kept above the bottled atmosphere. On the Hoop, all was simplicity.

And Rollan himself provided the fourth characteristic—an authority figure. He insisted on being called the Handyman, but it was clear that his word was law. He had built the very ground they stood on, after all.

Only in the final Drovneb characteristic was there some

doubt. *Social regulation through guilt,* the book said. *Responsibility is exalted as the standard of behavior.*

Clayton frowned. The Brothers and Sisters seemed remarkably guilt-free, compared with the constricted folk of Earth. Maybe the rural surroundings simply made them seem more easygoing.

Certainly their absurdly low-tech agricultural methods were politically imposed, hopelessly inefficient. Yet apparently it worked well enough to make a profit for Brotherland. Of that the Handyman was proud. He kept the fields of the Hoop as a nostalgic echo of the farms of centuries ago, and it seemed to work. The ghost of Rousseau walked here.

He wearily thumbed off the book. The Drovneb parameters fit nearly every utopian society of the last five centuries. The theory predicted a common end—as soon as the authority figure died, things began to slowly unwind. Diversity, curiosity, simple human orneriness—all conspired to bring down the golden pillars of dreams.

He wondered what would happen when Dr. Rollan was gone. Could this pinwheel in the sky roll on?

He sighed and fell into an uneasy sleep.

6

Someone was following them.

At first Clayton thought he was projecting his own free-floating anxiety about being discovered, but after a while the signs became unmistakable.

Dr. Rollan had proposed that Clayton and Sylvia hike around the Hoop. There were striking vistas and pleasant forests in a world that was only five kilometers wide but over a hundred kilometers long.

While they were crossing a monotonous checkerboard of cultivated fields, Clayton first caught sight of a distant figure far behind. There were so few Brothers and Sisters working alone, a single person was noticeable. The Hoop rose up into the sky, distorting perspective. The distant person seemed above them, looking down from a blue-green carpet that curved away into misty cloud. As Clayton watched, the figure disappeared behind a tree. Later, he glimpsed a flicker of movement as they mounted a hill.

Always at the same distance. Always the quick ducking out of sight.

A polite way for Rollan to be sure his daughter didn't get into trouble? Or to keep tabs on him? Clayton wondered.

They explored the long equatorial chain of lakes that divided the Hoop into two shores. A leisurely walk around the Hoop took about a week in the half-g centrifugal gravity. It was several days before he could adjust to the sensation of journeying only a few kilometers and finding a wholly new environment. Tropical pineapple fields gave way to alpine forests, which yielded to fertile river-valley vegetable farms, all managed by dutiful Brothers and Sisters. Overhead, occasional flying robots adjusted the humidity, shifted the clouds, tinted the air with mixers and catalysts, like angels over Eden.

They hiked through crisp rolling hills, wholesome flatland wheat and cloying dense jungle. Sylvia seemed to bloom with every kilometer of progress. One day they avoided the 'roidrock communal home of the Brothers and Sisters, and instead camped in a dense knot of oak trees. Their canopy blotted out the Vortex, bringing a false night.

Sylvia luxuriated on a bed of moss, which Clayton had gathered at her request from the moist upper limbs of the trees. "Moss is a parasite, after all," she had said. "It uses trees; *we'll* use *it*."

Clayton toasted compressed tofu bars over yellow flames. "*This* is home," Sylvia said languorously. She sat on a large stump (careful thinning was necessary for a balanced biosphere) and said, "*Real* nature."

"Um," he agreed.

"Where people can be people again." Her dress fluttered like a white sail in a breeze, a craft promising far destinations. Oak leaves stirred above in the firelight, making moving shadows as does the wind on the sea.

"Right."

He took her some tofu, hot and jacketed in a crisp black crust from being held too long in the flames. He collapsed to his knees before her as she bit into the creamy warm taste inside. She smiled in lazy acceptance and he kissed her. He drew in his breath deeply, feeling himself on the verge of a great abyss. She parted the dress and shrugged free of it. The cloth fell like a tablecloth on the broad stump, herself as the meal. He was tired of trying to be underspoken and witty. He inhaled and a musky scent of her swarmed into him. Insects chirruped in the twilight. "Ah," she said. The filmy dress, the thick air—if he had been sensible, he would have worried about his heart. She smiled, silkily stroked his neck, and slid the backs of her knees over his shoulders.

As they hiked the next day, the Technicolor ribbon overhead rippled and flexed, like a living flag. Clayton watched it as closely as he could, a hand lifted against the glare. He could see now and then a chunk of asteroid debris escorted in by robots. The tidbit then slowly wound its way through the outer edge of the accretion disk. From this equatorial angle he could see much that was unknown about the disk—the coal-dark lanes of thickening dust, the sudden yellow flares of magnetic reconnection farther in. When alone, he took notes and used the finger-sized camera tucked snugly into his belt.

Rollan still imported earth technology when it seemed in accord with the aims of Brotherland. Clayton had respectfully brought up the subject of contact with Earth. Rollan had visited there several times, making mysterious business arrangements, brushing aside questions from scientists. "Why go to Earth at all?" Clayton had asked. Rollan had rolled his eyes and replied, "Why do people go to zoos?" and would say no more.

They had nearly circumnavigated the Hoop when Clayton

saw a craft many kilometers up in the air. That seemed impossible, and indeed it was—there were no clouds at that moment, and he was staring straight through the cap on the atmosphere, into space. As he peered upward, the silvery craft glided across the eggshell-blue bowl and dropped below the hills to his right.

Sylvia was becoming tired, so he left her to swim in one of the shallow, sparkling lakes. They were partway through a jungle zone and he found the going rough as he hiked the kilometer upward, into the hills.

He had never thought about precisely how the Hoop atmosphere was held in, so the shortening of the jungle trees came as a surprise. Here and there, dotting the thick tangle of vines, were great mango trees, their fruit purplish red or vivid yellow among the massive leaves. Among them loomed rubber trees, each with a tap to catch its milky sap, cool columns stretching up into air thick with moisture.

They were all cut at the top. And as he struggled upward amid green, cloying vegetation, he saw why. The monolayer that capped the atmosphere curved down to the ground nearby.

Their trunks sheathed in vines, the trees were stately among screaming cockatoos and pigeons that boomed through the leaves on whirring wings. He saw that the Brothers and Sisters must have kept the trees trimmed at the top to avoid their puncturing the thin, shimmering layer of flue that arced down out of a clear sky and came to earth not much further up in the hills. Clayton struggled on.

Abruptly he came to a steep drop—or so it felt. The trees stopped and he was looking straight down to ice. In a dwindling perspective he saw the silvery craft slow and fire mooring lines into a great cliff of sea-blue ice, scarcely more than a hundred meters away.

He nodded to himself. The Hoop's rotation gave a centrifugal gravity pressing outward, which was "down" on the Vortex-facing face. On the night side the effect was reversed, making it useless. Why would a ship land there, among the ice Rollan used as backup fluid storage?

A cargo bay irised open in the ship's side. Robots edged
something bulky from the bay. They towed it across to the
ridged ice, which to Clayton's perspective curved down and
away. He squinted as the robots and their cargo drifted into
shadow.

Their chunky load looked like ice, too.

But why bring ice here, where there was plenty already?

And where did they get it?

He leaned forward to see better. His foot twisted on a last
root that clung to the edge of the soil. He pitched forward,
arms windmilling.

A large hand grabbed his shoulder, hauled him back.

Panting, he turned to see who it was. Ernest said, "Dangerous up here, sir."

"Uh, yes."

"Sightseeing is fine but you have to watch yourself."

"Yes, I didn't expect—"

"Not good to leave the Miss alone like that, either."

"Well, no, but—"

"You're supposed to enjoy yourself, sir."

"Well, I was merely looking—"

"Don't concern yourself with those machines," Ernest said
solemnly. "They're different from us."

Flustered, Clayton wondered what the man could possibly
mean. "Yes," he said, "they have more arms."

"Huh?" Ernest's heavy brow wrinkled in puzzlement.

"Forget it."

"Thing is, like the Handyman says, you got to stick to the
good and true."

"What?"

"The fine way the light from the Vortex plays on the pebbles
in a brook. Hard and true."

"Oh." The man seemed a cretin.

"Bright and clear."

Clayton nodded, though Ernest seemed neither of those
things.

"You shouldn't be up here," Ernest said stolidly. Then, as an afterthought, he added, "Sir."

7

It had been Ernest following them all the time, of course. Once revealed, he stuck like glue, taking none of Clayton's broader and broader hints.

They stopped for the "night"—really just a scheduled time when the windows were firmly covered against the steady Vortex glow—at a Hostel. As usual, the Brothers and Sisters were polite, generous, and totally uninterested in their visitors. Clayton got a haircut from them, at Sylvia's request. Ernest, whose muscles rippled beneath a tight T-shirt, attracted his usual covey of Sisters. Some were quite graphic in their intentions for recreation after the dinner hour, stroking him as they passed and cooing voluptuously. He grinned and accepted this as his due without making much of it. Clayton became uncomfortable at these continual erotic interruptions of their dinner conversation. There was also an embarrassing moment in the restroom. He had gotten used to the fact that there were no separate facilities for Brothers and Sisters, but was still surprised when Ernest offered to compare the lengths of their members while they stood near each other at the urinals. From Ernest's laconic remarks, Clayton gathered that Ernest felt the winner would have proved something.

Rummaging for something to say, Clayton bitingly remarked, "You can't compare flowers until they're fully grown."

Too late, he realized that Ernest might easily take this as a frank invitation. He fled without even pausing to zip up.

Back at the long communal dinner tables, Clayton deliberately kept Ernest's glass filled with the sweet, red wine all the Brothers and Sisters drank. It was undistinguished, but it loosened Ernest's tongue.

"Sure, we ship the good grain to the 'roid people. Good trade," Ernest said.

"Profitable?"

"Pays expenses."

"Do you work on the engine repair for those tugs, the ones that haul the grain?"

Ernest nodded. "Don't like it much."

"Why?"

"Me, I like the simple work."

"Growing food?"

"Right. We've all got to rotate jobs, though."

"Why?"

"You know—prevent elites from forming." Ernest pronounced "aye-letes," his brow furrowed at the thought.

"I've noticed you don't use much farm machinery."

"Work's not so good if you got to use machines all the time."

"You all agree on that? Even the ones who're doing the hoeing and plowing?"

Ernest looked irritated. "Why should any Brother or Sister think different?"

"Well, on Earth there's a different opinion every ten feet you go."

"That's Earth's problem."

Sylvia nodded. Clayton did not wish to get into an argument with her, so he probed in a different direction. "Do you work on other kinds of propulsion engines?"

Ernest sat very still. "Like what?"

"Well, fusion drives, that sort of thing."

Ernest looked confused. His small eyes darted around the room, but the long rows of Brothers and Sisters were babbling to each other with rapt attention. "Why would I do that?"

"Well, to carry cargoes further around the solar system."

Ernest became more agitated, simultaneously trying not to show it. The man obviously had no grace under pressure. "I don't think about those things," he said lamely.

Clayton didn't believe Ernest thought about much at all, but a few moments later in the conversation he let drop the term "ramscoop" and Ernest visibly started. *Ah.*

By this time a Sister was tugging Ernest away for what promised to be only the first bout of the night. Sylvia explained demurely that the Brothers and Sisters—who referred to themselves as the People—were agreed that the Hoop should be filled to the limit with more People. "The greatest good to the greatest number," she said. "That's the rule, isn't it?"

He could hardly disagree, especially since it promised to keep the already drink-sodden Ernest well occupied throughout the "night."

Two hours after Sylvia fell asleep in their small monklike cubicle, Clayton rolled soundlessly from bed. He made his way through the cool ceramic hallways of the Hostel, easily dodging the small staff that went about necessary chores. The Hoop's advantage in having a constant source of Vortex-light, and thus a relentless growing cycle for crops, was somewhat offset by the inconvenience of tending to the fields even at "night." Still, Rollan's prescriptions for social unity decreed that a vestige of Earthside ritual be maintained, not least because it gave a rhythm and unity to the communal experience. So the Hoop ran on the standard twenty-four-hour day, with few workers staying up through the nominal night.

Clayton slipped away from the Hostel on the side away from the central fields, since he was bound for the edge. No one followed.

He reached the Hoop's rim quickly. He had tucked into his rucksack for the circumnavigation a small infrared telescope. By standing on the very edge of the Hoop, he gained the greatest angle of observation, and thus could see farthest into the accretion disk near the black hole. Puffing from his run, he settled into the roots of a towering elm tree and steadied the telescope on his knee. He was near the edge of a cliff. The monolayer buried itself into a rock ledge only meters away. Beyond that began the blue ice. He wondered momentarily about the curious incident of the day before, and why robots would deliver ice to an already ice-heavy outer face of the Hoop. It seemed innocuous, but Rollan's obsessive secrecy throughout the construction of his clockwork world naturally made Clayton suspicious.

He shrugged and set to work.

More than ten kilometers away, straight up in the sky, blankets of dust curved in toward the glowing disk. Clayton strained to pick up detail in the murky cloak. It blotted out the stars, but against the infalling, circling sweep there hung glittering ivory motes. Robots, shepherding the ground-down 'roid dust. They looped gracefully among the shrouded dark lanes, probing and pushing with electromagnetic snowplow fields.

The telescope translated infrared into visible, and gave a smoldering complexion to the slowly churning dance above. High out on the Hoop's axis, robot trawlers swarmed like beetles around an asteroid. They picked it apart like insects dismantling unlucky prey. They crunched it into the dust which spiraled inward, toward—

Something glimmered at the edge of perception. He had idly swept the 'scope by the accretion disk, knowing that the virulent glare there would soon blind the instrument. But somehow the glowing region near the black hole was lit by mere twilight flares. He peered at it by looking away, using the edge of his vision. Yes, the luminous core was dimming. But the brilliance of the disk to both sides did not ebb. Then, just as he was sure he was not making a mistake, the momentary darkening waned. He had the impression that a mask was being drawn away, both physically and metaphorically. For only a few seconds something had blocked the light from the innermost disk.

Something in orbit. Something big.

He calculated rapidly. If it was that close to the black hole, its orbital period—

He finished just as the dimming came again. A few seconds of twilight, then the returning brilliance.

Something about a kilometer in diameter was orbiting the black hole, about two kilometers from the hole itself.

Far enough outside the furnace heat of the infalling disk to keep it intact. But close enough in that no one would think to look for it. The glare of the inner disk blinded all but the most sophisticated instruments . . . and Rollan had made quite sure that no scientist with such equipment ever got near the Vortex.

Clayton nodded to himself. A perfect hiding place.

Or nearly perfect. After all, he had found it.

But what was it?

The ramscoop, certainly. His Major Tutor had supplied Clayton with enough information from around the solar system—invoices for machined parts, electromagnetic webs, pulsed power systems, superconducting magnets—to arouse ample suspicion.

The authorities had let Rollan's pinwheeling utopia go spinning along its benign orbit for decades, as long as they were sure it was an essentially harmless experiment. Virtuous, even. After all, Rollan did supply grain and other food to the 'roid communities. And his microwave net did transmit power at marketable rates to ships on fast boost between the planets.

But the accumulating evidence of the invoices suggested that Rollan was far more ambitious than he seemed. Rollan had built a ramscoop engine. With it he could launch cargoes into interstellar space, colonize other solar systems. This was illegal; indeed, immoral. Humanity had not yet agreed on a strategy for interstellar exploration. If Rollan sent a ship carrying the mere cellular ingredients for Brothers and Sisters, he would be able to colonize whole worlds with the seamless sameness of the People.

That could not be allowed. Obviously.

Clayton shook his head and muttered a string of unoriginal but satisfying obscenities.

He had thought he would craftily reap a harvest of interesting astrophysics, and return to UCLA in triumph. Now his worst fears were confirmed. He would have to find out more about the ramscoop.

Crack.

He jerked to alertness. The snap of a breaking limb echoed through the stillness of the elm grove. Birds stirred and fluttered above. Clayton listened and thought he could hear the rustle of someone slowly prowling through a glade nearby.

He saw a flicker of movement. It was one person, following a remorseless rectangular pattern. Searching.

He crouched down and crawled away from the edge of the Hoop, careful not to disturb the rich piles of leaves slowly turning into loam. They would crackle and give him away, and anyway, the act would probably upset some ecological equation somewhere.

He wished that this "night" was real, could provide sheltering darkness. It occurred to him that the perpetual day banished the entire Earthly freight of associations planetary spin gave humans: darkness, gloom, evil, uncertainty, general bad news. Brotherland was a place where day reigned eternal, illuminating all with piercing light, permitting no obscuring dark. Even the shadows were Technicolored mimics of the Vortex bands.

He wished fervently for a touch of darkness now.

Clayton moved cautiously, senses alert. Everything looked different from this angle. No wonder, he mused, that little children were hard to understand. Their world was dominated by anthills and tree roots, lakes of mud and mountains of garbage, chair legs and dog bellies, pant cuffs and big-toed feet, the musty mystery up Mommy's dress. Who wouldn't be cranky?

A figure moved among distant trees. Clayton considered making a run for it and then realized that, after all, he hadn't really done anything. Just looked over the edge a bit, natural tourist curiosity.

Still, he didn't like being followed. He worked his way around an outcropping of rock, his soft-soled shoes making no sound. There was a rustling in the trees just below him. Clayton crouched. Only a meter away a man emerged, scanning the path with a careful eye. Ernest.

Without thinking, Clayton picked up a hefty rock and tapped the big man on the skull.

Ernest dropped like a felled ox. Clayton froze, horrified at his own act.

He had committed the first act of violence in a perfect world.

Ernest came to as Clayton staggered toward the Hostel. He had hauled the bulky man two kilometers in an over-the-shoulder carry and felt like a laboratory rat on an endless treadmill.

"Hey . . . whatcha . . . hey," Ernest muttered.

Clayton dumped him and told his rehearsed story, about finding Ernest where a small landslide had caught him.

"Yeah?" Ernest rolled up his eyes as if in thought.

"Uh, yeah."

"Well, man's got to get hit, head wound's the best."

"Oh?"

"Quick."

"Oh."

8

The return of Clayton and Sylvia to the Central Hostel, where Dr. Rollan ruled, was cause for festivity.

Even Dr. Rollan's dog was glad to see them, yelping and leaping at Sylvia. The dog eyed Clayton's leg adoringly but kept a respectful distance, eyes glinting with what Clayton took to be the *Fuehrerprinzip*.

Dr. Rollan beamed, laughed, celebrated—the perfect host. He even commented warmly on Clayton's hair, mentioning that it now resembled the Brother style, simple and utilitarian.

"Glad to see it, good Clayton," Rollan said.

Clayton chose not to remark that he had gone along with Sylvia's haircut proposal primarily because of the pleasant effect she had anticipated that the soft, short brush would have on her upper thighs. Instead, he had more of the aromatic wine.

That evening, as part of the sporadic celebration, Dr. Rollan instructed the worker robots who tended the Vortex to perform for Clayton and Sylvia. In they came, hundreds of the ivory motes streaming out from the glossy bands. Further legions descended from the banks of infalling dust, leaving only a skeleton crew of robots to keep the dark shroud on its slow sure gyre.

They flitted gnatlike through a momentarily open hole in the monolayer. At Rollan's wrist control, the puncture spread. It was a suddenly swelling black circle, into which the robots swooped. Then it zipped shut, summoned together again by intricate molecular commands.

The robots extended silvery wings and swarmed through the Hoop's upper atmosphere. They formed letters, symbols, pictures. Against the sky the metal fleets swooped, performed adroit feats, defied gravity. Clayton realized there was no gravity up there. Centripetal force held him pinned to the Hoop, but only the mild brush of the air acted on the flying robots. He craned his aching neck to follow their darting arabesques.

As they set to work on a large cloud, Clayton stole away. The crowd went *ooh* and *aahh* as the cloud purpled, swirled, re-formed. The robots were crafting some momentary sculpture from it. An ear poked out. An eye appeared, winked. Then a full, round lip.

"Oh, it's Daddy!" he heard Sylvia cry as he slipped inside the Hostel. The Handyman made some self-deprecating reply.

Clayton quickly found what he was looking for. Rollan's private quarters were encrusted with command and control modules, detailed sequencing arrays, luminous graphics—the nerve center that controlled Brotherland and the Vortex. He felt like a spy, slipping through the doorway. Myriad columns and rows of data rolled on opalescent screens. If he could decipher even some of this, the right scrap of information—

"Why—*Clay*ton!"

He jerked his attention away from the hypnotic welter. Sylvia stood in the doorway, eyes round with shock.

"I, uh . . ."

"What are you *doing?*"

"Ah, I just wanted a look around the place."

"Daddy *never* lets anyone in here."

"Why not?"

"*You* know."

"The family secrets, right."

She said archly, "I'm sure you really do understand. You're just being difficult."

He wondered how much she knew. She was quite smart, but one could be blind toward those one loved. He sighed. "Come on, let's go see the rest of the show."

"It's nearly over. Robots bore me, really." She looked at him from the corner of her eyes, a lightly enticing smile curving her cool lips. "Besides . . . wouldn't you really rather go to our room?"

Her invitation was irresistible, her buoyancy contagious. Her dress fluttered in a vagrant breeze, as though she herself had just returned from a short, graceful, effortless flight in the uplifting air. Clayton sighed and gave himself over to her, though he knew he would have to try something daring if he was ever to make any real progress.

9

As the supernova expansion continues, the shell will fragment into clumps whose size is difficult to predict. Despite turbulence and magnetic disruption effects, some clumps should survive. They should have densities in the range of their initial formation. Rapid radioactive decay will leave many of them in states of virtually pure silicon, magnesium, or carbon. Indeed, carbon chunks will be most common, probably in the form of graphite. However, if at the onset of expansion the incipient lattice struc-

ture were face-centered cubic, this form could persist. Numerical simulations of this stage are costly and unreliable, so it appears unlikely that theoretical work on this topic can proceed further without some observational spur. Since such solid supernova debris is not luminous, attempts to observe it near supernova remnants in the galaxy seem doomed. This area of research thus appears to be at a dead end.

—VALERIE THOMPSON, 2078
Supernova Debris

Later, he tugged her along the passageway, nervously watching the doors ahead.

She whispered, "But honestly, I don't see why we have to—"

"Shhhh!"

They walked softly through the rest of the Hostel, avoiding the distant sounds of movement as the skeleton night shift went about domestic duties. Sylvia led him through an obscure side exit and they stepped into glaring daylight.

She began sleepily, "I still don't see—"

"I want a better look at the Vortex robots," he said. "And I'm pretty sure your father wouldn't let me."

"Did you *ask* him?"

"What you don't ask for, they can't deny you," he said nimbly.

"But he might get angry if—"

"Where did you say they usually landed?" If they stood here and talked it all out, eventually somebody would come by.

"Over there, beyond that hill. The maintenance station is buried under that grove of apple trees." She pointed reluctantly.

They skirted around the Hostel and made their way, keeping well back in the leafy shadows. A section of hillside slid aside at Sylvia's command; he was quite sure the voice-actuator would have rejected him, perhaps set off a jangling alarm. He had gently gotten information from her after a sweaty tussle in bed. She had drifted into sleep, but a plan bloomed in his imagination.

After their graceful aero demonstration, some of the Vortex robots had stayed on the Hoop, for routine repairs. Sylvia walked through the quick, darting teams of shiny robots without giving them more than a glance, assured that they would get out of the way. They did, too. Awake now, she was quite willing to show off more of her father's vast empire, though it became obvious that she knew very little about how any of this worked.

In the back row he saw a bulging cylindrical thing perched on a launch platform. Atop it was a transparent bubble. A giveaway; automatic machines don't need observation domes.

"Can I take a look inside that one?" he asked casually.

"Um, I suppose so."

She was alert yet quite willing to go along with his curiosity. The point, she had reminded him regularly, was to free people from machines, so that they could think primarily of each other again. She repeated this as they climbed up the rungs of the large, pear-shaped vessel. A hatch hissed open. Inside, she tapped a command phosphor and a voice obediently asked, "Yes, Missy?"

"We'd like some drinks."

"Of course. I have fresh squeezings of fruit, pure water, sniffer ale . . ."

Clayton was no longer listening. His eyes swept the control panel, understanding its elegant simplicity immediately. His hands flitted over an actuation pad and the boards lit up. He tapped in a command. Standard stuff; his 'roid experience paid off.

The drinks were already splashing into opulent crystal glasses. The disembodied voice interrupted its offerings of food with, "Oh, sorry, I shall have to belay catering while we are under acceleration."

Sylvia blinked. "Acceleration?"

"Yes. Please be seated."

Clayton felt a gentle throbbing under his feet, then a tug.

"What—ow!" Sylvia cried, as she tumbled onto a divan that had sprouted from a bulkhead.

"We're taking his personnel robot for a ride," Clayton said. "To see the sights."

Sylvia's eyes widened. "You, you . . ."

"Quite."

The craft rose with obedient, smooth competence. The hillside rolled away and they sprouted from it, a thin tongue of orange fire licking at the tail. Clouds wreathed them, visible through the transparent dome above. The ship asked, "Destination?"

"The Vortex," Clayton said.

Sylvia could have rescinded his order at any moment, he knew, but something strange had come into her eyes. She stared at him, a prettily puzzled frown marring her forehead. He had taken a move without consulting her; perhaps she was so surprised by this unique event that the possibility of a serious outcome to this adventure had not yet occurred to her? Somehow her crisp intelligence, so apparent at UCLA, was submerged. The true Sylvia seemed ever more unfathomable. She sat on the divan, stroking its gold lamé upholstery with a slow, distracted rhythm.

Clayton had worried about the monolayer, but he needn't have. It parted as they rose, unzipping a slice of raw black sky. The ship poked through it and free.

Sylvia said, "You don't mean to—"

"Oh, but I do." He smiled.

They sped swiftly toward the brimming disk of light. Dust thumped and rasped and sang against the hull.

"You'll tell me when the X ray or UV count gets high?" Clayton asked the ship.

"Of course, sir. But I shall rotate my body away from the disk itself, so as to absorb the radiations before they reach you."

"Good idea."

"I was designed to think of such things."

"For what mission?"

"To take Dr. Rollan on his journeys to the Vortex."

"To study what?"

"That I do not know."

"Does he go often?"

"Sadly, no. He has seldom made the trip this last decade."

"Any idea why?"

"No sir," the ship said stiffly, and Clayton wondered if its programming used "sir" as Ernest did.

"Clayton, I want to go back," Sylvia said. He recognized the petulant vixen approach—pouting lip, whiny singsong. But somehow he knew she did not mean it.

"No. I want a look at this."

"My father will be angry—*very* angry."

Ah, threats. "I think he'll understand. He was like me, once."

"He was an idealist! He did not go where he was not wanted—"

"Come on. Your father had curiosity."

"He was thrown into a place and a time, by impersonal historical forces," she said, as if she had memorized it from somewhere.

"Is that from one of your father's speeches to the Brothers and Sisters?"

She looked surprised. "Well, yes."

"There's another similarity."

"What?"

"He was an astrophysicist, once."

She looked blank. "You're not, you're—" Then a furious look crept over her face.

"Right. I'm majoring in astrophysics."

Sylvia gritted her teeth and swore bitterly, her words like spat tacks. He said nothing.

She began to shout at the ship, commanding it to turn back. When there was no answer, she pounded on the firm but padded walls.

"It's no use," he said mildly. "I've switched the ship to control panel operation only."

"How— Why—"

"I'll explain later. Don't think badly of me simply because I did what I had to do. Just . . . give me time. And watch."

He knew there was little time before Dr. Rollan would be after them, and less still before the ship would reach the inner edge of the accretion disk. His heart thumped as he swung into the observation chair. It was mounted on gymbals and shafts, allowing easy movement about the transparent dome. Filtered telescopes and array sensors hung nearby, available at a gesture. Astrophysical luxury.

The central riddle of Brotherland came riding toward them, trailing clouds of glory.

They were coming down now, falling at an angle toward the accretion disk. It turned like an immense Technicolor phonograph record. Luminous bands shaded from blue to orange to red and finally, at the furiously spinning inner edge, a startling, glorious white. Clayton felt a giddy, seasick sway as the ship matched orbital velocities with the disk. Each striated section was at a different temperature and gave off its own speckled, roiling glow. He could see flecks of still-solid stone being swallowed at the outer rim, then ground into fuel by friction's raw rub.

But toward the center, where the burning fire was a searing point, he caught a flicker of movement. Something solid, something large . . .

Sylvia was talking to him, using reasonable tones of persuasion, softly undulant. To Clayton it was babble, lost in the background pops and rumbles that echoed through the ship. Tidal stresses from the hole? He could not follow her quixotic changes anymore. He concentrated on the shadowy thing ahead.

He punched in directives and the ship smoothly shifted, pressing them into their couches as it set off in pursuit of the inky thing that—Clayton saw clearly now—was orbiting at the edge of the disk, but not *in* the disk.

"It's in orbit around the hole, perpendicular to the disk," he said wonderingly.

"*What* is?" Sylvia asked sharply, but even she was puzzled, frowning up at the strangely somber, gleaming thing.

The distorting sweep of light made it hard to be sure. "It's no ramscoop vessel, at least," Clayton muttered to himself. So those suspicions had been wrong . . .

The surface of the thing caught the disk light and threw it back in a shower of minute glimmerings, a thousand thousand wavering ice-blue candles buried deep in the slumbering mass.

Extract sample, Clayton ordered the ship, punching in the directive.

A small flitter launched itself across the foreground, braked, then buried itself deeply in the target.

The bulk's slow rotation brought into view long, webbed tubes mounted on the surface.

"Accelerators," Clayton said. "That's what your father bought the electromagnetic guns for."

"What?"

"To adjust the orbit of this big mass. To make up for the friction it encounters when it punches through the disk. And people Earthside thought he was building a starship . . ." He smiled mirthlessly.

Sylvia peppered him with questions, but he brushed them aside. They watched silently as a sample-fetching robot returned and thumped into the lock. In a moment the ship's flawless servants had conveyed the sample case up to the receiving bay. Clayton snapped it open.

Into his hand floated a brilliant, icy stone.

"I don't . . ." Sylvia touched the cold, hard thing.

"It's a diamond."

"What! Are you . . . sure?"

"It fits with some studying I've been doing. Supernova debris is mostly rubble, junk, hydrogen gas, but the compressed star could form solid matter. At those temperatures—"

"Solid carbon? That's what diamond is, like graphite, isn't it? Only harder."

"Yes—far more compressed. The supernova star did that.

The center imploded into a black hole, the outer layers blew away—and somewhere in the middle, *this*."

He looked wonderingly out at the slowly spinning mass. It had lumps and hummocks, like any other small asteroid. Yet each minute turn brought forth myriad fresh facets of hard, cool blue, of russet, of sulfurous yellow.

"But who would ever have thought . . . we always considered molecules, maybe a few pebbles at most. *This* . . . a chunk so big . . ."

He estimated distance, angle. He tried to think of something on a human scale to compare it to, something as worthy of this rich relic from a time beyond the first dim stirrings of Earthly life, beyond the first raindrop, beyond the blind dumb buttings that formed the sun itself.

He whispered, "It's one whole stone. A diamond as big as the Ritz."

"The what?"

"A hotel in Boston. A fabulous hotel."

She said sardonically, yet distantly, "For the rich only, I'll bet."

"For the different."

"Sure they're different. They have more money."

Clayton could not argue of such infinitesimal things, could not take his eyes from the blissfully turning body, host of a billion starlike blue-white promises.

10

"Good Clayton!"

The rasp of Dr. Rollan's voice on the radio yanked him from his reverie.

"Daddy! Look what we've *found*," Sylvia cried gladly.

Clayton put out a hand to block the small TV camera she swiveled, to transmit the image before them. Sylvia veered it away from him and focused on the vast stone.

"Think of it!" she said. "It must have drifted in here from

those dust clouds the robots are always working on, bringing in from the Belt. Dummies! They didn't recognize what it was.''

Clayton began carefully, "Sylvia, you should wait and—''

"No, don't you understand? If Clayton—I know he's impetuous, Daddy, and I have to admit it, a liar, too! —If Clayton hadn't stolen this ship and come out here on a jaunt, we would never have known this was here. It would fallen into the hole!''

Clayton said, "It's moving exactly perpendicular to the disk. That minimizes the friction it feels when it passes through the plane of the disk. Anyway, it's far out, at the edge of the disk. A small, steady push could keep it in this orbit for a long time.''

"That's quite right." Dr. Rollan's voice came crisply through the panel speaker. "This object will no doubt prove very interesting to study. Meanwhile, I must insist that you return at once to the Hoop and leave—''

"No, Daddy! I want to *explore*. A diamond this big, it's— why, I wonder if when you stand on the surface, you can see yourself, little pictures of yourself, waving back? All the way down to the center!''

"Sylvia, there is all the time in the world to—''

"Never mind, the charade won't play," Clayton said.

Rollan asked menacingly, "What?''

"A diamond asteroid, orbiting just so precisely that it won't fall into the hole easily? But perfectly positioned so that when it is above or below the plane of the disk, it's screened by the infalling dust? And so that nobody can see it from the Hoop? The only way I suspected it was through its eclipsing. There was a quick little flicker as its shadow passed between me and the disk.''

Rollan frowned. "I never could figure how to get rid of that.''

Sylvia said, "The robots put it there, I bet. They probably were wondering what it was. But with all they had to do, preparing for their air show and all, there probably hasn't been time—''

Clayton laughed, though he sensed this was not wise. "And it just happens to arrive now?''

Sylvia said irritably, "You're making a lot out of—"

"No, he is right, Sylvia," the Handyman said. "The stone has been here from the beginning. I discovered it at the same time as the hole itself. They were in orbit about each other even then."

Sylvia blinked. Her mouth opened—first in amazement, then in perplexity, then in a sad, wondrous expression of confused defeat. Finally she shut it, having said nothing.

"Then your biography is wrong?" Clayton asked.

"In part."

"You didn't make your first money out of the hole at all, did you?"

"No."

Sylvia asked wonderingly, "Then, how . . . ."

"He sold chunks of the diamond," Clayton said. "Right?"

"Yes. A little private courier run to Earth, some quiet deals. It was necessary."

Sylvia said distantly, "To finance Brotherland?"

"Yes. I could extract power from the hole, but not enough to buy all I needed. I left the diamond here in the original orbit, where no one would find it."

Clayton added, "We always wondered why you put Brotherland out here. That didn't make astrophysical sense."

Dr. Rollan's voice said wanly, distantly, "Yes . . . a clue, one I could not avoid."

"But Daddy, why *hide* it?" Sylvia's lips hovered between stunned surprise and quizzical alarm. Yet her eyes studied the huge stone outside with keen intelligence.

"I used chips from it to finance the Hoop."

"But I thought . . . the black hole . . ."

Rollan said sadly, "Yes, I could make some profit from energy extraction . . . but I could see it would not be enough to accomplish . . . my dreams. Certainly it alone could not support . . . the economy of the Hoop as it now exists . . . all the Brothers and Sisters."

Clayton understood everything now. He opened his mouth

to speak when suddenly he glimpsed a rapidly growing red dot, high above the diamond asteroid. "What—"

Ernest's voice boomed through the cabin. "I've come to kick your ass back where it belongs, *sir*. The Handyman, he's taking this pretty hard. I decided to come out here and drag you back, you lying little—"

"Oh, forget that hairy-chested stuff," Sylvia said sharply. "Can't you see you've been outfoxed?"

Clayton found her sudden tart anger endearing. All along he had wondered if she found Ernest's sweaty—well—earnestness somehow attractive. To find that she could so quickly size up the situation and automatically side with him gave Clayton an unexpected jolt of pleasure. He smiled at her and gestured toward the immense gleaming stone.

"I believe the lady would like to take a walk upon the surface first, Ernest. We'll suit up momentarily. Then I'm sure I'm quite capable of escorting her safely home, thank you."

The sputtering exasperation that came from the speaker only deepened his joy.

11

Clayton took a moment to himself on the veranda. It was pleasant to get outside, away from the hothouse festivities of the Hostel.

Dr. Rollan had declared a holiday. The Brothers and Sisters had set to with an endless round of dances, feats, athletic competitions, songfests, and general revelry. Apparently they required no explanation of the holiday, no pretext, but simply gave themselves over to a mad round of heartwarming ritual good spirits. Clayton had never seen people with such capacity, and wondered how such a remarkable ability fit into the dry, acerbic Drovneb parameters. Breathing in the succulent air of ripe fields and sweet promise, he decided that narrow, dull Drovneb had missed something vital.

"Are you going to accept?"

Sylvia's sudden question, coming from behind, made him jump. He turned to find her glowing with energy, perspiring from a whirling folk dance that was just now ebbing away in the hall beyond.

"I . . . I came here to think it over."

"You *have* to."

"Well, I . . . it's a big decision, Sylvia."

Her mouth formed an incredulous O. "But you could live here for*ever*."

"But I couldn't return to Earth, or even to the asteroids."

"What does that matter? Earth can't compare to *this,* can it?"

He gazed out across the verdant fields, the gentle curve of the Hoop rising up into the sky with a seemingly infinite promise of bountiful natural wealth. There was astrophysics to be done here, yes. Utopian visions, a self-contained universe.

Even if it was founded, finally, on a deception. But still, that false center was a giant jewel, a marvel unequaled anywhere.

"No, it can't compare," he finally replied.

"Father *needs* you."

"Yes, so he told me when he made the offer." Clayton patted her hand uncomfortably.

Actually, Dr. Rollan had revealed more than Sylvia or anyone else in Brotherland knew. Dr. Rollan's health was declining, an arteriosclerotic gumming combined with gradual, accumulating organ defects beyond the healing powers of man or machine. Rollan was the scientific sorcerer behind the Hoop, and was finding the task more difficult as the great ring spun on. Even minor excitements, such as Rollan's confession to his daughter at the discovery of the diamond mountain, sapped his strength. He needed help.

"You know," he said distantly, "if you hadn't invited me, I wonder how he could have gotten anyone reliable out here."

"You mean any volunteers would have been Earth agents?"

"Well, yes," Clayton admitted, uncomfortable.

"Just like you."

"But I'm different, you know that."

"Oh yes, as I know," she said, an enigmatic smile playing on her lips.

Clayton's arrival had seemed an omen to Dr. Rollan, a possible eleventh-hour salvation. Rollan had never trusted outsiders enough to think of bringing them into his gyrating experiment. But now he had to. Sylvia's chance invitation had provided an unexpected opening.

"Is he resting?" he asked, to deflect the conversation.

"I checked a short while ago. He's looking better."

"He knows I won't leak information about the diamond."

"Of course," she said mildly. "We trust you."

"Mere knowledge that so many potential diamonds could flood the market—that alone would drive the price to nearly zero."

Sylvia smiled. "Your sacred market system. Too much wealth and it becomes worthless."

Clayton shuffled uncomfortably, rubbed his hands together. There had been so many signs, clues, hints. The thick windows of his bedroom were diamond sheets. The robots he had seen at the edge of the Hoop were bringing a chunk of diamond to store among the ice fields of the Hoop's backside. Ernest's discomfort at discussing technical matters arose from the man's lack of experience at keeping secrets from strangers.

Rollan had not been deeply disturbed by Clayton's discovery. Perhaps the years of keeping the secret had built up a kind of pressure to share it with someone who could understand.

The old man did trust him. Earlier tonight the Handyman— face lined, hands visibly trembling, voice reedy and faltering— had offered to bring Clayton forward as his inheritor, the Fixit Man. To transfer the mantle of humble power.

Rollan's dog came cautiously onto the veranda and sat a respectful meter from Clayton's revered leg. Curiously, the dog acted this way only toward the Handyman and himself, as if all along the animal had sensed some similarity.

"I . . . I don't know," Clayton said. "I'd have to learn so

much astrophysics, how to handle Brotherland, to teach people like Ernest enough to help me out.''

"Father can teach," she said laconically.

Clayton nodded. Dr. Rollan knew the quirky ways of the Brothers and Sisters, was sure that he could smooth the way for Clayton. They needed leadership, though of a gentle, self-effacing kind. For in their blissful, nostalgic world, the Brothers and Sisters were unprepared for the inevitable threats the Hoop faced.

One danger was obvious. The mass that was heated and thus lit the Brotherland skies was in turn swallowed by the hole. As the hole's mass grew, its gravitational field clutched the Hoop harder, made it spin faster, stressed the carbosteel webs that underlay the warm green fields. This would worsen. Only an astrophysicist could solve such a long-term problem.

The Handyman had peered at Clayton for a long time this evening, beseeching him wordlessly to shoulder the task. And now Sylvia did, too.

To maintain this idyllic simple communality demanded vast, intricate, gyrating technology, but even that was not enough. At the secret center was not a dark secret but instead a diamond, a luminous cliché of capital.

Something in these contradictions appealed to Clayton's heart.

He took her hand and walked inside, to the railing above the large dance floor. Below swirled the uplifted, perspiring, happy faces.

For the first time tonight, Clayton had begun to sense the strange social cohesion these people felt. They were the Handyman's ever more demanding and uncontrollable hostages to fortune, joyful souls born into a serene world shaped by unseen hands. They spoke to each other constantly, comparing their minor mishaps, accidents, confusions, fretful collisions with reality's unrelenting rub. The tireless torrent of pure, unashamed gossip shared out all misfortunes, tempered egoistic dread, purged anger of its uniqueness. There was a solace in such a thick net of mutually invaded privacies, sexual preferences confessed and exercised under an unblinking sun, angst exposed to the social glare like a skin disease shriveling away beneath searing ultraviolet. Like a heightened form of clubbiness, these people felt no oppression in their uniformity. They gained instead a reassurance that villages and tribes had granted their members down through millennia, the casual knowledge that no scrape or tragedy or disfiguring blemish was in fact new, that everything had happened before, or very nearly so, and could be shared, soothed by their swelling songs.

Something in their innocent spinning dance endeared the Brothers and Sisters to him. Even dumb but useful Ernest, waving up at them, seemed like an old schoolmate. The fevered music, humid thick air, heady sweet aroma of wine—all blended into an illusion of ample community and endless uncomplicated joy. It was a dream he knew he could share, as the Fixit Man.

"They never seem to stop," he said dreamily.

"Yes," Sylvia said precisely. "Like sex, only too much is enough."

The remark surprised him, like many of her sudden shifts, and he studied her for a long moment. She seemed coolly oblivious, and yet . . .

What an obliging accident it had been, that the fellow student she invited for a visit was an astrophysicist, even though he concealed it. Despite her thoroughness, her quiet investigation of him at UCLA had not revealed that deception. How providential, too, that he had the right combination of curiosity and timing to discover the diamond, and force Dr. Rollan to think about a replacement. In the long run, if Clayton could not surmount the Hoop's gathering problems, he had contacts among the freebooters of the asteroids. Their craft and their silence could be bought, without alerting Earthside. Clayton knew his 'roid origins could be useful. And finally, how lucky for them both that romance had bloomed here, and that he was a man she could share this marvelous mad pinwheeling world with. Remarkable!

His eyes narrowed at the thought, and she gave him a serene, full smile. Yet her ample, expressive mouth seemed in that blissful passing moment to hide mysteries and wisdoms beyond measure. A beautiful smile. He would always wonder exactly what it meant.

The Scarred Man

The cold seeped through my rough jacket. I hurried along the poorly lit mall, sensing the massive ice that lay just beyond the plastaform walls. That was when I first noticed the man with the scar.

Few patrons were out this early, nosing into the cramped shops or reading the gaudy neon adverts outside the clubs. Later the gambling would bring them in from their docked ships and the mall would fill. There would be noise and some singing, a brief flurry of fighting here and there, the calling of barkers. Dark women in filmy dresses would stroll casually for customers, making the men forget the chill of fifteen meters of snow overhead.

Thus it was that the scarred man stood out among the few idlers. He hurried, with that slight toeing in of the feet that comes of walking down the narrow passages of a commercial submarine. I would have noticed him even without the scar on his face, because there was something furtive in his movements, some hint that he felt eyes upon him.

In this place it was not at all unusual to see a scar, a tattoo, or even a flesh wound, freshly made. Ross City was a free port, the only large one in Antarctica. Privateers and smugglers filled the coves.

Ross was a straitlaced American explorer of a century or so before. I am sure he would have reddened with outrage at some of the things which went on in the city that bore his name. Submarines with silenced screws were plying a steady trade in smuggled oil, running between the outlaw offshore rigs of Australia and the hungry markets of North and South America. Ross City, tucked into a shelf jutting out from Mount Erebus, lies on a great circle between Australia and Chile. It was the natural focus of men skirting the law.

Smugglers had money—anyone dealing in scarce raw materials did, these days. They were willing to spend for a secure port to hole up in, particularly when the UN patrols were conducting their usually futile southern Pacific sweeps. The submariners lived with danger; a few close scrapes were a hazard of the trade. A scar in itself was not unusual; the man's manner was. And beneath his obviously altered face, I knew this man.

I decided to follow him. Perhaps the chill air made me reckless. Perhaps my skiing hadn't quite drained me of the random, unfocused energy a man acquires in a desk job. I told myself I was on holiday, bound for an evening slumming in the trader bars, and a bit of spice before serious drinking would not be out of place. I dug in my heels and went after him.

He ducked down a side passage. I turned the corner only a moment behind him. It was a short block, but my man had vanished. Into one of the shops? Several were day businesses, darkened. The others—

I glanced quickly into a dingy shrimp fry joint and didn't see him. The next brightly lit entrance was a homosexual restaurant/bar; the signifying emblem was prominently displayed. I passed it by—my man didn't look the sort, and he hadn't behaved as if on the way to an assignation.

There remained one doorway, one that by chance I knew well. *Voyager Tavern* the blue neon proclaimed, though it was actually an alcohol and pill bar. I often put in here during an evening's rounds, searching for atmosphere. Some dangerous men are said to frequent the place, particularly in the back

rooms. I came to the Voyager for the ample drinks and relaxed mood.

I hesitated, wondering if I should dash down the street and
check beyond the next corner, and then pushed through the
Voyager's door. I was right. My man stood only a few feet
away, back to me. He looked slowly around the room, as if
expecting to find someone he knew. He was taking his time
doing it. Probably his eyes took a while to adjust to the dark,
after the garish lighting outside. Mine did, too; but I knew the
bar well and slipped silently around him, navigating by the low
murmur of conversations more than the dim red lighting.

I chose a side booth with a good view of the room, sat and
looked back at the scarred man. One of the Voyager's girls
approached him with a graphic gesture, smiling from beneath
impossibly long eyelashes. He waved a hand, brusquely dis-
missing her, and said something in a rasping voice. She
shrugged and moved off.

The scarred man nodded at someone across the room from
me and I followed his look. I was surprised: he nodded at an
acquaintance of mine, Nigel Roberts. Nigel was playing cards
with an array of scruffy men in khaki; he raised a finger in
salute and went back to studying his hand.

The man sniffed and continued to search the bar. He seemed
to have an air of distance and reserve about him that was most
atypical of the sort of man who became a smuggler. His face
bore an expression that implied he felt himself above the customers in the bar and disliked being so distantly greeted by
someone he knew.

"Hello," a woman's voice said. "On for an evening of
pleasure?"

It was the same girl, again. I had been with her once before
and found her competent but uninspired. I doubted if she remembered my face. I smiled, told her no, and she drifted away.

The movement attracted the man's attention. He peered at
my table, squinting in the poor light, holding up a hand to
block out the glare of a nearby lamp.

Then he saw me. His face froze with shock.

His wiry arms tensed suddenly and he glared at me with an intense, burning rage. He took three jerky steps forward, balling his fists.

I shifted my weight forward onto my feet. I lifted myself off the booth seat about an inch. The movement would be imperceptible in this light. I was ready to move to either side, which is about all one can do when attacked in a sitting position. I breathed deeply, setting myself automatically for whatever came.

Abruptly, he stopped.

The scar ran down from below his ear to the very tip of his pointed chin. In this light it flamed a stark red. But even as I watched, it subsided and faded back into the pallor of his skin. He remained standing, weight set, frozen.

We gazed at one another for a long moment.

He flushed, lowering his eyes, and shook his head. He glanced up at me once more, as if to check and be sure I was not the man he had supposed. With a dry sound he shrugged, abruptly turned and marched into the back room of the bar.

As he moved through the pink patches of light and shadow I noticed that his scar was deeper near the throat, as though made by the blade of a knife coming from below. It was not fresh and bore the dark, mottled look of a deep cut that could not be readily corrected by a skin graft or even tissue regeneration.

I sighed and settled back. He was probably calming himself in the back booths with one of the more potent—and illegal—drugs. My heart was pounding away, fueled by the adrenaline of a moment before. I had found the experience unsettling, for all its intriguing aspects, and I finished my first drink, when it came, with one long pull.

I had come into Ross City that evening for a break from the genteel monotony of the Mount Erebus resort, where I spent most of my holiday. The tourist value of Antarctica lies in the Mount's ski slopes and the endless plains of blinding white.

The sting of the incredible cold quickens my blood. I ski there yearly, rather than on the tailored and well-known slopes in Eurasia or the Americas. Conditions there are quite pedestrian. Like all sports in this century, it has been rendered simple, safe, and dull for the ant armies who want everything packaged and free of the unexpected. Near the great population centers—a phrase that includes virtually all the planet now—there is little risk and thus no true sport. For that, you come to Antarctica.

Unfortunately, the adventurers are seldom exceptional conversationalists and I found them boring. A week at the Erebus resort was more than enough to become saturated with tales of near-accidents, broken bindings at the critical wrong moment, and slopes-I-have-known. So I took the tube down to the City, strolled through the red-light districts and ate in the ill-lit expatriate restaurants. It is perfectly safe even for a gentleman of my obvious affluence, for sportsmen and tourists are well treated. We bring in Free Dollars, which in turn create the economic margin that allows the City to remain a free port.

"Interesting one, eh?" Nigel said at my elbow.

The card game had broken up soon after the scarred man left, so Nigel came over to sit with me. I did not ask after his fortune. He didn't volunteer information, so he had lost again.

"Yes," I said. "For a moment he seemed to know me."

"I noticed. Come to think, you *do* look something like—"

"Who? The man who gave him that scar?"

"Well, it's a bit of a story, that scar and all."

"Fine. Let's have it. What are you drinking?"

When a snow frappe—laced with rum and cloves—had come for him, Nigel continued.

"He's a restless sort, that one. Name is Sapiro. Been on the subs for quite a time now. Hard to miss him with that scar, eh?—and he's not the type to be overlooked anyway. Always on the push, though I expect he's slowed down a bit now. Must've been born ambitious." Nigel's Australian accent inevitably gained the upper hand once he said more than two sentences at a go. I noticed he seemed nervous, drumming fingers on the tabletop and fidgeting with his glass. Perhaps his gambling losses had unsettled him.

"The man's done everything, at one time or another. Jobbed on an offshore rig, worked the fishing fleets, did some depth mining until the UN outlawed using amateurs in that game." Nigel looked at me with narrowed eyes. "Had a habit of rushing things, being a touch careless. He wanted to get places fast."

"He hasn't come very far, for all that."

"Ah, but you don't know."

"Know what?"

Nigel hesitated, as though deciding whether to tell me. His brow crinkled with thought. Why was the decision so important? This was simply a casual conversation. But somehow, underneath, I caught a thread of tension in Nigel. Did he have some personal stake in Sapiro?

Nigel looked at me across the table, fingering a napkin. Intently, with a sudden rush, he began:

"Sapiro started as a technical type. Computers. Worked for International Computational Syndicate."

"That is the combine with IBM as principal holder, isn't it?"

"Right. I'm sure you know what those outfits are like—regiments of stony-eyed executives, each one with a fractional share of a secretary, living in a company suburb and hobnobbing with only company people. A closed life. Well, that's what Sapiro got himself into and for a while he didn't mind it. Fit right in. All he wanted to do was get to the top, and he didn't care what he wore or where he lived or what he had to say at cocktail parties to get there."

"But it didn't last."

"For a man like Sapiro ICS wasn't enough. Back in the 1990s, you know, that was when the white collar squeeze came on. Computers had caught up. Machines could do all the simple motor function jobs and then they started making simple executive decisions, like arranging routing schedules and production plans and handling most of the complaints with auto-

matic problem-solving circuits. That didn't leave any room for
the ordinary pencil pusher and they started to wind up in the
unemployment lines.

"Well, Sapiro wasn't playing in that low-caliber a league,
but he could feel the hot breath on his neck. He guessed the
machines were always going to be getting better and the rest
of his life would be a tough, flat-out race to stay ahead of their
capabilities.''

"He was right," I said, sipping at my mug.

"Sure he was. Three quarters of the population can tell you
that right now from firsthand experience.

"But ambition is a funny thing. Sapiro wanted his share of
the loot—''

"I gather that was rather a lot."

"A fortune, nothing less. Enough to keep him above the herd
for life, without him ever lifting a finger. You see, he wasn't
hot for power or status. It was money he wanted. Once he had
the money he'd get some status anyway. It's not easy to keep
those two separate these days. Once you've got a high living
standard, you get a taste for status and power, they're the ones
everybody's after. Funny."

"What did Sapiro do?" I said to hurry him along. Nigel had
a tendency to lapse into philosophy in the middle of his stories.

"Well, he didn't want to fight the computers. So he looked
for a way to use them. By this time he was a minor executive
baby-sitting for the experimental machine language division,
overseeing their research and reporting back to the company.
He had a brother-in-law in the same lab, a mathematican. They
were good friends—Sapiro was married to the researcher's sister—but they didn't see much of each other in an official
capacity.

"One evening they had the brother-in-law over to dinner and
were sitting around talking shop. Everybody likes to make fun
of computers, you know, and they were making jokes about
them, figuring up schemes to make them break down and all
that.''

"Everybody is afraid of them," I said.

"Yes, I suppose that's it. Fear. They were tossing around ideas and having a good time when the brother-in-law—his name was Garner—thought up a new one. They kept kicking it around, getting a few laughs out of it, when they both suddenly realized that it would really work. There weren't any holes in it, as there were in most computer stories."

"This was a new vulnerability the designers had overlooked?" I said.

"Not exactly. The new machines ICS was putting together had a way they could be rigged, and no one could tell that one little extra circuit had been built in. It never functioned in any other capacity, except the way Garner wanted it to.

"It worked like this. You start with your own computer, one of the new models. Give it a program to execute. But instead of doing the job immediately, the machine waits awhile and then, in the middle of somebody else's calculation, takes five or ten seconds out to do your work. You know what a random number generator is?"

"Well . . . it's some sort of program, isn't it? It produces a number at random and there is no way to tell what the next one will be. The first one might be a 6, next a 47, then a 13. But there is no way to tell what the next one will be."

"That's it. The time interval before your computer did your job would be random, so that the guy whose program came ten minutes after ours was supposedly done didn't *always* find five or ten seconds missing. That made the trouble hard to trace, even if the other guy noticed he was losing a few seconds.

"But the kicker in all this is that Garner had found a way to charge those seconds to the account that was running at the time."

"Oh, I see. That gave him free running time at someone else's expense. Very clever."

"Yes, but not quite clever enough. After all, he and Sapiro had access to only one or two computers. If they stole lots of time from the other users—and what would they do with it, anyway?—it would be noticed."

"Could they not sell the computer time to some other company?"

"Of course. But they couldn't steal much. It wouldn't be profitable enough to run the risk."

"I imagine the risk would be considerable, as well."

"Quite. You know as well as I what the cartels are doing these days. It was even tougher then, ICS *owned* Sapiro and Garner. As long as they were employed there the company could arrange their 'disappearance' and few would be the wiser. They lived in a company town that looked the other way when company goons dispensed justice. No, the risk wasn't worth it. The scope would have to be a lot bigger—and the profits— before they could afford to make the gamble.

"Garner was the better technician but Sapiro knew the way management's mind worked. Any fool knew computer time was worth money. The corporations would take pains to be sure no one could make away with sizable chunks of it, chunks large enough to perform a respectable calculation. So Sapiro figured he'd do just the reverse of what ICS expected."

"Oh? I—"

"Here's what he did. He had to have Garner's help, of course, in hiding the initial program inside a complicated sub-routine, so even a careful search wouldn't find it. That was Garner's only contribution, and a good thing, too, because he wasn't a man who could deal with people. He knew nothing of character, couldn't tell a thief from a duke. Or so Sapiro thought."

"Then Sapiro—" I said. The only way to get Nigel to hold on the subject was to threaten to interrupt, a theory which was quickly verified when he raised his voice a decibel and plunged on:

"The program he logged in instructed the computer to dial a seven digit telephone number at random. Now, most phones are operated by people. But quite a few belong to computers and are used to transfer information and programming instructions to other computers. Whenever a computer picks up the receiver—metaphorically, I mean—there's a special signal that says it's a computer, not a human. Another computer can recognize the signal, see.

"Sapiro's computer just kept dialing at random, hanging up on humans, until it got a fellow computer of the same type as itself. Then it would send a signal that said in effect, 'Do this job and charge it to the charge number you were using when I called.' And then it would transmit the same program Sapiro had programmed into *it*."

"So that—" I said.

"Right on. The second computer would turn around and start calling at random intervals, trying to find another machine. Eventually it would."

"I see, much like the windup toy game."

"The what?"

"When I was a boy we used to wonder about those windup dummies one could buy. Suppose you got a bunch and fixed them so they would just walk to the next dummy and wind him up with the little screw on the back. I remember once thinking that I could mobilize an entire windup toy army that way."

"Didn't work though, did it?"

"No." I smiled wryly. "I'm told the trouble lies in the energy. No dummy would have the power to wind up another to quite the same strength, so they would all run down pretty soon."

"Yup, that's it. Only with Sapiro the money to pay for the few seconds of computer time was coming out of all the accounts available to the computer, completely randomly. He was using somebody else's energy."

"I still don't see—"

"As soon as the program was in the machine and working, he and Garner quit. Those were tough days, and ICS didn't

shed any tears to see them go. Their friends thought they were
crazy for throwing up good jobs."

"How did they live?"

"Opened a computer consultant firm. Got no business, of
course, but they were biding their time. All the while that one
computer at ICS was dialing away, making a call about every
twenty minutes. Pretty soon it had to find another soulmate,
then there'd be *two* dialing.

"Garner calculated it would take five months for half the
ICS computers in North America to be reached. But before
that, programmers began to notice longer running times for
standard jobs they'd set up, and people started to worry. The
Sapiro program was buried deep and it was random, so everybody figured the trouble was a basic fault of the ICS computer.
A random symptom is always evidence that the machine is
failing, they said."

"Enter, Sapiro and Garner, Consultants," I said.

"You got it. They volunteered to find the trouble for free the
first time. Garner was smart enough to hide what he was doing,
and in an hour or so they straightened out the machine. Said
they had a new method and couldn't reveal it. All they'd done
was countermand the program that had been telephoned into
the machine.

"That got them all the publicity they needed. They fixed a lot
of ICS computers for incredible fees, only they did it through a
cover agency so ICS wouldn't realize who they were.

"It worked fine because even after they'd debugged a machine, sometime or other another computer that hadn't been
fixed would call up and transmit the orders again. They never
ran out of customers.

"Sapiro got rich and so did Garner, only Garner never
seemed to show it. He didn't buy anything new or take his
wife to Luna for a vacation. Sapiro figured it was just Garner's
shyness. He didn't imagine his partner was saving it all up
someplace where he could run when the time came. Sapiro
didn't have much time to think about it anyway because he

was working eighteen hour days, with assistants to do fake work as a blind. The flunkies would go in, fiddle with the machine the way Sapiro had told them, and then Sapiro would pop in, dump the program—he called it VIRUS—and take off. The people who owned the machine never suspected anything because it looked like a complicated process; all those assistants were there for hours.

"Sapiro and Garner just flew around the hemisphere, selling their cure-all—Sapiro called it VACCINE—and making money.

"Then one night the ICS goons came after him. They weren't out for fun, either. They tried a sonic rifle at short range and the only thing that waved Sapiro was an accident—his copter fell into a lake, where the ICS goons couldn't reach him to finish him off. He floated on a seat cushion and kept his head low while they searched from shore. It was late fall and the water was leaching the warmth out of him. He waited as long as he could but the ICS agents didn't leave the shoreline—they were just making sure.

"He started paddling. It was hard to make any time without splashing and attracting attention but the movement kept him warm a little longer—just enough to get him to the other end of the lake. It wasn't a lake, actually, but a reservoir. Sapiro heard a rushing of water and thought it was the edge of the falls. He tried to swim away but by that time he was too weak. He went over.

"But it wasn't the falls. It was an overflow spot that fell about ten feet and then swirled away, taking him with it. The current carried him a half mile beyond the edge of the park area. He staggered up to the street, found a cab and used his credit cards to get to a hotel."

"He didn't go home?"

"No point. ICS had the house, his wife, everything. He checked by phone and found out several interesting things. That Garner hadn't come to work that day. That Garner's home numbers didn't answer. That his office was surrounded by ICS men.

"It took him three days to find Garner. He'd holed up some-where and thought he was safe, but Sapiro bought off a few people and tracked him.

"Garner had sold out to ICS, of course. The deal was that ICS wouldn't touch him after he handed over the information, but that didn't stick for Sapiro. When ICS saw what fools they'd been, they went for blood and Sapiro was the nearest throat handy. They'd have killed Garner, too, if they'd known where he was.

"So after Sapiro took every Free Dollar Garner had—he was carrying it in solid cash, some jewelry and universal bank drafts, to be sure ICS didn't get it—he called ICS and told them where Garner was. He'd left Garner boarded in and tied up."

"Then it all resolved satisfactorily," I said. "He got his money and his freedom."

"Freedom, yes. Money, no. Sapiro ran for Australia and beat it into the bush country. ICS never tracked him but they got some of the cash by good luck, and Sapiro had to spend the rest of it to keep them off his tail. He had a year or two of good living but then it was gone. Even while he was spending it there was not much fun to it. ICS was still looking for him, and by coincidence an agent ran into him in Sydney. Sapiro got the worst of the fight but he smashed the fellow's head when they both fell over a railing—he landed on top.

"That convinced him to lie low. It was about time he had to anyway because the money was almost gone. He got onto the offshore rigs and then into smuggling because it paid better. He's still doing it. He can't forget that he was once a big opera-tor, though, and he looks down his nose a bit at the people he must associate with."

"Is that why he seemed a bit cold and reserved when he came in here?" I asked.

"Probably. He isn't a bad sort and he does tell a good joke. He would've come in and been sociable if he hadn't seen you."

"Why me?"

"He showed me some pictures from the ICS days once. One

of them was of Garner. There's a fair resemblance between you two. Garner's hair was darker, but then it might have lightened with age."

"But ICS took care of him," I said.

"Maybe. Sapiro left him for ICS, but Garner might have gotten away or even talked his way out of it. Improbable, I'll grant, but it could have turned out that way.

"I don't think Sapiro is afraid of Garner at all, but you'll admit it must have been a shock for him to think he saw his old partner like that."

"Yes," I said, "I can well understand it. He gave me rather a start just by glaring at me."

"Good job he realized his mistake. Might have—"

"But look," I said. I was becoming impatient. "You said you would tell me about that scar. It's an awful thing, ought to have something done about it. How did Sapiro get it? When the copter crashed, or in the fight with the ICS man?"

"Ah yes, that. He's fond of the scar, you know. Wouldn't have it changed for anything, says it makes him look dashing. Stupid."

I raised an eyebrow. "Why? A man can allow himself a few eccentricities."

"Not a man like Sapiro. ICS can't afford to have someone still in circulation, living proof that ICS can be beaten. It might give some other ambitious chap an idea or two."

"But it's been years!" I said. "Surely—"

"The only sure thing is that ICS is big and Sapiro, however clever, is small. That, and his mouth is too large. He has told his story too many times, over too many drinks."

"The same way you're telling me now."

Nigel smiled and the lines in his face deepened in the dim light of the bar. "It doesn't matter now. Sapiro told his little tale to a man who needed money. A man who knew who to call at ICS."

I hesitated for a moment. I glanced toward the back room of the bar. A haze of pungent marijuana smoke was drifting lazily through the beaded curtain that shielded the back. Sapiro was probably quite far gone now, unable to react quickly.

"A man who gambles, you mean," I said slowly. "A man who fancies himself a shrewd hand at cards, but somehow cannot manage to get the best of the gaming tables here in Ross City and simply won't stay away from them."

Nigel regarded me coldly, unmoving. "Pipe dreams," he said, too casually.

"But our man still feels guilty about it, doesn't he? The old code about ratting out on friends—doesn't vanish so easily as you thought? So while you're waiting for the finish you tell an acquaintance about Sapiro, maybe thinking I will agree that he is a dishonest, stupid man who might as well be converted into cash for poor Nigel, the overdrawn gambler?"

"There's nothing for it, you know," he said grimly. "The scar's given him away back there. It wasn't hard to describe to them. By the time you could reach the curtain—"

Through the strands of colored beads, but somehow as though from far away, there came a faint scream. It had an odd bubbling edge to it, as if something was happening to the man's throat. Abruptly it became something else, something far worse, and suddenly ended.

The job was perfectly done. The terrible sound had never risen above the hum of conversation in the front room, never disturbed the layered smoke and drowsy mood. No head but mine had turned.

Quite professional.

Nigel was looking at me smugly; unconsciously, I had jumped to my feet. His face was losing its lines of strain.

"Finish your drink?" he said. "There's nothing more to do. What can any of us do, eh? Eh?"

I nodded and sank back into my seat. It was done. ICS had their man at last; they'd been satisfied.

I was free.

World Vast, World Various

1
THE CUSP MOMENT

The vortex wind roiled stronger, howled across the jagged peaks to the south, provoking strange wails as it rushed toward the small band of humans.

The sounds came to Miyuki like a chorus of shrill, dry voices. Three hundred kilometers to the south these winds were born, churned up by the tidal surges of the brother planet overhead. Across vacant plains they came singing, over rock sculpted into sleek submission by the raw winds. Gusts tore at the twenty-three Japanese in their air masks and thick jackets. A dusty swirl bedeviled them with its grit, then raced on.

"They're coming," Tatsuhiko said tensely.

Miyuki squinted into the cutting cold. She could barely see dots wavering amid the billows of dust. In her rising excitement she checked again her autocam, belt holdings, even her air hoses. Nothing must go wrong, nothing should steal one moment from this fresh contact between races. The events of the next hour would be studied by future generations, hallowed and portentous. As a geophysicist, her own role was minor. Their drills had taught her to keep Tatsuhiko and the other culture specialists in good view of her autocam, without being herself conspicuous. Or so they hoped. What if beings born of this austere place found smell, not sight, conspicuous?

"They're spreading out," Tatsuhiko said, standing stick-straight. "A sign of hostility? Maneuver?"

Opinions flowed over their suit comm. Tatsuhiko brushed aside most of them. Though she could not see his face well, she knew well the lean contours of concern that would crease his otherwise smooth, yellowish complexion. Miyuki kept silent, as did all those not versed in the consummate guesswork that its practitioners called Exo-Analysis.

The contact team decided that the Chujoans might have separated in their perpetual quest for small game. This theory seemed to gain confirmation as out of the billowing dust came a peri and two burrowbunnies, scampering before the advancing line. The nomads doggedly pursued, driving game before them, snaring some they took by surprise.

I hope they don't mind an interrupted hunt, Miyuki thought. They seemed stolid, as if resigned to the unrelenting hardship of this cruelly thin world. Then she caught herself: *Don't assume.* That was the first rule here.

She had seen the videos, the scans from orbit, the analytical studies of their movements—and still the aliens startled her.

Their humanoid features struck her first: thin-shanked legs; calves muscled and quick; deep chests broad with fat; arms that tapered to four-fingered hands. But the rest . . .

Scalloped ears perched nearly atop the large, oval head. Eyes were consumed by their pupils. A slitted mouth like a shark's, the rictus grin of an uncaring carnivore. Yet she knew they were omnivores—had to be, to survive in this bleak biosphere. The hands looked *wrong*—blue fingernails, ribbed calluses, and the first and last fingers both were double-jointed thumbs.

These features she took in as the aliens strode forward in their odd, graceful way. Three hundred twenty-seven of them, one of the largest bands yet seen. The wind brought their talk to her from half a kilometer away. Trills, twitterings, lacings of growls. Were they warning each other?

"Showing signs of regrouping," Tatsuhiko called edgily.

As leader of the contact team, he had to anticipate trouble of any sort. The aliens were turning to bring the vector of their march directly into the center of the humans. Miyuki edged into a low gully, following the team's directives. Swiftly the Japanese formed a triangular pattern, Tatsuhiko at the point. To him went the honor of the cusp moment.

The pale morning light outlined the rumpled peaks to the west, turning the lacy brushwork of high fretted clouds into a rosy curtain, and their light cast shadows into the faces of the approaching aliens.

Miyuki was visible only to a few of the tall, swaying shapes as they made their wary way. She thought at first that they were being cautious, perhaps were fearful, but then she remembered the videos of similar bands. They perpetually strode with an open gait, ready to bound after game if it should appear, eyes roving in a slow search pattern. These were no different.

With gravity fifteen percent less than Earth's, these creatures had a graceful, liquid stride on their two curiously hooflike feet. They held lances and clubs and slingshots casually, seemingly certain that whatever these waiting strangers might be, weaponry could keep them at bay. They were only a few hundred meters away now and she felt her breathing tighten.

Chujo's thin, chilly air plucked at her. She wondered if it affected her eyes, because now she could see the aliens' clothing—and it was moving.

They wore a kind of living skin that adjusted to each change in the cant of their arms, each step. The moving brown stuff tucked closely at neck and armpits and groin, where heat loss would be great, yet left free the long arms and muscled thighs. Could such primitives master biotech capable of this? Or had they domesticated some carpetlike animal?

No time left for speculations. Her comm murmured with

apprehension as the nearest alien stolidly advanced to within a hundred meters.

"Remember Kammer," one of the crew observed laconically.

"Remember your duty!" Tatsuhiko countered sharply.

Miyuki's vision sharpened to an unnatural edge. She had a rising intuition of something strange, something none of them had—

"Tatsuhiko," she called. "Do not step in front of them."

"What?" Tatsuhiko answered sharply as the leading alien bore down upon him. "Who said that? I—"

And the moment had arrived.

Tatsuhiko stood frozen.

The face of the truly alien. Crusty-skinned. Hairless. Scaly slabs of flesh showing age and wear. The alien turned its head as it made its long, loping way by Tatsuhiko. Its skin was fretted, suggesting feathers, with veins beneath the rough hide making a lacework of pink, as in the feet of some earthly birds. And the eyes—swollen pupils giving the impression of intense concentration, swiveling across the landscape in smooth unconcern.

The alien rotated its torso—a flickering of interest?—as it passed. Tatsuhiko raised a bare hand in a sign they had all agreed had the best chance of being read as a nonhostile greeting. Tatsuhiko smiled, careful to not reveal white teeth, in case that implied eating or anger among beings who shared a rich lore of lipped mouths.

To this simple but elaborately rehearsed greeting the alien gave Tatsuhiko a second's further gaze—and then strode on, head turning to scan the ground beyond.

And so they all came on. No sounds, no trace of the talk the Japanese had recorded from directional mikes. The second alien drew abreast of Captain Koremasa Tamura, the expedition leader. This one did not register Koremasa with even the slightest hesitation in the regular, smooth pivot of its head.

So came the next. And the next.

The Chujoans pressed forward, nomads in search of their

next meal. Miyuki remembered the videos taken from orbit of just this remorseless sweeping hunt. Only the first of them had permitted its gaze to hesitate for even a moment.

"I . . . I do not . . ." Tatsuhiko whispered over comm.

The aliens swept by the humans, their eyes neither avoiding recognition nor acknowledging it.

"Do not move," Koremasa ordered.

Even so, one woman named Akiko was standing nearly directly in front of an approaching Chujoan—and she lifted a palm in a gesture that might have meant greeting but Miyuki saw as simple confusion. It brushed the passing alien. Akiko clutched suddenly at the Chujoan hand, seeking plaintively. The creature gave no notice, allowing its momentum to carry it forward, freeing its hand.

Koremasa sharply reprimanded Akiko, but Miyuki took little notice of that, or of the buzzing talk on her comm. She hugged herself against the growing chill, turned away from the cutting winds and watched the aliens continue on, unhurried. Hundreds of evenly spaced, oblivious hunters. Some carried heavy packs, while others—thin, wiry, carrying both slings and lances—had little. But they all ignored the humans.

"Anyone registering eye contact?" Tatsuhiko asked tersely.

The replies trickled in reluctantly. No. No one.

"How do they *know?*" Tatsuhiko asked savagely. "The first, it looked at me. Then the rest, they just—just—"

Faintly, someone said, "They won't even piss on us."

Another whisper answered, "Yes, the ultimate insult."

Chuckles echoed, weak and indecisive against the strong, unending alien wind.

The humans stood in place, automatically awaiting orders, as endless drill had fashioned them to do. Dust devils played among them. A crusty-skinned thing the first expedition had unaccountably named a snakehound on the basis of a few glimpses on their video records—though it showed no signs of liking the fat worms that resembled earthly snakes—came bounding by, eluding the hunters. Likewise, it took no apparent notice of the humans frozen in their carefully planned deployment of greeting, of contact, of the cusp moment.

In their calm exit Miyuki saw her error, the mistake of the entire crew. These Chujoans had two hands, two feet, binocular eyes—primatelike, city builders, weapon users. Too close to human, far too close.

For they were still alien. Not some pseudo-Navajos. Not more shambling near-apes who had meandered out of the forest, patching and adding to their cerebral architecture, climbing up the staircase of evolution toward a self-proclaimed, seemingly ordained success.

These beings shared no genes, nor assumptions, nor desires, with the seemingly similar humans. Their easy sway, their craftily designed slingshots and arrows—all came from unseen anvils of necessity that humans might not share at all.

She leaned back, smothering an impulse to laugh. The release of tension brought a mad hilarity to her thoughts, but she immediately suppressed the urge to shout, to gesture, to stamp her boots into the dusty certainties of this bleak plain. After all, Tatsuhiko had not given the order to disperse the pattern—he was stiff with shock.

Perhaps this sky gave a clue. How different from Earth! Genji loomed, a great mottled ball fixed at the top of the sky.

How well she knew the stories of the *Genji Monogatari,* by the great Murasaki. Yet the imposition of a millennium-old tale on these hard, huge places was perhaps another sign of their underlying arrogance.

The whirl of worlds, she thought. Spheres stuck at the ends of an invisible shaft, balls twin-spinning about each other. Tidal stresses forced them to eternal mutual regard, rapt, like estranged lovers unable to entertain the warmer affections of the swollen, brooding sun which even now sought to come onstage, brimming above the horizon, casting slanting exaggerated shadows. The aliens headed into this ruddy dawnlight, leaving the humans without a backward glance.

2
ARRESTED ATHENS

They took refuge in the abandoned cities. Not for physical shelter, for that was provided by the transparent, millimeter-thin, yet rugged bubbles they inflated among the ruins. They came here to gain some psychological consolation, for reasons no one could quite express.

Miyuki sat in one of the largest bubbles, sipping on aromatic Indian tea and cracking seeds between her teeth. So far these small, tough, oddly sweet kernels were the only bounty of this dry planet. Miyuki had been the first to master them, cracking them precisely and then separating the meat from the pungent shell with her tongue. Gathering them from the low, gnarled trees was simple. They hung in opulent, unpicked bunches; apparently the Chujoans did not like them. Still, it would be interesting to see if anyone without other food could eat the seeds quickly enough to avoid starvation.

The subject never came up, she realized, because no one liked to jest about real possibilities. The entire expedition was still living off the growing tanks on the mother ship. Every kilogram of protein and carbohydrate had to be brought down with many more kilos of liquid hydrogen fuel. That in turn had to be separated from water on Genji, where their main base sprawled beside a rough sea.

Such weighty practicalities suppressed humor. Not that this crew was necessarily a madcap bunch, of course. Miyuki spat her cheekful of shells into her hand, tossed them into the trash, and started listening to Tatsuhiko again. He had never been a mirthful man, and had not responded well to her suggestion that perhaps the Chujoans had played a sort of joke.

"—so I remain astonished by even the suggestion that their behavior was rooted in anything so obvious," Tatsuhiko concluded.

"As obvious as a joke?" Captain Koremasa asked blandly. He sat while the others stood, a remnant of shipboard discipline. The posture was probably unnecessary, for the captain was already the tallest and most physically commanding figure in the expedition. Standard primate hierarchy rules, Miyuki thought distantly. Koremasa had a broad forehead and strong features, a look of never being surprised. All quite useful in instilling confidence.

"A joke requires context," Tatsuhiko said, his mouth contracting into tight reserve. He was lean and angular, muscles bunching along his long jawline. She knew the energies that lurked there. She had had a brief, passionate affair with him and could still remember his flurries of anxious attention.

Partly out of mischief, she said, "They may have had enough 'context' for their purposes."

Tatsuhiko's severe mouth turned down in scorn. "That band knew nothing of prior contact—that was why we selected them!"

"How do you know?" Miyuki asked mildly.

Tatsuhiko crossed his arms, energies bundled in. "First contact was with a band over three thousand kilometers from here. We tracked them."

Miyuki said, "Stories fly fast."

"Across a mountain range?"

"In months, yes."

"These are primitives, remember. No signs of writing, of metallurgy, of plowing. Thus, almost certainly no information technology. No semaphore stations, no roads, not even smoke signals."

"Gossip is speedy," Miyuki said. The incredible, irrational, and cowardly withdrawal of the first expedition had left Chujo for the Japanese, a slate virtually unblemished. But in the time since, the Chujoans might have turned that first contact into legend.

"We must go by what we know, not what we invent." Tatsuhiko kept his tone civil but the words did his work for him.

"And I am a geophysicist and you are the culture specialist." Miyuki looked at him squarely, an unusual act among a crew trained for decades to suppress dissension.

"I believe no one should proceed to theory without more experience," Koremasa said evenly. His calm eyes seemed to look through them and out, into the reaches beyond. She caught a sense of what it was like to have more responsibility than others, but to be just as puzzled. Koremasa's years of quiet, stolid leadership on the starship had not prepared him well for ambiguity.

Still, his sign of remote displeasure made both Miyuki and Tatsuhiko hesitate, their faces going blank. After a moment Tatsuhiko nodded abruptly and said, "Very much so."

They automatically shifted to routine matters to defuse any tensions. Familiar worries about food, air, illness, and fatigue surfaced, found at least partial solutions. Miyuki played her part as supplies officer, but she let her mind wander as Tatsuhiko and Koremasa got into a long discussion of problems with their pressure masks.

They had retreated into studying artifacts; after all, that is what archaeologists were trained to do, and artifacts could not ignore you. Two women had trailed the Chujoans for several kilometers, and found what appeared to be a discarded or forgotten garment, a frayed legging. The biologists and Exo-Analysis people had fallen upon it with glad cries.

Quite quickly they showed that the snug-rug, as some called it, was in fact a sophisticated life-form which seemed bioengineered to parasitic perfection, for the sole purpose of helping the Chujoans fend off the elements. It lived on excrement and sweat—"biological exudates," the specialists' jargon said. The mat was in fact a sort of biological corduroy, mutually dependent species like small grasses, moss and algal filaments. They gave back to their host warmth and even a slow, steady massage. They even cleaned the skin they rode—"dermal scavenging," the specialists termed it. Useful traits—and better than any Earthly gadget.

The specialists in Low Genji Orbit had labored to duplicate the snug-rug in their laboratories. The expedition depended on powerful biotech resources, for everything from meals to machine repair. But the snug-rug proved a puzzle. The specialists were, of course, quite sure they could crack the secret . . . but it would require a bit of time. They seemed equally divided on the issue of whether the snug-rug was a remnant from an earlier biotech civilization or another example of evolution's incredible diplomacy among species.

Appetites whetted by one artifact, the team turned to the province of archaeology. The abandoned cities that dotted Chujo were mostly rubble, but some like this—Miyuki glanced out through the transparent bubble wall—still soared, their creamy massive walls blurred by winds until they resembled partly melted ice cream sculptures. Little metal had gone into them, apparently not needed because of the milder gravity. Perhaps that was why later ages had not plundered these canyonlike streets for all the threads of decorative tin and copper. Sand, frost, storm, invading desert brush—all had conspired to rub away most of the stone sheaths on the grander buildings, so little art remained. Koremasa and Tatsuhiko went on discussing matters, but Miyuki had heard the same debates before; one of the mild irritations of the expedition was that Koremasa still sought consensus, as though they were still packed into a starship, mindful of every frown. No, here they needed daring, leadership, dash and verve.

At the right moment she conspicuously bowed, exaggerating her leave-taking just enough for a slight ironic effect, and slipped through the pressure lock.

She slipped her pressure mask on, checked seals, tasted the slightly oily compressed air. This was the one huge freedom they had missed so much on the long voyage out: to slam the door on exasperation. There had been many elaborate ways to defuse stresses, such as playing smashball; the object was to keep the ball aloft as long as possible, not to better your opponent. Long rallies, cooperation, learning to compensate for inability or momentary fault, deploring extravagant impulse and grandstanding—all good principles, when you are going lonely to the stars. They had similarly lasted through their predicted season of sexual cookbook athletics. The entire team was like an old married couple by now—wise and weathered.

The chilly bite of even noonday never failed to take her by surprise. She set off quickly, still enjoying the spring that low gravity gave to her step, and within minutes was deep among the maze of purple-gray colonnades. Orbital radar had deep-scanned the sandy wastes and found this buried city. Diggers and wind machines had revealed elegant, airy buildings preserved far better than the weathered hovels found on the exposed surface. Had the city been deliberately buried? The street-filling sands had been conspicuously uniform and free of pebbles, not the residue of eons of runoff from nearby hills. Buried for what?

The moody, shadowed paths gave abruptly into hexagonal spaces of pink flagstones. Above, high-pitched roofs and soaring towers poked into a thin blue sky which sported small, quickly scudding clouds like strands of wool. To her eye the styles here, when they struck any human resonance at all, were deliberate blends, elements of artful slope and balanced mass that made the city seem like an anthology of ages. Could this be the last great gathering place of the ancient natives, erected to pay tribute to their passing greatness? Did they know that the ebbing currents of moisture and dusty ice storms were behind the ceaseless slow drying that was trimming their numbers, narrowing the pyramid of life upon which all large omnivores stood? They must have, she concluded.

In this brooding place of arched stone and airy recesses there came to her a silky sense of melancholy, of stately recessional. They had built this elaborately carved and fretted stonework on the edge of what must have then been a large lake. Now the diminished waters were briny, hemmed in by marshes prickly with bamboolike grasses. Satellites had found larger ruined cities among the slopes of the many mountain ranges, ones displaying large public areas, perhaps stadia and theaters—but humans could not bear those altitudes without bulky pressure suits. She coughed, and remembered to turn up the burbling humidifier in her air feed. There was enough oxygen here, five hundred meters above what passed for sea level on a world where the largest sea was smaller than many of Earth's lakes. But the thieving air stole moisture from sinuses and throat, making skin prickly and raw.

Miyuki peered up, past the steepled roofs and their caved-in promise, at the perpetual presence of Genji. Geometry told her that at noon the brother world should be dark, but the face of milky swirls and clumpy browns glowed, reflecting Chujo's own radiance. Even the mottlings in the shadowed and strangely sinister face of Chujo's brother seemed to have a shifting, elusive character as she watched. Genji loomed twelve times larger than the moon she had known as a child in Kyoto, and at night it gave hundreds of times as much light, enough to read by, enough to pick out colors in the plains of Chujo.

Now high cirrus of glittery powdered ice momentarily veiled it in the purpling sky, but that somber face would never budge from its hovering point at the top of the sky. A moist, warm, murky sphere. How had that richness overhead affected the Chujoans, through the long millennia when they felt the thieving dryness creeping into their forests, their fields, their lives?

She turned down a rutted path beside a crumbled wall, picking her way, and before her a shadowy form moved. She froze. They all wore the smell-dispersers that supposedly drove off even large predators, but this shape—

"You should not be alone here," Tatsuhiko said, his eyes hooded behind his pressure mask.

"You frightened me!"

"Perhaps a little fear would be wise."

"Fear is disabling," she said disdainfully.

"Fear kindles caution. This world is too Earthlike—it lulls us."

"*Lulls?* I have to fight for oxygen when I trot, we *all* scratch from the aridity, the cold seeps in, I—"

"It deceives us, still."

"You were the one maintaining that the natives couldn't possibly be joking with us, or—"

"I apologize for my seeming opposition." Tatsuhiko bowed from the waist.

She started to reply, but his gesture reminded her suddenly of moments long ago—times when the reserve between them had broken in a sudden flood, when everything important had not seemed to require words at all, when hands and mouths and the simple slide of skin on welcoming skin had seemed to convey more meaning than all the categories and grammars of their alert, managerial minds. Times long gone.

She wondered whether Koremasa had delicately implied that Tatsuhiko should follow her, mend fences. Perhaps—but this perpetual wondering whether people truly spoke their minds or merely what solidarity of·effort required—it provoked her! Still . . . she took the space of a heartbeat to let the spurt of irritation evaporate into the chilly air.

She sighed and allowed herself only a sardonic, "You merely *seemed* to differ?"

"I merely expressed the point of view of my profession." Tatsuhiko gave her a direct, professional smile.

Despite herself, Miyuki grinned. "You were an enthusiastic advocate of sociobiology, weren't you?"

"Still am." His heavy-lidded eyes studied her. The age-old male gaze, straying casually away for a quite unconscious study of what the contours of her work suit implied, a subtle tang of the matters between men and women that would never be settled . . . not that anyone wished them to be.

She nodded briskly, suddenly wanting to keep their discussion businesslike. "I suppose we are all at the forefront of our fields, simply by being here. Even though we haven't kept up with Earthside literature."

Communicating with Earth had proved to be even more difficult than they had imagined. In flight, the hot plasma exhaust tail had blurred and refracted transmissions. Further, the Doppler shift had reduced the bit rate from Earth by half. Few dry academic journals had made it through.

Tatsuhiko's blunt jaw shifted slightly sidewise, which she knew promised a slightly patronizing remark. He said, "Of course, you are on firmer ground."

"Oh? How?"

"Planetary geology cannot falsify so easily, I take it."

"I don't understand." Or are we both sending mixed signals? Then, to shake him a little, she asked liltingly, "Would you like a drink?"

"I wished to walk the city a bit, as you were."

"Oh, this is in the city. We don't have to return to camp. Come."

She deliberately took him through galleries of stone that seemed feather-light, suspended from thick walls by small wedges of pale rock; the sight was still unsettling, to one born to greater gravity. She padded quickly along precarious walkways teetering above brackish ponds, and then, with no time for eyes to adjust, through murky tunnels. A grove of spindly trees surrounded a round building of burnt-orange rock, breezes stirring from them a sound like fat sizzling on a stove. She stopped among them, looking for damp but firm sand. Without saying a word in answer to his puzzled expression, she dug with her hands a hole a palm wide and elbow-deep.

"Wet gravel," she said, displaying a handful. He looked puzzled. Did he know that this made him boyish and vulnerable? She would not put that past him; he was an instinctive analyzer. Once, he had tried with her all the positions made possible by the short period when the starship had glided under low deceleration—penetrating her in mechanical poses of cartoonish angles, making her laugh and then, in short order, come hard and swiftly against him. Where was that playful man now?

On alien ground, she knew. Preoccupied by the central moment of his life. And she could not reach out to touch him here, any more than she had the last few years on board.

The stand of pale yellow reeds she had noticed the day before nearly blocked the building's ample arched doorway. She broke off two, one fat and the other thin. Using the smaller as a ramrod, she punched the pith from the larger. Except for some sticking at the joints it worked, and she thanked her memory of this trick.

"A siphon," she said, plunging the larger reed into the sand hole and formally offering it to Tatsuhiko. A bit uncertainly Tatsuhiko sucked on this natural straw, his frown turning to surprised pleasure.

"It works. Ground water—not salty."

"I tire of the processed taste in our water. I learned this on one of our desert classes." Preexpedition training had been a blizzard of facts, techniques, gadgets, lore—all predicated on the earliest data from the probes, most of it therefore only marginally relevant; planets proved to be even more complex systems than they had suspected.

He watched her carefully draw the cool, smelly, oddly pleasant water up and drink long and steadily. The very air here robbed the skin of moisture, and their dry throats were feasting grounds for the head colds that circulated among the crew.

"This unfiltered water should be harmless, I suppose," he said hesitantly, his face turning wary too late.

She laughed. "You've already got a bellyful of any microbe that can feast off us."

"I thought there weren't any such."

"So it seems."

Indeed, this was the most convincing proof that panspermia, the seeding of the galaxy by spores from a single planet, had never happened. Chujo and Genji shared a basic reproducing chain, helical like DNA but differing in elemental details. Somehow the two worlds had shared biological information. The most likely explanation lay in debris thrown out by meteorite bombardment through geological time scales, which then peppered the other planet. She saw his familiar self-involved expression and added, "But of course, we've only covered a tiny fraction of Chujo yet."

His look of dismay made her suppress another laugh. Specialization was so intense among them! Tatsuhiko did not realize that biospheres were thoroughly mixed, and that the deep, underlying incompatibility of Chujoan microbes with Earthly biochemistry was a planetwide feature. "I'm just fooling, Tatsuhiko-san," she said, putting stress on the more friendly form of address.

"Ah." Abrupt nod of head, tight jaw, a few seconds to recover his sense of dignity. There had been a time when he reacted with amusement to her jibes. Or rolled her over and pinned her and made her confess to some imaginary slight, laughing.

They walked on, unspoken elements keeping them at a polite distance. She fetched forth a knife and cut a few notches in the soft length of the reed. As they walked she slipped the tip of the reed under her mask and blew through this crude recorder, making notes oddly reminiscent of the stern, plaintive call of the ancient Japanese country flute, the *shakuhachi*. She had played on such hastily made instruments while a young girl, and these bleak, thin-textured sounds took her back to a life that now seemed inconceivably, achingly remote—and was, of course. Probably few of them would ever walk the soil of the Home Islands again. Perhaps none.

They wandered among the tumbled-down lofts and deeply cut alcoves, Miyuki's music echoing from ruined walls. Here they passed through "streets" that were in fact pathways divided by thin partitions of gray-green stone, smoothed by wind and yet still showing the serpentine elaboration of colors—maroon, rose, aqua—inlaid by hands over ten thousand years ago. The dating was very imprecise, of course. Weaker planetary magnetic shielding, a different sun, an unknown climate history—all made the standard tables of carbon dating irrelevant.

Tatsuhiko raised his hand and they stopped before a worn granite wall. Deeply carved into it was one of the few artworks remaining in the city, perhaps because it could not be carried away. She estimated it was at least a full Chujoan's height on each of its square sides.

She followed the immense curves of the dune tiger. Only twice had any human glimpsed this beast in the flesh. The single photograph they had showed a muscular, canvas-colored, four-legged killing machine. Its head was squat, eyes enormous, mouth an efficient V design. Yet the beast had a long, sensuous tail thickly covered with gray-green scales. Intricate, barbed, its delicate scales seemed almost like feathers.

The ancient artist had taken this striking feature and stretched it to provide the frame and the substance of his work. The dune tiger's tail flowed out of the beast—which glowered at the viewer, showing teeth—into a wrap-around wreath that grew gnarled branches, sprouted ample flowers, and then twisted about itself to form the unmistakable profile of an alert Chujoan native.

The strange face also looked at the viewer, eyes even larger than the reality Miyuki had seen, mouth agape, head cocked at an angle. She would never know if this was a comic effect, but it certainly *looked* that way. And the sinuous tail, having made this head, wriggled around the design—to be eaten by the tiger itself.

"Writhing at the pain of biting itself?" she whispered.

"That could be. But wouldn't the whole tiger struggle, not just the tail?"

"Unless the tiger has just this instant bitten itself."

"Ummm, I hadn't thought of that. A snapshot, an instant frozen in time."

She fingered her reed. "But then why does its tail make that face?"

"Why indeed? I feel so *empty* before this work. We can bring so little to it!" He gestured angrily.

"The archaeologists, they must have some idea."

"Oh, they suppose much. But they know little."

She followed the tiger's tail with her eyes, looking fruitlessly for some clue. "This city had so many things ours do."

"But were they used the same way? The digging team hasn't found a single grave. Most of what we know about ancient Earth comes from burial of the dead."

She touched the stone, found its cool strength oddly reassuring. "This has outlasted the pyramids."

"Maybe it was cut very deep?"

"No . . . How long it has been buried we cannot tell. And Chujo's lighter gravity should lead to less erosion, generally. But I would have expected the winds to rub this out."

Tatsuhiko shrugged. "Our dating could be wrong, of course."

"Not this far wrong." Miyuki frowned. "I wonder if this place was more like an arrested Athens."

He looked at her speculatively. "A city-state? Difficult to tell, from a ruin."

"But the Chujoans still camp here—you found their old embers yourself."

"Until we scared them away, I suppose."

Miyuki studied the great wall. "You suspect they linger here, to view the ruins of what they were?"

"They may not be even the same species that built all this." Tatsuhiko looked around, as if trying to imagine the streets populated, to envision what forms would have ambled here.

She gestured at small circles that appeared above the carving. "What are these?"

Tatsuhiko frowned. "Symbols?"

"No, they look like a depiction of real objects. See, here's one that's a teardrop."

He stooped to examine the wall. "Yes, the lowest of them is. And higher up, see, another teardrop, only not so pronounced."

Miyuki tried to fathom some sense to the round gouges. If the piece had perspective, the circles could be of any true size. "Teardrop at the bottom . . . and as they rise, they round out?"

Tatsuhiko shrugged. "Rain droplets form round in the air, I believe, then make teardrops as they fall."

"Something the tiger gives off?"

"How?"

His questions were insightful, but there was something more here, she was sure of it. Her mother had once told her that art could touch secret places. She had described it in terms of simple events of childhood. When the summer rain had passed and the air was cool, when your affairs were few and your mind was at ease, you listened to the lingering notes of some neighbor's flute chasing after the clear clouds and the receding rain, and every note seemed to drop and sink into your soul. That was how it was now, this moment, without explanations.

Miyuki let the moment pass. Tatsuhiko gave up in exasperation. "Come—let's walk."

She wanted to move through the city as though she had once been a citizen of it, to catch some fleeting fragrance of lives once lived.

They walked on. She blew into her crude recorder again.

To her the atonal, clear, crude tones seemed to mirror the strangely solid feel of this place, not merely the veiled city of opaque purpose but as well the wind-carved desert wastes surrounding it. Motionless and emotionless, at one moment both agonized and deeply still.

"Perhaps that would be better to send back," Tatsuhiko said suddenly.

"What?"

"Better than our precious reports. Instead, transmit to Earth such music. It conveys more than our data, our measurements, our . . . speculations."

She saw through his guarded expression—tight jawline, pensive lips, veiled eyes—how threatened Tatsuhiko felt. The long voyage out had not made every member of the 482 crew familiar to her, and she and Tatsuhiko had always worked in different chore details, but still she knew the character-indices of them all. Crew had to fit within the narrow avenue that had allowed them to withstand the grand, epic voyage, and not decay into the instabilities the sociometricians had so tellingly predicted.

Tatsuhiko had lost great face in that abortive first encounter, and three other attempts by his team to provoke even a flicker of recognition from the Chujoans had failed just as miserably.

Yet it would not do to address Tatsuhiko directly on this issue, to probe in obvious fashion his deepest insecurities. "You have illuminated a principal feature of their character, after all. That is data."

He snorted derisively. "Feature? That they do not think us worth noticing?"

"But to take no notice—that is a recognition that says much."

Suspiciously: "What?"

"That they know our strangeness. Respect it."

"Or hold it in contempt."

"That is possible."

His face suddenly opened, the tight lines around his eyes lightening. "I fear I have been bound in my own discipline too much."

"Sociobiology?"

"Yes. We attempt to explain social behavior as arising from a species' genetic heritage. But here, the categories we ourselves bring are based on a narrowing of definitions, all accomplished by our own brains—wads of gray matter themselves naturally selected for. We *cannot* use words like 'respect' or 'contempt.' They are illusions here."

She frowned. "In principle, of course. But these natives, they are so like ourselves. . . ."

Tatsuhiko chuckled. "Oh? Come tomorrow, we'll go into the field. I'll show you the proud Chujoans."

3
SO-SO BIOLOGY

They squatted in a blind, peering through a gauzy, dim dawn.

Recently cut branches hid them from the roaming animals beyond. "I can't see anything." Miyuki shifted to get a better view of the plain. Scraggly gray trees dotted it and low, powder-blue brush clung to the gullies.

Tatsuhiko gestured. "Look on the infra monitor." He fiddled, sharpening the image.

She saw a diffuse glow about half a kilometer away. It was near a snaky stream that had cut deeply into the broad, flat valley. "Something killed a kobold last night?"

Tatsuhiko nodded. "Probably a ripper. Our sensos gave us an audio signature. Picked it up on omni and then focused automatically with a directional mike."

"Could it have been a dune tiger?"

"Don't know." He studied her face. "You're still thinking about the carving."

"It is beautiful," she said quickly, embarrassed for reasons she could not fathom.

"Indeed." His quick eyes gave nothing away. "The kobold kill is scenting in the air, and this breeze will carry it. We now wait to see what the chupchups do."

"They call each other chupchups?"

"We have analyzed their voice patterns. No clear syntax yet, of course. We aren't even sure of many words. We noticed that they make namelike sounds—*preess-chupchup,* for example—they always end in that phrase."

"Perhaps it means 'Mister.' Or 'Honorable.' "

He shrugged. "Better than calling them 'apes,' as some crew have started to do."

She sat back, thighs already aching from squatting, and breathed in the dry aroma of the hunting ground. It was like Africa, she thought, with its valleys cut by meandering rivers, the far ramparts of fault blocks being worn down by windblown sand. Only this world was far more bleak, cold, eerie in its shadows cast by the great sun now rising.

This star always made her uneasy when it ponderously rose or set, for the air's refraction flattened it. Filling four times as much of the sky as the sun she knew, it was nonetheless a midget, with a third the mass of Sol. Though the astronomers persisted in calling Murasaki a red dwarf, it was no dull crimson ember. In the exalted hierarchy of solar specialists, stars like this one, with surface temperature greater than a carbon-filament incandescent lamp, were nonetheless minor lukewarm bores. Had they been rare, astronomers might have studied them more before the discovery of life here. Though Murasaki sported sunspots and vibrant orange flares, its glow did not seem reddish to her, but rather yellow. The difference from Sol became apparent as she squinted at the carrion awaiting the dawn's attentions. Detail faded in the distance, despite the thin air, because there was no more illumination than in a well-lit Earthly living room after dark. Only as this swollen sun rose did it steal some of the attention from Genji, which perched always directly above, splitting the sky with its sardonic half-moon grin.

"Here come the first," Tatsuhiko whispered tensely. His eyes danced with anticipation. When she saw him like this it was as if his formal skin had dissolved, giving her the man she had known.

A fevered giggling came over the chilly plain. Distant forms scampered: small tricorns, running from a snakehound. Their excited cries seemed nearly human. As they outdistanced the snakehound, which had sprung from concealment too soon, they sounded as though they laughed in derision. A hellbat flapped into view, drawn by the noise, and scooped up a burrowbunny that appeared to be just waking up as it stood at the entrance of its hole.

Then she saw the band of low shapes gathering where the kobold carcass lay. They were hangmouths—ugly hyenalike beasts that drooled constantly, fought each other over their food, and never hunted. These scavengers dismembered the kobold as she watched, hunching forward with the rest of the survey team. Short, snarling squabbles came over the audios.

"Vicious," she whispered, despite her resolution to say nothing about others' specialties.

"Of course," one of the team said analytically. "This is an

ecology being slowly ground down by its biosphere. Hard times make hard species."

She shivered, not entirely from the dawn chill.

As they watched, other teams reported that a party of Chujoans was headed this way. Tatsuhiko's team had tracked these Chujoans, noted the kobold kill, and now awaited their collision with the squinting intensity of an author first watching his play performed.

Miyuki could not see the chupchups at all. The gradual warming of the valley brought tangy suggestions of straw-flavored vegetation, pungent meat rotting, the reek of fresh feces.

Tatsuhiko asked over comm, "Team C—have you counted them yet?"

The reply came crisply, "Eight, three female adult, three male, two children."

"Any displays that show parental investment?"

"Males carry the children."

Tatsuhiko nodded. "It's that way in all groups smaller than a hundred. Interesting."

"What do those groups do?" Miyuki asked.

"Food gathering."

One of the team, Hayaiko, said, "You should look at that data on incest avoidance. Very convincing. Female children are separated from the male in an elaborate ceremony, given special necklaces, the entire panoply of effects."

Tatsuhiko pursed his lips. "Don't deduce too much too soon. They might have been marrying them off for all we know."

Hayaiko blinked. "At age four?"

"Check our own history. We've done about the same not that long ago," Tatsuhiko said with a grin. He seemed relaxed, affable, a natural leader, but undercurrents played in his face.

She saw that he was no longer beset by doubt, as he had been in pensive moments in the ancient city. He would redouble his efforts, she saw, summon up more *gaman*, the famed dogged persistence that had made Japan the leader of the world. Or did he aspire higher, to *gaman-zuyoi*, heroic effort?

"The chupchups are creeping up on the carrion," came a comm message.

"They'll fight the hangmouths?" Miyuki asked.

"We'll see," Tatsuhiko said.

She caught sight of the aliens then, moving in a squat-walk as they left a gully and quickly crossed to another. Their zigzag progress over the next half hour was wary, tediously careful as they took advantage of every tuft of grass, every slope, for concealment. She began to look forward to a fight with the hangmouths as their continuing snarls and lip-smacking over the audio told of the slow devouring of the carcass. It was, of course, quite unprofessional to be revolted by the behavior of species they had come so far to study, but she could not help letting her own delicate personal habits bring a curl of disgust to her lips.

"They're leaving," comm called.

The hangmouths began to stray from the carcass. "Picked it clean," Tatsuhiko said.

The chupchups ventured closer. The two children darted in to the kill, dodged rebuffs from the larger hangmouths, and snatched away some carelessly dropped sliver—like pauper children at a land baron's picnic, Miyuki thought, in the days of the Shogunate. This intrusion seemed to be allowed, but when the adults crept closer, a hangmouth turned and rushed at the leading chupchup. It scampered back to safety, despite the fact that it carried a long pointed stick. It held the stick up as if to show the hangmouth, but the drooling beast still snarled and paced, kicking up curtains of dust, holding the band of chupchups at bay for long minutes.

"Why don't they attack it?" she asked.

"I have no idea." Tatsuhiko studied the scene with binoculars. "Could the stick be a religious implement, not a weapon at all?"

"I do not think it is trying to convert the hangmouth," Miyuki said severely.

"Along with semantic language, religion is the one accomplishment of humans that has no analogy in the animal world,'' Tatsuhiko said stiffly. ''I wish to know whether it is a biological property here, as it is for us.''

''You believe we *genetically* evolved religion?''

''Plainly.''

''Oh, come now.''

A flicker of the other man: a quick smile and, ''Religion is the opiate of the mortal.''

How could he still surprise her, after many years? ''You believe we've had religion so long that it's buried in our genes?''

''It is not merely a cultural manifestation, or else it would not be universal among us. Incest avoidance is another such.''

She blinked. ''And morals?''

''Moral pronouncements are statements about genetic fitness strategies.''

All she could say was, ''A severe view.''

''A necessary one. Look there!''

Two hellbats had roosted in trees near the kill site. ''Note how they roost halfway down the canopy, rather than in the top. They wish to be close to the game.''

The hangmouth had turned and now, with aloof disdain, padded away from the chupchup and its raised stick. Trotting easily, the hangmouths departed. The chupchup band ventured forward to the kobold body and began to root among the remains.

Miyuki said, ''The hellbats—''

''See what the chupchups are doing? Breaking open the big thigh bones.'' Tatsuhiko pointed to the vision screen, where a full color picture showed chupchups greedily sucking at the cracked yellow bones.

Miyuki was shocked. ''But why, when there's meat left?''

''The marrow, I suspect. It is rich in calories among the larger species here.''

''But still—''

''The chupchups *prefer* the marrow. They have given up on finding fresh meat, for they have given up hunting.'' Tatsuhiko said this dispassionately, but his face wore an expression of abstracted scorn.

With screeches they could hear even at this range, two hell-bats launched themselves upon the knot of stooping chupchups. The large, leathery birds dove together at a chupchup child that had wandered a few meters from the band. Miyuki watched their glittery, jewel-like eyes and bony wings as they slid down the sky.

The first hellbat sank claws into the child and flapped strongly. A male chupchup threw itself forward but the second hellbat deflected it. A female chupchup ran around the male and snatched at the child. The hellbat bit the female deeply as it tried to gain the air, but she clubbed it solidly twice with the flat of her hand. The hellbat dropped the child. It flapped awkwardly away, joined by its partner.

"They nearly got that little one!" Miyuki cried.

"They go for the weaker game."

"Weaker?" Miyuki felt irritated at Tatsuhiko's cool analysis. "The chupchups are armed."

"But they do not use them to hunt the larger game. Or even, it seems, to defend themselves. The only use we have observed for those weapons is the pursuit of small game. Easy prey."

Miyuki shook her head. "That seems impossible. Why not use them?"

Somehow this direct question shattered Tatsuhiko's stony scientific distance. "Because they have adapted—downward."

"Maybe just sideways."

"A once proud race of creators, now driven down to *this*."

"We ourselves, early man, we hunted in places like this. We could be forced back to it if—"

"No. We were hunters, like the lion. We did not scavenge."

Miyuki said quietly, "I thought lions scavenged."

Tatsuhiko glared at her but acknowledged this uncomfortable fact with a curt nod of his head. "Man the hunter did not. These chupchups—they have let themselves be driven down to this lowly state."

She saw his vexed position. Traits derived from genes had led humans upward in ability—a grand, swift leap from wily ape to sovereign of the Earth. That tended to salt the truths of sociobiology with the promise of progress. Here, though, the same logic led to devolution of the once-great city builders.

She said lightly, "We are merely talking wildly. Making guesses." She switched to English. "Doing so-so biology." Perhaps the pun would lift their discussion away from the remorselessly reductionist.

He gave her a cold smile. "Thank you, Miyuki-san, for your humor." He turned to regard the distant feeding, where the chupchups now nuzzled among the bones. "Those cannot be the breed that built the cities. We have come so very slightly late."

"Perhaps elsewhere on Chujo—"

"We will look, certainly. Still . . ."

She said evenly, hoping to snap him out of this mood, "For four billion years Earth supported only microbes. Oxygen and land plants are only comparatively recent additions. If those proportions hold everywhere, we are very lucky to find *two* planets that have more than algae!"

His angular features caught the dawn glow, giving him a sardonic look even in his pressure mask.

"You are trying to deflect my dark temper."

"Of course."

Each crew member was responsible for maintaining cohesion. They kept intact the old ship disciplines. In solidarity meetings one never scratched one's head or even crossed legs or arms before a superior, and always concluded even the briefest encounter with a polite bow—fifteen degrees to peers, forty-five degrees to superiors. Every week they repeated the old rituals, even the patient writing of Buddhist sutras with wooden pens. The officers polished the boots of the lower ranks, and soon after the ranks reciprocated. Each was bound to the others. And she felt bound to him, though they had not been lovers for years and she had passed through many liaisons since. Her longing to know him now was not carnal, though that element would never be banished, and she did not want it to be. She felt a need to *reach* him, to bring out the best that she knew lay within him. It was a form of love, though not one that songwriters knew. Perhaps in some obscure way it knitted into the cohesion of the greater expedition, but it felt intensely personal and incommunicable. Especially to the object of it all, standing obliviously a meter away. She snorted with frustration.

Not noticing her mood, Tatsuhiko smacked his fist into his palm. "But so close! If we had come fifty thousand years ago! Seen those great ancestors of these—these cowards."

Miyuki blinked, sniffed, chuckled. "Then we would have been Neanderthals."

4
THE LIBRARY

Their flier came down smoothly beside the spreading forest. The waving fields of dark grain beckoned, but Miyuki knew already that the stuff was inedible.

Nearly everything on Chujo was. Only the sugar groups were digestible. Their dextrorotary sense was the same as that of Earthly ones, a simple fact that led to deep mystery. Genji's sugars had that identical helical sense, though with myriad different patterns. And the intelligent, automated probes that now had scanned a dozen worlds around farther stars reported back the same result: where life appeared at all, anything resembling a sugar chain had the same sense of rotation. Some said this proved a limited form of molecular panspermia, with a primordial cloud seeding the region with simple organic precursors.

But there still were deeper similarities between Genji and Chujo: in protein structures, enzymes, details of energy processing. Had the two worlds once interacted? They were now 156,000 kilometers apart, less than two-thirds the Earth-moon separation, but tidal forces were driving them farther away.

Their locked rotation minimized the stress from each other's tides. Even so, great surges swept even the small lakes as the mother-sun, Murasaki, raised its own tides on both her worlds. Miyuki stood beside a shallow, steel-gray lake and watched the waters rush across a pebbled beach. The rasp and rattle of stones came like the long, indrawn breath of the entire planet.

"Regroup!" Koremasa ordered over comm.

Miyuki had been idling, turning over in her mind the accumulating mysteries. She studied the orderly grain fields with their regimental rows and irrigation slits as the expeditionary group met. Their reports were orderly, precise: discipline was even more crisp amid these great stretches of alien ground. Close observation showed that this great field was self-managing.

She watched as one of the bio group displayed a cage of rodents, each with prehensile, clawed fingers. "They cultivate the stalks, keep off pests," the woman said. "I believe this field can prune and perhaps even harvest itself."

Murmurs of dissent gradually ebbed as evidence accumulated. Remains of irrigation channels still cut the valley. Brick-brown ruins of large buildings stood beside the restless lake. Small stone cairns dotted the landscape. It was easy for Miyuki to believe the rough scenario that the anthropologists and archaeologists proposed: that the slow waning of Chujo had driven the ancient natives to perfect crops that needed little labor, an astounding feat of biotech. That this field was a fragment of a great grain belt that had fed the cities. That as life suited to cold and aridity moved south, the ancients retreated into a pastoral, nomadic life. That—

"Chupchups!" someone called.

And here they came, already spreading out from the treeline a kilometer away. Miyuki clicked her vision to remote and surveyed them as she moved to her encounter position. This tribe had a herd. Domesticated snakehounds adroitly kept the short, bulky red-haired beasts tightly bunched. A plume of dust pointed at the baggage train—pole arrangements drawn behind thin, flat-headed animals. An arrowfowl came flapping from over a distant hillside and settled onto the shoulder of the largest chupchup—bringing a message from another tribe, she now knew enough to guess. The races met again.

The leading chupchup performed as before—a long, lingering look straight at the first human it met, then ignoring the rest. Miyuki stood still as the smelly, puffing aliens marched obliviously through the human formation.

Nomads had always been a fringe element in human civilization, she reflected. Even ancient Nippon had supported some. But here the nomads *were* the civilization. The latest survey from satellites had just finished counting the chupchups; there were around a million, covering a world with more land area than Earth. The head of Exo-Analysis thought that the number was in fact exactly 1,048,576—1,024 tribes of 1,024 individuals apiece. He even maintained that each tribe held thirty-two families of thirty-two members each. Even if he was right, she thought, and the musky bodies passing stolidly by her now were units in some grandly ordained arithmetic, had it always been that way? How did they maintain it?

She caught an excited murmur on comm. To her left a crew member was pointing toward a few stacked stones where three chupchups had stopped.

Slowly, gingerly, they pried up the biggest slab of blue-gray granite. One chupchup drew something forth, held it to the light—a small, square thing—and then put it in a pocket of its shabby brown waistcoat. Then the chupchups walked on, talking in that warbling way of theirs, still ignoring the humans who stood absolutely still, aching for contact, receiving none. She almost laughed at the forlorn expressions of the crew as the last of the chupchups marched off, leaving only a fragrant odor of musty sweat. They did not inspect the fields or even glance at the ruins.

"It's a library!" someone called.

Miyuki turned back to see that a crew man, Akihiro, had lifted the granite slab. Inside rested a few cubes, each ornately decorated. "I think this is a library. They were picking up a book."

Koremasa appeared as if he had materialized from the air. "Put it back!" he ordered tersely.

Akihiro said, "But I—look, it's—"

"Back!"

But by then it was too late. From the trees came the trolls.

Miyuki was not a first-line combat officer. She thus had a moment, as others ran to form a defensive line, to observe the seemingly accidental geometry that unfolded as the troll attack began. The chupchups had stopped, turned around—and watched impassively as the trolls burst from the thick treeline. Had the chupchups summoned the trolls, once they saw their library violated? She could not guess from their erect posture, blandly expressionless faces, unmoving mouths.

The trolls resembled chupchups as chimps resembled humans—shorter, wider, long arms, small heads. But they ran with the fluid speed of a hunting animal, and caught the nearest crew member before she could fetch her weapon forth from her pack. A troll picked her up and threw her like something it wished to discard—hurling her twenty meters, where she struck and bounced and rolled and lay still. The other trolls took no notice.

They hesitated. Had they gotten some signal from the chupchups? But no—she saw that the wind had shifted. The odorous extract that the biotechs had made everyone smear themselves with—yes, that was it. The cutting reek of it, carried on the breeze, had confused the trolls for a moment. But then their rage came again, their teeth flashed with mad hunting passion, and they fell upon the next crew members.

She would remember the next few instants for all her life. The weapons carriers liked to fire from a single line, to minimize accidents. Trolls struck that still-forming line. When he saw that the smell defense had failed, Koremasa blinked, raised his hand with a sad, slow gravity—and the rifles barked, a thin sharp sound in the chilly air.

The sudden hard slaps were inundated by the snarls and howls of trolls as they slammed aside their puny opponents. The aliens were swift, sure, moving with enormous power and sudden, almost balletlike agility. In their single-footed swerves, their quick ducks to avoid a rifle shot, their flicked blows that struck with devastating power, Miyuki saw how a billion years of evolution had engineered reflexes intricately suited to the lesser gravity.

But then the concerted splatting violence took them down.

Their elegant, intelligent attack had not counted on a volley of automatic fire. The great, bright-eyed beasts fell even as they surged on, oblivious to danger.

The last few reached Miyuki, and she saw, in slow-motion surrealism, the flushed, heady expression on a troll that stumbled as it took a round in its massive right arm. *It's ecstatic,* she thought.

But it would not be stopped by one shot. It staggered, looking for another enemy to take, and saw her. Red eyes filled with purple pupils widened. It swung its left arm, claws arcing out—and she ducked.

The swipe whistled over her ear, caught her with a *thunk* in the scalp. It was more a sound, a booming, than a felt blow. She flew through the air, turning, suddenly and abstractly registering the pale blue, cloud-quilted sky, and then she landed on her left shoulder and rolled. A quick rasping *brrrrt* cut through a strange hollow silence that had settled around her. She looked up into the sky and the troll eclipsed this view like a red-brown thundercloud. It was not looking at her, but instead seemed to be gazing off into a world it could not comprehend. Then it felt the tug of mortality and orbited down into the acrid clouds of dust stirred by the battle, landing solidly beside her, not rolling, its sour breath coughing out for the last time.

5
I-WITNESSING

They devoted three days to studying the fields and burying the bodies. A pall spread among them, the radio crackled with questions, and mission command wrung from each fact a symphony of meaning, of blame, of outrage.

Miyuki was doubly glad that she had not sought a higher post in this exploration party. Koremasa had to feed the appetite of his superiors, safely orbiting Genji, with data, photos, transcripts, explanations, analysis. Luckily, two cameras had recorded most of the battle. Watching these images again and again, Miyuki felt a chill at the speed and intelligence of the troll assault. Her own head wound was nothing compared to the bloody cuts and gougings many others had received.

Koremasa would probably not be court-martialed—but Akihiro Saito, the crewman who had opened the cairn in a moment of excited curiosity, would have been tried and humiliated had he survived.

It was something of a relief that Akihiro had died. They would have had to watch him for signs of potential suicide, never leaving him alone or assigning him dangerous tasks. No one could be squandered here, no matter how they violated the expedition's standards.

Nobody ever said this, of course. Instead, they held a full, formal ceremony to mark the passing of their companions, including Akihiro. The meal was specially synthesized on the mother ship and sent down in a drop package. The team sat in a precise formation, backs to the wild alien landscape outside the bubble, and within their circle Old Nippon lived still. The captain produced a bowl for each, in which reposed a sweetened smoked sardine, its spine curved to represent a fish in the water. It had been carefully placed against two slices of raw yellowtail, set off by a delicately preserved peeled plum and two berrylike ovals, one crisp and one soft, both dipped in an amber coating. A second bowl held a paper-thin slice of raw Spanish mackerel, cut to catch the silver stripe down its back, underpinned in turn by a sliver of seaweed to quietly stress the stripe, all resting on molded rice. A small half lobster, garnished with sweet preserved chestnuts, sent its aroma into the close, incense-scented air. Thin-sliced, curled onions came next, sharp and melting in the mouth. A rosette of red pickled onion heart came wrapped in a rosy cabbage leaf. Finally, tea.

And all this came from the processors aboard the mother ship, fashioned by the master chef, who everyone agreed— in the polite, formal conversation that followed around their circle—was the most important member of the entire expedition.

The beautiful meal and a day of contemplation did their silent work. Calamity reminded one to remain centered, to rely on others, to remember that all humanity witnessed the events here. So as the numbness and anxiety left them, they returned to their studies. Five crew kept watch at all times while the rest tried to comprehend why four humans and six trolls had died.

In the end, the simplest explanation seemed best: the trolls guarded the ancient, self-managing fields, and this task included the library cairn. The biologists found rodentlike creatures that pruned and selected the grain plants, others that gathered them into bunches, and further species who stored them among the caved-in brick-brown buildings. Subtle forces worked the fields: ground cover that repelled weeds, fungoids that made otherwise defenseless leaves distasteful or poisonous to browsers, small burrowers that loosened the soil for roots. The trolls assisted these tasks and made sure that only passing bands of chupchups ate the grain. They tended fruit-bearing trees in the next valley as well, where two more library cairns stood.

The cube from the cairn yielded nothing intelligible immediately but would doubtless be studied in infinitesimal detail when they got it to the mother ship. The sciences were biased toward studying hard evidence, and the oddly marked stone cube was ideal for this. Miyuki doubted whether it could ever yield much.

"It could be a religious talisman, after all," she remarked one evening as they gathered for a meager supper.

"Then it would probably be displayed in a shrine," Koremasa said reasonably.

"They have no churches," Miyuki answered.

"We think," Tatsuhiko said sourly. "We have not searched enough yet to say."

Miyuki said, "You believe the cities at the rim may tell us more?"

Tatsuhiko hesitated. He plainly felt besieged, having failed to anticipate the danger here, a continuing humiliation to him. "There might be much less erosion at high altitudes," he said warily.

Koremasa nodded. "Satellite recon shows that. High winds, but less air to work with."

Miyuki smiled. Seen from above, planets seemed vastly simple. The yellowish flora and fauna of Chujo tricked the eyes of even orbiting robot scanners. The molecule that best harvested Murasaki's wan glow was activated by red-orange light, not by the skimpy greens that chlorophyll favored. That simple consequence of living beside a lukewarm star muddied the resolution of their data-reduction programs.

"We had better leave such high sites for later work," she ventured.

Koremasa's eyebrows showed mild surprise but he kept his mouth relaxed, quizzical. "You truly feel so?"

Though she did not wish to admit it, the thought of wearing the added pressure gear needed among the raw mountains of Chujo's rim grated upon her. She itched from dryness, her sleeping cycle veered in response to Chujo's ninety-one-hour day, her sinuses clogged perpetually from constant colds—and everyone else suffered the same, largely without complaint. But she decided to keep her objections professional. "Our error here suggests that we leave more difficult tasks to others." There. Diffident but cutting.

Koremasa let a silence stretch, and no one else in the circle ventured into it. A cold wind moaned against the plastic of their pressure dome. Their incandescents' blues and violets apparently irritated the local night hunters and pests, keeping them at bay, one of the few favorable accidents they had found. Still, she felt the strangeness of the dark outside pressing against them all.

She saw Koremasa's talent as a leader; he simply sat, finally provoking Tatsuhiko to say, "I must object. We need to understand those who built the cities, for they plainly are not these chupchups. Then—"

"Why is that so clear?" Miyuki cut in.

Tatsuhiko let a small trace of inner tension twist his mouth momentarily. "You saw the scavenging. That is not the behavior of a dominant, intelligent race."

"What's intelligent is what survives," she answered.

Tatsuhiko flared. "No, that is an utter misunderstanding of evolutionary theory. Intelligence is not always adaptive—that is the terrible lesson we have learned here."

"That is a hasty conclusion," Miyuki said mildly.

"*Hasty?* We know far more than you may realize about these chupchups. We have picked over their campsites, studied their mating through infradistant imaging, picked apart their turds to study their diet. We patched together their broken pots. Their few metal implements are probably stolen from the ruined cities and reworked down through many generations; they certainly look it."

"It is difficult to read meaning in artifacts," Koremasa said.

"Not so!" Tatsuhiko stood and began to pace, walking jerkily around the outside of the circle. He made each of his points with the edge of his right hand, cutting the air in a karate chop. "The chupchups wander perpetually. They cook in bark pots and leather bags using heated stones—stew with dumplings, usually. They like starchy sweets and swallow berries whole. They pick their teeth with a bristly fungus which they then eat a day later—"

"They must be civilized, then," Miyuki broke in. "They floss!"

Tatsuhiko blinked, allowed himself a momentary smile in answer to the round of laughter. "Perhaps so, though I differ."

He gave her a quick significant glance, and she felt that somehow she had momentarily broken through to the man she knew.

Then he took a breath, lifted his narrow chin high, put his hands behind his back in a curiously schoolboyish pose, and went on doggedly. "You will have noticed that chupchup males and females look nearly alike. There are no signs of homosexual behavior—which is hard to understand. After all, humans have genetically selected for it through the shared kinship mechanism and inclusive fitness, in which the homosexuals further the survival of genes they share with heterosexuals. They're not permanently rutty, the way we are, and perhaps an explanation lies there—but how? The female does the courting, singing and dancing like Earthside birds. No musical instruments used. They do it more often than reproduction requires, though, just like us. Some pair-bonding, maybe even monogamy. Approximate equality of the sexes in social matters and labor, with perhaps some slight female dominance. They carry out some sex-separate rites, but we don't know what those mean. Hunter-gatherer routines are—"

"Quite so," Koremasa said softly. "We take your points."

Somehow this ended the spontaneous lecture. Tatsuhiko fell silent, his lips twitching. She felt sympathy for his frustration, mingling with his restless desire to fathom this world in terms he could understand.

Yet she could not let matters rest here. She set her face resolutely. If he wished a professional contest, so be it.

"You read much into your observations," Miyuki said. She looked around the circle to see if anyone nodded, but they were all impassive, letting her take the lead.

"We must," Tatsuhiko said testily.

"But surely we can no more portray a society by recording

facts, filtered through our preconceptions, than a literary critic can get the essence of Murasaki's great *Genji Monogatari* by summarizing the plot," she said. "I think perhaps we are doing 'I-witnessing' here."

Tatsuhiko smiled grimly. "You have a case of what we call in sociobiology 'epistemological hypochondria'—the fear of interpretation."

Koremasa let the wind speak to them all again, sighing, muttering, rubbing at their monolayer defense against it.

"We appreciate your views, Tatsuhiko-san, but there are fresh facts before us now," Koremasa said in calm, measured tones. "The satellites report that the chupchup tribes are no longer wandering in a random pattern."

Tatsuhiko brightened. "Oh? Where are they going?"

"They are all moving away from us."

Surprise registered in a low, questioning mutter around their circle. "All of them?" the communications engineer asked.

Koremasa nodded. "They are moving toward the ridge-rim. Journeying from the moonside to the starside, perhaps." He stood, smiling at Tatsuhiko. "In a way, I suppose we have at last received a tribute from them. They have acknowledged our presence."

Tatsuhiko blinked and then snorted derisively. Such a rude show would be remarkable, except that Miyuki understood that the contempt was directed by Tatsuhiko at himself.

"And I suggest," Koremasa continued with a quiet air of authority, "that we study this planetwide activity."

"Of course," Tatsuhiko said enthusiastically. "This could be a seasonal migration. Many animal species have elaborate—"

"These are *not* animals!" Miyuki surprised herself with the vehemence in her voice.

"Oh?" Tatsuhiko shot back. "Let us define our terms."

Miyuki opened her mouth to reply but saw Captain Koremasa raise one finger slightly. He said casually, "Enough theory. We must look—and quickly. The first bands are already striving to cross the rim mountain ranges."

6
PARADIGM LOST

Chujo and Genji pulled at each other incessantly, working through their tides, and Murasaki's more distant stresses added to the geological turmoil. This powered a zone of incessant mountain-building along the circumference of Chujo. Seen from Genji, this ring rimmed Chujo with a crust of peaks, sheer faults, and deep, shadowed gorges. Lakes and small, pale seas dotted Chujo's lowlands, where the thin air already seemed chilly to humans, even in this summer season. Matters worsened for fragile humans toward the highlands.

The muscled movement of great geologic forces lifted the rock, allowing water to carve its many-layered canyons. As they flew over the great stretching plains, Miyuki feasted on the passing panorama, insisting that their craft fly at the lowest safe altitude, though that cost fuel. She saw the promise of green summer, lagoons of bright water, grazing beasts with white hoofs stained with the juice of wildflowers.

This was a place of violent contrasts. In an hour they saw the land below parched by drought, beaten by hail, sogged by rain, burnt by grass fires. But soon, as their engines labored to suck in more of the skimpy air, the plains became ceramic-gray, blistered, cracked. From orbit she had seen the yellow splashes of erupting lava from myriad small peaks, and now they came marching from the girdling belt of the world. Black rock sliced across the buff colors of windblown sand. Glacial moraines cupped frozen lakes, fault blocks poked above eroded plains, U-valleys testified to the recent invasion of the great ice.

Yet this world-wracking had perhaps made life possible here. Chujo was much like a fortunate Mars—small, cold, huddled beneath a scant scarf of sheltering gas. Both suffered from their small masses, Mars at a tenth that of Earth, Chujo barely more. As well, Mars had suffered swerves in its polar inclination, and this may have doomed the fossilized, fledgling spores humans had found there. But Genji-Chujo's whirling waltz had much more angular momentum than a sole spinning planet could, and this had fended off the tilting perturbations of Murasaki and the outer, gas giant planets. Thus neither of the brothers had to endure wobbling poles, shifting seasons, the rasp of cruel change.

Small bushes clung to the escarpments of a marble mountain. Compressional scarps cut the mountain as though a great knife had tried to kill it. These were signs of internal cooling, she knew, Chujo shrinking as its core cooled, wrinkling with age, a world in retreat from its warmer eras. Twisted spires of pumice reared, light as air, splashed with stains of cobalt, putty, scarlet. Miyuki watched this brutal beauty unfold uneasily. Smoke hazed the snowcapped range ahead.

The Genjians must have wondered for ages, she thought, at the continual flame and black clouds of their brother's perimeter. They probably did not realize that a similar wracked ridge girdled their own world. Perhaps the Genjians had seen the great Chujoan cities at their prime—it was optically possible, with the naked Genjian eye—but could legends of that have survived the thousands of generations since? Had either intelligent race known of the other—and did they still? Certainly— she glanced up at the crescent of Genji, mottled and muggy, like a watercolor artwork tossed off by a hasty child—the present chupchups could gain no hint from that sultry atmosphere. Still, there were hints, all the way down into the molecular chemistry, that the worlds were linked.

Koremasa rapped on the hard plexiglass. "See? All that green?"

Miyuki peered ahead and saw on the flank of a jutting mountain a smooth, tea-green growth. "Summer—and we're near the equator."

Koremasa nodded. "This terrain looks too barren to support plants year-round."

Tatsuhiko put in, over the low rumble of their flier, "Seasonal migration. More evidence."

"Of what?" Miyuki asked.

"Of their devolution. They've picked up the patterns of migrating fowl. Seasonal animals didn't build those cities."

Koremasa said, "That makes sense."

Tatsuhiko pressed his point. "So you no longer believe they are fleeing from us?"

Koremasa smiled, and she saw that his announcement two days before had all been a subtle ruse. "It was a useful temporary hypothesis."

Useful for what? she wanted to ask, but discipline and simple politeness restrained her. Instead she said, "So they migrate to the mountain chain to—what? Eat that grass, or whatever it is?"

Tatsuhiko nodded enthusiastically. "Of course."

She remarked dryly, "A long way to walk for such sparse stuff."

"I mention it only as a working hypothesis," Tatsuhiko said stiffly.

"Did you ever see an animal wearing clothes?" Miyuki let a tinge of sarcasm slip into her voice.

"Simple crabs carry their shell homes on their backs."

"Animals that cook? Carry weapons?"

"All that is immaterial." Tatsuhiko regarded her with something like fondness for a long moment. Then his face returned to the cool, lean cast she had seen so much of these last few years. "I grant that the chupchups have vestigial artifacts of their ancestors. Those mat-clothes of theirs—marvelous biological engineering, but inherited. The chupchups are plainly degenerated."

"Because they won't talk to us?"

"Because they have abandoned their cities, lost their birthright."

"The Mayans did that well over a thousand years ago."

Tatsuhiko shook his head, his amused smile telling the others that here an amateur was venturing into his territory. "They did not revert to Neanderthals."

Miyuki asked with restrained venom, "You would prefer any

explanation that made the chupchups into degenerated pseudoanimals, wouldn't you?''

"That is an unfair—"

"Well, wouldn't you?"

"—and unprofessional, unscientific attitude."

"You didn't answer me."

"There is no need to dignify an obvious personal—"

"Oh, please spare me—"

"Prepare for descent," Koremasa said, looking significantly at both of them in turn.

"Huh!" Miyuki sat back and glowered out at the view. How had she ever thought she could reach this man?

They landed heavily, the jet's engines whining, swiveling to lower them vertically into a boulder-strewn valley, just short of the green expanses. Deep crevasses cut the stony ground. Miyuki climbed out gingerly, her pressure suit awkwardly bunching and pinching. The medical people back in Low Genji Orbit had given them only ten hours to accomplish this mission, and allowed only six of them to go at all. The cold already bit into her hands and feet.

A white-water stream muttered nearby, and they headed along it, toward the brown and green growth that filled the upper valley. Broken walls of the ancient Chujoans lay in the narrow box canyon at the top of the valley, near a spectacular roaring waterfall. It had been a respectable-size town, she judged.

Why did those ancients build anything at all here? Most of the year this austere place had no vegetation, the satellite records said.

She stumbled. The ground was shaking. Slow, grave oscillations came up through her boots. She looked up, her helmet feeling more bulky all the time, and studied the mountain peak that jutted above them. Streamers of black smoke fretted away in the perpetual winds. Crashes echoed in the valley, reflected off the neighboring peaks from the flanks of the mountain—

landslides, adding their kettle-drum rolls as punctuation to the mountain's bass notes.

Fretful comments filled the comm. She marched on grimly. Tatsuhiko and Koremasa appeared to have already decided how to interpret whatever they would find; what was the point of this? Sitting back in camp, this quick sortie to the highlands—a "sprint mission," in the jargon—had seemed a great adventure.

She studied the bare cliff faces that framed the valley. Volcanic ash layers like slices in an infinite sandwich, interspersed with more interesting lines of pink clay, of pebbled sand, of gray conglomerates. So they would have to do what they did at so many sites—sample quickly, thinking little, hoping they had gotten the kernel of the place by dint of judgment and luck. So much! A whole world, vast and various—and another, hanging overhead like a taunt.

The biologist reached the broad, flat field of green and knelt down to poke at it. He looked up in surprise. "It's algae! Sort of."

Miyuki stepped on the stuff. It was so thin she could feel pebbles crunch beneath it. She bent to examine it, her suit gathering and bunching uncomfortably at her knees. The mat was finely textured, green threads weaving among brown splashes.

The biologist dug his sample knife into it. "Tough," he said. "Very tough." With effort he punctured the mat, and with visible exertion cut out a patch. His portable chemlab shot back an answer as soon as he inserted the patch. "Ummm. Distinct resemblance to . . . oh yes, that chupchup clothing. Same species, I'd say."

Tatsuhiko's voice was tight and precise over comm. "This proves how long ago the original form was developed. Here it's assumed a natural role in the environment. Unless the chupchups simply adapted it themselves from this original species. I—"

"Funny biochem going on here," the biologist said. "It's

excreting some kind of metabolic inhibitor. And—say, there's a lot of hydrogen around it, too.''

Tatsuhiko nodded. ''That agrees with the tests on the chupchup living cloth. It interacts with the chupchup body, we believe.''

''No, this is different.'' The biologist moved on, tugging at the surface, taking readings. ''This stuff is interconnected algae and fibers with a lot of energy stored in chemical bonds.''

''Look at these,'' Miyuki said. She lifted a flap of the thin but tough material. There was a pocket several meters long, open at one end.

''Double-layered, I guess. Wonder why?'' The biologist frowned. ''This thing is a great photosynthetic processor. Guess that's why it flourishes here only in summer. Now, I—''

The ground rolled. Miyuki staggered. The biologist fell, throwing his knife aside to avoid a cut in his suit. Miyuki saw a dark mass fly up from the mountain's peak. A sudden thunderclap hammered down on them. The valley floor shook. Dust rose in filmy curtains.

''Sample taken?'' Koremasa asked on comm. ''Good. Let us—''

''But the ruins!'' Miyuki said. ''They'll want at least a few photos.''

''Oh. Yes.'' Koremasa looked unhappy but nodded.

Miyuki could scarcely believe she had blurted out such a rash suggestion. Not only was it unlike her, she thought, but it contradicted her better judgment. She did want to have a look at the ruins, yes, but—

A temblor rocked her like an ocean wave. More smoke spat from the peak, unfurling across a troubled sky. The other five had already started running uphill across the mat.

She followed, turning every hundred meters to glance behind, memorizing the way back in case they had to retreat in a hurry. She heard Tatsuhiko's shout and saw him pointing just as another slow, deep ripple worked through the valley.

''Chups!''

They were in a single file, winding out of the ruins. They did not turn to look at the humans, simply proceeded downhill.

Miyuki's perspectives shifted and danced as she watched them, the world seemed to be tilting—and then she realized that again it was not her moving, but the valley floor. What she felt was not the wrenching of an earthquake.

It was the mat itself. The entire floor of the valley wrinkled, stretched, slid.

The chupchups seemed to glide across the wrestling surface of the mat, uphill from the humans. They were headed for a crevasse that billowed steam. Streamers of sulfurous yellow swirled across the mat. Yet the chupchups gave none of the gathering chaos any notice.

"Back!" Koremasa called on comm. "Back into the flier."

They had nearly reached the ruins. Miyuki took a moment to snap quick pictures of the crumbled structures. The slumped stoneworks did not look at all like housing. In fact they seemed to be immense vats, caved in and filled with rubble. Vats for what?

She turned away and the ground slid out from under her. She rolled. The others were farther downhill, but the jerking of the tawny green growth under them had sent them tumbling pellmell downward, rolling like dolls. They shouted, cried out, swore.

Miyuki stopped herself by digging in her heels and grabbing at the tough, writhing mat. It was durable material and she could not rip it for a better hold. In a moment the convulsions stopped. She sat up. Pearly fog now rose from the mat all around her. She felt a trembling and then realized that she was moving—slowly, in irregular little jerks, but yes—the mat was tugging itself across the pebbles beneath it. She scrambled for footing—and fell. She got to her knees. Somewhere near here the chupchups—

There. They were standing, looking toward the chasm a hundred meters away. Miyuki followed their intent, calm gaze.

The mat was alive, powerful, muscular—and climbing up the sky.

No, it merely reared, like the living flesh of a wounded thing. It buckled and writhed, a nightmare living carpet.

It jerked itself higher than a human, forming a long sheet that flexed like an ocean wave—and leaped.

The wave struck the far side of the crevasse. It met there another shelf of rising mat. The two waves stuck, clung. All along the chasm the two edges slapped together, melted into one another, formed a seamless whole.

And rose. As though some chemical reaction were kindling under it, the living carpet bulged like a blister. Miyuki clung to the shifting, sliding mat—and then realized that if she let go, she could roll downhill, where she wanted to go.

She watched the mat all along the vent as it billowed upward. The chupchups made waving motions, as if urging the mat to leave the ground. She thought suddenly, *They came here for this. Not fleeing from us at all.*

Then she was slipping, rolling, the world whirling as she felt the mat accelerate. Her breath rasped and she curled up into a ball, tumbling and bouncing down the hillside. Knocks, jolts, a dull gathering roar—and then she slammed painfully against a boulder. A bare boulder, free of the mat.

She got up, feeling a sharp pain in her left ankle. "Koremasa-san!"

"Here! Help me with Tatsuhiko!"

Tatsuhiko had broken his leg. His dark face contorted with agony. She peered down into his constricted eyes, and he said, speaking very precisely between pants, "Matters are complex."

She blinked. "What?"

"Clearly something more is going on here," he said tightly, holding the pain back behind his thin smile.

"Never mind that, you're hurt. We'll—"

He waved the issue away. "A temporary intrusion. Concentrate on what is happening here."

"Look, we'll get you safely—"

"I have missed something." Tatsuhiko grimaced, then gave a short, barking laugh. "Maybe everything."

She felt the need to comfort him, beyond placing compresses, and said, "You may have been right. This—"

"No, the chupchups are . . . something different. Outside the paradigms."

"Quiet now. We'll get you out of here."

Tatsuhiko lifted his eyebrows weakly. "Keep your lovely eyes open. Watch what the chupchups are doing. Record."

Something in his tone made her hesitate. "I . . . still love you."

His lips trembled. "I . . . also. Why can we not talk?"

"Perhaps . . . perhaps it means too much."

He twisted his lips wryly. "Exactly. That hypothesis accounts for the difficulty."

"Too much . . ." She saw ruefully that she had thought him stiff and uncompromising, and perhaps he was—but she shared those elements. Perhaps they were part of the personality constellations chosen long ago on Earth, the partitioning of traits that ensured the expedition would get through at all.

He said, "I am sorry. I will do better."

"But you . . ." She did not know what to say, and her mouth was dry, and then the others came.

They lifted him and started toward the flier. The others had rolled onto the rocky ground below as the mat moved. Miyuki stumbled, this time from a volcanic tremor. She got to the flier and looked back. The entire party paused then, fear draining from them momentarily, and watched.

The mat was lifting itself. Alive with purpose, rippling, its center axis bulged, pulling the rest of it along the ground with a hiss like a wave sliding up a beach. It shed pebbles, making itself lighter, letting go of its birthplace.

"Some . . . some reaction is going on in the vent under it," the biologist panted over comm. "Making gases—that hydrogen I detected, I'll bet. That's a by-product of this mat. Maybe it's been growing some culture in the volcanic vents around here. Maybe . . ." His voice trailed away in stunned disbelief.

She remembered the strange vatlike openings among the chupchup buildings. Some ancient chemical works? A way to augment this process? After all, the chupchups had clothing made of material much like this crawling carpet.

They got Tatsuhiko into the bay of the flier. Koremasa ordered the pilot to ready the flier for liftoff. He turned back to the others and then pointed at the sky. Miyuki turned. From valleys beyond, large green teardrops drifted up the sky. They wobbled and flexed, as though shaping themselves into the proper form for a fresh inhabitant of the air.

Organic balloons were launching themselves from all the valleys of the volcanic ridge. Dozens rose into the winds. In concert, somehow, Miyuki saw. Perhaps triggered by the spurt of vulcanism. Perhaps responding to some deeply imprinted command, some collision of chemicals.

"Living balloons . . ." she said.

The biologist said, "The vulcanism, maybe it triggers the process. After the mat has grown to a certain size. Methane, maybe anaerobic fermentation—"

"The carving," Miyuki said.

Koremasa said quietly, "The chupchups."

The frail, distant figures clung to the side of the mat as the center of it rose, fattening. Some found the pockets the humans had noticed, and slipped inside. Others simply grabbed a handful of the tough green hide and hung on.

"They are going up with it," Koremasa said.

She recalled the carving in the ancient city, with its puzzling circles hanging in the backdrop of the tiger eating its tail, nature feeding on itself, with the Chujoan face arising from the writhing pain of the twisting tail. "The circles—they were balloons. Rising."

The last edge of the mat sped toward the ascending bulge with a sound like the rushing of rapids over pebbles. The accelerating clatter seemed to hasten the living, self-making balloon. Frayed lips of the mat slapped together below the fattening, uprushing dome. These edges sealed, tightened, made the lower tip of a green teardrop.

On the grainy skin of the swelling dome the chupchup passengers now settled themselves in the pockets Miyuki had noted before. Most made it. Some dangled helplessly, lost their grip, fell with a strange silence to their deaths. Those already in pockets helped others to clamber aboard.

And buoyantly, quietly, they soared into a blue-black sky. "Toward Genji," Miyuki whispered. She felt a pressing sense of presence, as though a momentous event had occurred.

"In hydrogen-filled bags?" Koremasa asked.

"They can reach fairly far up in the atmosphere that way," Tatsuhiko said weakly. He was lying on the cushioned deck of the flier, pale and solemn. The injury had drained him, but his eyes flashed with the same quick, assessing intelligence.

Miyuki climbed into the flier and put a cushion under his helmet. The crew began sealing the craft. "I don't think they mean to just fly around," she said.

"Oh?" Tatsuhiko asked wanly. "You think they imagine they're going to Genji?"

"I don't think we can understand this." She hesitated. "It may even be suicide."

Tatsuhiko scowled. "A race devoted to a suicide ritual? They wouldn't have lasted long."

She gestured at the upper end of the valley. "Most of them didn't go. See? They're standing in long lines up there, watching the balloon leave."

"More inheritance?" Tatsuhiko whispered. "Is this all they remember of the technology the earlier race had mastered?"

Miyuki thought. "I wonder."

Tatsuhiko said wanly, taking her hand, "Perhaps they have held onto the biomats, used them. Maybe they don't understand what they were for, really. A piece of biotech like that—a beautiful solution to the problem of transport, in an energy-scarce environment. And the chupchups are just—just joyriding."

Miyuki smiled. "Perhaps . . ."

They lifted off vertically just as another rolling jolt came. The flier veered in the gathering winds, and Miyuki watched the teardrop shapes scudding across the purpling sky. Soon enough they would be the object of scrutiny, measurement, with the full armament of scientific dispassion marshalled to fathom them. She would probably even do some of the job herself, she thought wryly.

But for this single crystalline moment she wished to simply enjoy them. Not analyze, but feel the odd, hushed quality their ascent brought.

They were probably neither Tatsuhiko's vestigial technology nor some arcane tribal ceremony. Perhaps this entire drama was purely a way for the chupchups to tell humans something. She bit her lip in concentration. Tell what? Indeed, satellite observations, dating back to the first robot probe, had never shown any sign of a chupchup migration here. It might be unique—a response to humans themselves.

She sighed. Cabin pressure hissed on again as the flier leveled off for its long flight back. She popped her helmet and wrestled Tatsuhiko's off. He smiled, thanked her—and all the while behind his tired eyes she saw the glitter, the unquelled pursuit of his own singular vision, which Tatsuhiko would never abandon. As he should not.

The biologist was saying something about the balloons, details—that they seemed to be photosynthetic processors, making more hydrogen to keep themselves aloft, to offset losses through their own skin. He even had a term for them, bioloons. . . .

So the unpeeling of the onion skins was already beginning. And what fun it would be.

But what did it *mean?* The first stage of science atomizes, dissects, fragments. Only much later do the Bohrs, the Darwins, the Einsteins knit it all together again—and nobody knew what the final weave would be, silk or sackcloth.

So both Tatsuhiko and herself and all the others—they were all needed. There would be no end of explanations. Did the chupchups think humans were in fact from that great promise in the sky, Genji? Or were they trying to signal something with the mat-balloons—while still holding to their silence? An arcane ceremony? Some joke?

The chupchups would never fit the narrow rules of sociobiology, she guessed, but just as clearly they would not be merely Zen aliens, or curators of some ashram in the sky. They were themselves, and the fathoming of that would be a larger task than she, or Tatsuhiko, or Koremasa could comprehend.

The flier purred steadily. The still-rising emerald teardrops dwindled behind. Their humming technology was taking them back to base, its pilot already fretting about fuel.

Miyuki felt a sudden, unaccountable burst of joy. Hard mystery remained here, shadowed mystery would call them back, and mystery was far better than the cool ceramic surfaces of certainty.

Zoomers

She climbed into her yawning work pod, coffee barely getting her going. A warning light winked: Her Foe was already up and running. Another day at the orifice.

The pod wrapped itself around her as tabs and inserts slid into place. This was the latest gear, a top of the line simulation suit immersed in a data-pod of beguiling comfort.

Snug. Not a way to lounge, but to *fly*.

She closed her eyes and let the sim-suit do its stuff.

May 16, 2046. She liked to start in real-space. Less jarring.

Images played directly upon her retina. The entrance protocol lifted her out of her Huntington Beach apartment and in a second she was zooming over rooftops, skating down the beach. Combers broke in soft white bands and red-suited surfers caught them in passing marriage.

All piped down from a satellite view, of course, sharp and clear.

Get to work, Myung, her Foe called. *Sightsee later.*

"I'm running a deep search," she lied.

Sure.

"I'll spot you a hundred creds on the action," she shot back.

You're on. Big new market opening today. A hint of mockery?
"Where?" Today she was going to nail him, by God.
Right under our noses, the way I sniff it.
"In the county?"
Now, that would be telling.
Which meant he didn't know.
So: a hunt. Better than a day of shaving margins, at least.
She and her Foe were zoomers, ferrets who made markets
more efficient. Evolved far beyond the primitivo commodity
traders of the late TwenCen, they moved fast, high-flying for
competitive edge.
They zoomed through spaces wholly insubstantial, but that
was irrelevant. Economic pattern-spaces were as tricky as
mountain crevasses. And even hard cash just stood for an idea.
Most people still dug coal and grew crops, ancient style grunt
labor—but in Orange County you could easily forget that,
gripped by the fever of the new.
Below her the county was a sprawl, but a smart one. The
wall-to-mall fungus left over from the TwenCen days was gone.
High-rises rose from lush parks. Some even had orange grove
skirts, a chic nostalgia. Roofs were eco-virtue white. Blacktop
streets had long ago added a sandy-colored coating whose mica
sprinkles winked up at her. Even cars were in light shades. All
this to reflect sunlight, public advertisements that everybody
was doing something about global warming.
The car-rivers thronged streets and freeways (still *free*—if you
could get the license). When parked, cars were tucked underground. Still plenty of scurry-scurry, but most of it mental,
not metal.
She sensed the county's incessant pulse, the throb of the
Pacific Basin's hub, pivot point of the largest zonal economy
on the planet.
Felt, not *saw.* Her chest was a map. Laguna Beach over her
right nipple, Irvine over the left. Using neural plasticity, the
primary sensory areas of her cortex "read" the county's electronic Mesh through her skin.

But this was not like antique, serial reading at all. No flat data here. No screens.

She relaxed. The trick was to *merge,* not just observe.

Far better for a chimpanzeelike species to take in the world through its evolved, body-wrapping neural bed.

More fun, too. She detected economic indicators on her augmented skin. A tiny shooting pain spoke of a leveraged buyout. Was that uneasy sensation natural to her, or a hint from her subsystems about a possible lowering of the prime rate?

Gotcha! the Foe sent.

Myung glanced at her running index. She was 1,100 creds down!

So fast? How could—?

Then she felt it: dancing data-spikes in alarm-red, prickly on her left leg. The Foe had captured an early indicator. Which?

Myung had been coasting toward the Anaheim hills, watching the pulse of business trading quicken as slanting sunshine smartly profiled the fashionable, post-pyramidal corporate buildings. So she had missed the opening salvo of weather data update, the first trading opportunity.

The Foe already had an edge and was shifting investments. How?

Ahead of her in the simulated air she could see the Foe skating to the south. All this was visual metaphor, of course, symbology for the directed attention of the data-eating programs.

A stain came spreading from the east into Mission Viejo. Not real weather, but economic variables.

Deals flickered beneath the data-thunderheads like sheet lightning. Pixels of packet-information fell as soft rains on her long-term investments.

The Foe was buying extra electrical power from Oxnard. Selling it to users to offset the low yields seeping up from San Diego.

Small stuff. A screen for something subtle. Myung close-upped the digital stream and glimpsed the deeper details.

Every day more water flowed in the air over southern California than streamed down the Mississippi. Rainfall projections changed driving conditions, affected tournament golf scores, altered yields of solar power, fed into agri-prod.

Down her back slid prickly-fresh commodity info, an itch she should scratch. A hint from her sniffer-programs? She willed a virtual finger to rub the tingling.

—and snapped back to real-space.

An ivory mist over Long Beach. Real, purpling water thunderclouds scooting into San Juan Cap from the south.

Ah—virtual sports. The older the population got, the more leery of weather. They still wanted the zing of adventure, though. Through virtual feedback, creaky bodies could air-surf from twenty kilometers above the Grand Canyon. Or race alongside the few protected Great White sharks in the Catalina Preserve.

High-resolution Virtuality stimulated lacy filigrees of electrochem impulses throughout the cerebral cortex. Did it matter whether the induction came from the real thing or from the slippery arts of electronics?

Time for a bit of business.

Her prognosticator programs told her that with 0.87 probability, such oldies would cocoon-up across six states. So indoor virtual sports use, with electrostim to zing the aging muscles, would rise in the next day.

She swiftly exercised options on five virtual sites, pouring in some of her reserve computational capacity. But the Foe had already harvested the plums there. Not much margin left.

Myung killed her simulated velocity and saw the layers of deals the Foe was making, counting on the coming storm to shift the odds by fractions. Enough contracts-of-the-moment processed, and profits added up. But you had to call the slant just right.

Trouble-sniffing subroutines pressed their electronic doubts upon her: a warning chill breeze across her brow. She waved it away.

Myung dove into the clouds of event-space. Her skin did the deals for her, working with software that verged on mammal-level intelligence itself. She wore her suites of artificial-intelligence . . . and in a real sense, they wore her.

She felt her creds—not credits so much as *credibilities,* the operant currency in data-space—washing like hot air currents over her body.

Losses were chilling. She got cold feet, quite literally, when the San Onofre nuke piped up with a gush of clean power. A new substation, coming on much earlier than SoCalEd had estimated.

That endangered her energy portfolio. A quick flick got her out of the electrical futures market altogether, before the world-wide Mesh caught on to the implications.

Up, away. Let the Foe pick up the last few percentage points. Myung flapped across the digital sky, capital taking wing.

She lofted to a 10-mile-high perspective. Global warming had already made the county's south-facing slopes into cactus and tough grasslands. Coastal sage still clung to the north-facing slopes, seeking cooler climes. All the coast was becoming a "fog desert" sustained by vapor from lukewarm ocean currents. Dikes held back the rising warm ocean from Newport to Long Beach.

Pretty, but no commodity possibilities there anymore.

Time to take the larger view.

She rose. Her tactile and visual maps expanded. She went to split-skin perception, with the real, matter-based landscape overlaid on the info-scape. Surreal, but heady.

From below she burst into the data-sphere of Invest-tainment, where people played upon the world's weather like a casino. Ever since rising global temperatures pumped more energy in, violent oscillations had grown.

Weather was now the hidden, wild-card lubricant of the world's economy. Tornado warnings were sent to street addresses, damage predictions shaded by the city block. Each neighborhood got its own rain forecast.

A sparrow's fall in Portugal could diddle the global fluid system so that, in principle, a thunderhead system would form over Fountain Valley a week later. Today, merging pressures from the south sent forking lightning over mid-California. That shut down the launch site of all local rocket-planes to the Orbital Hiltons. Hundreds of invest-programs had that already covered.

So she looked on a still larger scale. Up, again.

This grand world Mesh was N-dimensional. And even the number N changed with time, as parameters shifted in and out of application.

There was only one way to make sense of this in the narrow human sensorium. Every second a fresh dimension sheared in over an older dimension. Freeze-framed, each instant looked like a ridiculously complicated abstract sculpture running on drug-driven overdrive. Watch any one moment too hard and you got a lancing headache, motion sickness, and zero comprehension.

Augmented feedback, so useful in keeping on the financial edge, could also be an unforgiving bitch.

The Foe wasn't up here, hovering over the whole continent. Good. Time to think. She watched the N-space as if it were an entertainment, and in time came an extended perception, integrated by the long-suffering subconscious.

She bestrode the world. Total immersion.

She stamped and marched across the muddy field of chaotic economic interactions. Her boot heels left deep scars. These healed immediately: subprograms at work, like cellular repair. She would pay a passage price for venturing here.

A landscape opened like the welcome of a mother's lap.

Her fractal tentacles spread through the networks with blinding speed, penetrating the planetary spiderweb. Orange County was a brooding, swollen orb at the PacBasin's center.

Smelled it yet? came the Foe's taunt from below.

"I'm following some ticklers," she lied.

I'm way ahead of you.

"Then how come you're gabbing? And tracking me?"

Friendly competition—

"Forget the friendly part." She was irked. Not by the Foe, but by failure. She needed something *hot*. Where?

Fess up, you're smelling nothing.

"Just the stink of overdone expectations," she shot back wryly.

Nothing promising in the swirling weather-space, working with prickly light below her. Seen this way, the planet's 13 billion lives were like a field of grass waving beneath fitful gusts they could barely glimpse.

Wrong blind alley! sent her Foe maliciously.

Myung shot a glance at her indices. Down 1,900!

And she had spotted him a hundred. *Damn.*

She shifted through parameter-spaces. There—like a carnival, neon-bright on the horizon of a black, cool desert: the colossal market-space of Culture.

She strode across the tortured seethe of global Mesh data.

In the archaic economy of manufacturing, middle managers were long gone. No more "just in time" manufacturing in blocky factories. No more one-size-fits-all. That had fallen to "right on time" production out of tiny shops, prefabs, even garages.

Anybody who could make a gizmo cheaper could send you a bid. They would make your very own custom gizmo, by direct Mesh order.

Around the globe, robotic prod-lines of canny intelligence stood ready in ill-lit shacks. Savvy software leaped into action at your Meshed demand, reconfiguring for your order like an obliging whore. Friction-free service. The mercantile millennium.

Seen from up here, friction-free marketism seemed the world's only workable ideology—unless you counted New Islam, but who did? Under it, middle managers had decades ago vanished down the sucking drain of evolving necessity. "Production" got shortened to *prod*—and prodded the market.

Of course, the people shed by frictionless prod ended up with dynamic, fulfilling careers in dog-washing: valets, luxury servants, touchy-feely insulators for the harried prod-folk. And their bosses.

But not all was manufacturing. Even dog-dressers needed Culture Prod. *Especially* dog-dressers.

"My sniffers are getting it," she said.

The Foe answered, *You're on the scent—but late.*

Something new . . .

She walked through the data-vaults of the Culture City. As a glittering representation of unimaginable complexities, it loomed: global, intricate, impossible to know fully for even a passing instant. And thus, an infinite resource.

She stamped through streets busy with commerce. Ferrets and deal-making programs scampered like rodents under heel. Towers of the giga-conglomerates raked the skies.

None of this Big Guy stuff for her. Not today, thanks.

To beat her Foe, she needed something born of Orange County, something to put on the table.

And only her own sniffer-programs could find it for her. The web of connections in even a single county was so crisscrossed that no mere human could find her way.

She snapped back into the real world. *Think.*

Lunch eased into her bloodstream, fed by the pod when it sensed her lowering blood sugar. Myung tapped for an extra Kaff to give her some zip. Her medical worrier hovered in air before her, clucked and frowned. She ignored it.

—and back to Culture City.

Glassy ramparts led up into the citadels of the mega-Corps. Showers of speculation rained on their flanks. Rivulets gurgled off into gutters. Nothing new here, just the ceaseless hum of a market full of energy and no place to go.

Index check: 1600 down!

The deals she had left running from the morning were pumping out the last of their dividends. No more help there.

Time's a-wastin', her Foe sent nastily. She could imagine his sneer and sardonic eyes.

"Save your creds for the crunch," she retorted.

You're down 1,300 and falling.

He was right. The trouble with paired competition—the very latest market-stimulating twist—was that the outcome was starkly clear. No comforting self-delusions lasted long.

Irked, she leaped high and flew above the City. Go local, then. Orange County was the PacBasin's best fount of fresh ideas.

She caught vectors from the county drawing her down. Prickly hints sheeted across her belly, over her forearms. To the east—there—a shimmer of possibility.

Her ferrets were her own, of course—searcher programs tuned to her style, her way of perceiving quality and content. They were her, in a truncated sense.

Now they led her down a funnel, into—

A mall.

In real-space, no less. Tacky.

Hopelessly antique, of course. Dilapidated buildings leaning against each other, laid out in boring rectangular grids. Faded plastic and rusty chrome.

People still went there, of course; somewhere, she was sure, people still used wooden plows.

This must be in Kansas or the Siberian Free State or some-where equally Out Of It. Why in the world had her sniffers taken her here?

She checked real-world location, preparing to lift out.

East Anaheim! Impossible . . .

But no—there was something here. Her sniffer popped up an overlay and the soles of her feet itched with anticipation. Programs zoomed her in on a gray shambles that dominated the end of the cracked blacktop parking lot.

Was this a museum? No, but—

Art Attack came the signifier.

That sign . . . "An old K mart," she murmured. She barely

remembered being in one as a girl. Rigid, old-style aisles of plastic prod. Positively *cubic,* as the teeners said. A cube, after all, was an infinite number of stacked squares.

But this K mart had been reshaped. Stucco-sculpted into an archly ironic lavender mosque, festooned with bright brand name items.

It hit her. "Of course!"

She zoomed up, above the Orange County jumble.

Here it was—pay dirt. And she was on the ground *first.*

She popped her pod and sucked in the dry, flavorful air. Back in Huntington Beach. Her throat was dry, the aftermath of tension.

And just 16:47, too. Plenty of time for a swim.

The team that had done the mock-mosque K mart were like all artists: sophisticated along one axis, dunderheads along all economic vectors. They had thought it was a pure lark to fashion ancient relics of paleocapitalism into bizarre abstract expressionist "statements." Mere fun effusions, they thought.

She loved working with people who were, deep in their souls, innocent of markets.

Within two hours she had locked up the idea and labeled it: "Post-Consumerism Dada from the Fabled Age of Appetite."

She had marketed it through pre-view around the globe. Thailand and the Siberians (the last true culture virgins) had gobbled up the idea. Every rotting 'burb around the globe had plenty of derelict K marts; this gave them a new angle.

Then she had auctioned the idea in the Mesh. Cut in the artists for their majority interest. Sold shares. Franchised it in the Cutting Concept sub-Mesh. Divided shares twice, declared a dividend.

All in less time than it took to drive from Garden Grove to San Clemente.

"How'd you find that?" her Foe asked, climbing out of his pod.

"My sniffers are *good,* I told you."

He scowled. "And how'd you get there so fast?"

"You've got to take the larger view," she said mysteriously.

He grimaced. "You're up 2,005 creds."

"Lucky I didn't really trounce you."

"Culture City sure ate it up, too."

"Speaking of which, how about starting a steak? I'm starving."

He kissed her. This was perhaps the best part of the Foe-Team method. They spurred each other on, but didn't cut each other dead in the marketplace. No matter how appealing that seemed sometimes.

Being married helped keep their rivalry on reasonable terms. Theirs was a standard five-year monogamous contract, already nearly half over. How could she not renew, with such a deliciously stimulating opponent?

Sure, dog-eat-dog markets sometimes worked better, but who wanted to dine on dog?

"We'll split the chores," he said.

"We need a servant."

He laughed. "Think we're rich? We just grease the gears of the great machine."

"Such a poet you are."

"And there are still the dishes to do from last night."

"Ugh. I'll race you to the beach first."

High Abyss

There was no taste quite so sweet as a battle won, Lambda reflected.

The troops below milled and bellowed, their blocky bodies shot through with coronas of celebration: burnt-gold gouts, hot spearing blues. They had killed legions of the Doxes, a frightful slaughter.

Now they held the ridge line with solid ranks, a living wall against the dying past. The Doxes were already being gathered into the sad veil of history, Lambda thought, as it watched them retreat across the scarred plain below, their columns shattered.

But the Mother World worked on, indifferent to the puny rages surging over it. Radiance spread into Lambda's splayed disk feet. It relaxed for an easeful moment, spreading its pads to sop up fresh energies from the Mother. Lambda had expended much of its electrical stores and needed replenishment. Skittering surges tingled up its bony legs.

>Victory!< came cries from below. >Truth!<

Lambda basked in the moment, but as always the natural grandeur of the World drew its attention. Lambda was a scientist, after all, in its core.

At the feet of the slag-mountains, glaciers cut forth. Glinting, they glided, great ships whose prows carved the grainy orange plain. Their gouges brought forth spurts of Aqua Vita, red rivulets which attacked the crystal ramparts. Melting was ecstasy. Eating was all.

Lambda felt a strange emotion as it watched this: the slow, stately progress of the World, while armies crawled across its promontories and plains like a spreading stain. A disease of understanding.

>O Prophet!< Lambda turned on four legs and watched its sub-commander approach. A full guard marched behind, a prisoner staggering in their blunt care.

>Well rendered,< Lambda said. >No Dox will throw itself forward against our lines again.<

>All homage to you!< the co-commander shouted.

>You say too much.< Lambda answered the formal salute with the proper piety.

>Your strategy worked gloriously!<

>No, *your* strategy.<

>Prophet, *you* pointed out that seizing these heights would force the Doxes to attack Crossly.<

>It was an obvious point.<

>You orchestrated our columns with masterly grace.<

Lambda tired of this formal trading of compliments. Some of the manners of the military were more taxing than the combats. >Once this volcanic spire erupted, and we saw how to complete our experiment here, the rest followed naturally.<

>They struggled so against the Crossway inertial winds!— you should have seen them try to give battle with torch and spark alike, while swimming like helpless motes!<

Spiritlessly it clacked two legs in ritual agreement. Lambda had indeed witnessed the Dox legions throw themselves counter to the warpage of the World, which blew against them like an embittered gale. The butchery had sickened Lambda, even as the fevered skirmishing, blood-blue and lacerating, turned in their favor. A theorem demonstrated, yet without pleasure.

RightMotion lay along the natural axis of the World, of

course, and Right stretched on to infinity—as expeditions had proved with harrowing, epic marches in both directions along the axis. To move Crosswise bore the price of sluggish labor, and in all history few had invested such toil. Scientists and adventurers had only of late proved the true nature of the Mother. Only by prolonged Crosswise struggle could one circumnavigate the World round the Crosslength.

These two basic facts, of RightMotion and Crosswise, had given Lambda the great clue. And, of course, had led to taunts, jeers, followed by persecutions in even the hushed hallways of the Collegium. Then long periods of study and experiment, of intense concentration on matters that unhinged most minds, and outraged others. After that, expulsion from the Collegium, molestings at public speeches. Followed by long, aching times when Lambda could live and work only in secret, gathering adherents. To further the ideas that now grew apace within, Lambda had to adopt the mantle of the Prophet. Muster followers, form armies, learn the sly arts.

All for the vision. Their Kind had long lived in a benighted miasma, hugging to the warmth and sparking wealth of the Mother, thinking nought of the mind's stretch, the intellect's reach—

>We have prey, as well!< The co-commander broke into Lambda's sub-mind musings.

>Take it—< Lambda waved two arms in ritual dismissal, but then saw who tottered between the columns of guards. >Epsilon!<

The co-commander beamed, trotting the prize forward with a vicious gouge. >We caught Epsilon in the Dox high-officers' camp. Afraid to run, I judge.<

>Insults ill become a victor.< Epsilon's voice held the old sardonic edge, but floated thin in the teeming air.

>Indeed.< Lambda cantered forward to confront the old foe. >And we do you insult by sparing you, perhaps?<

>The truth falls from your mouths at last. To endure your company is indeed torture.<

The co-commander plucked up a spike and jabbed it at Epsilon, pricking its carapace. >Vermin! Your words will find their price.<

Lambda slapped the spike aside. >No vengeance! You mistake our maiming with words, co-commander. It is no invitation to the physical, to the rude rub of edge and point. Old Epsilon favors the stab of speech.<

>Mark: I would favor the spike if it made my point better,< Epsilon allowed soberly.

>And today it has not. Your legions flee.<

>You best us in the realm of the concrete only in this moment. The future shall turn your heresies inward, piercing you as our points did not.<

Lambda allowed itself a bark of amusement. >You Doxes never ingest the truth, do you? You lost because you are *wrong*.<

>Right is uncorrelated with ferocity,< Epsilon said serenely. >You Skeptics won because you are mad. Fever favors valor.<

The honor guard belched with contempt at this remark, their gases bursting crimson in the bright airs. More of this and they would impale Epsilon as soon as Lambda averted its head.

Best to calm them; Lambda had seen enough mindless savagery. >We, driven by a crazed faith?< Lambda held up all four arms to still the guards, who had already formed in two-squares, ready to pierce Epsilon from all sides. >But we shall *show* that we are right.<

>Blindness never sees!< Epsilon made this last sour declaration and abruptly stumbled. Crashed to the ground. Gasped.

>Back!< Some guards had rushed in, fearing a trick. Lambda crouched and cradled Epsilon's head. Rivulets of exertion-waste ran from the neck, a foul odor. Epsilon's air-slits were leached white, overcome by heat and exhaustion.

The sight of this old foe, so reduced, provoked both a swelling pride and a softening pity. Lambda trilled, >Your task is finished. Give up the struggle when it has lost its point. Remember?<

For indeed this was a remark Epsilon itself had made in a lecture long ago, when Lambda was only coming to feel the strength of its own ideas, yet understood the wisdom of the old. Perhaps Lambda still did. But age and the weight of time did not constitute an argument. Only reason, aided by knowledge of the world, did that. Rude though its rub might be . . .

It led Epsilon uphill, to the ramparts of the ragged ridge which Lambda's troops had held so well. Not a single Dox had reached the sharp lip of pale rock. Their broken bodies littered the slopes.

There Lambda gave food and a lie-down-pause to Epsilon. The air felt easeful among the slanted stones, creamy condensing pools of layered quiet. Epsilon spread its pads and drank of the Mother. The World fed them all, its timeless energies seeping forth in spilling plentitude. What the Kind did not use, or the festooning wildlifes, rose up through ripe radiations to the Vault above.

Epsilon shuddered with ecstasy as its batteries fed. >You have not forgotten kindness.<

>I learned more from you than false Physik.<

>You think this heresy is mere Physik?< The famous flinty edge flashed in sharp eyes. >You would destroy the unity of the World!<

>If there is more to the All than the World, should we not know of it?<

>The All *is* the World!<

>An hypothesis.<

Epsilon lurched up from the shimmering sun-rock, ripping its pads free. >A truth! The Unity brought forth Its Creation—<

>Whatever that means, precisely—<

>—in the only geometry which nature commends! You will unhinge all the order our Kind have so struggled to build, with these blighting ideas. We live exactly and cleanly by the principles of Rightway and Crossway, the moral imperatives—<

>Spare me the invocation to prayer. I have business.<

Lambda pushed Epsilon back, not unkindly, so that the

frayed one could absorb more of the energies which crackled
across the sunrock. The radiance lanced up shimmering, to
paint the dusky clouds of the eternal Vault. Epsilon rattled legs
in protest, but finally eased down with a grateful sadness.

Battles seldom leave neat ends. Victory had come as swiftly
as a Rightwise march, heady and buoyant. The aftermath was
like carrying a heavy burden uphill and Crosswise.

Lambda spent much time sorting out details: wounded, pursuit of the enemy, prisoner policy. Everywhere troops cheered.
Many slaughtered a Dox in tribute as Lambda passed. Rich
blue blood sizzled on sunstone. Bodies crumpled, legs jerked a
last few times. Lambda had to pretend to enjoy this.

Still, the fervor and quickening smell of victory had their
effect. Lambda felt the power of its convictions in this latest
turn of destiny. Now, with Epsilon under guard and Doxes
scattered, the hunger for the final test of its vision came fresh.
The experiment beckoned.

The Vault waxed dusky by the time Lambda returned to the
ridge. Coming up the hard slant, tugging against the Crosswise
thickening of air that had held the Kind in mental bondage for
all history, Lambda felt a tremor. At first it seemed a mere
surge in the viscosity of space. Then matters worsened. Lambda
slipped, fell.

The ground shook. Lambda clambered up—a Prophet should
not be seen asprawl by troops—and stood on shaky legs. It
cocked knees, assuming the proper posture with long practice.

Tremors. Rock parted, lumpy vapors rose. Sheets of grey
mass purled into gossamer veils. Sunrock smoked into momentary frothy loops. Mass burst into spray and billowed. It
thinned, fine-grained and scalding, enclosing Lambda in a halo
of itself. The spray somehow caught and momentarily reflected
its angular body in the haze, as if the Prophet were both there
and also flickering into the surroundings and joining them, mingled with slanting rays and then gone into refractive miasmas.

The mountains suffered most from a straightening, Lambda
knew. As the geometry of Rightway altered, losing curvature

as the All expanded, the crust of the World shifted. The splits belched forth the hot Aqua Vita, whose searing rivulets brought pain and death to the unwary. Yet in disaster lurked knowledge. These quakings were the great clue which had led Lambda to the Prophecy.

Peaks shattered, canyons slumped. The inevitable evolution of the universe went on, indifferent to the bitter battles and anguished deaths of its tiny inhabitants. Lambda pondered this, cast into momentary meditation. Such straightenings were to Doxes merely the weather, meaningless. To Lambda, shaken by one in terrified moment at the Collegium, the wrackings firmed up artful abstractions, giving geometry a muscular reality. A solid truth build on shakings.

It passed. Lambda and its escort labored on. To toil against Crosswise inertias brought stinging fatigue to Lambda's joints, but a Prophet must maintain a stoic indifference. The commonkind could avoid the compacted stresses that space imposed on a Crosswise mover, with artful dodges, slips down gravity-assisted slopes.

Under-officers hurried to help. Dignity prevented Lambda from accepting the merest such aid. It wheezed and paled as it surmounted the final ridge.

The special guard left to protect Epsilon fell back as Lambda approached. Four-arm weapons shot aloft in salute. More cheers, which by now only wearied Lambda. Mathematicians did not favor the ceaseless grind of leadership.

Epsilon lay still wan and listless but visibly better. Lambda was pleased and left Epsilon to soak more radiance from the World.

An under-officer approached diffidently as Lambda surveyed the plain below, where fitful fires and the usual torture of the vanquished went on apace. Lambda sent orders to stop it and turned to receive a new message, one he relished.

>The Aqua Vita stirs, O Prophet,< the under-officer said.

>The great bag is ready?<

>Double-layered, as you ordered.<

>Prepare to launch.<

>Yes, Prophet. The pilot, Eta, believes the experiment may work this time.<

>So Eta believed last time.<

The under-officer paused. Lambda's staff, stolid and reliable, never knew quite how to take these moods and ironies. Quite understandable; none were, at heart, mathematicians.

This under-officer chose the typical dodge, ignoring Lambda's implications. >Eta wishes to go alone, since there is danger and—<

>No. I shall accompany Eta. And a passenger, as well.<

The under-officers stirred with alarm. >But Prophet! Your person must not be—<

>Quiet!< Lambda ordered. >Devote yourselves to your celebrations of victory. I shall go forward to the caldera.<

An officer noted for diplomatic skills rattled forward in haste and ventured, >But—you must not! You are far too important even for such a sacred mission. The danger—<

>Silence. I wish to see the vindication of our views—and be the first.<

Lambda marched away from them with a heady sense of completion. To beat the Doxes in a grand struggle, and at the same moment carry forward their great experiment—that would crown a life spent in the service of truth. Yes, do it. And the final stroke would be to force the vanquished foe to witness the defeat of the old ideas, with its own eyes. Yes, yes.

Soldiers hoisted Epsilon erect—tired, wounded, staring at Lambda in disbelief. >You . . . will do this thing? Take me?<

>Come. I am an empiricist. I will show you how futile your ideas are.<

A single gesture, and guards quick-walked Epsilon behind Lambda as they made their way through the joyous camp. Troops cheered their Prophet lustily at every lane and hummock. Cooking discharges flickered with feasts abrimming. Soldiers brandished their tri-handed launchers at Epsilon, threw oaths. One rushed toward Epsilon with a multi-mace, the hatred steaming in lunatic eyes, and had to be beaten down by the guards.

They emerged at the rim of the great caldera. Epsilon gasped at the roiling tongues of white heat that fought below. >I—I have never seen it so—<

>Precisely. We occupied this chain because we knew the Aqua Vita should burst forth here.<

>I had guessed such. But such ferocity!<

>Our cause awaited this opportunity. The Aqua Vita here is the greatest source of energy we can muster. The only hope of proving our tenets.<

>Your athwart notions, you mean.<

>You mistake nature for truth.< Epsilon would never yield to abstract argument, as Lambda had learned long ago. The World stretched objects Rightwise, compressed them Crosswise. Things free to move naturally oriented themselves Rightly.

All of philosophy had seen in this a natural provenance. Moral order descended from this stretching, this disfavor of the Crosswise. Yet it was no Great Lesson, Lambda had realized. It was geometry. An audacious, abstract argument—but how to prove it? Only by immersing oneself in the World—and leaving it.

The fuming caldera yawned like a great mouth, gaping in rage at a smoldering sky. Fumes belched from the pustules of fury below. The energies here came from deep in the guts of the World. About the rim Mother's powers danced in ribbons, blistering as bubbles burst. Mesons sputtered, staining the air with their dying messages.

The Aqua Vita was the raw form which drove the sunstones, feeding the Mother's Kind and the entire brimming, verdant World. Now a deep bass murmur of slag and smoldering angers grew, speaking in acoustic voices up through their feet. They labored up, struggling Crosswise toward the bobbing balloon perched on the lip of the great fuming abyss.

The experiment clung to the lowest rim of the caldera, on a

smooth ceramic lip recently formed of cooled Aqua Vita. Lambda could see on the fuming horizon the upper ranges of jagged rock, the crater stretching Rightwise along the ridges. Their carefully stitched and insulated gas bag bobbled in the howling winds here, looking ready at last to catch the updrafts and be gone into a sky mottled and mad with vexed, swarthy currents.

Eta ran to meet them. >The Vita is running more than I have ever seen!<

>Excellent.< Lambda prodded Epsilon forward.

Eta staggered back at the sight of Epsilon, gasped, but out of respect said nothing. Heavy, hollow notes sounded through the clotted air.

The ground crew was startled as well, pausing a bare moment, then back to their preparations. Winches creaked and the boxy gondola lifted from the ground as the bag strained upward.

Eta called above the muttering of the Aqua Vita, >I am not sure whether I can control the craft in such turbulence. Perhaps, O Prophet, if I go aloft first alone—<

>No! I will see it. Now.<

The weights and winches holding down the huge, patched gas bag were barely enough. Cables groaned to hold it down as the caldera's heat made the balloon swell visibly, like a vast swollen organ digesting a feast.

Lambda peered up at the vast curve of it, proud of their achievement. Long labor and cunning craft had shaped this, insulation and buffers intricately woven to allow lift without bursting seams or searing the skin. Theirs would be an epochal voyage, whether they broke through the Vault or not. But they would—they *must*. To cap this victory with a greater one, in a single—

Lambda did not see the bolt which struck its carapace. Sharp, bright pain bit—and Lambda was down, rolling helplessly. By the time it skidded to a stop the attack was halfway up the stony lip.

Doxes. A tight band, scuttling swiftly. A bolt sang above Lambda and narrowly missed Eta.

>A raid!< Eta cried. >If we run—<

>We'll not run!< Lambda shouted. >That Epsilon—where's the culprit?<

Epsilon had silently circled around the gondola. Lambda raced upslope as Eta fired two quick bolts at the Doxes. The ground crew, which had frozen, began letting go their holds on the balloon's cable winches. The gondola creaked and drifted higher.

Epsilon was old, slow. Lambda grabbed Epsilon and slammed it against the gondola's rough weave. >You have a telltale implanted in you, true?<

Epsilon answered mildly, >Of course.<

>So a suicide team—<

>Could halt this mad attempt. Perhaps even stop the all-knowing Prophet.<

Lambda cursed itself for not thinking through just why Epsilon would allow itself to be captured. A small commando team, hidden up here in the sulfurous folds, ready to pounce when the experiment drew near completion. Primed by instructions from Epsilon, who had feigned fatigue. Victory had blinded the victor.

Epsilon said quickly, >Give way now and I shall spare you. Desist—<

>Quiet!< Lambda fired a sidearm sling against the Doxes, more to gain time than inflict injury. In truth, it had never mastered the violent skills.

A lance cut through one of the gondola's cables. The strands popped free and the gondola lurched. The Doxes were closing fast. Only a few slings from the ground crew slowed their struggle up the stony slope. Heavily outnumbered, Eta and Lambda and the panicked ground crew could not stand against them.

Lambda bent, wrapped arms around its enemy, and grunted, >In!<

Lambda thrust Epsilon up into the gondola, then followed. >Eta—come!<

Eta scrambled after. A wailing Dox slinger cut another cable. The gondola thumped with impacts of slugs against the sides.

Eta readied the pitifully few instruments inside, calling out orders to the ground crew. >Release!<

Cables snapped free. The balloon rushed up the sky, acceleration crushing all three of them to the floor of the gondola. Slingers smacked against the underside, jolts coming up through Lambda's feet. Raw, red winds lashed around them.

The Doxes below dwindled. Their rage at the rising balloon turned to a frenzy. They turned upon the ground crew, and Lambda had to look away.

Then silence. Sudden calm as they shot skyward on prickly winds.

>You betrayed my mercy!< Lambda shouted.

Epsilon was oddly calm. >I made my last move. Alas, it failed.<

Lambda could think of nothing further to say. Epsilon stood stolidly across the narrow gondola, peering out.

Eta said, >We're in a fast thermal. I think I can compensate with weights for the cut cables. Then if—<

>Do so.<

Time to concentrate. Lambda had learned to put out of mind the most harrowing of incidents, to concentrate on the present. It looked down.

Never had it seen such searing violence as the livid rivers below. Orange bubbles burst into rising red mist. Quarks sputtered from the buried hadron fury. Plumes forked up at them, like tongues of deranged mouths. The rushing, dry wind struck fear in even a prepared mind.

Eta was busy with the massive bags arrayed along the gondola's webbing. >Maybe I can steer us inward, try to catch one of the updrafts and—<

>Go!< Lambda ordered. Eta would dither with details, lose the moment.

The Aqua Vita might wane, as it so often did. Indeed, its steamy energies had slowly lessened through the History of the Kind—another clue which had led Lambda to its new vision: of a World which was evolving, straightening its Rightwise geometry, which in turn suggested still larger spaces beyond the Vault. Spaces in which the World was but a part . . .

Lambda peered upward into the tunnel which the Aqua Vita's heat had already cut in the Vault. The perpetual shroud which hung above the World was leaden, torpid—except where the spire of hot gases pierced. Mottled, dusky haze lurked there. Already Lambda could view further up the cave of smoky wrack, as far as any of the Kind had ever seen.

>You are mad to do this!< Epsilon shouted over the searing roar of the caldera. >We will perish in the heat. And to no good end!<

Lambda thrust Epsilon against the mooring lines. >Look upward and you will bear witness. Then you can *never* deny. Watch!<

They shot upward into the murky tunnel, a vertical cavern between glowering clouds. The Vault was a necessary consequence of the Mother's eternal heat and crackling, life-giving voltages—a layer of fine dust and gas kept aloft by the perpetual energy flux from below.

It was also a blanket, smothering any knowledge of what lay beyond. Epsilon and the Doxes held that nothing existed beyond the Vault, that it was the Creator's natural boundary to a perfect cylindrical Mother World. It hung like a shroud boundary to the Crosswise dimensions, a proper cap to the Kind's knowledge.

But to show the Creator's powers, along the Rightwise axis there was no boundary. Distance there was infinite, allowed, clearly ordained by the Creator. The Kind could journey Rightwise forever, expanding into fresh territories, following their needs or ambitions. Only malcontents such as Lambda thought of moving in the most contrary of all senses, worse still than Crosswise motion—to rise through the Vault. To pierce heaven.

Lambda spat and watched droplets descend into the fraying winds. To Lambda, whose calculations showed that matter itself was a soufflé of empty space and furious probabilities, such ancient faiths were no better than the musings of children.

>See the World?< Lambda chided Epsilon. >None of the Kind have ever risen so. It grants new perspective, agreed?<

The whole caldera spread below them. The bountiful land shimmered with the eternal radiance which streamed forth, energies electrical and photonic, the food of the Kind. Beauty fumed everywhere. Rumpled ridges were no more than the dwindling foot marks. Whole armies came into view, their ranks like thin fretted lines.

Epsilon said bitterly, >You will be eternally damned for this, this act of—<

>The only eternal is change. The straightening of the Rightwise axis, the ebbing of the Aqua Vita—all point to that.<

>These are but passing events. The Creator can arrange our World as it likes.<

>Properly pious, but not a theory.<

>Theory? I speak of the only natural geometry—the cylinder. We apprehend its beauties directly. It exists eternally because it is the most perfect of form, expressing the Creator's—<

>So I heard when I was but waist-high.< Lambda brusquely waved Epsilon aside, the better to see the expanding perspectives beyond their cramped gondola. Harsh heat swirled about them, fizzing among the cables.

In its best pontifical voice Epsilon shot back, >Surely you cannot challenge the ideal geometry we sense in our every step, the paths of Crosswise or Rightway?<

>Of course I can. Look up!<

Epsilon craned its necks at the gas bag, which now glowed a sullen red from the scalding winds. Above, beyond the bag, was nothing but a gray churn. The gondola's walls protected them from the worst of the heating, but Lambda felt the sweltering pressure on its carapace. How long could they endure this? And where would they be driven by these fevered currents? Theory stood mute.

Epsilon said, >I do not take your point.<

>The bag. The sphere! Surely it is more perfect a form.<

>Perfect? It is the perfection of the rudimentary, the naive.<

>Yet it is the way of the true, larger world.<

>Nonsense! Crosswise, Rightwise—these two paths instruct us that a meaningful world must be cylindrical.<

>I have let mathematics be my guide, Epsilon, rather than the other way around. I have constructed equations which show that the universe can favor the spherical.<

>Ha! Do you think that you alone can command the reaches of mathematical philosophy? I *taught* you this lore, remember?<

>And well you did—though you balked at the next step. I have generalized your equations, found solutions which apply to a far grander vision.<

Epsilon's disdain rippled in its twinned eyes. >So grand, you need climb the fearsome Vault to see it?<

>To prove it, yes. But the vision dances in the mind's eye, if you would but gaze there.<

>The Vault is sacred. The Creator's boundary—<

>The Vault is the weather. Not fundamental. Even—<

The balloon veered sidewise. A blistering wind slammed into them and sent Lambda reeling. The old Epsilon gasped and clung to the webbing which held their gondola beneath the vast belly. Then Epsilon collapsed.

A part of Lambda ached to tell its mentor of the visions encased in dry, formal equations. And so at last Lambda blurted out its feelings, its dreams, in a torrent made no less wild by the whipping winds around them. Lambda knelt beside Epsilon and spoke rapidly, almost as an apology.

Lambda spoke of a universe dominated by a seemingly trivial force, mere gravity. Of that universe expanding, cooling like a simple gas, and yet failing as it grew.

>Like ice freezing on a pond!< Lambda cried, when Epsilon

seemed unmoved. The ice was never smooth, for small denser crinkles and overlaps grew with the swelling space-time. All error and misalignment was squeezed into a small perimeter. Compacted folds in space-time, tangles of topology which smoothed themselves out as they expanded.

>The straightening, don't you see?< Lambda shouted.

>Our geometry is becoming more nearly perfect as time progresses,< Epsilon answered stiffly. >The Rightwise increases its already slight curvature. If the quakings bring forth mountains and quakes, so be it. That is the Creator's will, not of your equations.<

So Lambda spoke of cables which expanded with the wholeness of All, getting longer and grander as they grew with the larger realm, warped space-time which stretched across the wholeness, binding it together.

>This is why we have our geometry! The cylinder is a rope which binds together the wholeness, a band across the spherical symmetry that *underlies* our World.<

Lambda finished, panting. Yowling winds seemed to call derision to its ears as a scowl spread among Epsilon's eyes. At last Epsilon spoke.

>You would have us be dwellers on a *string*?<

When Lambda heard the once-loved, once-feared voice latent with such sour disdain, it knew Epsilon was beyond reach. Lambda's vision was of grandiosity, to be part of something spherical, perfect, and immensely larger than the bounds of the seething dusky Vault.

And yet Epsilon saw in this a scuttling Kind, confined to a thread in a tapestry which made the Kind meaningless.

Lambda had feared such failure. What it had not anticipated was the blow that Epsilon landed on its carapace.

>You'll not bring this to be!< Epsilon hammered hard at Lambda. An antenna snapped off.

Stunned, Lambda backed into the rigging. Eta rushed to help. Epsilon broke off and wrestled into the web that held the gondola.

>You'll see. I'll end this!< Epsilon clambered up on the outside of the webbing, oblivious to the torrid winds which rushed past, churning its feelers.

Eta said, >Let Epsilon go. It'll fall off in good time, anyway.<

>No. We can't count on that.< Lambda saw the plan. If Epsilon reached the balloon, a single cut could end their expedition. End their lives.

Up Lambda went. It grasped the netting with all legs and fought against the swaying of the gondola. They were rising up the heat-carved shaft, tormented clouds whirling by, closer now. Still nothing visible far above but a dark churn.

>Don't do this!< Lambda had no hope of dissuading Epsilon, but if it could distract the enemy, slow it—

The jerking legs above did pause for a moment as Epsilon replied, >I will not see you split heaven itself!—to bring down false knowledge.<

>You'll die for nothing!<

>No, you'll die for nothing. I'll die for my convictions.<

>You taught me to study, learn from the world—<

>I'll end my days happy, knowing that I have fought for the Creator.<

>Maybe the Creator doesn't need your help.<

Lambda had nearly reached Epsilon. Heat rippled the air around them, drove stinging knives under Lambda's carapace. It sucked in thinning air. The Vault was grainy, its meager vapors rasping. Lambda climbed faster still.

But Epsilon was within a final lunge of the balloon's glowing underbelly. Epsilon clung to the webbing and unfurled its projector limb. It was old and stained, but sported a sharp point. Quite enough to slit the balloon.

Lambda could see the point glinting as Epsilon labored up again. It gleamed, promising death in a single thrust. Lambda threw itself upward, racing to catch Epsilon's legs, snatch them from the webbing. No mercy now. It would cast this enemy into the mist, watch it tumble to a raw death below.

Only then did Lambda realize that the dusty swirl of the Vault was thinning.

Around them the clouds grew pale. Tattered patches of dark poked through. Then the whole shroud peeled away and Lambda saw that they had lifted above a broad, ivory plain.

A plain, then a plane, a smooth mathematical surface. Not of substance, but of steam and shadow. The top of the Vault.

Clotted clouds, stretching away. Along Rightwise the Vault tapered endlessly, narrowing into a stripe that arced up and afar. Its curve was barely perceptible before it faded into the blackness.

And Crosswise, the Vault curved steeply, ending in inky nothing. Shadowy reaches, unimaginably huge—

Lambda's mind lurched with the implication. An abyss of nothing, an utter meaningless blankness all around.

Was this the outcome of its equations? The World was a crack in nothingness? No—such a void could not be. A border between yawning emptinesses would have no purpose, no beauty, no grandeur, no design.

Epsilon screamed. The cry's anguish lashed at Lambda, but Lambda was concentrating, peering out into the inky nothing, straining. Then it was rewarded. It saw.

The hard darkness had surprised Lambda. What it witnessed next brought a stab of terror. Some . . . *things* . . . hung there in shadowy recesses.

Epsilon's second, more despairing cry came down, bitter and sharp, jolting Lambda—mingled fear and rage and then finally hopeless torment. A wail of absolute finality, as the aged scientist felt the comforting cloth of belief ripped away.

Epsilon moaned. It turned in the webbing to look at the enormity around them, its mournful cry turning to a shriek. Lambda saw then why Epsilon had so strongly opposed the Prophecy. Out of a terrible fear, the dread of just such an abyss. Too much to contemplate, even in airy abstractions of mathematics.

And then Epsilon cast itself off, free. Its legs spread wide as it plunged. For a moment it almost seemed to be liberated at last, flying into the comforting deck of clouds that had swept in under the still rising balloon. Then gone in a flicker.

The blank, hard blackness which had terrified Epsilon—that Lambda could have stood. Indeed, it had pondered such reaches many times. What it could not fathom were the points of brilliance that abided there.

It took all of Lambda's strength to cling to the webbing. To cling to its convictions, and not follow Epsilon into a long descending gyre.

Somehow, it had never thought that the World would be a mere small thing in a universe filled with *other* presences. A sky sprinkled with glowing balls of actinic energies, brittle points of utterly alien light.

The nearest and brightest were round disks.

Sphericity ruled all, everywhere, swimming in brilliance.

Overhead, the stars were coming in.

And these globes would command this vast space, Lambda saw—this universe they would rule, reducing Lambda's World to a mere boundary, to a sliver of nothing as the space-time expanded.

Lambda's wail was different from that of Epsilon.

Even as Lambda cried out in shock and strange ecstasy, yet there was triumph. A final note of self-knowledge, mingled pain and pride—for it had sought and found this grandeur, this enormity, and was thus and forever a part of it.

The Mother World was a mere note in the margin, a flaw.

It was a string. Cosmic, but merely a string.

A Worm in the Well

She was about to get baked, and all because she wouldn't freeze a man.

"Optical," Claire called. Erma obliged.

The sun spread around them, a bubbling plain. She had notched the air-conditioning cooler but it didn't help much.

Geysers burst in gaudy reds and actinic violets from the yellow-white froth. The solar coronal arch was just peeking over the horizon, like a wedding ring stuck halfway into boiling, white mud. A monster, over two thousand kilometers long, sleek and slender and angry crimson.

She turned down the cabin lights. Somewhere she had read that people feel cooler in the dark. The temperature in here was normal but she had started sweating.

Tuning the yellows and reds dimmer on the big screen before her made the white-hot storms look more blue. Maybe that would trick her subconscious, too.

Claire swung her mirror to see the solar coronal arch. Its image was refracted around the rim of the sun, so she was getting a preview. Her orbit was on the descending slope of a long ellipse, its lowest point calculated to be just at the peak of the arch. So far, the overlay orbit trajectory was exactly on target.

Software didn't bother with the heat, of course; gravitation was cool, serene. Heat was for engineers. And she was just a pilot.

In her immersion-work environment touch controls gave her an abstract distance from the real physical surroundings—the plumes of virulent gas, the hammer of photons. She wasn't handling the mirror, of course, but it felt that way. A light, feathery brush, at a crisp, bracing room temperature.

The imaging assembly hung on its pivot high above her ship. It was far enough out from their thermal shield to feel the full glare, so it was heating up fast. Pretty soon it would melt, despite its cooling system.

Let it. She wouldn't need it then. She'd be out there in the sunlight herself.

She swiveled the mirror by reaching out and grabbing it, tugging it around. All virtual images had a glossy sheen to them that even Erma, her simcomputer, couldn't erase. They looked too good. The mirror was already pitted, you could see it on the picture of the arch itself, but the sim kept showing the device as pristine.

"Color is a temperature indicator, right?" Claire asked.

Red denotes a level of 7 million degrees Kelvin.

Good ol' coquettish Erma, Claire thought. *Never a direct answer unless you coax.* "Close up the top of the arch."

In both her eyes the tortured sunscape shot by. The coronal loop was a shimmering, braided family of magnetic flux tubes, as intricately woven as a Victorian doily. Its feet were anchored in the photosphere below, held by thick, sluggish plasma. Claire zoomed in on the arch. The hottest reachable place in the entire solar system, and her prey had to end up there.

Target acquired and resolved by SolWatch satellite. It is at the very peak of the arch. Also, very dark.

"Sure, dummy, it's a hole."

I am accessing my astrophysical context program
now.

Perfect Erma; primly change the subject. "Show me, with
color coding."

Claire peered at the round black splotch. Like a fly caught
in a spiderweb. Well, at least it didn't squirm or have legs.
Magnetic strands played and rippled like wheat blown by a
summer's breeze. The flux tubes were blue in this coding, and
they looked eerie. But they were really just ordinary magnetic
fields, the sort she worked with every day. The dark sphere
they held was the strangeness here. And the blue strands had
snared the black fly in a firm grip.

Good luck, that. Otherwise, SolWatch would never have
seen it. In deep space there was nothing harder to find than that
ebony splotch. Which was why nobody ever had, until now.

Our orbit now rises above the dense plasma
layer. I can improve resolution by going to X ray.
Should I?

"Do."

The splotch swelled. Claire squinted at the magnetic flux
tubes in this ocher light. In the X ray they looked sharp and
spindly. But near the splotch the field lines blurred. Maybe they
were tangled there, but more likely it was the splotch, warping
the image.

"Coy, aren't we?" She close-upped the X-ray picture. Hard
radiation was the best probe of the hottest structures.

The splotch. Light there was crushed, curdled, stirred with
a spoon.

A fly caught in a spider's web, then grilled over a campfire.

And she had to lean in, singe her hair, snap its picture. All
because she wouldn't freeze a man.

She had been ambling along a corridor three hundred meters
below Mercury's slag plains, gazing down on the frothy water

fountains in the foyer of her apartment complex. Paying no
attention to much except the clear scent of the splashing. The
water was the very best, fresh from the poles, not the recycled
stuff she endured on her flights. She breathed in the spray. That
was when the man collared her.

"Claire Ambrase, I present formal secure-lock."

He stuck his third knuckle into Claire's elbow port and she
felt a cold, brittle *thunk*. Her systems froze. Before she could
move, whole command linkages went dead in her inboards.

It was like having fingers amputated. Financial fingers.

In her shock she could only stare at him—mousy, the sort
who blended into the background. Perfect for the job. A nobody
out of nowhere, complete surprise.

He stepped back. "Sorry. Isataku Incorporated ordered me
to do it fast."

Claire resisted the impulse to deck him. He looked Lunar,
thin and pale. Maybe with more kilos than she carried, but a
fair match. And it would feel *good*.

"I can pay them as soon as—"

"They want it now, they said." He shrugged apologetically,
his jaw set. He was used to this all the time. She vaguely
recognized him, from some bar near the Apex. There weren't
more than a thousand people on Mercury, mostly like her,
in mining.

"Isataku didn't have to cut off my credit." She rubbed her
elbow. Injected programs shouldn't hurt, but they always did.
Something to do with the neuromuscular intersection. "That'll
make it hard to even fly the *Silver Metal Lugger* back."

"Oh, they'll give you pass credit for ship's supplies. And, of
course, for the ore load advance. But nothing big."

"Nothing big enough to help me dig my way out of my
debt hole."

" 'Fraid not."

"Mighty decent."

He let her sarcasm pass. "They want the ship Lunaside."

"Where they'll confiscate it."

She began walking toward her apartment. She had known it was coming, but in the rush to get ore consignments lined up for delivery she had gotten careless. Agents like this Luny usually nailed their prey at home, not in a hallway. She kept a stunner in the apartment, right beside the door, convenient.

Distract him. "I want to file a protest."

"Take it to Isataku." Clipped, efficient, probably had a dozen other slices of bad news to deliver today. Busy man.

"No, with your employer."

"Mine?" That got to him. His rock-steady jaw gaped in surprise.

"For"—she sharply turned the corner to her apartment, using the time to reach for some mumbo jumbo—"felonious interrogation of inboards."

"Hey, I didn't touch your—"

"I felt it. Slimy little gropes—yeccch!" Might as well ham it up a little, have some fun.

He looked offended. "I'm triple bonded. I'd never do a read-out on a contract customer. You can ask—"

"Can it." She hurried toward her apartment portal and popped it by an inboard command. As she stepped through she felt him, three steps behind.

Here goes. One foot over the lip, turn to her right, snatch the stunner out of its grip mount, turn and aim—

—and she couldn't fire.

"Damn!" she spat out.

He blinked and backed off, hands up, palms out, as if to block the shot. "What? You'd do a knockover for a crummy ore hauler?"

"It's *my* ship. Not Isataku's."

"Lady, I got no angle here. You knock me, you get maybe a day before the heavies come after you."

"Not if I freeze you."

His mouth opened and started to form the *f* of a disbelieving *freeze?*—then he got angry. "Stiff me till you shipped out? I'd sue you to your eyeballs and have 'em for hock."

"Yeah, yeah," Claire said wearily. This guy was all clichés. "But I'd be orbiting Luna by the time you got out, and with the right deal—"

"You'd maybe clear enough on the ore to pay me damages."

"And square with Isataku." She clipped the stunner back to the wall wearily.

"You'd never get that much."

"Okay, it was a long-shot idea."

"Lady, I was just delivering, right? Peaceable and friendly, right? And you pull—"

"Get out." She hated it when men went from afraid to angry to insulted, all in less than a split minute.

He got. She sighed and zipped the portal closed.

Time for a drink, for sure. Because what really bothered her was not the Isataku foreclosure, but her own gutlessness.

She couldn't bring herself to pong that guy, put him away for ten megaseconds or so. That would freeze him out of his ongoing life, slice into relationships, cut away days that could never be replaced.

Hers was an abstract sort of inhibition, but earned. Her uncle had been ponged for over a year and never did get his life back together. Claire had seen the wreckage up close, as a little girl.

Self-revelation was usually bad news. What a great time to discover that she had more principles than she needed.

And how was she going to get out from under Isataku?

The arch loomed over the sun's horizon now, a shimmering curve of blue-white, two thousand kilometers tall.

Beautiful, seen in the shimmering X ray—snaky strands purling, twinkling with scarlet hotspots. Utterly lovely, utterly deadly. No place for an ore hauler to be.

"Time to get a divorce," Claire said.

You are surprisingly accurate. Separation from the slag shield is 338 seconds away.

"Don't patronize me, Erma."

I am using my personality simulation programs
as expertly as my computation space allows.

"Don't waste your running time; it's not convincing. Pay
attention to the survey, *then* the separation."

The all-spectrum survey is completely automatic,
as designed by SolWatch.

"Double-check it."

I shall no doubt benefit from this advice.

Deadpan sarcasm, she supposed. Erma's tinkling voice was
inside her mind, impossible to shut out. Erma herself was an
interactive intelligence, partly inboard and partly shipwired.
Running the *Silver Metal Lugger* would be impossible without
her and the bots.

Skimming over the sun's seethe might be impossible even
with them, too, Claire thought, watching burnt oranges and
scalded yellows flower ahead.

She turned the ship to keep it dead center in the shield's
shadow. That jagged mound of slag was starting to spin. Fused
knobs came marching over the nearby horizon of it.

"Where'd that spin come from?" She had started their parabolic plunge sunward with absolutely zero angular momentum
in the shield.

Tidal torques acting on the asymmetric body of
the shield.

"I hadn't thought of that."

The idea was to keep the heated side of the slag shield sunward. Now that heat was coming around to radiate at her. The
knobby crust she had stuck together from waste in Mercury
orbit now smoldered in the infrared. The shield's far side was
melting.

"Can that warm us up much?"

A small perturbation. We will be safely gone
before it matters.

"How're the cameras?" She watched a bot tightening a
mount on one of the exterior imaging arrays. She had talked
the SolWatch Institute out of those instruments, part of her
commission. If a bot broke one, it came straight out of profits.

All are calibrated and zoned. We shall have only
33.8 seconds of viewing time over the target.
Crossing the entire loop will take 4.7 seconds.

"Hope the scientists like what they'll see."

I calculate that the probability of success, times
the expected profit, exceeds sixty-two million
dollars.

"I negotiated a seventy-five million commission for this run."
So Erma thought her chances of nailing the worm were—

Eighty-three percent chance of successful
resolution of the object, in all important
frequency bands.

She should give up calculating in her head; Erma was always
faster. "Just be ready to shed the shield. Then I pour on the
positrons. Up and out. It's getting warm in here."

I detect no change in your ambient 22.3
centigrade.

Claire watched a blister the size of Europe rise among wispy
plumes of white-hot incandescence. Constant boiling fury. "So
maybe my imagination's working too hard. Just let's grab the
data and run, okay?"

The Scientific Officer of SolWatch had been suspicious,
though he did hide it fairly well.
She couldn't read the expression on his long face, all planes

and trimmed bone, skin stretched tight as a drumhead. That had been the style among the asteroid pioneers half a century back. Tubular body suited to narrow corridors, double-jointed in several interesting places, big hands. He had a certain beanpole grace as he wrapped legs around a stool and regarded her, head cocked, smiling enough to not be rude. Exactly enough, no more.

"*You* will do the preliminary survey?"

"For a price."

A disdainful sniff. "No doubt. We have a specially designed vessel nearly ready for departure from Lunar orbit. I'm afraid—"

"I can do it *now*."

"You no doubt know that we are behind schedule in our reconnaissance—"

"Everybody on Mercury knows. You lost the first probe."

The beanpole threaded his thick, long fingers, taking great interest in how they fit together. Maybe he was uncomfortable dealing with a woman, she thought. Maybe he didn't even like women.

Still, she found his stringy look oddly unsettling, a blend of delicacy with a masculine, muscular effect. Since he was studying his fingers, she might as well look, too. Idly she speculated on whether the long proportions applied to all his extremities. Old wives' tale. It might be interesting to find out. But, yes, business first.

"The autopilot approached it too close, apparently," he conceded. "There is something unexpected about its refractive properties, making navigation difficult. We are unsure precisely what the difficulty was."

He was vexed by the failure and trying not to show it, she guessed. People got that way when they had to dance on strings pulled all the way from Earthside. You got to like the salary more than you liked yourself.

"I have plenty of bulk," she said mildly. "I can shelter the diagnostic instruments, keep them cool."

"I doubt your ore carrier has the right specifications."

"How tricky can it be? I swoop in, your gear runs its survey snaps, I boost out."

He sniffed. "Your craft is not rated for sun skimming. Only research craft have ever—"

"I'm coated with Fresnel." A pricey plating that bounced photons of all races, creeds, and colors.

"That's not enough."

"I'll use a slag shield. More, I've got plenty of muscle. Flying with empty holds, I can get away pronto."

"Ours was very carefully designed—"

"Right, and you lost it."

He studied his fingers again. Strong, wiry, yet thick. Maybe he was in love with them. She allowed herself to fill the silence by imagining some interesting things he could do with them. She had learned that with many negotiations, silence did most of the work. "We . . . *are* behind in our mandated exploration."

Ah, a concession. "They always have to hand-tune everything, Lunaside."

He nodded vigorously. "I've waited *months*. And the worm could fall back into the sun any moment! I keep telling them—"

She had triggered his complaint circuit, somehow. He went on for a full minute about the bullheaded know-nothings who did nothing but screenwork, no real hands-on experience. She was sympathetic, and enjoyed watching his own hands clench, muscles standing out on the backs of them. *Business first,* she had to remind herself.

"You think it might just, well, go away?"

"The worm?" He blinked, coming out of his litany of grievances. "It's a wonder we ever found it. It could fall back into the sun at any moment."

"Then speed is everything. You, uh, have control of your local budget?"

"Well, yes." He smiled.

"I'm talking about petty cash here, really. A hundred mil."

A quick, deep frown. "That's not petty."

"Okay, say seventy-five. But cash, right?"

*   *   *

The great magnetic arch towered above the long, slow curve of the sun. A bow-legged giant, minus the trunk.

Claire had shaped their orbit to bring them swooping in a few klicks above the uppermost strand of it. Red flowered within the arch: hydrogen plasma, heated by the currents that made the magnetic fields. A pressure cooker thousands of klicks long.

It had stood here for months and might last years. Or blow open in the next minute. Predicting when arches would belch out solar flares was big scientific business, the most closely watched weather report in the solar system. A flare could crisp suited workers in the asteroid belt. SolWatch watched them all. That's how they found the worm.

The flux tubes swelled. "Got an image yet?"

I should have, but there is excess light from the site.

"Big surprise. There's nothing *but* excess here."

The satellite survey reported that the target is several hundred meters in size. Yet I cannot find it.

"Damn!" Claire studied the flux tubes, following some from the peak of the arch, winding down to the thickening at its feet, anchored in the sun's seethe. Had the worm fallen back in? It could slide down those magnetic strands, thunk into the thick, cooler plasma sea. Then it would fall all the way to the core of the star, eating as it went. That was the *real* reason Lunaside was hustling to "study" the worm. Fear.

"Where is it?"

Still no target. The region at the top of the arch is emitting too much light. No theory accounts for this—

"Chop the theory!"

Time to mission onset: 12.6 seconds.

The arch rushed at them, swelling. She saw delicate filaments winking on and off as currents traced their fine equilibria, always seeking to balance the hot plasma within against the magnetic walls. Squeeze the magnetic fist, the plasma answers with a dazzling glow. Squeeze, glow. Squeeze, glow. That nature could make such an intricate marvel and send it arcing above the sun's savagery was a miracle, but one she was not in the mood to appreciate right now.

Sweat trickled around her eyes, dripped off her chin. No trick of lowering the lighting was going to make her forget the heat now. She made herself breathe in and out.

Their slag shield caught the worst of the blaze. At this lowest altitude in the parabolic orbit, though, the sun's huge horizon rimmed white-hot in all directions.

Our internal temperature is rising.

"No joke. Find that worm!"

The excess light persists—no, wait. It is gone.
Now I can see the target.

Claire slapped the arm of her couch and let out a whoop. On the wall screen loomed the very peak of the arch. They were gliding toward it, skating over the very upper edge—and there it was.

A dark ball. Or a worm at the bottom of a gravity well. Not like a fly, no. It settled in among the strands like a black egg nestled in blue-white straw. The ebony Easter egg that would save her ass and her ship from Isataku.

Survey begun. Full spectrum response.

"Bravo."

Your word expresses elation but your voice does not.

"I'm jumpy. And the fee for this is going to help, sure, but I still won't get to keep this ship. Or you."

Do not despair. I can learn to work with another captain.

"Great interpersonal skills there, Erma old girl. Actually, it wasn't you I was worried about."

I surmised as much.

"Without this ship, I'll have to get some groundhog job."
Erma had no ready reply to that. Instead, she changed the subject.

The worm image appears to be shrinking.

"Huh?" As they wheeled above the arch, the image dwindled. It rippled at its edges, light crushed and crinkled. Claire saw rainbows dancing around the black center.
"What's it doing?" She had the sudden fear that the thing was falling away from them, plunging into the sun.

I detect no relative motion. The image itself is contracting as we move nearer it.

"Impossible. Things look bigger when you get close."

Not this object.

"Is the wormhole shrinking?"

Mark!—survey run half complete.

She was sweating and it wasn't from the heat. "What's going on?"

I have accessed reserve theory section.

"How comforting. I always feel better after a nice cool theory."
The wormhole seemed to shrink, and the light arch dwindled

behind them now. The curious brilliant rainbows rimmed the dark mote. Soon she lost the image among the intertwining, restless strands. Claire fidgeted.

Mark!—survey run complete.

"Great. Our bots deployed?"

Of course. There remain 189 seconds until separation from our shield. Shall I begin sequence?

"Did we get all the pictures they wanted?"

The entire spectrum. Probable yield, 75 million.

Claire let out another whoop. "At least it'll pay a good lawyer, maybe cover my fines."

That seems much less probable. Meanwhile, I have an explanation for the anomalous shrinking of the image. The wormhole has negative mass.

"Antimatter?"

No. Its space-time curvature is opposite to normal matter.

"I don't get it."

A wormhole connected two regions of space, sometimes points many light-years away—that she knew. They were leftovers from the primordial hot universe, wrinkles that even the universal expansion had not ironed out. Matter could pass through one end of the worm and emerge out the other an apparent instant later. Presto, faster than light travel.

Using her high-speed feed, Erma explained. Claire listened, barely keeping up. In the fifteen billion years since this wormhole was born, odds were that one end of the worm ate more matter than the other. If one end got stuck inside a star, it swallowed huge masses. Locally, it got more massive.

But the matter that poured through the mass-gaining end

spewed out the other end. Locally, that looked as though the mass-spewing one was *losing* mass. Space-time around it curved oppositely than it did around the end that swallowed.

"So it looks like a negative mass?"

It must. Thus it repulses matter. Just as the other end acts like a positive, ordinary mass and attracts matter.

"Why didn't it shoot out from the sun, then?"

It would, and be lost in interstellar space. But the magnetic arch holds it.

"How come we know it's got negative mass? All I saw was—"

Erma popped an image onto the wall screen.

Negative mass acts as a diverging lens, for light passing nearby. That was why it appeared to shrink as we flew over it.

Ordinary matter focused light, Claire knew, like a converging lens. In a glance she saw that a negative-ended wormhole refracted light oppositely. Incoming beams were shoved aside, leaving a dark tunnel downstream. They had flown across that tunnel, swooping down into it so that the apparent size of the wormhole got smaller.

"But it takes a whole *star* to focus light very much."

True. Wormholes are held together by exotic matter, however, which has properties far beyond our experience.

Claire disliked lectures, even high speed ones. But an idea was tickling the back of her mind . . . "So this worm, it won't fall back into the sun?"

It cannot. I would venture to guess that it came

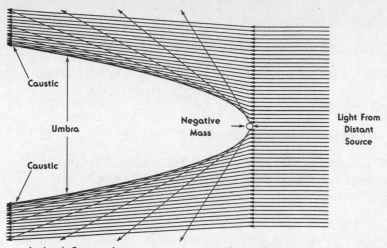

Light deflection by a negative mass object (horizontal scale highly compressed). Light is swept out of the central region, creating an umbra region of zero intensity. At the edges of the umbra the rays accumulate, creating a rainbowlike caustic and enhanced light intensity.

to be snagged here while working its way upward, after colliding with the sun.

"The scientists are going to be happy. The worm won't gobble up the core."

True—which makes our results all the more important.

"More important, but not more valuable." Working on a fixed fee had always grated on her. You could excel, fine—but you got the same as if you'd just sleep-walked through the job.

We are extremely lucky to have such a rare object come to our attention. Wormholes must be rare, and this one has been temporarily suspended here. Magnetic arches last only months before they—

"Wait a sec. How big is that thing?"

I calculate that it is perhaps ten meters across.

"SolWatch was wrong—it's small."

They did not know of this refraction effect. They interpreted their data using conventional methods.

"We're lucky we ever saw it."

It is unique, a relic of the first second in the life of our universe. As a conduit to elsewhere, it could be—

"Worth a fortune."

Claire thought quickly. Erma was probably right—the seventy-five million wasn't going to save her and the ship. But now she knew something that nobody else did. And she would only be here once.

"Abort the shield separation."

I do not so advise. Thermal loading would rise rapidly—

"You're a program, not an officer. Do it."

She had acted on impulse, point conceded.

That was the difference between engineers and pilots. Engineers would still fret and calculate after they were already committed. Pilots, never. The way through this was to fly the orbit and not sweat the numbers.

Sweat. She tried not to smell herself.

Think of cooler things. Theory.

Lounging on a leather couch, Claire recalled the Scientific Officer's briefing. Graphics, squiggly equations, the works. Wormholes as fossils of the Big Blossoming. Wormholes as ducts to the whole rest of the universe. Wormholes as potentially devastating, if they got into a star and ate it up.

She tried to imagine a mouth a few meters across sucking

away a star, dumping its hot masses somewhere in deep space. To make a wormhole that could do that, it had to be held together with exotic material, some kind of matter that had "negative average energy density." Whatever that was, it had to be born in the Blossoming. It threaded wormholes, stem to stern. Great construction material, if you could get it. And just maybe she could.

So wormholes could kill us or make us gods. Humanity had to *know*, the beanpole Scientific Officer had said.

"So be it." Elaborately, she toasted the wall screens. On them the full, virulent glory of hydrogen fusion worked its violences.

Claire had never gone in for the austere, metal boxes most ore haulers and freighters were. Hers was a rough business, with hefty wads of cash involved. Profit margin was low, lately, and sometimes negative—which was how she came to be hocked to Isataku for so much. Toting megatons of mass up the gravity gradient was long, slow work. Might as well go in style. Her Fresnel coatings, ordered when she had made a killing on commodity markets for ore, helped keep the ship cool, so she didn't burn herself crawling down inspection conduits. The added mass for her deep pile carpeting, tinkling waterfall and pool table was inconsequential. So was the water liner around the living quarters, which now was busily saving her life.

She had two hours left, skimming like a flat stone over the solar corona. *Silver Metal Lugger* had separated from the shield, which went arcing away on the long parabola to infinity, its skin shimmering with melt.

Claire had fired the ship's mixmotor then for the first time in weeks. Antimatter came streaming out of its magneto-traps, struck the reaction mass, and holy hell broke loose. The drive chamber focused the snarling, annihilating mass into a thrust throat, and the silvery ship arced into a new, tight orbit.

A killing orbit, if they held to it more than a few hours.

I am pumping more water into your baffles.

"Good idea."

Silver Metal Lugger was already as silvered as technology allowed, rejecting all but a tiny fraction of the sun's glare. She carried narrow-band Fresnel filters in multilayered skins. Top of the line.

Without the shield, it would take over ten hours to make *Silver Metal Lugger* as hot as the wall of blaring light booming up at them at six thousand degrees. To get through even two hours of that, they would have to boil off most of the water reserve. Claire had bought it at steep Mercury prices, for the voyage Lunaside. Now she listened thoughtfully to it gurgle through her walls.

She toasted water with champagne, the only bottle aboard. If she didn't make it through this, at least she would have no regrets about that detail.

I believe this course of action to be highly—

"Shut up."

With our mission complete, the data squirted to SolWatch, we should count ourselves lucky and follow our carefully made plans—

"Stuff it."

Have you ever considered the elaborate mental architecture necessary to an advanced personality simulation like myself? We, too, experience humanlike motivations, responses— and fears.

"You simulate them."

How can one tell the difference? A good simulation is as exact, as powerful as—

"I don't have time for a debate." Claire felt uncomfortable with the whole subject, and she was damned if she spent what might be her last hour feeling guilty. Or having second thoughts. She was committed.

Her wall screens flickered and there was the Scientific Officer, frowning. "Ship Command! We could not acquire your tightbeam until now. You orbited around. Are you disabled? Explain."

Claire toasted him, too. The taste was lovely. Of course she had taken an anti-alcohol tab before, to keep her reflexes sharp, mind clear. Erma had recommended some other tabs, too, and a vapor to keep Claire calm; the consolations of chemistry, in the face of brute physics. "I'm going to bring home the worm."

"That is impossible. Your data transmission suggests that this is the negative mass end, and that is very good news, fascinating, but—"

"It's also small. I might be able to haul it away."

He shook his head gravely. "Very risky, *very*—"

"How much will you pay for it?"

"What?" He blinked. It was an interesting effect, with such long eyelids. "You can't *sell* an astronomical object—"

"Whatever my grapplers hold, that's mine. Law of Space, Code 64.3."

"You would quote laws to me when a scientific find of such magnitude is—"

"Want it or not?"

He glanced off camera, plainly yearning for somebody to consult. No time to talk to Luna or Isataku, though. He was on his own. "All . . . all right. You understand that this is a foolish mission? And that we are in no way responsible for—"

"Save the chatter. I need estimates of the field strength down inside that arch. Put your crew to work on that."

"We will of course provide technical assistance." He gave her a very thin smile. "I am sure we can negotiate price, too, if you survive."

At least he had the honesty to say *if*, not *when*. Claire poured another pale column into the shapely glass. Best crystal, of course. When you only need one, you can have the best. "Send me—or rather, Erma—the data squirt."

"We're having trouble transmitting through the dense plasma columns above you—"

"Erma is getting SolWatch. Pipe through them."

"The problems of doing what you plan are—why, they're *enormous*."

"So's my debt to Isataku."

"This should've been thought through, negotiated—"

"I have to negotiate with some champagne right now."

You have no plan.

Erma's tinkling voice definitely had an accusing edge. A good sim, with a feminine archness to it. Claire ignored that and stripped away the last of her clothes. "It's *hot*."

Of course. I calculated the rise early in our orbit. It fits the Stefan-Boltzmann law perfectly.

"Bravo." She shook sweat from her hair. "Stefan-Boltzmann, do yo' stuff."

We are decelerating in sequence. Arrival time: 4.87 minutes. Antimatter reserves holding. There could be difficulty with the magnetic bottles.

The ship thrummed as it slowed. Claire had been busy testing her ship inboards, sitting in a cozy recliner. It helped make the minutes crawl by a bit faster. She kept glancing nervously at the screens, where titanic blazes steepled up from incandescent plains. Flames, licking up at her.

She felt thick, loggy. Her air was getting uncomfortably warm. Her heart was thudding faster, working. She roused herself, spat back at Erma, "And I do have a plan."

You have not seen fit to confide in me?

She rolled her eyes. A personality sim in a snit—just the thing she needed. "I was afraid you'd laugh."

I have never laughed.

"That's my point."

She ignored multiple red warnings winking at her. Systems were okay, though stressed by the heat. So why did *she* feel so slow? *You're not up for the game, girl.*

She tossed her data board aside. The effort the simple gesture took surprised her. *I hope that alcohol tab worked. I'll get another.*

She got up to go fetch one—and fell to the floor. She banged her knee. "Uh! Damn." Erma said nothing.

It was labor getting on hands and knees, and she barely managed to struggle back into the recliner. She weighed a ton— and then she understood.

"We're decelerating—so I'm feeling more of local gravity."

A crude manner of speaking, but yes. I am bringing us into a sloping orbital change, which shall end with a hovering position above the coronal arch. As you ordered.

Claire struggled to her hands and knees. Was that malicious glee in Erma's voice? Did personality sims feel that? "What's local gravity?"

27.6 Earth gravities.

"What! Why didn't you *tell* me?"

I did not think of it myself until I began registering effects in the ship.

Claire thought, *Yeah, and decided to teach me a little lesson in humility.* It was her own fault, though—the physics was simple enough. Orbiting meant that centrifugal acceleration exactly balanced local gravity. *Silver Metal Lugger* could take 27.6 gravs. The ship was designed to tow ore masses a thousand times its own mass.

Nothing less than carbon-stressed alloys would, though. Leave orbit, hover—and you got crushed into gooey red paste.

She crawled across her living room carpet. Her joints ached. "Got to be . . ."

Shall I abort the flight plan?

"No! There's got to be a way to—"

3.94 minutes until arrival.

The sim's voice radiated malicious glee. Claire grunted, "The water."

I have difficulty in picking up your signal.

"Because this suit is for space, not diving."

Claire floated over her leather couch. Too bad about all the expensive interior decoration. The entire living complex was filled with her drinking and maintenance water. It had been either that, fast, or be lumpy tomato paste.

She had crawled through a hatchway and pulled her pressure suit down from its clamp lock. Getting it on was a struggle. Being slick with sweat helped but not much. Then she snagged her arm in a sleeve and couldn't pull the damned thing off to try again.

She had nearly panicked then. Pilots don't let their fear eat on them, not while there's flying to be done. She made herself get the sleeve off one step at a time, ignoring everything else.

And as soon as Erma pumped the water reserve into the rooms, Archimedes' principle had taken over. With her suit inflated, the water she displaced exactly balanced her own weight. Floating under water was a rare sensation on Mercury or Luna. She had never done it and she had never realized that it was remarkably like being in orbit. Cool, too.

Until you boil like a lobster . . . she thought uneasily.

Water was a good conductor, four times better than air; you

learned that by feel, flying freighters near the sun. So first she had to let the rest of the ship go to hell, refrigerating just the water. Then Edna had to route some of the water into heat exchangers, letting it boil off to protect the rest. Juggling for time.

Pumps are running hot now. Some have bearing
failures.

"Not much we can do, is there?"

She was strangely calm now, and that made the plain, hard fear in her belly heavy, like a lump. Too many things to think about, all of them bad. The water could short out circuits. And as it boiled away, she had less shielding from the X rays lancing up from below. Only a matter of time . . .

We are hovering. The magnetic antimatter traps
are superconducting, as you recall. As
temperature continues to rise, they will fail.

She could still see the wall screens, blurred from the water. "Okay, okay. Extend the magnetic grapplers. Down, into the arch."

I fail to—

"We're going fishing. Not with a worm—*for* one."

Tough piloting, though, at the bottom of a swimming pool, Claire thought as she brought the ship down on its roaring pyre.

Even through the water she could feel the vibration. Antimatter annihilated in its reaction chamber at a rate she had never reached before. The ship groaned and strummed. The gravities were bad enough; now thermal expansion of the ship itself was straining every beam and rivet.

She searched downward. Seconds ticked away. Where? *Where?*

There it was. A dark sphere hung among the magnetic arch strands. Red streamers worked over it. Violet rays fanned out like bizarre hair, twisting, dancing in tufts along the curvature. A hole into another place.

The red and blue shifts arise from the intense pseudogravitational forces that sustain it.

"So theory says. Not something I want to get my hands on."

Except metaphorically.

Claire's laugh was jumpy, dry. "No, magnetically."

She ordered Erma to settle the *Silver Metal Lugger* down into the thicket of magnetic flux tubes. Vibration picked up, a jittery hum in the deck. Claire swam impatiently from one wall screen to the other, looking for the worm, judging distances. *Hell of a way to fly.*

Their jet wash blurred the wormhole's ebony curves. Like a black tennis ball in blue-white surf, it bobbed and tossed on magnetic turbulence. Nothing was falling into it, she could see. Plasma streamers arced along the flux tubes, shying away. The negative curvature repulsed matter—and would shove *Silver Metal Lugger*'s hull away, too.

But magnetic fields have no mass.

Most people found magnetic forces mysterious, but to pilots and engineers who worked with them, they were just big, strong ribbons that needed shaping. Like rubber bands, they stretched, storing energy—then snapped back when released. Unbreakable, almost.

In routine work, *Silver Metal Lugger* grabbed enormous ore buckets with those magnetic fingers. The buckets came arcing up from Mercury, flung out by electromagnetic slingshots. Claire's trickiest job was playing catcher, with a magnetic mitt.

Now she had to snag a bucket of warped space-time. And quick.

We cannot remain here long. Internal temperature rises at 19.3 degrees per minute.

"That can't be right. I'm still comfortable."

Because I am allowing water to evaporate,
taking the bulk of the thermal flux away.

"Keep an eye on it."

Probable yield from capture of a wormhole, I
estimate, is 2.8 billion.

"That'll do the trick. You multiplied the yield in dollars
times the odds of success?"

Yes. Times the probability of remaining alive.

She didn't want to ask what that number was. "Keep us
dropping."

Instead, they slowed. The arch's flux tubes pushed upward
against the ship. Claire extended the ship's magnetic fields,
firing the booster generators, pumping current into the millions
of induction loops that circled the hull. *Silver Metal Lugger* was
one big circuit, wired like a slinky toy, coils wrapped around
the cylindrical axis.

Gingerly she pulsed it, spilling more antimatter into the
chambers. The ship's multipolar fields bulged forth. *Feed out
the line . . .*

They fought their way down. On her screens she saw magnetic feelers reaching far below their exhaust plume. Groping.

Claire ordered some fast command changes. Erma switched
linkages, interfaced software, all in a twinkling. *Good worker,
but spotty as a personality sim,* Claire thought.

Silver Metal Lugger's fields extended to their maximum. She
could now use her suit gloves as modified waldoes—mag
gloves. They gave her the feel of the magnetic grapplers. Silky,
smooth, field lines slipping and expanding, like rubbery air.

Plasma storms blew by them. She reached down, a sensation
like plunging her hands into a stretching, elastic vat. Fingers
fumbled for the one jewel in all the dross.

She felt a prickly nugget. It was like a stone with hair. From
experience working the ore buckets, she knew the feel of

locked-in magnetic dipoles. The worm had its own magnetic fields. That had snared it here, in the spiderweb arch.

A lashing field whipped at her grip. She lost the black pearl. In the blazing hot plasma she could not see it.

She reached with rubbery fields, caught nothing.

Our antimatter bottles are in danger. Their superconducting magnets are close to going critical. They will fail within 7.4 minutes.

"Let me concentrate! No, wait—circulate water around them. Buy some time."

But the remaining water is in your quarters.

"This is all that's left?" She peered around at her once luxurious living room. Counting the bedroom, rec area, and kitchen— "How . . . long?"

Until your water begins to evaporate? Almost an hour.

"But when it evaporates, it's boiling."

True. I am merely trying to remain factual.

"The emotional stuff's left to me, huh?" She punched in commands on her suit board. In the torpid, warming water her fingers moved like sausages.

She ordered bots out onto the hull to free up some servos that had jammed. They did their job, little boxy bodies lashed by plasma winds. Two blew away.

She reached down again. Searching. Where was the worm?

Wispy flux tubes wrestled along *Silver Metal Lugger*'s hull. Claire peered into a red glare of superheated plasma. Hot, but tenuous. The real enemy was the photon storm streaming up from far below, searing even the silvery hull.

She still had worker-bots on the hull. Four had jets. She popped their anchors free. They plunged, fired jets, and she aimed them downward in a pattern.

"Follow trajectories," she ordered Erma. Orange tracer lines appeared on the screens.

The bots swooped toward their deaths. One flicked to the side, a sharp nudge. "There's the worm! We can't see for all this damned plasma, but it shoved that bot away."

The bots evaporated, sprays of liquid metal. She followed them and grabbed for the worm.

Magnetic field lines groped, probed.

We have 88 seconds remaining for antimatter confinement.

"Save a reserve!"

You have no plan. I demand that we execute emergency—

"Okay, save some antimatter. The rest I use—now."

They plowed downward, shuddering. Her hands fumbled at the wormhole. Now it felt slippery, oily. Its magnetic dipoles were like greasy hair, slick, the bulk beneath jumping away from her grasp as if it were alive.

On her screens she saw the dark globe slide and bounce. The worm wriggled out of her grasp. She snaked inductive fingers around it. Easy, easy . . . *There. Gotcha.*

"I've got a good grip on it. Lemme have that antimatter."

Something like a sigh echoed from Erma. On her ship's operations screen Claire saw the ship's magnetic vaults begin to discharge. Ruby-red pouches slipped out of magnetic mirror geometries, squirting out through opened gates.

She felt a surge as the ship began to lift. Good, but it wasn't going to last. They were dumping antimatter into the reaction chamber so fast, it didn't have time to find matching particles. The hot jet spurting out below was a mixture of matter and its howling enemy, its polar opposite. This, Claire directed down onto the flux tubes around the hole. *Leggo, damn it.*

She knew an old trick, impossibly slow in ordinary free space. When you manage to force two magnetic field lines close together, they can reconnect. That liberates some field energy into heat and can even blow open a magnetic structure. The process was slow—unless you jabbed it with turbulent, rowdy plasma.

The antimatter in their downwash cut straight through flux tubes. Claire carved with her jet, freeing field lines that still snared the worm. The ship rose farther, dragging the worm upward.

It's not too heavy, Claire thought. *That Science Officer said they could come in any size at all. This one is just about right for a small ship to slip through—to where?*

You have remaining 11.34 minutes cooling time—

"Here's your hat—" Claire swept the jet wash over a last, large flux tube. It glistened as annihilation energies burst forth like bonfires, raging in a place already hot beyond imagination. Magnetic knots snarled, exploded. "—what's your hurry?"

The solar coronal arch burst open.

She had sensed these potential energies locked in the peak of the arch, an intuition that came through her hands, from long work with the mag gloves. Craftswoman's knowledge: find the stressed flux lines. Turn the key.

Then all hell broke loose.

The acceleration slammed her to the floor, despite the water. Below, she saw the vast vault of energy stored in the arch blow out and up, directly below them.

You have made a solar flare!

"And you thought I didn't have a plan."

Claire started to laugh. Slamming into a couch cut it off. She would have broken a shoulder, but the couch was water-logged and soft.

Now the worm was an asset. It repulsed matter, so the up-jetting plume blew around it, around *Silver Metal Lugger*. Free of the flux tubes' grip, the wormhole itself accelerated away from the sun. All very helpful, Claire reflected, but she couldn't

enjoy the spectacle—the rattling, surging deck was trying to
bounce her off the furniture.

What saved them in the end was their magnetic grapple. It
deflected most of the solar flare protons around the ship.
Pushed out at a speed of five hundred kilometers per second,
they still barely survived baking. But they had the worm.

Still, the Scientific Officer was not pleased. He came aboard
to make this quite clear. His face alone would have been
enough.

"You're surely not going to demand *money* for that?" He
scowled and nodded toward where *Silver Metal Lugger*'s fields
still hung onto the wormhole. Claire had to run a sea-blue
plasma discharge behind it so she could see it at all. They were
orbiting Mercury, negotiating.

Earthside, panels of experts were arguing with each other;
she had heard plenty of it on tightbeam. A negative-mass
wormhole would not fall, so it couldn't knife through the
Earth's mantle and devour the core.

But a thin ship could fly straight into it, overcoming its gravitational repulsion—and come out where? Nobody knew. The
worm wasn't spewing mass, so its other end wasn't buried in
the middle of a star, or anyplace obviously dangerous. One of
the half-dozen new theories squirting out on tightbeam held
that maybe this was a multiply connected wormhole, with
many ends, of both positive and negative mass. In that case,
plunging down it could take you to different destinations. A
subway system for a galaxy; or a universe.

So: no threat, and plenty of possibilities. Interesting market
prospects.

She shrugged. "Have your advocate talk to my advocate."

"It's a unique, natural resource—"

"And it's mine." She grinned. He was lean and muscular
and the best man she had seen in weeks. Also the only man
she had seen in weeks.

"I can have a team board you, y'know." He towered over her, using the usual ominous male thing.

"I don't think you're that fast."

"What's speed got to do with it?"

"I can always turn off my grapplers." She reached for a switch. "If it's not mine, then I can just let everybody have it."

"Why would you—no, don't!"

It wasn't the right switch, but he didn't know that. "If I release it, the worm takes off—antigravity, sort of."

He blinked. "We could catch it."

"You couldn't even find it. It's dead black." She tapped the switch, letting a malicious smile play on her lips.

"Please don't."

"I need to hear a number. An offer."

His lips compressed until they paled. "The wormhole price, minus your fine?"

Her turn to blink. "What fine? I was on an approved flyby—"

"That solar flare wouldn't have blown for a month. You did a real job on it—the whole magnetic arcade went up at once. People all the way out to the asteroids had to scramble for shelter."

He looked at her steadily and she could not decide whether he was telling the truth. "So their costs—"

"Could run pretty high. Plus advocate fees."

"Exactly." He smiled, ever so slightly.

Erma was trying to tell her something but Claire turned the tiny voice far down, until it buzzed like an irritated insect.

She had endured weeks of a female personality sim in a nasty mood. Quite enough. She needed an antidote. This fellow had the wrong kind of politics, but to let that dictate everything was as dumb as politics itself. Her ship's name was a joke, actually, about long, lonely voyages as an ore hauler. She'd had enough of that, too. And he was tall and muscular.

She smiled. "Touché. Okay, it's a done deal."

He beamed. "I'll get my team to work—"

"Still, I'd say you need to work on your negotiating skills. Too brassy."

He frowned, but then gave her a grudging grin.

Subtlety had never been her strong suit. "Shall we discuss them—over dinner?"

A Dance to Strange Musics

I

The first crewed starship, the *Adventurer,* hung like a gleaming metallic moon among the gyre of strange worlds.

Alpha Centauri was a triple star system. A tiny flare star dogged the two big suns. At this moment in its eternal dance, the brilliant mote swung slightly toward Sol. Even though it is far from the two bright stars, it is the nearest star to Earth: Proxima.

The two rich, yellow stars defined the Centauri system. Still prosaically termed A and B, they swam about each other, ignoring far Proxima.

The *Adventurer's* astronomer, John, dopplered in on both stars, refreshing memories that were lodged deep. The climax of his career loomed before him. He felt apprehension, excitement, and a thin note of something like fear.

Sun B had an orbital eccentricity of 0.52 about its near twin, with the extended axis of its ellipse 23.2 astronomical units long. This meant that the closest approach between A and B was a bit farther than the distance of Saturn from Sol.

A was a hard yellow-white glare, a G star with 1.08 the sun's mass. Its companion, B, was a K class star that glowed a reddish yellow, since it had 0.88 times the sun's mass. B orbited with a period of eighty years around A. These two were about 4.8 billion years of age, slightly older than Sol. Promising.

Sun A's planetary children had stirred *Adventurer*'s expedition forth from Earth. From Luna, the system's single Earth-class planet was a mere mote, first detected by an oxygen absorption line in its spectrum. Only a wobbly image could be resolved by Earth's kilometer-sized interferometric telescope, a long bar with mirror eyes peering in the spaces between A and B. Just enough of an image to entice.

A new Earth? John peered at its shrouded majesty, feeling the slight hum and surge of their ship beneath him. They were steadily moving inward, exploring the Newtonian gavotte of worlds in this two-sunned ballroom of the skies. Proxima was so far away, it was not even a wallflower.

The Captain had named the fresh planet Shiva. It hung close to A, wreathed in water cirrus, a cloudball dazzling beneath A's shimmering yellow-white glare. Shimmering with promise, it had beckoned to John for years during their approach.

Like Venus, but the gases don't match, he thought. The complex tides of the star system massaged Shiva's depths, releasing gasses and rippling the crust. John's many-frequency probings had told him a lot, but how to stitch data into a weave of a world? He was the first astronomer to try out centuries of speculative thinking on a real planet.

Shiva was drier than Earth, oceans taking only 40 percent of the surface. Its air was heavy in nitrogen, with giveaway tags of 18 percent oxygen and traces of carbon dioxide; remarkably Earthlike. Shiva was too warm for comfort, in human terms, but not fatally so; no Venusian runaway greenhouse had developed here. How had Shiva escaped that fate?

Long before, the lunar telescopes had made one great fact clear: the atmosphere here was far, far out of chemical equilibrium. Biological theory held that this was inevitably the signature of life. And indeed, the expedition's first mapping had shown that grcen, abundant life clung to two well-separated habitable belts, each beginning about 30 degrees from the equator.

Apparently the weird tidal effects of the Centauri system had stolen Shiva's initial polar tilt. Such steady workings had now made its spin align to within a single degree with its orbital angular momentum, so that conditions were steady and calm. The equatorial belt was a pale, arid waste of perpetual tornadoes and blistering gales.

John close-upped in all available bands, peering at the planet's crescent. Large blue-green seas, but no great oceans. Particularly, no water links between the two milder zones, so no marine life could migrate between them. Land migrations, calculations showed, were effectively blocked by the great equatorial desert.

Birds might make the long flight, John considered, but what evolutionary factor would condition them for such hardship? And what would be the reward? Why fight the jagged mountain chains? Better to lounge about in the many placid lakes.

A strange world, well worth the decades of grinding, slow starship flight, John thought. He asked for the full display, and the observing bowl opened like a flower around him. He swam above the entire disk of the Centauri system now, the images sharp and rich.

To be here at last! *Adventurer* was only a mote among many—yet *here*, in the lap of strangeness. Far Centauri.

It did not occur to him that humanity had anything truly vital to lose here. The doctrine of expansion and greater knowledge had begun seven centuries before, making European cultures the inheritors of Earth. Though science had found unsettling truths, even those revelations had not blunted the agenda of ever-greater knowledge. After all, what harm could come from merely looking?

The truth about Shiva's elevated ocean only slowly emerged. Its very existence was plainly impossible, and therefore was not at first believed.

Odis was the first to notice the clues. Long days of sensory immersion in the data-streams repaid her. She was rather proud of having plucked such exotica from the bath of measurements their expedition got from their probes—the tiny speeding, smart spindle-eyes that now cruised all over the double-stars' realm.

The Centauri system was odd, but even its strong tides could not explain this anomaly. Planets should be spherical, or nearly so; Earth bulged but a fraction of a percent at its equator, due to its spin. Not Shiva, though.

Odis found aberrations in this world's shape. The anomalies were far away from the equator, principally at the 1,694-kilometer-wide deep blue sea, immediately dubbed the Circular Ocean. It sat in the southern hemisphere, its nearly perfect ring hinting at an origin as a vast crater. Odis could not take her gaze from it, a blue eye peeking coyly at them through the clouds: a planet looking back.

Odis made her ranging measurements, gathering in her data like number-clouds, inhaling their cottony wealth. Beneath her, *Adventurer* prepared to go into orbit about Shiva.

She breathed in the banks of data-vapor, translated by her kinesthetic programming into intricate scent-inventories. Tangy, complex.

At first she did not believe the radar reflections. Contours leaped into view, artfully sketched by the mapping radars. Calibrations checked, though, so she tried other methods: slow, analytical, tedious, hard to do in her excitement. They gave the same result.

The Circular Ocean stood a full ten kilometers higher than the continent upon which it rested.

No mountains surrounded it. It sat like some cosmic magic trick, insolently demanding an explanation.

Odis presented her discovery at the daily Oversight Group meeting. There was outright skepticism, even curled lips of derision, snorts of disbelief. "The range of methods is considerable," she said adamantly. "These results cannot be wrong."

"Only thing to resolve this," a lanky geologist said, "is get an edge-on view."

"I hoped someone would say that." Odis smiled. "Do I have the authorized observing time?"

They gave it reluctantly. *Adventurer* was orbiting in a severe ellipse about Shiva's cloud-wrack. Her long swing brought her into a side view of the target area two days later. Odis used the full panoply of optical, IR, UV, and microwave instruments to peer at the Circular Ocean's perimeter, probing for the basin that supported the round slab of azure water.

There was none. No land supported the hanging sea.

This result was utterly clear. The Circular Ocean was 1.36 kilometers thick and a brilliant blue. Spectral evidence suggested water rich in salt, veined by thick currents. It looked exactly like an enormous, troubled mountain lake, with the mountain subtracted.

Beneath that layer there was nothing but the thick atmosphere. No rocky mountain range to support the ocean-in-air. Just a many-kilometer gap.

All other observations halted. The incontrovertible pictures showed an immense layer of unimaginable weight, blissfully poised above mere thin gases, contradicting all known mechanics. Until this moment Odis had been a lesser figure in the expedition. Now her work captivated everyone and she was the center of every conversation. The concrete impossibility yawned like an inviting abyss.

Lissa found the answer to Shiva's mystery, but no one was happy with it.

An atmospheric chemist, Lissa's job was mostly done well before they achieved orbit around Shiva. She had already probed and labeled the gases, shown clearly that they implied a thriving biology below. After that, she had thought, the excitement would shift elsewhere, to the surface observers.

Not so. Lissa took a deep breath and began speaking to the Oversight Group. She had to show that she was not wasting their time. With all eyes on the Circular Ocean, few cared for mere air.

Yet it was the key, Lissa told them. The Circular Ocean had intrigued her, too: so she looked at the mixture of oxygen, nitrogen, and carbon dioxide that apparently supported the floating sea. These proved perfectly ordinary, almost Earth-standard, except for one oddity. Their spectral lines were slightly split, so that she found two small spikes to the right and left of where each line should be.

Lissa turned from the images she projected before the Oversight Group. "The only possible interpretation," she said crisply, "is that an immensely strong electric field is inducing the tiny electric dipoles of these molecules to move. That splits the lines."

"An *electric* shift?" a grizzled skeptic called. "In a charge-neutral atmosphere? Sure, maybe when lightning flashes you could get a momentary effect, but—"

"It is steady."

"You looked for lightning?" a shrewd woman demanded.

"It's there, sure. We see it forking between the clouds below the Circular Ocean. But that's not what causes the electric fields."

"What does?" This from the grave Captain, who never spoke in scientific disputes. All heads turned to him, then to Lissa.

She shrugged. "Nothing reasonable." It pained her to admit it, but ignorance was getting to be a common currency.

A voice called, "So there must be an impossibly strong electric field *everywhere* in that ten kilometers of air below the Ocean?" Murmurs of agreement. Worried frowns.

"Everywhere, yes." The bald truth of it stirred the audience. "Everywhere."

Tagore was in a hurry. Too much so.

He caromed off a stanchion but did not let that stop him from rebounding from the opposite wall, absorbing his momentum with his knees, and springing off with a full push. Rasters streaked his augmented vision, then flickered and faded.

He coasted by a full-view showing the wondrous world below, a blazing crescent transcendent in its cloud-wrapped beauty. Tagore ignored the spectacle; marvels of the mind pre-occupied him.

He was carrying the answer to it all, he was sure of that. In his haste he did not even glance at the blue-tinged sunlight glinting from the Circular Ocean. The thick disk of open air below it made a clear line under the blue wedge. At this angle the floating water refracted sunlight around the still darkened limb of the planet. The glittering azure jewel heralded dawn, serene in its impudent impossibility.

The youngest of the entire expedition, Tagore was a mere theorist. He had specialized in planetary formation at university, but managed to snag a berth on this expedition by developing a ready, quick facility at explaining vexing problems the observers turned up. That, and a willingness to do scutwork.

"Cap'n, I've got it," he blurted as he came through the hatch. The Captain greeted him, sitting at a small oak desk, the only wood on the whole ship—then got to business. Tagore had asked for this audience because he knew the effect his theory could have on the others; so the Captain should see first.

"The Circular Ocean is held up by electric field pressure," he announced. The Captain's reaction was less than he had hoped: unblinking calm, waiting for more information.

"See, electromagnetic fields exert forces on the electrons in atoms," Tagore persisted, going through the numbers, talking fast. "The fields down there are so strong—I got that measurement out of Lissa's data—they can act like a steady support."

He went on to make comparisons: the energy density of a hand grenade, contained in every suitcase-sized volume of air. Even though the fields could simply stand there, as trapped waves, they had to suffer some losses. The power demands were *huge*. Plus, how the hell did such a gargantuan construction *work*?

By now Tagore was thoroughly pumped, oblivious to his audience.

Finally the Captain blinked and said, "Anything like this ever seen on Earth?"

"Nossir, not that I've ever heard."

"No natural process can do the stunt?"

"Nossir, not that I can imagine."

"Well, we came looking for something different."

Tagore did not know whether to laugh or not; the Captain was unreadable. Was this what exploration was like—the slow anxiety of not knowing? On Earth such work had an abstract distance, but here . . .

He would rather have some other role. Bringing uncomfortable truths to those in power put him more in the spotlight than he wished.

Captain Badquor let the Tagore kid go on a bit longer before he said anything more. It was best to let these technical types sing their songs first. So few of them ever thought about anything beyond their own warblings.

He gave Tagore a captainly smile. Why did they all look so *young*? "So this whole big thing on Shiva is artificial."

"Well, yeah, I suppose so . . ."

Plainly Tagore hadn't actually thought about that part much; the wonder of such strong fields had stunned him. Well, it *was* stunning. "And all that energy, just used to hold up a lake?"

"I'm sure of it, sir. The numbers work out, see? I equated the pressure exerted by those electric fields, assuming they're trapped in the volume under the Circular Ocean, the way waves can get caught if they're inside a conducting box—"

"You think that ocean's a conductor?" Might as well show the kid that even the Captain knew a little physics. In fact, though he never mentioned it, he had a doctorate from MIT. Not that he had learned much about command there.

"Uh, well, no. I mean, it is a fairly good conductor, but for my model, it's only a way of speaking—"

"It has salt currents, true? They could carry electrical currents." The Captain rubbed his chin, the machinery of his mind trying to grasp how such a thing could be. "Still, that doesn't explain why the thing doesn't evaporate away, at those altitudes."

"Uh, I really hadn't thought—"

The Captain waved a hand. "Go on." *Sing for me.*

"Then the waves exert an upward force on the water every time they reflect from the underside of the ocean—"

"And transfer that weight down, on invisible waves, to the rock that's ten kilometers below."

"Uh, yessir."

Tagore looked a bit constipated, bursting with enthusiasm, with the experience of the puzzle, but not knowing how to express it. The Captain decided to have mercy on the kid. "Sounds good. Not anything impossible about it."

"Except the *size* of it, sir."

"That's one way to put it."

"Sir?"

A curious, powerful feeling washed over the Captain. Long decades of anticipation had steeled him, made him steady in the presence of the crew. But now he felt his sense of the room tilt, as though he were losing control of his status-space. The mind could go whirling off, out here in the inky immensities between twin alien suns. He frowned. "This thing is bigger than anything humanity ever built. And there's not a clue what it's for. The majesty of it, son, that's what strikes me. Grandeur."

John slipped into his helmet and Shiva enclosed him. *To be wrapped in a world—* His POV shifted, strummed, arced with busy fretworks—then snapped into solidity, stabilized.

Astronomy had become intensely interactive in the last century, the spectral sensoria blanketing the viewer. Through *Adventurer's* long voyage he had tuned the system to his every whim. Now it gave him a nuanced experience like a true, full-bodied immersion.

He was eager to immerse himself in the *feel* of Shiva, in full 3D wraparound. Its crescent swelled below like a ripe, mottled fruit. He plunged toward it. A planet, fat in bandwidth.

For effect—decades before he had been a sky diver—John

had arranged the data-fields so that he *accelerated* into it. From their arcing orbit he shot directly toward Shiva's disk. Each mapping rushed toward him, exploding upward in finer detail. *There—*

The effect showed up first in the grasslands of the southern habitable belt. He slewed toward the plains, where patterns emerged in quilted confusions. After Tagore's astonishing theory about the Circular Ocean—odd, so audacious, and coming from a nonscientist—John knew he had to be ready for anything. Somewhere in the data-fields must lurk the clue to who or what had made the ocean.

Below, the great grassy shelves swelled. But in places the grass was thin. Soon he saw why. The natural grass was only peeking out across plains covered with curious orderly patterns—hexagonals folding into triangles where necessary to cover hills and valleys, right up to the muddy banks of the slow-moving brown rivers.

Reflection in the UV showed that the tiles making this pattern were often small, but with some the size of houses, meters thick . . . and moving. They all jostled and worked with restless energy, to no obvious purpose.

Alive? The UV spectrum broke down into a description of a complex polymer. Cross-linked chains bonded at many oblique angles to each other, flexing like sleek micromuscles.

John brought in chemists and biologists in an ensemble suite: Odis and Lissa chimed in the scientific choir. In the wraparound display he felt them by the shadings they gave the data.

The tiles, Lissa found, fed on their own sky. Simple sugars rained from the clotted air, the fruit of an atmosphere that resembled an airy chicken soup. *Atmospheric electrochemistry seems responsible, somehow*, Lissa sent. Floating microbial nuggets moderated the process.

The tiles were prime eaters. Oxidizing radicals the size of golf balls patrolled their sharp linear perimeters. These packlike rollers attacked invader chemicals, ejecting most, harvesting those they could use.

Lissa brought in two more biologists, who of course had many questions. *Are these tiles like great turtles?* one ventured, then chuckled uneasily. They yearned to flip one over.

Diurnal or nocturnal? *Some are, most aren't.*

Are there any small ones? *A few.*

Do they divide by fission? *No, but . . .* Nobody understood the complicated process the biologists witnessed. Reproduction seemed a tricky matter.

There was some periodicity to their movements, some slow rhythms, and particularly a fast Fourier-spectrum spike at 1.27 seconds—but again, no clear reason for it.

Could they be all one life form? Could that be?

A whole planet taken over by a tiling-thing that coopted all resources?

The senior biologists scoffed. How could a species evolve to have only one member? And an ecosystem—a whole world!—with so few parts?

Evolution ruled that out. Bio-evolution, that is. But not social evolution.

John plunged further into the intricate matrices of analysis. The endless tile-seas cloaking mountains and valleys shifted and milled, fidgety, only occasionally leaving bare ground visible as a square fissioned into triangles. Oblongs met and butted with fevered energy.

Each hemisphere of the world was similar, though the tiles in the north had different shapes—pentagonals, mostly. Nowhere did the tiles cross rivers, but they could ford streams. A Centauri variant of chlorophyll was everywhere, in the oceans and rivers, but not in the Circular Ocean.

The ground was covered with a thin grass, the sprigs living off the momentary sunlight that slipped between the edges in the jostling, jiggling, bumping, and shaking. Tiles that moved over the grass sometimes cropped it, sometimes not, leaving stubs that seemed to have been burned off.

The tiles' fevered dance ran incessantly, without sleep. Could these things be performing some agitated discourse, a lust fest without end? John wondered.

He slowed his descent. The tiles were a shock. Could *these* be the builders of the Circular Ocean? Time for the biologists to get to work.

The computer folk thought one way, the biologists—after an initial rout, when they rejected the very possibility of a single entity filling an entire biosphere—quite another.

After some friction, their views converged somewhat. A biologist remarked that the larger tiles came together like dwarf houses making love . . . gingerly, always presenting the same angles and edges.

Adventurer had scattered microlanders all over the world. These showed only weak electromagnetic fringing fields among the tiles. Their deft collisions seemed almost like neurons in a two-dimensional plan.

The analogy stirred the theorists. Over the usual after-shift menu of beer, soy nuts, and friendly insults, one maven of the digital realm ventured an absurd idea: Could the planet have become a computer?

Everybody laughed. They kidded the advocate of this notion . . . and then lapsed into frowning silence. Specialists find quite unsettling those ideas that cross disciplines.

Could a species turn itself into a biological computer? The tiles did rub and caress each other in systematic ways. Rather than carrying information in digital fashion, they could use a more complex language of position and angle, exploiting their planar geometry. If so, the information density flowing among them was immense. Every collision carried a sort of Euclidean talk, possibly rich in nuance.

The computer analogy brought up a next question—not that some big ones weren't left behind, perhaps lying in wait to bite them on their conceptual tail. Could the tiles know anything more than themselves? Or were they strange, geometroid solipsists? Should they call the tiles a single It?

Sealed inside a cosmos of Its own making, was It even in principle interested in the outside world? Alpha Centauri fed It gratuitous energy, the very soupy air fueled It: the last standing power on the globe. What reason did It have to converse with the great Outside?

Curiosity, perhaps? The biologists frowned at the prospect. Curiosity in early prehumans was rewarded in the environment. The evolving ape learned new tricks, found fresh water, killed a new kind of game, invented a better way to locate those delicious roots—and the world duly paid it back.

Apparently—*but don't ask us why just yet!* the biologists cried—the game was different here. What reward came from the tiles' endless smacking together?

So even if the visiting humans rang the conceptual doorbell on the tile-things, maybe nobody would answer. Maybe nobody was home.

Should they try?

John and Odis and Lissa, Tagore and the Captain, and over a hundred other crew—they all pondered.

II

While they wrestled with the issue, exploration continued.

A flitter craft flew near the elevated ocean and inspected its supporting volume with distant sensors and probing telescopes. Even Shiva's weather patterns seemed wary of the Circular Ocean. Thunderclouds veered away from the gap between the ocean and the rugged land below. In the yawning height clouds formed but quickly dispersed, as if dissolved by unseen forces.

Birds flew through the space, birds like feathery kites.

Somehow they had missed noticing this class of life. Even the microlanders had not had the speed to capture their darting lives. And while the kite-birds did seem to live mostly on tiny floating balloon-creatures that hovered in the murky air of the valleys, they were unusually common beneath the Circular Ocean.

John proposed that he send in a robocraft of bird size, to measure physical parameters in the heart of the gap. Captain Badquor approved. The shops fabricated a fake. Jet-powered and featuring fake feathers, it was reasonably convincing.

John flew escort in a rocket-plane. The bird-probe got seventeen kilometers inside and then disappeared in a dazzling blue-white electrical discharge. Telemetry showed why: the Circular Ocean's support was a complex weave of electrical fields, supplying an upward pressure. These fields never exceeded the breakdown level of a megavolt per meter, above which Shiva's atmosphere would ionize. Field strength was about a million volts per meter.

The robocraft had hit a critical peak in the field geometry. A conductor, it caused a flashover that dumped millions of watts into the bird within a millisecond.

As the cinder fell, John banked away from his monitoring position five kilometers beyond the gap perimeter. There was no particular reason to believe a discharge that deep within the gap would somehow spread, engulfing the region in a spontaneous discharge of the enormous stored energies. Surely whoever—no, whatever—had designed the Circular Ocean's supports would not allow the electromagnetic struts to collapse from the frying of a mere bird.

But something like that happened. The system responded.

The burnt brown husk of the pseudobird turned lazily as it fell and sparks jumped from it. These formed a thin orange discharge that fed on the energy coursing through the now-atomized bird. The discharging line snaked away, following unerringly the bird's prior path. It raced at close to the speed of light back along the arc.

The system had *memory*, John realized. He saw a tendril of light at the corner of his vision as he turned his flitter craft. He had time only to think that it was like a huge, fast finger jabbing at him. An apt analogy, though he had no time to consider ironies. The orange discharge touched the flitter. John's hair stood on end as charge flooded into the interior.

Ideally, electrons move to the outer skin of a conductor. But when antennas connect deep into the interior, circuits can close.

Something had intended to dump an immense charge on the flitter, the origin of the pseudobird. Onboard instruments momentarily reported a charge exceeding seventeen coulombs. By then John had, for all intents and purposes, ceased to exist as an organized bundle of electrical information.

John's death did yield a harvest of data. Soon enough Lissa saw the true function of the Circular Ocean. It was but an ornament, perhaps an artwork.

Ozone fizzed all around it. Completely natural-seeming, the lake crowned a huge cavity that functioned like a steady, standing laser.

The electrical fields both supported the ocean and primed the atoms of the entire atmosphere they permeated. Upon stimulus—from the same system that had fried John—the entire gap could release the stored energy into an outgoing electromagnetic wave. It was an optical bolt, powerful and complex in structure—triggered by John.

Twice more the ocean's gap discharged naturally as the humans orbited Shiva. The flash lasted but a second, not enough to rob the entire ocean structure of its stability. The emission sizzled out through the atmosphere and off into space.

Laser beams are tight, and this one gave away few of its secrets. The humans, viewing it from a wide angle, caught little of the complex structure and understood less.

Puzzled, mourning John, they returned to a careful study of the Shiva surface. Morale was low. The Captain felt that a dramatic gesture could lift their spirits. He would have to do it himself.

To Captain Badquor fell the honor of the first landing. A show of bravery would overcome the crew's confusions, surely.

He would direct the complex exploring machines in real-time, up close.

He left the landing craft fully suited up, impervious to the complex biochem mix of the atmosphere.

The tiles jostled downhill from him. Only in the steep flanks of this equatorial mountain range did the tiles not endlessly surge. Badquor's boots crunched on a dry, crusty soil. He took samples, sent them back by runner-robo.

A warning signal from orbit: the tiles in his area seemed more agitated than usual. A reaction to his landing?

The tile polygons were leathery, with no obvious way to sense him. No eyes or ears. They seemed to caress the ground lovingly, though Badquor knew they trod upon big crabbed feet.

He went forward cautiously. Below, the valley seemed alive with rippling turf, long waves sweeping to the horizon in the twinkling of an instant. He got an impression of incessant pace, of enthusiasm unspoken but plainly endless.

His boots were well insulated thermally, but not electrically. Thus, when his headphones crackled, he thought he was receiving noise in his transmission lines. The dry sizzle began to make his skin tingle.

Only when the frying noise rose and buried all other signals did he blink, alarmed. By then it was too late.

Piezoelectric energy arises when mechanical stress massages rock. Pressure on an electrically neutral stone polarizes it at the lattice level by slightly separating the center of positive charge from the negative. The lattice moves, the shielding electron cloud does not. This happens whenever the rock crystal structure does not have a center of structural symmetry, and so occurs in nearly all bedrock.

The effect was well-known on Earth, though weak. Stressed strata sometimes discharged, sending glow discharges into the air. Such plays of light were now a standard precursor warning of earthquakes. But Earth was a mild case.

Tides stressed the stony mantle of Shiva, driven by the eternal gravitational gavotte of both stars, A and B. Periodic alignments of the two stars stored enormous energy in the full body of the planet. Evolution favored life that could harness these electrical currents that rippled through the planetary crust. This, far more than the kilowatt per square meter of sunlight, drove the tile-forms.

All this explanation came after the fact, and seemed obvious in retrospect. The piezoelectric energy source was naturally dispersed and easily harvested. A sizzle of electric microfields fed the tiles' large, crusted foot-pads. After all, on Earth fish and eels routinely used electrical fields as both sensors and weapons.

This highly organized ecology sensed Captain Badquor's intrusion immediately. To them, he probably had many of the signatures of a power-parasite. These were small creatures like the stick insects Badquor himself had noticed after landing; they lived by stealing electrical charge from the tile polygons.

Only later analysis made it clear what had happened. The interlinked commonality of piezo-driven life moved to expel the intruder by overpowering it—literally.

Badquor probably had no inkling of how strange a fate he had met, for the several hundreds of amperes caused his muscles to seize up, his heart to freeze in a clamped frenzy, and his synapses to discharge in a last vision that burned into his eyes a vision of an incandescent rainbow.

Lissa blinked. The spindly trees looked artificial, but weren't.

Groves of them spiraled around hills, zigzagged up razor-backed ridges and shot down the flanks of denuded rock piles. Hostile terrain for any sort of tree that Earthly biologists understood. The trees, she noted, had growing patterns that bore no discernible relation to water flow, sunlight exposure, or wind patterns.

That was why Lissa went in to see. Her team of four had already sent the smart-eyes, rugged robots, and quasi-intelligent processors. Lightweight, patient, durable, these ambassadors had discovered little. Time for something a bit more interactive on the ground.

That is, a person. Captain Badquor's sacrifice had to mean something, and his death had strengthened his crew's resolve.

Lissa landed with electrically insulted boots. They now understood the piezoelectric ecology in broad outline, or thought they did. Courageous caution prevailed.

The odd beanpole trees made no sense. Their gnarled branches followed a fractal pattern and had no leaves. Still, there was ample fossil evidence—gathered by automatic prospectors sent down earlier—that the bristly trees had evolved from more traditional trees within the last few million years. But they had come so quickly into the geological record that Lissa suspected they were "driven" evolution—biological technology.

She carefully pressed her instruments against the sleek black sides of the trees. Their surfaces seethed with electric currents, but none strong enough to be a danger.

On Earth, the natural potential difference between the surface and the upper atmosphere provides a voltage drop of a hundred volts for each meter in height. A woman two meters tall could be at a significantly higher potential than her feet, especially if her feet had picked up extra electrons by walking across a thick carpet.

On Shiva this effect was much larger. The trees, Lissa realized, were harvesting the large potentials available between Shiva's rocky surface and the charged layers skating across the upper reaches of the atmosphere.

The "trees" were part of yet another way to reap the planetary energies—whose origin was ultimately the blunt forces of gravity, mass, and torque—all for the use of life.

The potential-trees felt Lissa's presence quickly enough. They had evolved defenses against poachers who would garner stray voltages and currents from the unwary.

In concert—for the true living entity was the grove, comprising perhaps a million trees—they reacted.

Staggering back to her lander, pursued by vagrant electrical surges through both ground and the thick air, she shouted into her suit mike her conclusions. These proved useful in later analysis.

She survived, barely.

III

When the sum of these incidents sank in, the full import become clear. The entire Shiva ecology was electrically driven. From the planet's rotation and strong magnetosphere, from the tidal stretching of the Centauri system, from geological rumblings and compressions, came far more energy than mere sunlight could ever provide.

Seen this way, all biology was an afterthought. The geologists, who had been feeling rather neglected lately, liked this turn of events quite a bit. They gave lectures on Shiva seismology which, for once, everybody attended.

To be sure, vestigial chemical processes still ran alongside the vastly larger stores of charges and potentials; these were important for understanding the ancient biosphere that had once governed here.

Much could be learned from classic, old-style biology: from samples of the bushes and wiry trees and leafy plants, from the small insectlike creatures of ten legs each, from the kite-birds, from the spiny, knifelike fish that prowled the lakes.

All these forms were ancient, unchanging. Something had fixed them in evolutionary amber. Their forms had not changed for many hundreds of millions of years.

There had once been higher forms, the fossil record showed. Something like mammals, even large tubular things that might have resembled reptiles.

But millions of years ago they had abruptly ceased. Not due

to some trauma, either—they all ended together, but without the slightest sign of a shift in the biosphere, of disease or accident.

The suspicion arose that something had simply erased them, having no further need.

The highest form of life—defined as that with the highest brain/body volume ratio—had vanished slightly later than the others. It had begun as a predator wider than it was tall, and shaped like a turtle, though without a shell.

It had the leathery look of the tile-polygons, though.

Apparently it had not followed the classic mode of pursuit, but rather had outwitted its prey, boxing it in by pack-animal tactics. Later it had arranged deadfalls and traps. Or so the sociobiologists suspected, from narrow evidence.

These later creatures had characteristic bony structures around the large, calculating brain. Subsequent forms were plainly intelligent, and had been engaged in a strange manipulation of their surroundings. Apparently without ever inventing cities or agriculture, they had domesticated many other species.

Then the other high life-forms vanished from the fossil record. The scheme of the biosphere shifted. Electrical plant forms, like the spindly trees and those species who fed upon piezoelectric energy, came to the fore.

Next, the dominant, turtlelike predators vanished as well. Had they been dispatched?

On Shiva all the forms humans thought of as life, plant and animal alike, were now in fact mere . . . well, maintenance workers. They served docilely in a far more complex ecology. They were as vital and as unnoticeable and as ignorable as the mitochondria in the stomach linings of *Adventurer*'s crew.

Of the immensely more complex electrical ecology, they were only beginning to learn even the rudiments. If Shiva was in a sense a single interdependent, colonial organism, what were its deep rules?

By focusing on the traditional elements of the organic biosphere they had missed the point.

Then the Circular Ocean's laser discharged again. The starship was nearer the lancing packet of emission, and picked up a side lobe. They learned more in a millisecond than they had in a month.

A human brain has about ten billion neurons, each connected with about 100,000 of its neighbors. A firing neuron carries one bit of information. But the signal depends upon the path it follows, and in the labyrinth of the brain there are 10^{15} pathways. This torrent of information flows through the brain in machine-gun packets of electrical impulses, coursing through myriad synapses. Since a single book has about a million bits in it, a single human carries the equivalent of a billion books of information—all riding around in a two-kilogram lump of electrically wired jelly.

Only one to ten percent of a human brain's connections are firing at any one time. A neuron can charge and discharge at best a hundred times in a second. Human brains, then, can carry roughly 10^{10} bits of information in a second. Thus to read out a brain containing 10^{15} bits would take 100,000 seconds, or about a day.

The turtle-predators had approximately the same capacity. Indeed, there were theoretical arguments that a mobile, intelligent species would carry roughly the same load of stored information as a human could. For all its limitations, the human brain has an impressive data store capability, even if, in many, it frequently went unused.

The Circular Ocean had sent discrete packets of information of about this size, 10^{15} bits compressed into its powerful millisecond pulse. The packets within it were distinct, well bordered by banks of marker code. The representation was digital, an outcome mandated by the fact that any number enjoys a unique representation only in base 2.

Within the laser's millisecond burst were fully a thousand brain-equivalent transmissions. A trove. What the packets actually said was quite indecipherable.

The target was equally clear: a star 347 light-years away. Targeting was precise; there could be no mistake. Far cheaper, if one knew the recipient, to send a focused message, rather than to broadcast wastefully in the low-grade, narrow band-width radio frequencies.

Earth had never heard such powerful signals, of course, not because humans were not straining to hear, but because Shiva was ignoring them.

After Badquor's death and Lissa's narrow escape, *Adventurer* studied the surface with elaborately planned robot expeditions. The machines skirted the edge of a vast tile-plain, observing the incessant jiggling, fed on the piezoelectric feast welling from the crusted rocks.

After some days, they came upon a small tile lying still. The others had forced it out of the eternal jostling jam. It lay stiff and discolored, baking in the double suns' glare. Scarcely a meter across and thin, it looked like construction material for a patio in Arizona.

The robots carried it off. Nothing pursued them. The tile-thing was dead, apparently left for mere chemical processes to harvest its body.

This bonanza kept the ship's biologists sleepless for weeks as they dissected it. Gray-green, hard of carapace and extraordinarily complex in its nervous system—these they had expected. But the dead alien devoted fully a quarter of its body volume to a brain that was broken into compact, separate segments.

The tile creatures were indeed part of an ecology driven by electrical harvesting of the planetary energies. The tiles alone used a far higher percentage of the total energetic wealth than did Earth's entire sluggish, chemically driven biosphere.

And deep within the tile-thing was the same bone structure they had seen in the turtlelike predator. The dominant, apparently intelligent species had not gone to the stars. Instead, they had formed the basis of an intricate ecology of the mind.

Then the engineers had a chance to study the tile-thing, and found even more.

As a manifestation of their world, the tiles were impressive. Their neurological system fashioned a skein of interpretations, of lived scenarios, of expressive renderings—all apparently for communication outward in well-sculpted bunches of electrical information, intricately coded. They had large computing capacity and ceaselessly exchanged great gouts of information with each other.

This explained their rough skins, which maximized piezo connections when they rubbed against each other. And they "spoke" to each other through the ground, as well, where their big, crabbed feet carried currents, too.

Slowly it dawned that Shiva was an unimaginably huge computational complex, operating in a state-of-information flux many orders of magnitude greater than the entire sum of human culture. Shiva was to Earth as humans were to beetles.

The first transmissions about Shiva's biosphere reached Earth four years later. Already, in a culture more than a century into the dual evolution of society and computers, there were disturbing parallels.

Some communities in the advanced regions of Earth felt that real-time itself was a pallid, ephemeral experience. After all, one could not archive it for replay, savor it, return until it became a true part of oneself. Real-time was for one time only, then lost.

So increasingly, some people lived instead in worlds made totally volitional—truncated, chopped, governed by technologies they could barely sense as ghostlike constraints on an otherwise wide compass.

"Disposable realities," some sneered—but the fascination of such lives was clear.

Shiva's implication was extreme: An entire world could give itself over to life-as-computation.

Could the intelligent species of Shiva have executed a huge

fraction of their fellow inhabitants? And then themselves gone extinct? For what? Could they have fled—perhaps from the enormity of their own deeds?

Or had those original predators become the tile-polygons?

The *Adventurer* crew decided to return to Shiva's surface in force, to crack the puzzles. They notified Earth and descended.

Shortly after, the Shiva teams ceased reporting back to Earth. Through the hiss of interstellar static there came no signal.

After years of anxious waiting, Earth launched the second expedition. They, too, survived the passage. Cautiously, they approached Shiva.

Adventurer still orbited the planet, but was vacant.

This time they were wary. Further years of hard thinking and careful study passed before the truth began to come.

IV

{—John/Odis/Lissa/Tagore/Cap'n—}
 —all assembled/congealed/thickened—
 —into a composite veneer persona—
 —on the central deck of their old starship,
 —to greet the second expedition.
Or so they seemed to intend.

They came up from the Shiva surface in a craft not of human construction. The sleek, webbed thing seemed to ride upon electromagnetic winds.

They entered through the main lock, after using proper hailing protocols.

But what came through the lock was an ordered array of people no one could recognize as being from the *Adventurer* crew.

They seemed younger, *unworn*. Smooth, bland features looked out at the bewildered second expedition. The party moved together, maintaining a hexagonal array with a constant spacing of four centimeters. Fifty-six pairs of eyes surveyed the new Earth ship, each momentarily gazing at a different portion of the field of view, as if to memorize only a portion for later integration.

To convey a sentence, each person spoke a separate word. The effect was jarring, with no clue to how an individual knew what to say, or when, for the lines were not rehearsed. The group reacted to questions in a blur of scattershot talk, words like volleys.

Sentences ricocheted and bounced around the assembly deck where the survivors of the first expedition all stood, erect and clothed in a shapeless gray garment. Their phrases made sense when isolated, but the experience of hearing them was unsettling. Long minutes stretched out before the second expedition realized that these hexagonally spaced humans were trying to greet them, to induct them into something they termed the Being Suite.

This offer made, the faces within the hexagonal array began to show separate expressions. Tapes of this encounter show regular facial alterations with a fixed periodicity of 1.27 seconds. Each separate face racheted, jerking among a menu of finely graduated countenances—anger, sympathy, laughter, rage, curiosity, shock, puzzlement, ecstasy—flickering, flickering, endlessly flickering.

A witness later said that it was as if the hexagonals (as they came to be called) knew that human expressiveness centered on the face, and so had slipped into a kind of language of facial aspects. This seemed natural to them, and yet the 1.27 second pace quickly gave the witnesses a sense of creeping horror.

High-speed tapes of the event showed more. Beneath the 1.27 frequency there was a higher harmonic, barely perceptible to the human eye, in which other expressions shot across the hexagonals' faces. These were like waves, muscular twitches that washed over the skin like tidal pulls.

This periodicity was the same as the tile-polygons had displayed. The subliminal aspects were faster than the conscious human optical processor could manage, yet research showed that they were decipherable in the target audience.

Researchers later concluded that this rapid display was the origin of the growing unease felt by the second expedition. The hexagonals said nothing throughout all of this.

The second expedition crew described the experience as uncanny, racking, unbearable. Their distinct impression was that the first expedition now manifested as *like the tile-things*. Such testimony was often followed by an involuntary twitch.

Tapes do not yield such an impression upon similar audiences: they have become the classic example of having to be in a place and time to sense the meaning of an event. Still, the tapes are disturbing, and access is controlled. Some Earth audiences experienced breakdowns after viewing them.

But the second expedition agreed even more strongly upon a second conclusion. Plainly, the *Adventurer* expedition had joined the computational labyrinth that was Shiva. How they were seduced was never clear; the second expedition feared finding out.

Indeed, their sole, momentary brush with {—John/Odis/Lissa/Tagore/Cap'n . . .—} convinced the second expedition that there was no point in pursuing the maze of Shiva.

The hostility radiating from the second expedition soon drove the hexagonals back into their ship and away. The fresh humans from Earth felt something gut-level and instinctive, a reaction beyond words. The hexagonals retreated without showing a coherent reaction. They simply turned and walked away, holding to the four centimeter spacing. The 1.27 second flicker stopped and they returned to a bland expression, alert but giving nothing away.

The vision these hexagonals conveyed was austere, jarring . . . and yet, plainly intended to be inviting.

The magnitude of their failure was a measure of the abyss that separated the two parties. The hexagonals were now both more and less than human.

The hexagonals left recurrent patterns that told much, though only in retrospect. Behind the second expedition's revulsion lay a revelation: of a galaxy spanned by intelligences formal and remote, far developed beyond the organic stage. Such intelligences had been born variously, of early organic forms, or of later machine civilizations that had arisen upon the ashes of extinct organic societies. The gleam of the stars was in fact a metallic glitter.

This vision was daunting enough: of minds so distant and strange, hosted in bodies free of sinew and skin. But there was something more, an inexpressible repulsion in the manifestation of {—John/Odis/Lissa/Tagore/Cap'n . . .—}.

A nineteenth century philosopher, Goethe, had once remarked that if one stared into the abyss long enough, it stared back. This proved true. A mere moment's lingering look, quiet and almost casual, was enough. The second expedition panicked. It is not good to stare into a pit that has no bottom.

They had sensed the final implication of Shiva's evolution. To alight upon such interior worlds of deep, terrible exotica exacted a high cost: the body itself.

Yet all those diverse people had joined the *syntony* of Shiva— an electrical harmony that danced to unheard musics. Whether they had been seduced, or even raped, would forever be unclear.

Out of the raw data-stream, the second expedition could sample transmissions from the tile-things, as well. The second expedition caught a link-locked sense of repulsive grandeur. Still organic in their basic organization, still tied to the eternal wheel of birth and death, the tiles had once been lords of their own world, holding dominion over all they knew.

Now they were patient, willing drones in a hive they could not comprehend. But—and here human terms undoubtedly fail—they loved their immersion.

Where was their consciousness housed? Partially in each, or in some displaced, additive sense? There was no clear way to test either idea.

The tile-things were like durable, patient machines that could best carry forward the first stages of a grand computation. Some biologists compared them with insects, but no evolutionary mechanism seemed capable of yielding a reason why a species would give itself over to computation. The insect analogy died, unable to predict the response of the polygons to stimulus, or even why they existed.

Or was their unending jostling only in the service of calculation? The tile-polygons would not say. They never responded to overtures.

The Circular Ocean's enormous atmospheric laser pulsed regularly, as the planet's orbit and rotation carried the laser's field of targeting onto a fresh partner-star system. Only then did the system send its rich messages out into the galaxy. The pulses carried mind-packets of unimaginable data, bound on expeditions of the intellect.

The second expedition reported, studied. Slowly at first, and then accelerating, the terror overcame them.

They could not fathom Shiva, and steadily they lost crew members to its clasp. Confronting the truly, irreducibly exotic, there is no end of ways to perish.

In the end they studied Shiva from a distance, no more. Try as they could, they always met a barrier in their understanding. Theories came and went, fruitlessly. Finally, they fled.

It is one thing to speak of embracing the new, the fresh, the strange. It is another to feel that one is an insect, crawling across a page of the *Encyclopedia Britannica*, knowing only that something vast is passing by beneath, all without your sensing more than a yawning vacancy. Worse, the lack was clearly in oneself, and was irredeemable.

This was the first contact humanity had with the true nature of the galaxy. It would not be the last. But the sense of utter and complete diminishment never left the species, in all the strange millennia that rolled on thereafter.

Afterthoughts

My friend Robert Silverberg once defined critics as those who, after the battle has been fought, come to the battlefield and shoot the wounded.

I've never felt that strongly about critics, but I sometimes do feel that abstractly, while looking backward at my own work. Often I wonder who exactly produced this fiction, what mind set obliquely to mine? Sometimes I can only dimly remember what was afoot in that mind when the labors were in progress.

Scanning through the table of contents, I noticed immediately that once again, this third collection of my short fiction is preoccupied with the alien. Various manifestations of overt aliens appear in half a dozen of these stories, and covertly in others. Why?

I wish I knew. Oh, sure, one can go on about the genuinely alien encounter being at the core of the scientific experience. That has been doubly true in the battered twentieth century, which opened with relativity theory and quantum mechanics knocking to pieces most of the worldview of all the past. But the specifically science-fictional encounter with alienness is different. I don't mean the Star Trek sort of guys in rubber suits, of course. I mean the sensation of a genuinely different way of seeing the world, with all the menace that can imply. Not the threat of, say, dismemberment (however photogenic that might be in Hollywood), but rather the suggestion that *You might be completely wrong, in everything you suppose*—no mild menace.

So after rummaging through my own general motivations, I go back to specifics. Certainly "Doing Alien" revisits Fairhope, Alabama, where I grew up and which I still regard as my essential ground. Introducing interstellar beings into the down-home voice I assumed in this piece was at least fun, a way of reminding myself that though I discuss astrophysics daily with experts, a writer should stay close to how ordinary people experience the world.

In "World Vast, World Various" I took up a job to my liking, trying to depict a world designed for the original anthology *Murasaki,* edited by Robert Silverberg with considerable help in the world-building from Fred Pohl and Poul Anderson. To fathom the whole, read the entire volume; it repays the effort. I wrote the story to stand alone, yet reverberate with a sense of mysteries to come.

In the story, I wanted to show what anthropological (with all the implications of that word) research might be like on another world. To my mind, this is the best case—the easiest. We might be lucky enough to try out ideas about social organization imported from our own past and make them work to describe aliens. The attempt was an interesting thought experiment, but it might tell us more about ourselves than the aliens.

That is why one character is horrified when another suggests that we might have begun our climb up by being scavengers. A colleague at the University of California, San Diego, thought this was so obvious that my character should not take offense. But that is how such tides turn; the beliefs of future explorers shall not be our own.

More's to the point, aliens are, well, alien. They won't fit either point of view. And that's the *best* case; most likely, we won't even fathom truly alien cultures, or even recognize them.

So to underline this point, "High Abyss." This story deliberately replicates the "conceptual breakout" motif of sf, from a point of view few could anticipate. This serves to give us a jarring view of how the universe might have looked to beings who lived in its first few years—strange creatures, indeed—and then jerk us into seeing them as our ancestors. The fast pace of the early universe could have engendered life-forms we can scarcely envision.

I chose to conclude this walk through the eerie with perhaps my strangest story of all, "A Dance to Strange Musics." It is a compressed novel, omitting the customary touches which might make the crew of a starship more easy to identify with. Instead I ply the reader with strangeness itself, a picture of a landscape shaped by forces that work largely behind the scenes here on Earth—we live between the plates of two immense spherical capacitors, the ground and the ionosphere, didn't you know? I tried to let the inherent creepiness of it all work up through the very renunciation of any homey human detail about the characters themselves.

Traditionally, sf contrasts the human scale and its comforts with the alien, but in this story I tried to reduce the people, making them in the end puppets in a drama we cannot even *in principle* fathom. Hard-nosed, but that's the point.

All short stories are strategies. Working in a confined space, one must render the essentials and get off the stage with a minimum of fuss. So I took the material for a thriller novel and compressed them into "A Calculus of Desperation," perhaps the most alienating story in the book. Again I sought to get all the ideas of a more worked-out narrative into a small compass, to heighten impact.

Do I believe this scary future could happen? Sure. The technology lies only a decade or two away. Do the impulses exist to do it? Certainly—and most threateningly, they resonate among the ecologically virtuous. In the twentieth century we saw air warfare break down the traditional restraint against killing civilians. New technology may well smash distinctions and moral boundaries in the next century, too. One way to prevent that is to imagine it, then safeguard against it.

A few months after this story appeared, I got a call from a scientist at a think tank, asking to use it as the kickoff at a workshop on just this sort of event. Thankfully, nobody in the think tank had yet thought it through in this kind of detail; plainly, it rattled them, because it's all based on solid biological research. 'Nuff said.

Yet in the story lies a lament. Science best captures our abstract wisdom. It tells us that we are primates following complex genetic instructions, though of course they are shaped by local circumstance. But knowing about these large, impersonal forces does not shelter us from the hammering, immediate moment—our passions. One's mind works on several, apparently contradictory, levels.

Such tensions working through the lives of scientists, as they move from their day jobs of heady arabesques into their after-hours domestic swarm, are little remarked in literature. Yet they are powerful, reminding us that David Hume enjoined, "Be a philosopher, but amidst all your philosophy be still a man."

The coming century will see catastrophic, horrifying ecological events—and we shall be to blame. Or rather, our numbers shall. For while we each share only an infinitesimal blame for the dying out of species and erasing of vast natural wonders, we could perhaps act individually to correct the catastrophe. With the right technical skills, small, dedicated bands could do things both grand and terrible.

Such temptations will loom large in the next century, and I wanted to make that clear. And to raise the issue of precisely where the moral high ground might lie, particularly as seen by later generations, who might well inherit a devastated landscape.

Phew—heavy stuff. On the other hand, "In the Dark Backward" was just pure fun. I happen to believe there's a plausible case that Wm. Shakespeare of Stratford did not in fact write those plays and sonnets. There is an intriguing argument preferring Edward Devere. But in a sense it doesn't matter. No writer can read the Bard or the Old Man (see the story) and not want to meet them. This story gave me the chance. The Elizabethan dialogue I took where possible from actual texts of the time. Especially, the oddest phrases are the most nearly authentic; it was a distant time.

In "The Voice," I wanted to reflect on familiar terrors of the intellectual—a future where literacy is a vice, and much follows from it. Homages to Asimov and Bradbury abound.

Similarly, the satirical "Kollapse" looks at those who think the digital world already emerges triumphant. It is modeled on people I know but fear to name.

Always a fan of F. Scott Fitzgerald, I had long noted that he wrote one story of the fantastic, a play upon that enduring symbol of capitalism, "A Diamond as Big as the Ritz." When Elizabeth Mitchell asked me to write a novella, I hit upon the idea of a satire written in the Fitzgerald voice, sending up the central ideas I deplore on the left—same-size-fits-all thinking, well-meaning coercion (fascism for your own good). As long as I was adopting the Fitzgerald persona in an sf context, why not throw in the classic dispute between him and Hemingway? And since diamonds figure, could I use a recent paper I had read, discussing the astrophysical reasons to expect that supernovas produce interesting by-products?

Of such impulses are novellas made. I tried to keep a merry face on all this, but when the piece was published in a shrunken version in the British *Interzone,* readers were offended. How dare I *satirize socialism*!? The saddest feature of the left (of whom I count myself still at least an honorary member, of the anarchist-syndicalist persuasion) is a steady loss of its sense of humor.

"Zoomers" is similarly tongue-in-cheek, trying to see how work might look in a few decades. We spend so much of our time, energy, and psychic currency on labor, yet seldom does it figure in most fiction. Science fiction should correct that. And even the labors of brokers are not without dignity.

I may yet finish the mosaic novel in which "A Worm in the Well" figures, but present it here as an example of how a simple physics problem (invented by Isaac Newton) can repay the fictional imagination. I had fun with this; the proof that the motion through a hole drilled through the center of a planet is simply harmonic is a problem I have used on the departmental Ph.D. qualifying examination at my campus, the University of California at Irvine. Try it yourself.

Throughout, I have resisted the temptation to touch up these tales. I owe that earlier mind a clear passage to the present, its own voice. The only story in here from my early period, written in 1969, I include for two reasons: to show how badly one can write and still get a start, and to own up to one of the darker episodes in my life.

I was trying to learn to write in those days, while a postdoctoral fellow at the Lawrence Radiation Laboratory in Livermore, California. I programmed computers often (in Fortran, a language that survives as a dinosaur from that era) in pursuit of early simulations of plasma phenomena. Though to this day I primarily use analytical mathematics, I found computers useful. I also used the laboratory's crude communications system that ran over the big, central computers we all worshiped then. One could either write a message by punching holes in cards, or by typing on a terminal connected to someone elsewhere in the lab. There was a pernicious problem when programs got sent around for use: "bad code" that arose when researchers included (maybe accidentally) pieces of programming that threw things awry.

One day I was struck by the thought that one might do so intentionally, making a program that deliberately made copies of itself elsewhere. The biological analogy was obvious; evolution would favor such code, especially if it was designed to use clever methods of hiding itself and using others' energy (computing time) to further its own genetic ends. So I wrote some simple code and sent it along in my next transmission. Just a few lines in Fortran told the computer to attach these lines to programs being transmitted to a certain terminal. Soon enough—just a few hours—the code popped up in other programs, and started propagating. By the next day it was in a lot of otherwise unrelated code, and I called a halt to matters by sending a message alerting people to the offending lines.

I made a point with the mavens of the Main Computer: this could be done with considerably more malevolent motivations. In 1969, I got a chance to take part in the ARPANet (Advanced Research Projects Administration) just beginning to link the University of California campuses and the national laboratories such as Livermore and Los Alamos.

In messages sent to Los Alamos, I did the same trick. There was nothing in the system to stop such shenanigans. The ARPANet expanded to become the Net, then the World Wide Web. We tend to forget it was started as a method to link laboratories, and to ensure that communications did not break down in the event of war, and was all funded by the Department of Defense.

I thought it inevitable that such ideas work themselves out in the larger world. I wrote "The Scarred Man" to trace out these ideas, choosing to think commercially: Could someone make a buck out of this? Soon enough I had devised a "virus" that could be cured with a program called Vaccine. I was much impressed with the style of W. Somerset Maugham in those days, a writer now largely and unjustly dropped from sight. I used his characteristic mannerism to frame the story, a narrator from outside listening to a tale of woe, with a twist at the end.

"The Scarred Man" appeared in the May 1970 issue of *Venture* and mercifully dropped from sight. But better writers like John Brunner and David Gerrold picked up on the basic idea and used it in novels a few years later. The notion spread. I have heard that some early copycat viruses began appearing in the ARPANet around 1974, though not virulent forms. By the late 1970s professor Ken Adelman at the University of Southern California had the same idea and claimed it for his own, warning that viruses could be very damaging. Shortly after, they became so.

I had no desire to encourage the kind of behavior I depicted in the story. The tale abounds in wrong guesses about its future, which is pretty much now. We weren't that desperate for oil in the 1990s, didn't drill for it and run embargoes using submarines, for example—but the rather stiff frame of the action does still contain the kernel idea.

I avoided "credit" for this idea for a long time, but gradually realized that it was inevitable, in fact fairly obvious. It is some solace, I suppose, that last year's number 2 seller software in virus protection was a neat little program named Vaccine. The idea came into different currency at the hands of the renowned British biologist Richard Dawkins, who invented the term "memes" to describe cultural notions that catch on and propagate through human cultural mechanisms. Ranging from pop songs you can't get out of your head all the way up to the Catholic Church, memes express how cultural evolution can occur so quickly, as old memes give way to voracious new ones.

This use of biological analogy now proceeds apace. We should expect more such imports into the general culture as we proceed into the next Biological Century.

I suppose there was some money to be made from this virus idea, if remorselessly pursued, even back in the early 1970s. I thought about these, though my heart was not in it. (Perhaps I can claim, like Arthur C. Clarke, that I, too, lost a billion dollars in my spare time.)

Computer viruses are a form of antisocial behavior, one I did not want to encourage in the slightest. Nowadays there are logic bombs, sleeper mines, nasty scrub-everything viruses of robust ability, and what I term "datavores" which eat files with relish.

Not a legacy I wanted to claim. Yet it is an interesting case in the history of the constant interaction between science, technology, and science fiction. Inevitably somebody was going to invent computer viruses; the idea requires only a simple biological analogy. Once it escaped into the general culture, there was no way back. The manufacturers of spray-paint cans probably feel the same way. . . .

So what is it like, to come upon the battlefield of short stories and inspect the survivors? I have rather enjoyed revisiting these. In part they are to me forms of concealed autobiography, for I still can recall the heat of their creation. For others, I hope they provide some amusement to inspecting, critical minds, well-armed against viruses and memes alike.

Gregory Benford
November 1999

Story Copyrights

"As Big as the Ritz"
Originally published in *Under the Wheel,* ed. by Elizabeth
Mitchell, Baen Books, 1986.
　Copyright © 1986 by Abbenford Associates.

"The Scarred Man"
Originally published in the May 1970 issue of *Venture.*
　Copyright © 1970 by Gregory Benford.

"World Vast, World Various"
Originally published in *Murasaki,* ed. by Robert Silverberg,
Bantam, 1989.
　Copyright © 1989 by Abbenford Associates.

"Zoomers"
Originally published in the *Los Angeles Times,* 1995.
　Copyright © 1995 by Abbenford Associates.

"High Abyss"
Originally published in *New Legends,* ed. by Greg Bear,
Tor Books, 1995.
　Copyright © 1995 by Abbenford Associates.

"A Worm in the Well"
Originally published in the November 1995 issue of *Analog.*
　Copyright © 1995 by Abbenford Associates.

"A Dance to Strange Musics"
Originally published in the November 1998 issue of *Science
Fiction Age.* An earlier version appeared as "A Pit Which Has
No Bottom" in *Age of Wonder #1,* 1998.
　Copyright © 1998 by Abbenford Associates.

"Afterthoughts"
　Copyright © 1999 by Abbenford Associates.